PRAISE

"Wickedly delightful and addictively delicious, Kaylie Smith's *Phantasma* is the decadent feast that every romantasy lover dreams of. Dark magic, fraught danger, exhilarating trials, and a simmering-hot romance abound within its pages. Even long after closing the book, readers will be haunted by the tenacity of headstrong Ophelia and her sinfully gorgeous Phantom. And there's a cat!"

—Sophie Kim, #1 *Sunday Times* bestselling author of *The God and the Gumiho*

"Easily one of my favorite reads this year! Make it *Caraval*, but for grown-ups, where everything is darker, bloodier, spicier, and full of twists and turns. Kaylie Smith has created an absolute page-turner with their inventive games, creepy setting, and a swoony love interest that will gladly have you offering up the key to *your* heart."

—Nisha J. Tuli, international bestselling author of *Trial of the Sun Queen*

"Spellbinding, suspenseful, and spicy, *Phantasma* is a darkly romantic romp that will take your breath away. Smith has deftly woven the nine levels of hell into a tale that's as swoon-worthy as it is bloody, and readers will love following Ophelia through a game of wit and nightmares. Combined with thoughtful neurodivergent rep and twists I didn't see coming, this is a story that kept me reading long into the night!"

—M. K. Lobb, author of the Seven Faceless Saints duology

"Sinister, seductive, and delightfully dangerous. Straight off the streets of the Big Easy, readers will be craving more with every brilliantly crafted level in this game of secrets and forbidden desires. *Phantasma* is the perfect concoction of dark opulence, sizzling hot romance, and unforgiving gore."

—Alexis L. Menard, author of *House of Bane and Blood*

ENCHANTRA

Also by Kaylie Smith

WICKED GAMES

Phantasma

ENCHANTRA

KAYLIE SMITH

FOREVER

NEW YORK   BOSTON

Copyright © 2025 by Kaylie Smith

Cover art and design by Alexandra Purtan. Cover copyright © 2025 by Hachette Book Group, Inc.

Forever
Hachette Book Group
1290 Avenue of the Americas, New York, NY 10104
read-forever.com
@readforeverpub

Published in the UK by Second Sky in 2025. An imprint of Storyfire Ltd., Carmelite House, 50 Victoria Embankment, London EC4Y0DZ, United Kingdom

First Forever Edition: April 2025

Forever is an imprint of Grand Central Publishing. The Forever name and logo are registered trademarks of Hachette Book Group, Inc.

The publisher is not responsible for websites (or their content) that are not owned by the publisher.

The Hachette Speakers Bureau provides a wide range of authors for speaking events. To find out more, go to hachettespeakersbureau.com or email HachetteSpeakers@hbgusa.com.

Forever books may be purchased in bulk for business, educational, or promotional use. For information, please contact your local bookseller or the Hachette Book Group Special Markets Department at special.markets@hbgusa.com.

Fox art by Taylor Navis

Library of Congress Control Number: 2024952748

ISBNs: 9781538770801 (paperback), 9781538775837 (Barnes & Noble special edition)

Printed in the United States of America

CCR

10 9 8 7 6 5 4 3 2 1

For the brave souls who burned the bridges between themselves
and their demons. And for those still trying to light the match—
we'll wait for you.

And for Deanna, Becca, and Night,
who helped me stay sane so this book could exist.
Thanks for always answering my calls.

CONTENT GUIDANCE

This book contains explicit sexual content, blood, death, light gore, drug references, heavy alcohol use, self-harm, and drink spiking with a magical aphrodisiac. An in-depth list of content is available at the author's website.

HIERARCHY OF PARANORMAL BEINGS

KING OF THE DEVILS

|

PRINCE OF THE DEVILS

|

DEVILS

|

DEMONS

OFFSPRING OF A DEVIL & ANOTHER
PARANORMAL BEING

|

WRAITHS

OFFSPRING OF A DEMON & ANOTHER PARANORMAL BEING

OTHER IMMORTAL PARANORMAL BEINGS	MORTAL PARANORMAL BEINGS
VAMPIRES	NECROMANCERS
SHAPESHIFTERS	SEERS
FAMILIARS	WITCHES
GHOSTS	SPECTERS

CLASSIFICATIONS OF WRAITHS

SHADOW WRAITHS

MOST COMMON TYPE OF WRAITH, CAN CONTROL SHADOWS AS
WELL AS TURN INTO SHADOWS THEMSELVES TO MOVE THROUGH
THE DARKNESS AT GREAT SPEEDS. THEIR SHADOWS HAVE HEALING
ABILITIES. THEY REFUEL THEIR MAGIC WITH DEEP SLEEP.

LIGHT WRAITHS

CAN CONTROL LIGHT AND FIRE AND, IN SOME CASES, CAN USE
LIGHT TO TRANSPORT THEMSELVES LONG DISTANCES. THEY HAVE
THE ABILITY TO HEAL OTHERS AT A RAPID SPEED. THEY USE THE SUN
TO REFUEL THEIR MAGIC.

BLOOD WRAITHS

CAN CONTROL AND WIELD BLOOD. CAN ALSO CONTROL OTHERS
BY GIVING THEM SOME OF THEIR OWN BLOOD. THEY REFUEL THEIR
MAGIC BY DRAINING ENERGY FROM OTHER LIVING THINGS.

VOID WRAITHS

RAREST TYPE OF WRAITH. CAN TURN THEMSELVES AND OTHERS
INVISIBLE, AND CAN ALSO CONTROL LIGHT AND SHADOWS. THEY
CAN RIP OPEN PORTALS BETWEEN DIFFERENT PLACES AND LINEAR
PLANES, AND THEY CAN PAUSE TIME IN VERY SMALL INTERVALS,
THOUGH IT COSTS THEM A GREAT DEAL OF ENERGY.

"I am out with lanterns, looking for myself."

—Emily Dickinson

PROLOGUE

Darkness

Hell was made of swirling darkness and secrets just like the man in front of her.

"I loathe you," she swore as the black tendrils of magic that slithered from his hands wrapped around her wrists and throat, shoving her back into the labyrinth's wall. The sensual energy that always buzzed over her skin whenever he was this close made her grit her teeth as she resisted the shot of attraction slowly heating up her veins. The last time his shadows were wrapped around her like this, there was much less clothing between them.

He followed after his shadows, stalking forward until his chest pressed into hers.

"Love. Loathing. Same passion, different names," he told her. "And how easily and swiftly the line can be blurred, don't you think?"

"No," she seethed. "I don't think it will ever be anything but crystal clear to me that I *hate* you."

Leaning down slowly, until his lips were right next to her ear, he said, "Prove it."

THE BEGINNING

OMENS

Genevieve Grimm's first murder was in the heart of Rome.

At the beginning, the crows had shown up one at a time. Squawking in the background of her morning walks to the pasticceria that had become her favorite place to get breakfast. Their jam tarts one of the things she would miss dearly when she left Rome behind to delve into the unknown ahead.

Every morning for the last week she'd packed and repacked her trunks, worried she might be choosing the wrong gowns or forgetting her favorite perfume—or any of the other things she thought might make the best first impression. In the afternoons she explored the city, attempting to visit every significant landmark within a few days, so that her sister, Ophelia, would never suspect she had strayed from their agreed itinerary.

Or that was the excuse she gave herself, anyway.

Really, she was stalling. Thinking that perhaps it was a mistake to pin so many hopes on a stranger who didn't even know she existed. Or that she should wait for a clear-cut sign before uprooting all her sister's carefully laid plans.

It had been at breakfast a few days ago, at the pasticceria, when she'd first recognized that the crows were behaving strangely. One of the little fiends had watched her from a blooming, pink oleander tree while she sipped hot chocolate outside the pastry shop and flipped through a book—a grimoire from Ophelia's collection that she had snuck into her trunk. She'd looked back at the bird, and there was something a bit too shrewd in its gaze. Something unnatural. But the thought that it might be *supernatural* had never crossed her mind.

Neither did the prospect that the feathered beasts would turn into full-blown omens.

The next day, however, the first crow was joined by another, trading shrieks as she walked to the Porta Portese flea market, and again as she walked back to the town house Ophelia had arranged for the duration of the trip. It was that night that the pair had turned into a trio, tapping their beaks against her bedroom window well into the witching hours.

But despite it being clear that there was something off about the birds, Genevieve still wasn't ready to face her suspicion as to why they were pursuing her. Only after her visit to the Colosseum, where she should have been an indistinguishable face amongst a sea of equally clichéd tourists, did the crows become impossible to ignore.

She'd dressed for the day as drably as she was capable of, hoping it might help mitigate any unwanted attention from the birds. Her gown was made of blush chiffon, the hem and sleeves adorably ruffled, and her loose golden-brown curls were swept up in a simple chignon atop her head. She didn't bother with gloves or any sort of jewelry—like herself, corvids enjoyed shiny things a bit too much.

Her effort was rewarded when her walk to the ancient amphitheater was uneventful. Her stroll staying even-paced as she made her way further and further from the town house without spotting a single one of the feathered fiends. Nor was she bothered while she followed a guide around the magnificent attraction.

No, it wasn't until the sun finally dropped below the horizon, turning everything from warm gold to cold silver, and she stepped back outside with the rest of her tour group, that the caws of the murder came with it. A crow was perched on every single rooftop and streetlamp, and the scene of a hundred beady gazes locking onto her face in the middle of the bustling crowd would likely never fade from her memories. Nor would the echo of the burning sensation in her lungs as she ran through the cobblestone streets of Rome while the birds chased after her in a frenzy of shrieks and wings.

The crows never harmed her, never left her with a single scratch on her skin as they swooped too low for comfort and sent the crowds around her screaming in terror. Nor did they pull a hair out of place on her head. They only offered the inescapable feeling of being rushed.

She'd hoped for a sign and she'd certainly gotten one.

"I'll go!" she shouted at the birds. "I just need a little longer!"

Then they *did* get a little too close to her—their wings brushing against her hair, her back, her skirts—as they pushed her toward the town house faster and faster.

She pounded up the path to her front door, her fingers fumbling for the gilded key in her cape's pocket as the birds swooped through the air and began to land on the window ledges and the balcony above. She shoved the key into the lock and listened for the click before pushing herself inside and spinning for the stairs.

I just had to ask for a sign, she admonished herself in her mind. *Now I can't put it off any longer.*

Throwing open the double doors to the primary suite, she hauled a trunk up onto the bed. She cringed as frantic pecking reverberated against the windows of the far wall. Talons scraped over the glass and sent a hair-raising screech through the air as inky feathers fluttered over the panes.

Tossing dresses, skirts, and undergarments onto the bed, she muttered, "It's in here somewhere."

When she finally reached the bottom of the case and plucked out the item she was searching for, the pecking hushed.

It was a black envelope embossed with an intricate filigree

design, the swirling patterns foiled in glittering silver. Its matching wax seal featured an image of a thorned branch adorned with wild roses and berries, a large letter "S" embedded in the center. Inside was a piece of velvety parchment more luxurious than any paper she'd ever felt, and the words elegantly scrawled across it were in rich sapphire ink.

Genevieve pulled the letter from its already torn sleeve, unfolding it as a heavy sensation settled over her shoulders. Her blood began to heat as she read it once again.

From the desk of the Enchantra Estate

Dearest Tessie,

My deepest apologies that it has taken me so long to get back to you. The situation with my family has grown increasingly complicated over the years and I'm afraid that time got away from me. I won't bore you too much with the details.

I know there is much we have to discuss, even beyond the topics of your letters, and so I must <u>insist</u> the two of us do so in person.

I must express my most ardent regret that we left things the way we did and that I neglected to reach out before now, but I would very much like to rectify my mistakes.

Enclosed is a small gift for your travel expenses. Please do not take it as charity, for I know how you are, but as rather I have more than I, or my kin, know what to do with, and it's the least I can offer in order to reunite our acquaintance. I know the spring equinox is soon, but I insist you visit us before its eve, as I will have a brief sabbatical from my duties to Knox. I demand you visit, actually. Plus, the demonberries will be perfectly ripe.

See you very soon.

Your old friend,
Barrington Silver

When she'd opened the letter for the first time back home, she had noticed that the ink of some of the letters had bled ever so slightly, making parts of certain words appear thicker than the others. Revealing an all-too-familiar shape amongst the lines.

A crow.

"Damned fucking birds," she muttered.

The omen was blatant now—as was the sensation emanating from the parchment. The slight buzz of warmth was one that she'd been training herself to recognize in recent months. Magic.

I know the spring equinox is soon, but I insist you visit us before its eve.

Genevieve had always intended to leave Rome with plenty of time before the equinox, but between her nerves and all the city's attractions...

Better late than never, right?

She shoved the invitation back inside the pages of her diary and clasped her trunks closed. It was time.

Behind her the murder reached a crescendo, their beaks hitting the glass panes so hard she wasn't sure how they hadn't yet shattered. Their caws were thunderous as their frantic wings continued to beat in sync with her heart.

"I'm going," she grunted as she hauled her luggage off the bed, the weight of the trunks nearly too heavy.

But when she finally turned around, ready to go, the birds had disappeared.

The Eve of the Spring Equinox

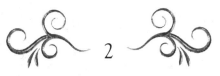

2

THE INVITATION

Afternoon light filtered in through the window, swathing the first-class sleeping car in an enchanting golden hue. The Tuscan countryside just outside was likely one of the most breathtaking sights she'd ever behold, but she could hardly even look at it as it rushed past, her nerves on fire as the train barreled toward its destination.

The last of the lunch carts rolled down the hall outside her roomette, the sound of glasses and plates rattling against each other slowly fading away as it passed. She tapped her foot on the ground in a steady rhythm of impatience as she waited for the train to make its next stop.

The journey through the Italian countryside had been uncomfortable, exhausting, and, worst of all, *tedious.* At first she'd tried rereading the books in her trunk, but after confirming that the plague of crows following her was likely the result of magic known as a hex, she quickly became bored.

Reaching her right hand over to her left, she attempted to fiddle with a ring that she continued to forget she no longer wore. She dropped both hands back into her lap with a frustrated sigh. Being trapped within the same four walls without a single interesting soul to talk to was Genevieve's personal version of Hell. She felt she'd done enough of that growing up in Grimm Manor.

While her late mother, Tessie Grimm, had trained her sister in the art of Necromancy, Genevieve had been stuck with nothing but her stuffed animals and dolls to talk to. As the eldest, Ophelia would be the only one to inherit their mother's magic, and it had taken Genevieve years to realize how their mother's focus on Ophelia had made her feel like an only child. And left her with a constant need to be in a crowd. Or someone else's bed.

Genevieve had become accustomed to hiding her own magic, terrified of her mother finding out about her power and sheltering her like Ophie. She told herself she wanted nothing to do with Tessie Grimm's outlandish world. Then her mother had died, just a few months ago, and Ophelia had taken over their family's legacy. Instead of their mother's approach, Ophelia had decided to embrace her Necromancer title by becoming a sort of problem-fixer for every paranormal being who arrived on Grimm Manor's doorstep in recent months—Witches, Ghosts, Vampires, Devils—and it made Genevieve realize just how willfully naïve she'd been about the world.

Her experience in Phantasma—the Hellish competition that she and Ophelia had entered this past autumn—had made her want to learn as much as she could about such paranormal things. The competition itself had not worried Genevieve a great deal when she'd entered. She'd known that her particular brand of inherited magic—from her and Ophelia's father—would make it easy to avoid all of the physical horrors and trials within the Devil's Manor. But it had been frustrating to think that if she did not have such magic, she would likely have not gotten past a single day in the competition.

There had been plenty of opportunities for Genevieve to tell Ophelia about her newfound desire to learn. But every time Genevieve had tried, she'd found herself unable to admit how foolish she'd been. How she'd been running from her family, from herself, for so long.

Nor had she been ready to admit the *largest* reason she'd stopped scorning the paranormal. Because she was no longer trying to win the affections of a man who'd never loved her...

A whistle sounded overhead, slicing through her thoughts to announce that the train would soon be approaching its next stop—Florence. The closest city to her final destination.

Genevieve's reflection in the window perked up.

She was so close now. So close to discovering another family like hers.

She dug into the pocket of her cape and pulled out a photograph. She had found it in her mother's room, hidden away with other keepsakes from the life Tessie Grimm had led before settling down in New Orleans. A life that even Ophelia knew nothing about.

The sepia-colored picture showed a man standing next to Tessie Grimm, his arm slung over her shoulders in a way that made their comfort with one another very apparent. But what always drew Genevieve's eye was the fact that they were both wearing matching heart-shaped lockets.

From the moment she found the photograph, Genevieve had found herself asking the same questions. She knew that her mother's locket was connected to her family's lineage, that it had always been meant to pass on to Ophelia upon their mother's death. Was the man in the picture a Necromancer, too? Did he have children? Were any of them...like her?

And so her curiosity grew over the years. Until she could no longer resist it.

She flipped the photograph in her hands and read the names on the back, written in her mother's elegant script.

Barrington Silver and Tessie Grimm.

The blast of the steam whistle echoed a second time, and Genevieve shoved the photograph deep into the pocket of her cape. The rhythmic clatter of the train's wheels over the tracks gradually diminished as they approached the new station, the soft hum of the engine slowly quieting as she stood to gather her things.

Despite the invitation's directive to visit Enchantra *before* the eve of the equinox, she couldn't imagine Mr. Silver would turn her away. Firstly, because of the fervor in which his note had been written. There were deep indentations in the paper where the pen had nearly pierced through with the intensity of his strokes. And secondly, because if he refused to speak with her after tormenting her with that hex, she might be tempted to murder him.

Perhaps that last sentiment wasn't exactly fair. After all, the invitation was addressed to her mother, and she should probably never have opened it. Not to mention the guilt she felt for initiating the correspondence with Mr. Silver months before her mother's death, hoping to reconnect them in order to get exactly this sort of invitation. She'd sent six letters, signing each of them with Tessie Grimm's name. But by the time she finally received a letter back, her mother was gone...

A quick rap against her roomette's door startled her out of her thoughts.

"Miss Grimm," the familiar attendant greeted her politely, his thick Italian accent filled with warmth. He had voluminous sable hair and a youthful face. They had shared a few brief conversations over the journey, a nice interruption in the maddening solitude. "Do you wish for me to pack you a meal to go?"

Genevieve shook her head. She was much too excited to eat. "No, thank you, Luca. But if you could help me with one of my trunks, I'd very much appreciate it."

Luca dipped his chin in a nod. "Of course, Miss Grimm."

He stepped forward to gather the larger of the trunks before ducking back out into the hall and pausing for her to follow. She didn't bother lingering or looking back at the stuffy little room, just followed Luca down the narrow hall, relieved to finally be moving on. As they walked, her hip bumped against her trunk and into the wall uncomfortably, her knuckles knocking painfully into the wood paneling as she adjusted her grip. If there was one thing that irked her so far about this continent, it was that everything was much too small for her ample curves and the space she took up.

Checking over her shoulder to make sure the coast was clear from behind, she unfurled a tiny bit of her magic and extended it down her left arm and to the trunk in her hand, making it—and her fist—completely disappear.

When she and Luca finally made it to the front of the train, she returned her hand and luggage to a solid state once more before the small crowd of passengers and employees spotted anything odd. With a gentle hiss, the train doors slid open, revealing the bustling station nestled in the middle of a charming city, the colorful fashion of the crowds and the floral fragrance in the air the clearest signs of spring despite the suddenly cloudy sky above. The crisp breeze was sharp as it hit her skin, the season here so much different from the one back home. More vibrant.

She let Luca step off onto the weathered platform before them and waited for him to set her second trunk on the ground before allowing him to assist her down as well. He gave her a small bow as she procured a folded wad of crisp bills from the gilded case hanging from the chatelaine around her waist beneath her cape.

A warm smile stretched over his face as she pressed the tip into his palm. "It was a pleasure to meet you, Miss Grimm. I shall miss your colorful company."

"I am devastated for you," she told him sincerely, bending down to haul up both of her trunks, ready to leave the train long behind. "Try not to fall into too heavy a depression from my noticeable absence in your life."

He chortled as she turned and pushed herself through the scattered throng of travelers, toward a line of pristinely uniformed men near the station's entrance. She flicked her eyes over each of them with faux admiration and waited to see who might take the bait.

The first one to fold was a middle-aged man with a thick beard and a gnarled cane.

"Hai bisogno di un passaggio, bella ragazza?" he asked.

"I'm sorry," Genevieve told him. "I don't know much Italian. Do you speak English by chance?"

"English, no," he told her, shaking his head. He lifted his cane and pointed to another driver a few carriages to the left. "Morello."

"Grazie," she said before hurrying toward the other man.

This man was handsome, only a year or two her elder, with dark, combed-back hair and hazel eyes that crinkled when he smiled. Which he very much did as she approached.

"Are you Morello?" she checked, giving him a flattering smile.

"I am," he told her. "How may I help you?"

She dropped her bags at his feet. "I'm going to an address a few miles outside of the city. I have a map with all of the details."

She pulled out the hand-drawn map she'd also stolen from her mother's keepsakes and held it up for him. He bit his lip, and for a second she wondered if perhaps he didn't understand the slight drawl of her accent, but as his eyes shifted to the right, toward a father and son hugging each other goodbye, she realized he was only taking a moment to consider her question.

A shriek rang out overhead.

Genevieve looked to the sky, glaring at a trio of crows circling above.

I'm trying! she wanted to scream at them.

She peeled her gaze away from the creatures and cleared her throat to regain Morello's attention, making sure her next words dripped with the sort of saccharine Southern drawl that always seemed to hypnotize the marks she set her sights on.

"I promise to tip handsomely," she told him. "It's probably a bit further than you'd be used to driving, but it would mean the world to me if you could oblige."

His hazel eyes widened at the pleading expression on her face, glazing over ever so slightly, and she knew she was about to get her way.

With a vigorous nod, he bent down to scoop up her bags. He glanced at her hand, clearly checking for a ring, as he said, "No problem, Miss...?"

"Grimm," she provided.

"Miss Grimm," he acknowledged. "Right this way."

It was nearly three hours later that the carriage finally rolled down the long, winding driveway of Barrington Silver's estate. Genevieve brushed back the velvet curtain covering the cab's window and peered outside to take in the romantic landscape that stretched out around her. The birds continued to fly just ahead, chaperoning her through a much clearer sky than the one back at the station.

At least they're quiet now, she thought as her gaze dropped back to the horizon.

Nestled within the rolling hills of the countryside, the vineyard unfolded like a canvas of nature's finest artistry. Rows and rows of staked vines stretched out over the meticulously pruned fields, flowering trees adding splashes of color in every direction while the golden sun combed through their branches. As the carriage continued down the drive, a massive gate came into view. The swirling details of its silver metalwork were so intricate that they almost obscured the name spelled within its ornate design.

Enchantra.

The carriage rolled to a stop, and she heard Morello call out her name with confusion. When the cab's door swung open a beat later, his eyes were filled with concern.

"Miss Grimm, I worry your directions may have contained a mistake."

She lifted a brow. "Why is that?"

He beckoned, offering his hand to help her from the carriage, his boots crunching over the gravel.

A moment later they were standing before the silvered gate. Her eyes traced over the thorned vines entangled amongst the steel bars and narrowing in on the peculiar purple berries that dripped through the spaces between them and littered the ground at their feet.

She pulled the invitation from her pocket once more, Morello watching with rapt curiosity, and, as she had thought, the vines and berries were the exact ones embossed on its wax seal.

"This is definitely the right place," she confirmed to herself.

Morello looked from the envelope to the estate beyond the gates. "But..."

And he was right. There was absolutely a *but.*

Past the gates, as far as she could see, there was nothing but a sprawling, empty field.

3

BERRIES

I can take you back to the city," Morello assured her. "No extra charge."

Genevieve continued to stare through the gates. Something about the scene before her was scratching at the back of her mind...

"Miss Grimm?" Morello pressed.

For a moment she wondered if she should take this as a sign to accept his offer and return to the station. And then something beyond the gate *shimmered*. Like a mirage.

She blinked and it was gone.

A series of belligerent caws sounded above. Genevieve looked up at the sky, now turning black with the promise of rain. The three crows were now circling in an endless loop of anticipation.

She'd come all this way, risked too much trouble, dreamed about this for too long, to go back now.

There's something here for me, she thought. *There must be.*

Squaring her shoulders, Genevieve turned to Morello and stated, "I will not be leaving. I appreciate the ride and do hope you return safely before this weather rolls in."

"But I cannot abandon you here," Morello insisted. "If it's a place to stay that you need I—"

"You can and you will leave me here." She gave a flick of her hand. "I'll be just fine."

"There's nothing else around for miles," he protested. "You cannot possibly expect me to strand a lady in the middle of nowhere."

She sighed. She forgot how deeply entranced some men became with the illusion of sweet innocence she'd crafted—but she didn't have time to let this one down easy. She needed him to *go*.

Channeling the haunting stares her mother and sister were capable of, she fixed the most bone-chilling expression she could muster onto her face. Of course, Genevieve didn't have all the creepy details of a Necromancer working for her like they did—the icy eyes, the pallid complexions—but she'd have to make do.

Reaching inside of herself for a kernel of her magic, she began to make her form flicker in and out of its invisible, non-corporeal state as she crooned, "Who said I was a *lady*?"

Morello balked, stumbling back from her as she continued to flex her magic, his hazel eyes dancing from shock to terror as whatever charm he thought might have drenched her before melted away entirely.

She advanced a step. "Unless you want to end up as one of those whispered legends...of a man who wandered off with a *beautiful* stranger into the middle of nowhere only to disappear and never be heard from again...I suggest you leave. *Now*."

Morello swallowed and backed toward the carriage, though, to his credit, he didn't run.

"One can be only so intimidating when gifted with such a darling appearance, I suppose," she mused beneath her breath.

While Ophelia's icy gaze was often described as unsettling, Genevieve's eyes were a warm, *inviting* cerulean, framed by thick lashes and a heart-shaped face—which had the most *endearing* freckles smattered across the bridge of her nose and pink cheeks. Not to mention her voluptuous figure—which made the soft lines of her curves anything but sharp, even in a corset. Details her suitors had fawned over time and time again.

Your freckles are adorable.

You have the most beautiful eyes.

You're so sweet, you couldn't hurt a fly.

She'd bet good money Farrow Henry had regretted letting that last one roll off his tongue. He would hardly recognize the person who had frightened Morello away.

And frightened she had, because now Morello was scrambling up into his driver's seat, sans promised tip, and snapping the horse's reins to pull away as fast as he could. As the sound of the carriage faded into the distance, it was replaced by the sky's sudden grumbling. She glanced up to see several dark clouds rolling in and sighed. Her outfit was likely going to get ruined.

She turned back to the gate, squinting into the distance beyond it anew, gripping the silver bars and ignoring the stray thorns that dug into her palms as she concentrated.

A beat. And...*aha.*

The shimmer of magic.

"I know you're there," she whispered.

As if her words had awoken something, the sudden feeling that she was being watched sent a tingle down her spine. She glanced over her shoulder, but there was nothing behind her except the winding driveway and the rows and rows of berry-covered vines.

Squawk.

Genevieve jumped, tilting her face upward to find one of the large crows landing atop the gate's arch. She watched, cautious, as it began to peck at the berries dripping from the sculpted steel.

Plus, the demonberries will be perfectly ripe.

Genevieve reached up to pluck one of the bright, purplish berries from its vine, holding it up in front of her face to inspect. It wasn't quite a grape, nor was it a blueberry, but despite its strangeness, it certainly made her mouth water.

Of course they do, she could imagine Farrow's voice saying. *You're a Demon yourself, after all.*

Genevieve gritted her teeth.

She had entered Phantasma in part to escape him, but she'd found the manor's hallways crowded with wispy illusions of Farrow, lurking in every cobweb-filled corner. His face had appeared to her in the middle of the night when she couldn't sleep—and in her nightmares when she could—and he had somehow managed to follow just one step behind her everywhere she went, even after she'd escaped the haunted house's bleeding walls.

He was in the reflection of her hot chocolate at every café. In the heat of every fire. In the faces of the few lovers she'd had since he shattered her heart to pieces. Some days the agony of what happened between them lingered in a way that made everything she thought she knew about herself hazy. Like all this time she'd thought she'd been breathing clean air, but now she realized the smoke had just taken a while to suffocate her.

She had hoped maybe the unwanted memories would stop when she finally left New Orleans, but as the dull memory of ocean-blue eyes watching her through a wall of orange flames flickered through her mind now, she knew no amount of distance would take the burn of his memory away.

Ophelia might be the Necromancer, but Genevieve dealt with Ghosts just the same. Only hers were still alive.

Forget him, she ordered herself as she popped the fruit onto her tongue, relishing the sweet taste of the juice that flooded her mouth when she cracked open its icy exterior with her teeth.

"*Mmm,*" she hummed in satisfaction.

She picked another. And another.

The berries were delicious enough that she didn't notice the change occurring around her at first. When her eyes refocused, the last berry she'd plucked dropped to the ground in her slackened hand as the magic veil she'd seen rippling in the air finally lifted beyond the gates.

Stretching across the grounds in front of her was an intricate hedge maze, the lush green walls too tall for her to see what it might hide in its center. But even the looming labyrinth couldn't block out the glittering silver villa it sat in front of. Two squared structures that looked like towers bookended the front façade, stretching so high into the gloomy sky above that they nearly kissed the clouds. The entire stone exterior was encrusted with pearls of silver and draped in the same climbing, thorned vines as the gate. She could see that the driveway continued just beyond the locked entryway, forking before it reached the hedge maze and circling around to either side of the estate. And all of it was dusted in untouched, powdery white.

Snow? How odd . . .

She pressed herself closer to the bars as if it would make her vision clearer, confirming that she wasn't hallucinating the flurries of ice covering everything beyond the gates. The silver fence enclosed the entire perimeter as far as she could see, but with the sheer size of the grounds, and the eyes of a mere mortal, she couldn't tell exactly how far back the property actually went.

"I suppose I'll have to just go see for myself," she said, but before she summoned her magic, she hesitated.

She wondered whether this decision was going to be as irrevocable as some of the others she'd made. Once she stepped beyond the gates, she knew whatever she found might change her, and she'd already changed so much over the last year. Her reflection in the mirror not the naïve girl she used to be.

Yet all those changes were precisely what had led her to Enchantra now. There was something more waiting beyond the bars, the answer to a need she'd had for a very long time. A history that she hoped might help her understand why her mother had never been able to give her what she needed. Companion-ship that might make her feel like there was somewhere she might fit in outside of Grimm Manor.

Squawk.

Genevieve straightened herself up and glared at the crow, then let her magic warm in her veins as she turned herself non-corporeal long enough to slide through the bars. Once she slipped free of the gate and became solid once more, she padded down the remainder of the driveway, following its fork to the right to avoid the pruned labyrinth ahead.

A moment later the strange feeling of being watched flooded over her once again. She paused.

"Hello?" she called, peering into the thick bushes.

When a brief rustling sounded from within the hedges, she sucked in a sharp breath. A shadowy form suddenly leaped from the wall of greenery, and Genevieve let out a yelp of surprise as she stumbled backward, tripping over her skirts and barely catching herself before she crashed to the ground.

As she righted herself, her gaze clashed with a set of glowing amber eyes. A black fox.

The creature tilted its head at her as it fixed itself into a much too self-aware position, sitting with its front paws carefully crossed on the ground. As if it were waiting for an explanation on why she was trespassing.

"I was invited," Genevieve insisted to the fox despite how ridiculous it felt. "See, I have an invitation—"

The sable creature lunged forward and snatched the paper from her grasp before diving back into the maze.

"*Hey!*" she yelled as she swiped at the fluffy tip of its tail, but it squirmed right out of her grasp and disappeared. "Are you fuck-ing *kidding* me?"

She instinctually shifted into her invisible state and plunged into the greenery after it. On the other side of the hedge, she found herself within one of the labyrinth's many winding corridors as the fox skittered away to her right. She picked up her skirts and ran after it.

Fortunately for her, as the critter led her deeper into the maze, it began to slow its pace, thinking itself safe. Unfortunately for it, her invisibility made it rather easy to sneak up from behind.

As she became solid, she snatched the fox into the air by its scruff, letting it wriggle violently in her clutch as she tried to pry the black envelope from its maw with her free hand. It only locked its jaw tighter.

She clucked her tongue at the creature. "*Drop it!*"

The fox made a low, keening sound in its throat as its shrewd, gold eyes glared at her in a way that was much too humanlike.

"Don't you growl at me! *You're* the menace here," she chastised as she continued to yank at the invitation. "If you don't let go, I shall have to—"

Before she could finish her threat, the fox, and the envelope, evaporated into thick black smoke. Genevieve blinked in disbelief.

What in the Hell just happened? she wondered, her heart pounding as she slowly turned around, looking for an explanation.

Squawk.

Her gaze snapped to the sky.

"Shoo!" she yelled at the crow as it dipped a bit too low in the air. She'd had enough. "I've arrived! You did your job! It's time for you to *fuck off* and—"

Before she could finish, the bird dropped to the ground with a lifeless thud. She stared for a tense beat, taking in its engorged belly.

The berries . . . ?

"Well, that can't be good," she muttered as her vision slowly grew blurry. She tried to take a step back, to leave the puzzling maze, but everything around her was beginning to spin and her feet were refusing to work.

A moment later the world slipped away entirely.

There was something cold and wet nudging at Genevieve's face as the shadows crept back ever so slightly from the edges of her mind. Rapid, sniffled breaths huffed against her cheek before she was lifted from the ground and cradled against something hard and warm.

"Farrow?" she muttered, trying to pry her eyes open, to break her way out of the hold she was in. But she was too weak to fight, and whoever it was felt sturdier than Farrow, anyway. Their scent...sharp mint cut by something sweet...was nothing like the musky cologne Farrow used to drown himself in.

"Apuell abon, Umbra," a deep, unfamiliar voice murmured.

And somehow she knew exactly what that voice was saying. *Good girl, Umbra.*

Genevieve couldn't make out the rest of their words as the shadows flooded her mind once more, the sounds all mushing together. She tried one last time to open her eyes, to see who was there, but all she managed to glimpse was a brief flash of gold before the darkness swallowed her completely.

The nightmare was always the same.

He stood over her with a lit match as she desperately tried to disappear.

"You're a Demon. I wish I'd never met you. And now you'll fucking burn."

When Genevieve finally awoke, it was on the outside of Enchantra's gates, next to her trunks, with no recollection of how she got there and a bitter taste in her mouth.

4

WARMEST WELCOME

Genevieve sat up with a groan, a chill deep in her bones as she grimaced at the awful taste clinging to her tongue.

"What the *Hell*..." she whispered to herself as she rubbed her throbbing temples.

When she glanced over to the gates, she saw nothing beyond them, yet something in the back of her mind was telling her that was *wrong*. She shifted onto her knees and leaned forward, narrowing her eyes at the peculiar berries hanging around the bars.

A flicker of a memory flashed through her mind. Of her plucking one of the berries and putting it on her tongue...

Then another moment came back. Of her walking through the bars and watching a glittering villa appear before her eyes, a leafy labyrinth sprawling before it. The dead crow. The fox.

Have I gone mad?

She took a deep breath and reached out to wrap her hands around the bars and pull herself to her feet—

—and yelped in pain.

She snatched her hands back from the metal, cradling them against her chest as she let out a furious hiss at the searing buzz of magic that lingered on her skin. And everything suddenly sharpened in her mind. She had absolutely not gone mad. There had been a crow. A fox. A mysterious figure...carrying her...

She pushed herself back onto her feet, glancing down to brush off her dress and nearly choking at how dirty and rumpled it'd become. She huffed as she grabbed up her trunks, turning to the gate with rigid resolve as she reached for her magic and passed through the silver bars once more. As soon as she was back on the other side, it was as if a thick, hazy film had been peeled away from her senses. There, the hidden estate appeared once again in its full glory. She wondered whether the berries had done exactly as they were supposed to, but when she was put back on the other side, their magic was meant to make her forget what she had seen.

"Magic is such a thorn in my side," she grumbled, remaining in her non-corporeal state as she stepped right into the outer leafy wall of the hedge maze. She passed straight through the bushes, and the empty corridors between them, before finally finding herself clear of the labyrinth on the complete opposite side, yards away from the front porch of the expansive villa. As she approached the white marble steps, she noted the same scrawling letter "S" embossed into the double doors.

Returning to her solid form, she dropped her luggage on the porch before rocking up onto the balls of her feet to lift the silver knocker. The knocker's ring was an intricately crafted circlet of thorned vines, their points biting into her palm as she slammed it down with a heavy, metallic clang to announce her arrival.

For a long minute nothing happened. The silence in the air was eerie, the lack of life around, in general, alarming. Before she had time to lose her nerve, however, the door on the right heaved open. Genevieve sucked in a breath at the strange power that began to crackle in the air as a figure stepped up to the threshold, leaning one shoulder against the door's frame as their shrewd gaze took her in. A gaze that was an oddly familiar shade of amber.

The golden-eyed stranger stood a little less than a foot over her own—*very respectable*—five feet and five inches. His disheveled black hair was a bit longer than the preferred style of the men in New Orleans, combed back haphazardly and curling ever so slightly at the ends. His face was conventionally attractive—square jaw, sharp cheekbones, perfectly straight nose—in a way that may have leaned toward boring on anyone else. But the golden hoop that was pierced through his full bottom lip and the hypnotizing gold of his eyes enticed Genevieve in a way that was *sinful.*

He was wearing a tailored black shirt that was stark against his ivory complexion, a silk waistcoat affixed overtop and perfectly cut to his muscular frame. His pleated black trousers hung flatteringly at his waist, secured with a matching leather belt that was encrusted with onyx gems. He had stacks of obsidian rings adorning most of his fingers, and despite the sharp, unmistakable edge of darkness clinging to the air around him, there was something very intentional and refined about his appearance. So unlike the bland bachelors back home, who thought less effort translated to *stylish* for whatever reason. And certainly a complete departure from the man with golden hair and blue eyes that she saw in her nightmares.

Night and day.

Genevieve shook off the thought of Farrow, chastising herself for letting him run amok in her mind, and refocused her attention on the stranger in front of her. She cleared her throat.

"Hello," she greeted with a vibrant smile.

He said nothing as he scrutinized her as carefully as she had him, and it was an effort not to shift under the intensity of his gaze.

She lifted her chin. "My name is Genevieve Grimm."

"And?" he drawled. "What the fuck do you want?"

She hadn't necessarily expected the warmest welcome for showing up unannounced after the invitation's proposed dates, but the ire in his words truly puzzled her.

"May I come in?" she requested.

"No," he stated, his voice not particularly loud, but inarguably firm. "Anything else?"

"Yes. I want a *fucking* audience with Barrington Silver, and I'm not leaving until I get one," she told him.

For the briefest of seconds, she could've sworn the corners of his mouth twitched upward, but a blink later and his scowl had only deepened.

"I think you're lost," he told her, a threat simmering beneath the tight words. "Turn around and go back to wherever the Hell you came from. You're trespassing."

With that, he slammed the door right in her face.

For a moment she could only gape in disbelief.

When she recovered, a grunt of annoyance sounding in her throat, she grabbed for the silver knocker once again. His manners were ghastly, but she'd gone through too much trouble coming all this way to let a single boorish man stop her now. Hopefully he was just part of the staff, someone to scare away anyone who might accidentally stumble upon the estate.

Though he definitely *looked* like he could be a Necromancer.

She slammed the heavy knocker down once, twice, three times. When both doors wrenched open this time, there was a foreboding swirl of shadows dancing in the background, creating a smokelike halo around the stranger's broad frame. As the shadows began to spill out of the doorway, Genevieve rocked back on her heels, her breathing turning shallow as the inky wisps began to curl around her. The skin of her arms began pebbling at the unfamiliar power that shrouded him, but she stayed planted in place, refusing to give up any ground despite her instincts screaming at her to run.

Unless Ophelia has been hiding some of her abilities from me, I think it's safe to say that he's not a Necromancer, at all.

"Do you not understand when you are unwanted somewhere?" he growled.

"About as well as you understand how to treat a guest, I presume," she retorted, her voice a bit breathier than she would have liked. "But as I was *saying*, I have a letter from the head of this estate inviting me to Enchantra. And don't try to claim I've gotten the wrong place. The name is written on the front gate."

"So it is," he agreed as he crossed his arms, the shadows still wriggling around him like serpents poised to strike. "Why don't you show me this supposed invitation, then?"

She reached into her pockets, but when she didn't find the envelope, the memory hit her. *The fox.*

She glanced back to the stranger's face and saw that a taunting smirk had replaced the scowl on his lips.

"You know *exactly* where my invitation is," she accused, jabbing a finger in his face.

He said nothing, and when she tapped her foot with impatience, his eyes tracked the motion, the glint in them shifting to something akin to amusement. Though the tight clench of his jaw might argue otherwise.

"So, how does it work?" She propped a hand on her hip. "The fox. Is it some sort of magical illusion? A trained pet? Or was that *you*? Do you possess some sort of shapeshifting ability? What *are* you exactly?"

Because, Necromancer or not, he was undoubtedly *something*. And though he looked like he was only five or six years older than her, the sheer *presence* of him made her wonder whether the youth of his appearance was deceiving.

"What are *you*?" he retorted. "Besides trouble, I mean. How in the Hell did you get past the reinforcements on the gate a second time?"

"Aha!" she exclaimed, satisfaction flooding through her. "*You* put me back on the other side after I fainted. Were you not going to make sure I woke up? That I wasn't *dead?*"

"Wouldn't have been my concern if you were," he told her, a look of boredom settling in his peculiar gold eyes.

"You're an absolute cad," she commented, wrinkling her nose. "Your attitude is horrendous."

The smile that curled onto his lips at her insult was dangerous.

He leaned down, until his eyes were level with hers, their noses nearly touching. "Don't want to deal with my attitude? *Leave.*"

She balled her hands into fists. "*No.* I already told you—I'm not leaving until I speak to Mr. Silver. And especially not until I know that whatever hex was put on me has been lifted. Do you know what it's like to be followed around by hundreds of screaming birds everywhere you go?"

His expression turned mocking. "Equally enjoyable as this conversation?"

"I was invited here, and you know it," she maintained as if he hadn't spoken.

"I believe someone named Tessie was invited. And specifically requested to arrive *before* the eve of the equinox according to said invitation," he countered. "That deadline has passed, and you said your name was Juniper—"

"*Genevieve,*" she corrected.

"—therefore, the invite doesn't apply to you at all. I'll warn you one last time—*leave.*"

The slam of the door in her face was less unexpected this time.

She stood there for a long minute, trying to decide whether she wanted to risk vacating the grounds without confirmation that her little murder problem had been taken care of by simply coming here. Except the stranger had made the mistake of rousing her curiosity—and her stubbornness—and she found herself much more interested in finding out what he was so determined to keep her from discovering inside the house. Not to mention she was not sure that she could live with the idea of leaving him to think he had won.

I deserve to find others like me, she reminded herself. *If I find Barrington and show him the photograph, I'm sure he'd want that for me, too.*

Besides, what was worse? Coming so close to everything she'd been wanting for so long and walking away like a coward—or dealing with another insufferable man?

Those are a dime a dozen, she thought.

After collecting her baggage, she shifted herself into her noncorporeal form and passed right through the door before she could give it another thought. When she let herself solidify on the other side, dropping her trunks onto the gray-and-white-checkered floor of the foyer, she'd expected to find the hostile stranger still lingering there. But there was nothing around except ominous silence.

5

SPECTER

The foyer was grand in the way that only people with more wealth than they know what to do with could make things grand. Its ceiling was a mosaic of the night sky, encrusted with what she'd like to assume were diamonds for the glittering stars. The top halves of each wall were covered in jewel-toned murals of the Italian countryside. Shining foil details highlighted the strokes of the swirling clouds and flowering trees. The bottom halves were adorned with the most intricate wainscoting she'd ever seen, the molding painted a rich midnight blue.

The star of the scene, however, was the chandelier. Six tiers of pear-shaped crystals scattered specks of rainbow light across the room. Taper candles were nestled into the opulent sconces that hung every five or so feet along the walls. And every inch of the room was covered in dust.

Decaying opulence. What a waste.

On the far side of the foyer was a set of enormous wooden doors wedged between two marble pillars. To her left was a corridor that seemed to lead to the main part of the villa, windows stretching along its front wall to allow the natural light—or, in the present case, the snowstorm's gloom—to flood between the rich plum curtains. Large rectangular frames draped in taupe drop cloths were affixed along every wall, and Genevieve couldn't help but approach one of the hidden pieces, wondering why anyone would cover so much art. Except that when she brushed back the thick material, she saw that it wasn't art at all—it was a silvered mirror.

How odd . . .

To her right was a hallway, its left side lined with doors. On the opposite wall, however, was a row of enormous oil portraits, all framed in scrolling silver. Genevieve started down the hall, wondering whether she might be able to find someone in one of the rooms, but the strangeness of the first portrait caught her attention and brought her to a halt.

The painted girl was not much older than Genevieve, with striking white hair that fell to her waist and wispy bangs that parted on either side of her forehead to frame her face. Her eyes were pitch-black beneath her thick lashes, a jarring contrast to the rest of her fair features. As were her wine-colored lips, set in a way that made it seem like she knew a secret the viewer did not. She was posed on a silver velvet wingback chair in an ice-blue gown, and at her feet sat a full-grown snow leopard.

Genevieve blinked twice at the large spotted cat.

Surely not a pet, she thought as she shuffled over to the next portrait.

This one depicted a man whose facial structure looked very reminiscent of the girl beside him. Instead of pale hair and dark eyes, however, his unruly tresses were the color of ink, almost navy, tucked behind his ears, where large sapphire jewels dangled from each lobe. And his eyes . . . they were such a pale gray they were nearly white.

Genevieve shivered. *If I ever thought Ophie's eyes were creepy . . .*

The man was propped up on the same chair as the girl, and though there was no leopard at his feet, there *was* a black owl perched on his shoulder. Its glare painted in a way that seemed to follow the viewer.

Before Genevieve could move down to the next painting, a

thud echoed from somewhere overhead. She spun and hurried back toward the foyer, hoping to find a staircase that could take her to whoever was making the racket. Hopefully the owner of the estate himself. Or at least someone other than the golden-eyed stranger.

She noticed now that the set of double doors at the back were slightly ajar. She strutted toward them and hauled one open, stopping in her tracks as she took in the room on the other side. A grand ballroom. The sort that she often imagined as the backdrop of her daydreams.

High above her head, the ceiling was adorned with lively frescoes depicting battles between various paranormal and ephemeral beings—Devils with red talons ripping apart Shapeshifters in the middle of their transformations, Reveries spilling their opalescent blood into the mouths of Vampires, Angels ripping off one another's wings. The walls were draped in golden curtains tied back to reveal the tall arched windows that allowed silvery light to spill over the marble dance floor and illuminate more covered mirrors on the wall across from them. Between two of those windows was an enormous, gilded clock. The Roman numerals of its hours sat in the center of twelve large circles, all of them black except the current hour—four—which was as gold as its faceplate. And at the farthest corner of the ballroom, she caught a glimpse of exactly what she'd been looking for—a grand staircase. The steps led to a second-story landing, where a balcony surrounded three sides of the dance floor.

Genevieve moved toward the carpeted stairs, running her fingers over the gilded banister to leave a clean trail through the thick dust as she climbed, eyes searching through the shadows ahead for anything living. When she reached the landing, she noticed something out of the corner of her eye, unfurling like smoke.

Her head snapped toward the fox. "*You.*"

The fox gave a taunting swish of its tail before spinning and scurrying away. Genevieve gave chase, following it around a sharp corner to the left and into a wide corridor lined with closed doors. She squinted into the dark, but either the fox was blending in perfectly with the shadows, or it was gone.

"Hello?" she called out as she slowly made her way down the hall. "Anyone up here?"

She approached the first door to her right and twisted its knob, surprised to find it unlocked as she pulled it open. The room was . . . empty. No bed, no furniture, just a plain white box. She shut the door and checked the next room. Empty.

What a peculiar waste of space . . .

"Who the Hell are *you?*" someone hissed.

Genevieve reared back from the empty room's threshold and spun to find someone standing at the mouth of the corridor. They had spoken in a language Genevieve didn't recognize, and certainly shouldn't have understood, and yet every word had been crystal clear in her mind.

As they came closer, Genevieve realized it was the girl from the painting. Except her ghostly-white hair had been chopped into a sleek, blunt bob, the strands barely reaching the tops of her shoulders as they swished with the swiftness of her approaching stride.

"How did you get in here?" the girl demanded in that same language as her gaze roamed over the state of Genevieve's dress.

"Through the front door," Genevieve answered as she smoothed her hands over the boning of her bodice. She must look horribly unkempt. Definitely not her idea of a good first impression.

The girl snorted. "You've got gall, you know. If you're one of Knox's guests—you're early. And absolutely fucked. The Hunt is *tomorrow.*"

The Hunt?

"Not that you'll be there, since your funeral will be tonight," the girl continued, her tone too nonchalant for the words she was speaking.

"I don't know what you're talking about," Genevieve told her. "And how could I understand you before? You weren't speaking English..."

"Are you daft?" the girl asked, genuinely concerned now as she scrutinized Genevieve's face. "How exactly did you end up here?"

Oh. "There's this black fox—"

"Umbra?" The girl's eyes narrowed shrewdly now. "Did *Rowington* let you in here?"

Umbra. Rowington.

Genevieve filed those names away for later. "*Let* isn't necessarily the right word—"

"Ellin?" a deep voice echoed from around the corner, and for a moment Genevieve's stomach churned with worry over the confrontation that was about to occur, but when she and *Ellin* turned toward the voice, Genevieve was relieved to find it was not the golden-eyed bastard at all. No, this man was just a bit leaner, his raven hair perfectly combed back, the sides slightly more cropped than the top. The skin of his chest peeking out beneath his half-unbuttoned shirt was tattooed with crude tally marks, as were the slivers of his wrists right above his cuffs. The most striking detail about him, however, was the crimson color of his eyes.

Well, his eyes and the fact that he was perhaps the most attractive person Genevieve had ever seen. It was startling how handsome he was, honestly. Enough to make her blush.

"Ellington, you're dawdling," the man drawled around what looked to be a lollipop hanging out the corner of his mouth, his strut unhurried. And again Genevieve noted that he was speaking the same language the girl had been before, yet she had no problem understanding him. "Rowin already made up all of our rooms, and he's going to be cross if he finds out I got blood all over my—"

The man paused abruptly when he finally spotted Genevieve, then swung his gaze back to Ellin, his scarlet eyes narrowing into a brotherly glare. And Genevieve was pretty sure he was: the girl's brother, that is. Not only because of the clear resemblance—in the sharp slopes of their noses, the shapes of their eyes and mouths, their pitying, judgmental stares—but because the expression on his face was the sort of look only a sibling could give you right before they helped you clean up a mess and then extorted a favor out of you for it. Ophelia had worn that exact expression many times in their childhood.

"What the *fuck*, Ellin?" the man said as he pulled the cherry-red sucker from his mouth. "Did you leave the Hellmouth open again? Have the last two centuries not made you tired of watching Knox slaughter people?"

What the Hell is he talking about?

Ellin propped her hands onto her hips. "*I* did not let her in. I just found her here, asshole. Rowin is the one to ask—"

"*Rowin?*" He cut her off, eyebrows shooting up in disbelief.

Ellin shrugged. "She mentioned Umbra."

The man flicked his gaze over to Genevieve. "You're here with Rowin?"

"If I am?" Genevieve asked, mostly because she didn't quite understand what they might be getting at, but his previous words were still ringing in the back of her mind like an alarm.

Have the last two centuries not made you tired of watching Knox slaughter people?

Knox. That was the name Barrington had mentioned in his

letter. Something about having a brief break from his duties to *Knox*.

"If you're with Rowin, I have quite a few questions," the man said, switching to English just as easily as Ellin had. "But if you aren't, I think it'd be more humane to put you out of your misery before Knox or Grave find you here." He casually unsheathed a blade from his belt with his free hand.

"Sevin, not over the carpet," Ellin sighed.

Genevieve was careful not to give a reaction, despite her quickening pulse at the sight of the knife and the lingering threat in his words. What in the fuck was wrong with the residents of this household?

"I am with Rowin," Genevieve rushed out as *Sevin* shifted on his feet, waiting for her response.

"Fantastic, because I've spilled too much blood already," Sevin admitted at the same time that Ellin asked, "With Rowin in what way?"

Before Genevieve could answer either of them, there was a sudden shout from somewhere downstairs. The siblings exchanged a loaded look.

"Did that sound like Grave?" Ellin wondered.

Genevieve cautiously backed a step away. They didn't seem to notice.

The smile that unfurled on Sevin's lips was terrifying. "I want a front-row view of Grave's face when he sees *her*."

Ellin huffed. "What in the Hell do you think Rowin's up to? He couldn't possibly be trying to attempt—"

Genevieve shifted into her invisible state, letting the rest of their discussion fade behind her as she slipped past them and hurried back toward the stairs. She dashed across the ballroom floor and sighed in relief once she made it back to the foyer, turning solid only so she could collect her bags. Before she managed to grasp onto their handles, however, she was being pushed back against a wall.

She glanced up into furious amber eyes.

Rowin.

Genevieve tried to sidestep from between him and the wall, but he simply pressed his palms against the flat surface on either side of her and caged her in place with his arms.

He was *really* starting to piss her off.

"You're a *Specter?*" he demanded between clenched teeth.

"Do you have some sort of issue with that?" she snapped, itching to bring her knee up between his legs and *make* him move out of her way.

"What I have an issue with is the fact that you clearly don't know how to fucking listen," he growled, dragging her thoughts back to the present. "If I had known you were capable of getting through the wards on the gate, I wouldn't have bothered to help you recover from the demonberries. Do you have absolutely any idea what you've done? What game you're now playing? I suspect you don't, or you would never have come here."

"What the fuck is your problem?" she demanded before letting her magic flood through her and slipping through his form. He spun. "And your siblings threatening to *put me out of my misery?* What is wrong with all of you?"

"Don't ask questions you don't want the answers to," he warned.

"Oh, I guarantee I'm dying to know whatever ludicrous explanation you have for your ghastly hospitality," she told him. "I grew up in a house full of dead people, and it was less hostile than this. Were you all raised by the animals in your portraits? Do you have rabies? Or should I be concerned about the water?"

He stared down at her with an unreadable expression for a long moment. Then, "You met my siblings?"

Genevieve lifted a brow at his abrupt change in subject but still gave a nod of confirmation. "Ellin and Sevin, right?"

"Anyone else?" he interrogated.

"No, thank goodness. Or else I might have had to start using both hands to count all the threats I've received in the last half hour," she muttered. "And who is Knox? And Grave? What is *the Hunt*? Where is Barrington Silver? Why is it that they spoke to me in a language I don't know and yet somehow it still made sense?"

"You'll be getting those answers soon enough," he promised, his tone making the words sound almost like a threat. "I hope there isn't anyone waiting on you. A parent or a spouse who—"

He stiffened now, cutting himself off, and the way he was suddenly regarding her made her shift on her feet. His eyes began to darken as he flicked his gaze down to her...hands?

She glanced down at her suede gloves. Dyed a lovely blush color and trimmed with fur, they were her favorite pair because of their little pearl button details. But she didn't think the gloves' craftsmanship was what he was admiring.

"Are you married?" he asked, eyes narrowing in on her left ring finger.

Genevieve tucked her hand into her chest. "And what business would that be of yours?"

What an odd question.

The smile that began to unfurl at the corners of his mouth made alarm bells go off in the back of her mind. "You truly have no idea what sort of trouble you've gotten yourself into."

"Then I'll leave," she insisted, but when she tried to take a step toward her luggage, he blocked her path yet again.

"Leaving stopped being an option the second you set foot in this house," he told her.

"*Move*," she ordered. "I've had enough of being in your presence."

He huffed a laugh. "Well, you may want to find a way to get used to it."

"What do you mean?" she fumed. She was exhausted from the day's travel and desperately needed a proper bath and a hot meal. She had no energy to decipher any more cryptic threats.

His smile turned grim, but he didn't offer any more explanation. All he said was, "Umbra."

The shadows she'd seen swirling around him earlier began to reappear, slowly spilling out from *him*, the smokelike tendrils forming shadowy limbs. She watched in awe as a few of the inky wisps broke away and transformed into the fox. Genevieve glared at the fluffy creature as it wove itself affectionally between Rowin's legs. Umbra blinked wide yellow-orange eyes back at her—the color of them an exact match to Rowin's—and again Genevieve wondered what sort of being he was.

"Umbra, would you mind watching over our *guest* while I go find my father?" he requested the fox, the word *guest* sounding like a placeholder for something much more unsavory.

Before any of them could move, however, someone said, "Rowington."

Rowin's head snapped to his left as a tall figure appeared next to them in a swirling cloud of deep violet smoke.

"You know if Knox arrives and the mirrors are still covered, he'll be cross," the voice continued as the purple wisps of magic fully dispersed in the stale air.

Genevieve's mouth dropped open at the sight of the new arrival. She would have recognized this man anywhere.

Barrington Silver.

6

Familiar

The first thing Genevieve noticed as she stared at Barrington was that the locket he had worn in the photograph with her mother was nowhere to be seen.

The second thing was that, while the photo must have been taken at least a couple of decades ago, the man didn't seem to have aged a day since.

Immortal.

Genevieve's mother had held powerful magic, but she had aged like any ordinary woman. Barrington Silver was no Necromancer. He was some other kind of being entirely.

A cold feeling of fear and disappointment settled in Genevieve's stomach. She had made a mistake coming here. This family was definitely not like her own. Back in Grimm Manor, hunting down the reason for the matching lockets had seemed like a stroke of genius. But now she knew it had been nothing but desperate hope.

Barrington was taller than Rowin—though not by much—with pure salt hair and bright purple irises. The resemblance between them was crystal clear when they were side by side, except Barrington seemed *warm.*

Perhaps that is simply the effect of knowing him for so long through a photograph, she thought. *Or the fact that Rowin has been nothing but insufferable since the moment he opened the door—and his mouth.*

"If you don't mind, I'd like to go now." Genevieve said as she flicked her eyes between the two men.

Barrington's gaze snapped over to Genevieve as if he hadn't realized she'd been standing there. His face drained of color as he took her in. Like he was seeing a Ghost.

"Father," Rowin greeted dryly. "There's been an...occurrence."

"What have you *done?*" Barrington growled at Rowin.

Rowin's expression remained smooth. "I tried to stop her from coming in, but she doesn't respond very well to threats."

"But I'm leaving now," Genevieve insisted before the strange tension bubbling between the men could boil over. "I just wanted to ask you a few questions. And then you can lift the wards on your gate and I'll—"

"I already told you that leaving was no longer an option," Rowin threw at her. "The magic on the front gates will fry you if you go back there now."

"I'm afraid you don't seem to understand what's happening here, dear girl," Barrington agreed, his eyes still shining with a bit of disbelief as he took a step toward her. "It isn't your fault, of course—"

"We'll have to disagree on that front," Rowin bit out. "She was warned away *several* times."

"But the wards are not ours to lift," Barrington finished as if Rowin hadn't spoken. "You should never have been allowed to set foot inside Enchantra."

"Why? What is going on?" Genevieve demanded.

"She's a fucking *Specter,*" Rowin snapped. "What else did you want me to do? Maim her so she couldn't walk back in?"

Genevieve made an indignant noise.

Rowin gave her an unsympathetic look before addressing his father again. "She made her own bed, and now she'll have to lie in it. Which, incidentally, could be a *win* for me. Don't you think that has a nice *ring* to it?"

Barrington gave his son an odd look; then his eyes lit up with an emotion Genevieve didn't understand. He flicked his gaze between her and Rowin like he'd had some sort of epiphany, but he didn't bother saying what it was. Rowin gave his father a nod.

"Stop with the silent conversation," Genevieve demanded.

"You're right, we're being rude. Rowington, why don't you go inform your siblings of what's happening," Barrington suggested.

Rowin readily stalked away, and Barrington turned his full attention on Genevieve.

"You're Tessie Grimm's daughter," he stated.

Genevieve raised her brows in surprise at his recognition. She was not the daughter that favored Tessie Grimm. Not in any way.

"Yes. I am," she confirmed.

"Ophelia?"

She shook her head. "My name is Genevieve. Vivi, if you'd like. Ophelia is my sister."

Barrington's eyes fluttered shut for a moment. "What, exactly, has your mother told you about me?" he said.

"Nothing." The answer was automatic, instinctual. Truthfully, it wouldn't have mattered what he'd asked, as long as the question started with *what has your mother told you?* The answer to any question beginning that way would always be the same. "But I found a photograph of you and her. And I read some of your old letters. I thought maybe you were also a Necromancer. I was hoping. . . . well, it doesn't matter now."

"Damn it, Tessie," Barrington muttered, pinching the bridge of his nose as if he were starting to get a migraine. "It seems there has been some confusion. I would very much like to return you home to your mother, but today is the one day of the year that visiting Enchantra is...catastrophic. Leaving will not be straightforward, and I will need your cooperation."

"My cooperation with *what?*" she asked.

He sighed and beckoned for her to follow him. "Come. The house still needs to be prepared. And since my children refuse to do anything useful in this household, an extra pair of hands would be valuable."

He walked over to one of the covered mirrors on the wall of the foyer and Genevieve helped him pull down its drop cloth in a cloud of dust. She coughed, waving her hand in the air to shoo away the dust as Barrington moved on to the next mirror. She huffed and followed.

"I want to know who Knox is. And what is the Hunt? Who controls the wards on the gates? How come I can understand what you're saying even when it isn't in English? What exactly do you want me to cooperate with?" she demanded as he went from mirror to mirror, uncovering them. "And why the Hell are there so many mirrors in this house?"

"You certainly are Gabriel White's daughter," Barrington murmured.

Her inhale was sharp. "You've met my father? I thought per-haps you and my mother had stopped speaking before..."

"I met him very, very briefly," Barrington said. He turned sharply and began to walk toward the ballroom's entrance. She stayed on his heels.

"When I said the wards on the estate were not mine to lift, it is because they were made by a very powerful Devil named Knox," he explained as he hooked a right inside the ballroom. "His magic is also the reason you're able to understand our first language—the language of Hell. Many different types of beings will soon walk these halls, and the translation magic allows us all to understand each other. Soon you will not even notice the switch between tongues."

"Wait, Knox is a *Devil?*" Genevieve stopped in her tracks. "I've dealt with enough Devils in my lifetime already."

"Not any like Knox," Barrington promised as he ripped down another drop cloth, this covering one of the enormous mirrors that paralleled the arched windows on the far wall. "Surprising him with an uninvited guest, today of all days, would usually result in us cleaning up a lot of blood. But, fortunately, Rowington is the most practical of my children."

"You've lost me," she admitted. "So you work for this Devil?"

"I don't just work for him, Miss Grimm. I am his Familiar," Barrington revealed, a dark edge to his words. "Do you have any experience with Familiars?"

"I've…heard of them," she said as they walked back toward the front of the house now.

Genevieve thought back to the classification of paranormal beings she had studied in Grimm Manor. Familiars were creatures with no magic of their own who were bound to a powerful host like a Devil. They were classed as immortals, because their lifespans were bound to those of their hosts. If a host lived eternally, so would their Familiar.

It was rare for a human to become a Familiar, though. Mostly they were animals.

The animals in the portraits, Genevieve realized as they made their way across the foyer, to the hallway of paintings. The snow leopard. The owl. *Umbra.*

"The bonds between a Familiar and its host are practically unbreakable," Barrington continued. "Which is why I've been stuck with Knox for as long as I can remember and why most people choose animals over sentient beings. Imagine being tied to someone you hate for eternity."

"Why did you agree to such a bond then?" she wondered.

"It was a foolish endeavor on my part," he admitted. "A mortal man who discovered the world of paranormal beings and became unsatisfied with his fleeting life."

He scoffed at himself as they made it to the painting in the very center of the hallway, the only one that was covered up. To its right was a portrait of Barrington himself, though he did not have a Familiar like the others. It was only him, staring at the viewer with his violet eyes, though she swore at certain angles his irises had a familiar sheen of gold.

"Through my work for Knox I met my wife, Vira," Barrington said as he gently uncovered the painting next to his own. "As you can see, she is a Demon."

The woman in the painting looked to be Ophelia's age, maybe a little older, but the illusion of youth was broken by the heaviness in her crimson eyes. Her hair was white as snow, a single black streak running through it, and her smile was warm despite her pallid complexion.

"We were married, with Knox's permission, and eventually went on to have our seven children: Gravington, Covington, Rowington, Remington, Sevington, Wellington, and Ellington." He waved his hand at the other portraits down the hallway.

Despite his solemn tone, Genevieve had to stop herself from giggling. All their names were utterly *tragic*.

Again, Genevieve thought back to her studies of magical beings.

"If your wife is a Demon and you were once mortal, that would make your children..."

"Wraiths, yes."

Genevieve fought the urge to shudder. She knew little of Wraiths, and none of it was good. The books said they were made from darkness itself, that they craved the blood and souls of others. Thankfully, Barrington did not seem to notice her alarm.

"Due to my work with Knox," he said, "I missed a lot of my children's formative years. By the time they became adults, I knew I needed to find a way to ... retire."

"Mr. Silver, what does any of this have to do with my questions?" Genevieve implored. "I just want to leave."

"You asked me about the wards—and the Hunt," he told her as he beckoned her back toward the foyer. "While I was researching ways to sever my bond to Knox, my wife became very sick. A rare illness called Crimson Rot. When Knox heard of her ailment—and perhaps also of my desire to be rid of him— he offered me a bargain."

Genevieve's eyes widened.

Bargains with Devils were not simple agreements. They were rooted in deep magic, with dangerously specific terms that bound both parties. Devils used them to prey on the desperate or weak-minded. Genevieve might have learned nothing from her mother, but even she knew that making a bargain with a Devil could only ever lead to disaster.

"There is no cure for Crimson Rot." Barrington's voice became hushed now. "But there are temporary fixes—rare and stupefyingly expensive elixirs—that prolong death for about a year at a time. And, as luck would have it, Knox has access to a supply."

Barrington paused now, in the center of the foyer, the light of the chandelier bouncing off the exposed mirrors illuminating the devastation on his face.

"I didn't realize what I was agreeing to. Not fully. Or maybe I did, and I just convinced myself otherwise. Knox had set his eyes on my children, and what he proposed was the Hunt. A game that he designed as a punishment, because I wanted to break my bond. And a spectacle for every gambler and sick fanatic in Hell. He made it sound like the children would only need to go through the Hunt once, and on that basis I convinced them to agree. But the wording of his contract...was too clever for me. They have been forced to play every single year since."

"And this game affects my ability to leave how?" Genevieve pressed, though the pieces of the puzzle were already starting to click into place in her mind. Her chest began to tighten.

"Today is the day that Knox's magic locks in the players of the Hunt," Barrington explained. "At midnight sharp, anyone who set foot within Enchantra today, aside from Knox and myself, will officially be a player. They cannot escape until they either win the Hunt or they're..."

"They're *what?*" she whispered, though she sensed she already knew the answer.

"Killed, obviously," someone else announced.

7

THE PROPOSAL

Genevieve spun to find Rowin leaning against the molding of the hallway's opening, watching her with an inscrutable expression.

"Have you talked to the others?" Barrington prompted.

Rowin nodded. "They're not pleased with me, but that's nothing new. You and I should probably discuss a few more things before Knox's arrival."

Barrington nodded. He turned to gently take Genevieve by her elbow. "Come, girl, let's get you to the drawing room. I think you need to sit down."

"What I *need* is to stop being yanked around by strangers," Genevieve said as she ripped herself from his grip and dug in her heels. She speared Rowin with a glare. "What do you mean by win or be *killed?*"

"Do those words have alternate meanings I don't know about?" Rowin taunted. "You either win the Hunt or you're killed in it. So I hope your penchant for verbal sparring translates to some sort of physical capability as well."

Genevieve turned back to Barrington. "But you said that they've been playing this game for years. If everyone except the winner is killed—"

She cut herself off as the realization hit her. *Immortals.* They're all immortals.

"When we are killed in the Hunt, Knox's magic burns our souls from our corporeal forms and then rips our bodies out of this linear plane to transport both parts of us back to Hell," Rowin explained.

That sounded…ghastly. It was also frighteningly powerful magic—that much was clear even to Genevieve. Souls were delicate, and if Knox's magic could transport one from this plane to the Other Side in an instant, he was a powerful Devil indeed.

"Then we get to live out the remainder of the year under Knox's command," Rowin said, his voice dripping with bitterness.

"The winner, on the other hand, gets to stay here until the Hunt begins anew," Barrington finished. "But a mortal…a mortal's body cannot survive being separated from its soul without dire consequences, Miss Grimm."

"And I'm mortal," Genevieve whispered.

"You catch on quick," Rowin snorted.

She spun to bare her teeth at him. "You're an *ass.*"

He smirked. "Are words the only claws you've got?"

"Come closer and let's see," she crooned.

Rowin made to step forward, but Barrington raised a hand between them and barked, "*Enough.*" He narrowed his eyes at Rowin. "Go wait in the study. I'll be there in just a moment."

Genevieve watched with mild shock as Rowin began to transform into a shapeless tangle of shadows and smoke. One moment his figure was there, and the next it had melted into the darkness of the hallway and disappeared altogether.

"I cannot stand the thought of our cursed game harming one of Tessie's daughters," Barrington told her, his tone a bit firmer than before. "There is a way to keep you safe. It just requires some careful—"

A resounding crash echoed through the house.

Barrington sighed deeply. "Please excuse me. My children are clearly determined to drive me even madder than usual today. Make yourself comfortable in the drawing room down the hall."

And with that, Barrington Silver disappeared, leaving only a plume of purple smoke.

Genevieve had decided that finding the drawing room and waiting to see whatever solution Barrington arrived at would be a lot less exhausting than risking—what was it Rowin said? Being *fried* by the front gates?

The room was surprisingly warm, the mismatched antique furniture and fresh flowers in crystal vases making it feel both intimate and inviting. There was a set of chairs just across from the small couch, a mahogany coffee table between them, and an inset cupboard, made of the same reddish wood, spanning the entire wall at the back of the room. The shelving above the cupboard was filled with different bottles of liquor and glassware. In front of that, there was a long, marble bar lined with velvet-topped stools.

"Well, well, look who's joined us," an amused voice declared.

Genevieve stiffened as she scanned the room for the owner of the voice.

A smile curled up on Sevin's lips as her gaze locked with his, and he shifted the sucker in his mouth to the side, creating a bulge in his left cheek. Genevieve regarded him with skepticism as he pushed off the far wall and strutted closer.

"You pulled quite the stealthy disappearing act earlier. Are you the quiet type, then?" he questioned, a mischievous gleam in his crimson gaze as he pulled the sucker from his mouth to point it at her. "Or do you like to scream?"

Genevieve crossed her arms. "I think perhaps my new goal in life will be making sure you never know that answer."

He clucked his tongue in disappointment. "How do you feel about daggers?"

She narrowed her eyes. "In what way? Craftsmanship? Effectiveness? How I think one would look in your side?"

His grin stretched wider. "Just wondering how prepared you are to take a stabbing or two."

A bark of laughter rang out from the doorway as Ellin strode into the room.

"And what could she possibly do to prepare for that, Sevin?" Ellin flicked her gaze to Genevieve. "My advice is to simply not get stabbed. And if you do—don't bleed out."

As if that was something Genevieve could control.

"You'll have to excuse Ellin," Sevin apologized. "She doesn't have much experience with how fragile mortals are. Or how easy it is to drain them of blood."

Genevieve stiffened. She'd forgotten that the Silver children were Wraiths. *Was the blood and soul eating true, then?*

Before she could ask, however, Ellin tossed herself into a chair and complained, "Why would I spend enough time with mortals to know that? They're incredibly dull."

"I don't think *dull* is going to be this one's problem," Sevin commented with a grin as he slid his gaze back to Genevieve. "Is it?"

Genevieve didn't deign to respond as she sidestepped the coffee table and turned toward the exit. She was beginning to feel like a cornered hare in their presence. And the topic of her being stabbed or bleeding had come up one too many times. Barrington said he knew a way to spare her from whatever little game was being played in this cursed house, and Genevieve hoped to Hell he was telling the truth.

"Even if she is a bore," Ellin reasoned. "Rowin's plan is going to make things interesting. Maybe she'll even give you some competition in the voting for Favored."

Before Genevieve could snap at either of them, Rowin suddenly appeared in the room amongst his swirling shadows. Followed moments later by his father.

"Out," Barrington barked at Ellin and Sevin.

Ellin made a show of how inconvenient it was for her to be getting kicked out, while Sevin winked at Genevieve.

"Good luck," Sevin told his brother as he exited. "You look *darling* together."

Ellin snorted while Genevieve narrowed her eyes in confusion.

"Why don't you have a seat, Genevieve?" Barrington suggested as he waved a hand at the couch in the center of the sitting area.

She lifted her chin. "No, thank you."

Rowin rolled his eyes at her refusal.

"I know this is all overwhelming," Barrington told her. "But I'm afraid it may only get more distressing from here."

"More distressing than being told I may be forced into a game where my only option to escape is being *killed*?" she asked dryly.

"Yes," Barrington claimed.

It was at this moment that she really saw Barrington's age. His face might have been youthful, but his eyes held the weight of several lifetimes' experience as a parent. Meanwhile, Rowin was watching without an ounce of emotion on his face. As if he were made of stone.

"We don't have much time before Knox arrives and we lose the chance to speak freely," Barrington told her. "Now, there have never been any contestants other than my children in the Hunt.

Others have tried to enter. But the Hunt was designed specifically for those with the name *Silver*."

Out of the corner of her eye she saw Rowin move. Shoving his hands in the pocket of his trousers as his gold eyes flashed with . . . anticipation?

"Tessie would never forgive me if I let you go into this game without assistance." Barrington's voice had grown thicker with each word he spoke, and if there was ever a time for her to speak up about her mother's death, it was clearly now. Except the next words out of his mouth stopped the confession balancing on the tip of her tongue cold. "It has been decided that you will enter the Hunt as Rowington's wife."

For a moment the entire world stopped. Genevieve knew she'd heard him wrong—that the word *wife* had not just left his mouth.

The Hunt was designed specifically for those with the name Silver.

A wild laugh bubbled out of her.

"It's the only way two winners are allowed," Barrington continued. "A loophole Knox offered one of my other sons long ago, when his spectators had grown bored with the usual events of the Hunt. Any of my children can take up the same loophole should they desire."

She swung her gaze to Rowin. "You're going to just stand there and let your father ask me to take your hand in marriage?"

"Are you suggesting you'd like me to ask? And on my knees?" Rowin drawled. "That is what mortals do, correct?"

The idea of him getting on his knees for her heated her blood in a way that was even more baffling than the conversation they were having, but somehow she managed to keep her tone even as she snapped, "It's *one* knee, and obviously that is *not* what I'm suggesting. I'm suggesting you tell him that this is a ludicrous fucking idea!"

"Unfortunately, that I cannot do," Rowin stated evenly, his gaze locking with hers. "Because it was my idea."

She nearly choked.

"A marriage is the only way you will survive the Hunt, Genevieve," Barrington agreed.

"While I appreciate your lack of confidence in my ability to take care of myself," Genevieve told them, every word dripping with indignation, "I was hoping you would be finding a way for me to get out of this ordeal entirely. If the proposal is having to play your wretched game *and* get *married*, I think I'd rather play alone. Believe it or not, this wouldn't be my first deadly contest. Have you heard of Phantasma? I entered the Devil's Manor last year and, as you can see, I survived just fine."

She had seven golden stars marked into her skin to prove it.

Barrington shook his head. "Playing by yourself is not an option. Knox would kill you instead. And it's the very least I owe Tessie—to make sure you have a fighting chance."

She curled a lip at him in distaste.

"It's not a risk I'll take," Barrington maintained. "Not to mention it'd be equally beneficial to Rowington. A true win-win."

She propped a hand on her hip as she faced Rowin and taunted, "Ah, so I'm a *benefit*? And you made it sound as if you were doing *me* a favor."

"You're potentially a benefit," he corrected. "If you somehow learn how to listen in the next twenty-four hours."

"Well, I'm all ears right now," she pointed out. "Why don't you explain to me how I'm so beneficial to you?"

"Knox's loophole states that if one of us gets married and convinces their spouse"—his eyes darkened at that word—"to join the Hunt, they can play together for one season, and there's a special reward if they win. The couple is permanently released from the Hunt. There's a catch, of course. If a couple loses that first game, then the new family member is locked into the Hunt with the rest of us. Forever. At least if they're immortal."

"Which we have established that I am not," she reminded.

Rowin's mouth pressed into a grim line as she caught Barrington's wince.

"You're both being serious," she realized as she flicked her eyes between the two of them. "You both really think I'm going to agree to get *married* to a stranger?"

"I'm sure you could do worse," Rowin told her.

She would never admit aloud how right he was. Instead, she declared, "Even if I lowered my standards to the depths of Hell, I doubt you'd be able to reach them."

Rowin opened his mouth, probably to give her a biting retort, but Barrington was quicker.

"Might I remind you that Knox could arrive at any point. If the two of you don't learn how to be amicable and *quick*, Genevieve isn't going to survive the night," Barrington admonished. "No, not just amicable, you need to be *partners*. Fooling Knox and his spectators is going to take extreme measures from you both—no fighting in public, no insulting each other, as many public displays of affection as you can manage."

"You've truly *lost your minds*," Genevieve scoffed.

"And you will lose your life if you do not cooperate," Barrington snapped.

Genevieve curled her lip in disdain. "Do *not* talk to me like that, Mr. Silver. You are not *my* father."

Out of the corner of her eye she swore she saw Rowin smile.

"I'm sorry." Barrington sighed deeply, combing a hand back through his hair. "I just don't know how to convey to you the danger you're in. Knox will kill you if he finds you here. Unless he finds that you are part of the family. Even if you agree to play with Rowington, the two of you will need to show every sign of being in love."

"So I don't just have to go along with your asinine plan. I have to look like I'm *enjoying* it?"

"Knox will be watching you closely. And all of his spectators, too, as soon as the game begins. The mirrors are enchanted so that viewers in Hell can spy into the house. That's why looking glasses are in all of the common spaces. And why my children have an irritating habit of covering them up."

"Can't I marry one of the others instead?" she suggested.

"No," Rowin stated. "This was my idea. Therefore, you're mine. If anyone is winning freedom from the Hunt, it's me."

Genevieve was instantly flustered. Whether from fury or the fact that no man had ever called her his before, she wasn't sure.

Either way, she made sure to swear, "I will never be yours."

Rowin pulled something from his pocket. "This ring might claim otherwise soon enough."

"A ring," Genevieve said as she glanced down at the silver band he now presented.

There was a long moment of silence.

And then Genevieve ran.

WICKED REFLECTION

Genevieve wasn't entirely sure where she was going as she hastily made her way down the empty corridor. All she knew was that she needed to get *away*.

She dashed across the foyer to the hallway of portraits and noticed that the first door to her left was now halfway open. She cautiously peered inside and was relieved to find that it was an empty powder room, every wall adorned in a dusty, blue jacquard wallpaper that made her eyes cross with its hectic pattern. After turning the lock on the door with an echoing click, she braced her hands on the marble vanity.

Rings. Weddings. Devils. Games. It's all too fucking much. I wanted to find a companion to talk to about my childhood trauma, not a damned husband.

She gulped down a few deep breaths. She reached out with a shaky hand to twist on the faucet over the vanity's sink and splashed her face with a few handfuls of cold water before grabbing one of the neatly folded towels atop the cabinet and patting her skin dry.

When she lifted her gaze back to the mirror, a scream began clawing its way up her throat as she took in the wicked reflection now staring back at her. Though it was her own face, her cerulean irises had changed to a deep violet, and her mouth was pulled into a ghastly, too-wide smile.

What lovely little creature do we have here?

Genevieve backed away from the vanity until she hit the wall behind her, the room too narrow to put a comfortable distance between her and the monstrous illusion in the mirror. The crooning voice had unmistakably been inside her mind. Something that she'd experienced only once before, inside Phantasma, with a Devil named Sinclair.

"Who are you?" she demanded, her eyes never breaking from the unnatural violet gaze in the mirror as she worked to keep her words even.

The voice laughed. *Some refer to me as the master of the house. Others refer to me as Knox. Lady's choice. And you are…?*

It was Genevieve's turn to laugh. She was not about to give a Devil her name.

Oh, come now, you can tell—

A sudden pounding cut through the room.

"Genevieve, open the door," a deep voice that was becoming all too familiar called from the other side.

As perturbed as Genevieve was by the idea of letting Rowin think he could boss her around, she was more keen to escape the Devil's presence. She twisted the door's lock, but as quickly as it clicked open, it snapped right back into place.

Let him wait, lovely. I'm not done with you yet.

Genevieve opened her mouth to shout to Rowin, but when she tried to speak, no words would come out.

She glanced back to the mirror, and a rumbling laugh permeated her mind as something speared out of its surface and latched onto her wrists. Purple strings. She tried to free herself from the strings' clutches, but it was no use. The glittering threads only tightened as they dragged her forward. She lurched right into the vanity, the edge of the countertop hitting her stomach and making her grunt with pain.

Stop resisting and this will be a lot easier for you.

The strings gave another painful yank, nearly pulling her arms out of their sockets, until she finally let out a defeated hiss.

"*Alright*," she growled between clenched teeth as she climbed onto the vanity of her own volition.

The mirror in front of her began to ripple as the Devil urged her forward, and Rowin's knocking became even more impatient. As she tumbled through the strange portal, however, everything went utterly silent. It quickly became clear that wherever she'd been transported to was meant to be an exact replica of the powder room, except...mirrored. The strings were still twined around her wrists, but now they stretched out of the door into what she presumed would be this mirror-realm's version of the corridor back in Enchantra.

Come find me, lovely.

Genevieve climbed down from the vanity and lunged for the door with determination, following the strings through the hallway, through the reversed layout of the house, and across the foyer to the front entry. She noted, in the back of her mind, that it seemed much brighter here. Less dusty and certainly much quieter with the absence of the Silver family.

When she threw the front door open, she gasped at what she found beyond the porch.

The walls of the labyrinth were blanketed in blooming roses. All in shades of fuchsia, blush, and lavender, the gleaming sun overhead making them stretch toward the sky. Gone was the slush of snow and the bite of cold. Instead, she was met by a warmth that made her want to shed her cape and gloves, the latter of which she did pry off before tucking them into her pockets.

As if in a trance, she made her way toward the maze. The violet strings tugging more gently now—guiding instead of insisting. She wove her way around the twists and turns of the hedges, the sound of trickling water growing louder until she finally reached the labyrinth's heart. A square clearing decorated with the same checkered flooring of the foyer inside. Only a small perimeter of grass outlined the gray-and-white marble. In the center was an exquisite silver fountain, its streams of water spouting down from the mouths of a few very familiar animals.

A sudden swirl of deep purple smoke began to churn through the air in front of her as a figure took shape. A strangled gasp fell from her lips and she found herself staring back at the imposter she'd seen in the mirror. This version of herself had the same violet eyes and harsh smile, but instead of her ensemble's blush details, the imposter wore a gown of violet and black. As if they were dressed for a funeral.

"Hello, lovely," Genevieve's imposter-self rasped in Knox's voice.

"What sort of game is this?" Genevieve hissed. "Why do you look like me?"

The imposter's brows rose. "Do I? Well, that is certainly interesting."

Genevieve swallowed as Knox began circling her like a vulture, eyes flicking hungrily over every inch of her form.

"Why did you bring me here?" Genevieve demanded, impatient when he didn't offer anything more.

"I don't usually visit Enchantra until the masquerade, but today I sensed that something was different. Imagine my surprise when I peered through that mirror and found your pretty face staring back at me."

"What do you want?"

"No, I think the question is what do *you* want? *You* appear to have broken into *my* house."

"I—" Genevieve's mind raced. Barrington had said that Knox would kill her if he knew the truth. "I'm Rowington Silver's fiancée."

She couldn't believe she'd let those words past her lips. She still had no intention of following the Silvers' ludicrous scheme, but she would do whatever it took to get out of this nightmare alive.

A dangerous smile spread across Knox's face, and he looked her over once again. "Rowington has found himself a bride?"

Genevieve nodded. She couldn't bring herself to speak the lie again.

"And he's going to attempt…"

She nodded again.

"What joyful news," the Devil said, drawing closer. "The wedding is tonight then?"

Genevieve swallowed. And then nodded once more.

"I hope Rowington prepared you for what you're getting yourself into, lovely. If I announce the two of you are playing as a couple, my patrons are going to get excited. Which means there better be no cold feet on either you or Rowington tonight. Because if my spectators decide to pull their wagers, there will be consequences. When I lose, *everyone* loses."

"Very dramatic," Genevieve said dryly.

Knox paused his steps, facing her head-on now. It was eerie, staring back at herself like this.

"I must say, I am utterly *dying* to know what Rowin thinks he's going to do with you. A simple mortal. But I do love a good romantic tragedy." A sniff of amusement. "He's always been selfish, that one. Nearly two decades of freedom and it's still not enough for him."

"Freedom? Remaining unconfined while your family is trapped in Hell is not freedom. But I'm sure you already know that."

The smile on the imposter's face tightened. "You and Rowin are cut from the same cloth, I see."

Genevieve worked very hard not to make a face at that.

"You're going to play a little game now," Knox said. "Consider it a preliminary assessment of how you might fare in the Hunt."

"I'm not—" she began. But before she could finish, the imposter version of herself, and the purple strings, evaporated into thin air. Genevieve took that as her cue to leave.

She made to dash through an opening between the hedged walls, but the gap that led into the interior corridors shifted to the left. Stopping short of getting a face full of leaves and roses, she blinked in disbelief. She adjusted and tried to exit a second time, but the opening moved away once again.

"That's the wrong way out," a cheery voice called from behind her.

She turned to see Sevin, leaning next to another gaping exit on the far side of the square clearing, arms crossed over his chest as he watched her in amusement.

"You aren't real," she stated.

"Are you sure?" the illusion of Sevin asked with a tilt of his head.

"Yes," she said, unmoved. Aside from the fact that she knew better than most the illusions a Devil could create, there were certain details missing that made it clear this was an imposter. No lollipop hanging out of his mouth. And no spark of amusement in his eyes.

"We might not be the real thing, but I bet we could inflict pain just the same," a second voice commented on her right.

Genevieve whipped around to find Rowin, his expression a mask of apathy as he gave her a once-over. Whatever features were off about this version of him were not as easy for her to determine. His hair was shorter, perhaps. His outfit less impeccably tailored.

"Let's get this over with, shall we?" Rowin suggested, cutting through her thoughts as he started for her.

When he lunged forward, Genevieve scrambled back, narrowly avoiding the tip of the dagger he suddenly had gripped in his hand. As he righted himself to attack again, she reached over to rip out a handful of leaves and vines from the labyrinth's wall. He shot forward with the dagger once more, and she let it go through the palm of her left hand while she shoved the handful of foliage right into his mouth.

A burst of pain went through her hand and reverberated all the way up her arm as Rowin spit out the leaves with a decent amount of surprise. She gawked down at the knife protruding from her palm, blood spilling from the wound like a waterfall and splashing down the front of her cape and dress. Without a sound, Genevieve reached up to grab the hilt of the knife and pull it out of her wound, letting it clatter to the ground at their feet.

You should run, she told herself. *Move.*

But she could hardly do anything but stare at the blood ruining her gown.

The corners of Rowin's mouth turned down in dissatisfaction, and that was when she realized what was so off about this imposter. He was missing his lip ring.

A shame, since that might possibly be the only thing I enjoyed about him.

The illusion procured another dagger from thin air.

"May I suggest you start running, sweetheart?" Sevin called out with a laugh.

As if she'd been doused with cold water, Genevieve's shock finally wore off. Ducking beneath Rowin's raised arm, Genevieve hauled herself toward the opening of the labyrinth yet again, only this time it stayed in place. She sprinted down the first interior corridor, several pairs of footsteps echoing around her as Rowin, Sevin, and at least one other unseen figure gave chase. Something whipped past her head, and she gritted her teeth as a nick of pain began to burn along the top of her left cheekbone and a trickle of warm blood slid down her face. She made to hook the next right, but the moment she did, she face-planted into one of the flowering hedges. Spitting leaves out of her mouth, the irony not lost on her, she saw that the maze was once again moving itself around to trap her.

"A mortal," a gruff, unfamiliar voice scoffed just behind her. "Easy win."

Genevieve spun, but before she could make out the details of the stranger's face, his dagger descended. She tried to reach out for her magic, but the spark she could usually feel burning in her core was nowhere to be found, and the stranger rammed his blade through her right shoulder. At first the pain ripping through her nearly buckled her knees, and the only thing keeping her upright was her grip tangled in the branches at her sides. When she heard her attacker's huff of laughter, however, something inside her snapped. She unclenched her grip from the hedge and reached out to grab the knife by its blade mid-arc, hissing as its sharpened edge sliced into her already-wounded palm. The hulking stranger hesitated just long enough for her to rip the dagger from his grasp. She quickly adjusted her grip to its hilt and then rammed the dagger as deep into his right eye socket as it would go.

When she managed to dislodge the blade from his face, she slammed it into the side of his neck next. Over and over she hacked at him as her rage and fear twisted together into an unintelligible knot inside her. By the time his body finally slumped to the ground, she was heaving with the effort of her fury. Left frozen in shock at what she had done.

But the stillness didn't last long as another dagger whipped toward her, nearly lodging itself in the soft flesh of her abdomen before she dodged out of the way and stumbled back into the hedge—

—except the opening in the wall had shifted once again. She crashed to the ground, hard. She couldn't really remember the last time she'd taken a physical blow like that. For years she'd relied on her magic to avoid the discomfort of being human— while desperately trying to appear human as well.

I am so fucked up, she thought.

She wasn't sure who had thrown that last one, or whose footsteps were thundering toward her now, but she was sure she'd had enough. She braced herself against the agony still tearing through her body and lurched back to her feet, taking off through the maze once more. And either Knox had gotten all the assessment he needed, or she had found a dose of pure luck, because she managed to puzzle her way out of the labyrinth without any more trouble from moving walls or murderous siblings.

She tore through the house for the powder room, and as she clambered up onto the vanity and spilled through the mirror, back into reality, she heard one final thought.

This is going to be fun.

As Genevieve fell to the ground with a heavy thud, the door to the bathroom wrenched open, splintering where the lock had resisted and sending slivers of wood scattering to the floor.

She squeaked in surprise as she blinked up at Rowin, her mind still trying to understand what had just happened.

"Fuck. You spoke with Knox? What did he—" Rowin said, but Genevieve was already scrambling forward.

Crawling over the splintered wood, she wedged herself past him and out of the powder room, hauling herself to her feet and toward the front door. Back toward Enchantra's gate.

She was going to get away from this house, this family, if it killed her.

9

GRAVE MISTAKE

The chill in the evening air was biting compared to the fire in her lungs as she pushed her feet as fast as they'd go.

She flexed the magic in her veins as she dashed out down the front porch steps and met the beckoning entrance of the maze. She could feel the freezing air even in her Specter state, but she ignored it as she passed deeper and deeper into the maze. Her heart racing so erratically that her magic was flickering in and out, and when she heard heavy footsteps crunch in the snow not too far behind, her hold on her power broke entirely.

"*Damn it,*" she hissed as she paused and tried to regain control. But her concentration was utterly shot, and her reservoir of magic was running low from exhaustion. She could hear someone gaining on her and knew that she had essentially trapped herself in her haste.

Someone shouted behind her, making her feet mobilize once more as she began assessing her place in the labyrinth. The ten-foot walls of greenery made it hard for her to determine how deep she'd already gone, but at least these walls weren't moving like they had been in the mirror-realm. So, she started guessing. Left at the first fork, right at the second. Every other turn she made seemed to lead to a dead end, and when she rounded one corner a bit too tightly, a sprig of thorns sliced through her sleeve and into her skin. She hissed in pain as she looked down at the fresh blood seeping from the jagged wound, thinking the thorns might as well have been talons for how easily they cut through the fabric of her cape.

"That looks like it might have hurt."

Genevieve yelped in surprise and stopped short, her chest heaving as she scanned the darkness for *him*.

"Do *not* come any closer," she spat.

Rowin tilted his head at her, hands shoved deep in his pockets, his golden eyes glowing in the moonlight. "Sevin was right. You do look like a helpless little rabbit."

An offended scoff sounded from her throat. He took a step closer.

"You're going to get devoured here," he told her. "But I imagine the spectators are going to enjoy it. You might even edge out Sevin as this year's Favored. If you stay alive long enough."

She shuffled back a step. "What the fuck are you talking about?"

"I'd appreciate it if you stopped trying to scare my bride, Remi," a deep voice said from behind her.

Rowin's sharp scent of mint and honey suddenly enveloped her, and she twisted around to watch him approach. She swung her gaze between the two men in disbelief. Aside from the hoop pierced through Rowin's lip and a few other nearly indistinct details, the two of them looked like exact replicas of each other.

Identical twins.

"For fuck's sake, there's *two* of you?" Genevieve exclaimed.

Remi shrugged. "Our enemies are equally disappointed."

"Leave us," Rowin ordered his twin. "Father wants you to help Sevin and Ellin set up for the ceremony. He and Knox are discussing plans to update the masquerade invitations in the study, and he said that you could meet them in there."

Remi countered with a shrug. "As if I care about helping you set up something that's going to release you from this eternity of Hell while the rest of us are stuck with Knox forevermore."

Bitterness laced Remi's words, but not the kind held by envious strangers when they see others receive something *they* wanted. No, this kind was much more complicated. It was the sort of bitterness you had when it was someone you *loved* getting something you wanted. Your happiness for them confounded by your anger. Of not wanting to hurt them by taking it away, but perhaps deluding yourself into thinking you deserved it more, and that didn't make you a terrible person.

It was a feeling she'd grown up with. One that had created a wedge between her and Ophelia for far too long. But the day she'd realized that Ophie would always be their mother's priority, and that Ophelia didn't even wish that were so, was the day she'd found peace. She'd watched as the pressure of upholding their family's legacy had slowly stripped away Ophie's hopes and dreams for her own life, and she'd known it was not her sister she ought to be angry with.

"We can have this fight later," Rowin told his brother.

"When?" Remi asked, stepping forward. "The next time you decide to pay us a visit in Hell? The next time you write us to tell us what's going on in your life? You haven't done either of those things in nearly two decades, so I won't hold my breath."

"And I thought my household deserved the award for most tragically dramatic," Genevieve muttered, mostly to herself.

Rowin's eyes snapped to her face, irritation heating his gaze.

Remi huffed a humorless laugh. "I hope she's everything you deserve, Rowin."

Genevieve watched as Remi began doing that strange shadow thing she had seen Rowin do earlier, the wisps of darkness slowly enveloping him until he disappeared.

"You really don't know when to be *quiet*, do you?" Rowin growled as he turned on her.

"It's never been a talent of mine," she agreed.

In two steps, he was in front of her, walking her backward until she felt the prickling twigs of the labyrinth's wall poking at her spine.

"From here on out you are either on my side or in my fucking way," he told her, enunciating every word carefully, so close that their chests were pressed together, and she swore she could feel his heartbeat. "You have no idea what I'm putting on the line to save your ass. Knox appeared just after you ran away, and he's speaking with my father now. But he could decide to join us any second. Even this conversation is a risk."

"I thought we already established that *I'm* the one with all the risk, while you stand to reap a very big reward," she retorted.

"High rewards are bred from high risks," he explained. "If you die in the Hunt, we *both* lose, and everything I've been working toward goes out the window."

"Then why are you so insistent that we work together?" she implored.

"Because, yes, the reward I'll get if we *do* win is worth the odds. And . . ." His jaw clenched as his words trailed off.

"And?"

"And you stepped into the house on *my* watch. Therefore you're my burden to bear," he muttered.

"I will never be your *anything* to bear," she vowed with a scowl.

"You're going to have to be very careful not to talk like that from now on. Knox is already anticipating tripling his spectator list and the amount of wagers on this year's game. If you want to be the one to tell him all of this is a ruse, be my guest."

She swallowed, and a corner of his mouth lifted.

"That's what I thought. The marriage ceremony must be

completed before midnight. My father is explaining to Knox that we left it late because we wanted my family to attend. And Knox himself, of course. As far as he's concerned, we've had a whirlwind romance, and we were eagerly awaiting his blessing on our union." Rowin flicked his eyes over the bloody state of her dress. "His excitement about the money he's going to make seems to be outweighing his suspicions. For now. All we have to do is keep up our façade."

"I'm not the girl for this," she whispered, more to herself than him. "I can't pretend to be in love with someone I'm not."

"I'm sure you can pretend just fine," he murmured, as he raised his hand and began to twirl one of the curls that framed her face around his index finger. "Think of it as playing a character. Inside the walls of Enchantra you're no longer Genevieve Grimm. You're my wife." He tucked the strand of hair he'd been playing with behind her ear, letting his fingertips graze her cheeks ever so lightly and making her suck in a breath as she resisted the urge to lean into the touch. "In front of everyone you'll smile and pretend like you actually enjoy my company. There can be *no arguing*." A wicked glint entered his eyes as he said that last bit, and she shifted her gaze away before she could blush at how attractive she found that look. "And when we aren't fighting for our lives during the Hunt, if there's a moment we can play up for the viewers' entertainment, a kiss—"

That snapped her right out of his trance.

Fuck, how had he done that?

"No. There will be no kissing, no pretending, no *wedding*," she spat at him now, placing both her hands on his chest and shoving him away from her as hard as she could. He didn't budge.

He sighed in frustration. The expression of sincerity and heat he'd been wearing moments before melting away in an instant. It made her stomach churn.

"Might I remind you this is equally, if not entirely, your fault," he told her. "*You* decided to open an invitation that was not yours. You decided to break into the house despite my very clear warnings to leave. And what sort of mother forgets to mention the sadistic curse her *dear friend's* family have been suffering through for centuries—"

"The sort that's *dead*," Genevieve seethed, cutting him off before his words could slice into her any deeper.

At Genevieve's statement, Rowin stiffened. She glared up at him, hoping the revelation made him feel terrible. Before he could offer any sort of empty condolence, however, someone called his name from somewhere outside of the maze. Sevin.

"We need to get inside," Rowin told her, his tone only slightly softer than before. "As I said—the ceremony needs to be completed by midnight."

He began to turn away, but when she didn't move, he paused with an expectant look.

"No," she maintained. "This is absurd."

"Have we not already established that you do not have any other options? If you make me chase you any further, I'll—"

"You'll what?" she pressed. "Kill me? Isn't that likely to be my fate, anyway? At least if I make you do it, now, I'll save myself some trouble."

"You really think death by my hand would be better than taking it in marriage?"

"And if I do?"

His smile turned devious, and her heart began to thunder in her chest at the sight.

"You know what, trouble? Let's make our own little wager."

She held her breath.

"You manage to make it out of this labyrinth and get to the

front gate before I do—without using your magic—and I'll give you the choice. Play on your own or play with me. If I win, however, you come back inside and put on a damned wedding dress."

"You already know your way through the maze," she accused.

"I'll give you a head start, then," he allowed.

"Fine. When—"

"*Now.*"

Genevieve whirled around and darted out of the corridor without a second of hesitation as soon as the word crossed his lips. The sound of her blood rushing in her ears was so loud that she could barely hear her own footsteps pounding through the snow.

Two right turns and she finally happened upon the heart of the labyrinth. It looked just as it had in the mirror-realm that Knox had led her to. Except the circular pool at the base of the fountain was frozen solid in this reality, the arched streams of water unmoving. As she fled past, she saw that every angle showcased a different animal carved into its glittering tiers. A large mink. A serpent. A wolf. An owl. The rest blurred together as she ran.

She didn't know how long it took her to get out of the maze, how many frustrating dead ends or false exits she'd run into, but when the gleaming, thorny gates appeared ahead, with Rowin nowhere in sight, she nearly wept with relief. Inches before she reached the gate, however, a shadowy form appeared right in her path. She smacked straight into Rowin's suddenly solid figure, ricocheting off his chest and slipping on the snowy ground.

"Took you long enough," he drawled as he quickly wrapped an arm around her waist to steady her back on her feet.

She ripped herself from his embrace. "*You said no magic!*"

He smirked. "No, I said *you* couldn't use magic."

She wanted to scream. To lash out at him for fooling her with such an easy trick. She knew better than to make deals without choosing her words precisely.

"You lost," he stated, stepping past her with a beckoning wave. "Let's get this over with."

But she didn't follow him. Instead, she lunged forward, slamming her hands into the bars of the gate, entirely unconcerned by the frozen thorns wrapped around them digging into her wound. But that little bit of pain was the least of her worries. When a jolt of agony seared through her body the moment she touched the bars, she cried out, a pulse of power erupting around her and sent her tumbling backward with a heavy thud.

No. No. No.

She scrambled to her feet, shifting into her non-corporeal form to try again. As she went to pass through, however, it jolted her right out of her Specter state.

"*What the fuck?*" she hissed as she looked down at her now-solid hands.

Whatever enchantment coated the metalwork now seemed to nullify her Specter abilities. She tried once more, and the cold metal sent her flying back. Her skin felt like it had been set aflame. A feeling she knew all too intimately.

She turned and retched into the snow.

When she'd thoroughly emptied the contents of her stomach, she swiped the back of her hand across her mouth as she watched the flurries of snowflakes fall from the sky, feeling them dissolve on her feverish cheeks and coat her lashes. No. No. Fucking Hell, this could not be happening. If she couldn't leave, it meant she was trapped in yet another treacherous game. She'd made such a grave mistake coming here.

She reached over to touch the ring on her left finger in comfort. Remembered it was gone. Heaved once more.

Boots crunched through the snow, pausing next to her. She didn't bother to look up as Rowin crouched down to her level.

"I warned you there was no getting out," he reminded her. "Getting sick over it now is a little pathetic, really."

Pathetic.

Genevieve tensed at the word. A word she knew all too well. One that haunted her during the witching hours when she couldn't sleep. The anger that had been slowly extinguishing in her belly reignited instantly. Not just anger, *spite.* Because as devastated as she was that she'd trapped herself yet again, spite would give her strength. She was used to doing things out of spite. Excelled at it, actually.

Flashes of last year's Mardi Gras parade went through her mind. A carefully choreographed scene involving Farrow walking in on her and Basile Landry in the throes of...

She quickly shook the memories away, refocusing all her anger on the man in front of her instead. She twisted around and launched herself at him. He grunted in surprise as she pinned him down, straddling his waist.

"You're an absolute *bastard*—" she seethed.

In a blink he rolled her over until her back was pressed into the dirty ground, the melting ice soaking through her dress. She let out a shriek of frustration as she tried to reach up between them and claw at his face. He easily gathered both her wrists in one hand while he flattened the other on the ground next to her head to hold the brunt of his weight off her.

"And you're half wild," he observed, a spark igniting in his golden eyes.

She bucked her hips, trying to shove him off her, but likely only proving his point further.

"I'm not going to let you go unless you promise to behave," he threatened.

She gave a bitter laugh. "Then I suppose we'll have to stay like this forever."

He stared at her for a long, tense moment, and something about the intensity of his gaze made her breath hitch. She suddenly realized how close they were. How much of his body she could feel pressed along every inch of her own. The sculpted planes of his stomach, the hardness of his...

He rolled off her, blithely climbing back up to his feet in one fluid motion. She sighed in relief, until a blink later, when she found herself being lifted and thrown over his shoulder like a sack of flour. Never had she been manhandled like this before.

She growled with rage as she pounded her fists against his back. But his stride never faltered as he stalked toward the house.

"You're a fucking *brute*!" she snarled.

She felt his shoulders shake with laughter. "You're going to tire yourself out long before you hurt me, trouble."

Her jaw clenched as she pulled her punches, the blood rushing to her head giving her a migraine. Then she did the only other thing she could think of: she bit him. In the ass.

His grunt of surprise echoed well into the cold night around them, but he never loosened his hold.

10

COLD FEET

I am writing this in a room with no mirrors just in case I start crying. Which would be an odd thing to mention if I wasn't trapped in another mansion run by a Devil. This one seems even more vain than the other Devil I know, if you can believe it, given his clear obsession with mirrors.

I...am in such deep shit.

Fuck. Fuck. Fuck.

I promised Ophelia I'd be turning over a new leaf on this trip. That I'd curb my sailor's mouth. A bit hypocritical considering her own tongue has become equally as corrupt since spending so much time with Salem.

I also promised to be a bit more careful with my spontaneous urges...

I worry that I have only become worse since leaving New Orleans.

Part of me blames ~~him~~ for taking away so much of my joy that being reckless is the only thrill I have left. Another part of me knows I cannot possibly blame ~~him~~ for everything forever.

It's just that this situation is a new level of _fucked_ even for me.

I am about to get _married_. Yes. _Married_. Days from my twenty-second birthday. To a man I've known mere hours and whom I find infuriating.

But he won't be the first man I've attempted to marry that I've loathed. We can only hope this engagement will have a better ending.

Ophelia is going to murder me. If I manage to make it out of this house alive.

I'm pretty sure I've said that before.

X,

Genevieve

Alright, the specifications for your dress have been passed along," Rowin informed her as he strode back into the drawing room. She hurried to tuck her pen between the pages of her diary and shove the journal into the pocket of the dress she'd changed into after throwing away the one she'd ruined in the snow.

When he'd gotten her back inside, she'd refused to answer any of his or Barrington's questions on what she might like for their ridiculous farce of a wedding. Sevin had eagerly requested a chocolate fountain but was quickly dismissed. The moment Rowin mentioned that she could request any sort of extravagant gown she'd like, however, she perked up. Just a little.

At least one part of this should be enjoyable.

After Barrington and Sevin disappeared to take care of all the last-minute details, Rowin suggested giving her a tour of Enchantra before it was time for them to get ready.

"Why?" she questioned.

He gave her a bored look. "Because you'll be grateful for it when you get caught between rooms with no idea where to hide."

"Won't you be hiding with me? Isn't that the point of all of this?" she demanded.

"Believe it or not, we're not going to be sewn together at the hip after we take our vows," he drawled. "Which means there might be a point that we get separated. And if one of us dies, we *both* die—and I'm not the one who is most at risk for causing that. So, why don't you save us another ten minutes of arguing and get up?"

She huffed and stood from the drawing room's couch, trudging behind him as she tried to think of anything else she'd rather be doing less.

Phantasma didn't even make that list.

The first ten or so minutes were spent trailing after Rowin while he pointed out every little nook and cranny he thought might be a beneficial place for her to note, lecturing her about how each round of the Hunt would consist of a slightly different version of the game, with its own set of rules. The versions were seemingly endless, but he suggested that each of his siblings had their favorites and would likely stick to those.

"Do you?" she asked as they made their way into the ballroom now. "Have a favorite game I should know about?"

His expression turned thoughtful as he led her across the expansive marble dance floor. "I've really enjoyed the one where I ask you to do something, and you simply refuse to fucking do it."

"What a coincidence, I love that game, too," she remarked as they reached the foot of the grand staircase. "You know, if you tried being *nice* to me you might find—"

Before she could finish her thought, he was suddenly right before her. Her breath hitched as the length of his body pressed into hers, his arm coming up to wrap around her waist as he bent her back against the stair's banister. His eyes became half-lidded as he leaned his mouth down to her left ear, leaving her hands trapped between their bodies, her palms splayed flat against the taut muscles of his stomach.

"Relax," he demanded under his breath, "and try to pretend like you enjoy being this close to me. We have an observer."

Genevieve took a shaky breath as Rowin's lips leaned in close enough to brush against the pulse in her throat, but before they could make full contact, he straightened and glanced toward the top of the stairs.

"Ah, it's Grave," he muttered.

Genevieve glanced over and saw a man standing at the top of the stairs. A very *large* man. One who was slightly familiar...

The unidentified stranger from the mirror-realm, she realized. It had to be. A moment later and he blinked entirely from sight.

"I thought it might be Knox," Rowin explained.

"They both have a certain hostile aura about them," Genevieve allowed, her words still a bit breathless from how close he'd just been to having his lips on her skin.

A spark of shocked amusement flitted through his eyes, but it was gone as quickly as it had come, his mask of stone back in place as he prompted, "Shall we continue?"

She stared at him, dazed.

It confounded her how smoothly he'd changed from hot to cold, how easy it was for him to pretend at such intimacy while her heart did acrobatics in her chest.

"I think I'm done with the tour," she told him, refusing to meet his eyes. "I need time to do my hair before the ceremony."

He raised a brow. "You're skipping strategy to make sure your hair is perfect?"

She shrugged. "If I'm going to be dragged down the aisle, I at least want to look incredible. You only get a first wedding once."

"You're mortal. You only die once," he muttered as he left her to continue up the steps without a backward glance.

Genevieve huffed as she stomped off in the opposite direction, making her way back to the drawing room. She knew he was right, that there were much more important things for her to be worrying about than her hair or if they were going to get the details of her dress right, but she still wasn't sure the direness of the situation had fully set in.

"The Hunt this, Devils that," she muttered to herself as she walked through the foyer. "If I have to look awful on my wedding day, *I'm* going to be the scariest thing in this house—"

A grunt suddenly echoed through the corridor with the portraits, and Genevieve paused.

She padded in the direction of the sound and noticed that the door to one of the rooms on the left was cracked open, an odd hissing noise now coming from inside. She slowed her stride and tiptoed toward the open crack to peek in, waiting for her eyes to adjust to the darkness until she could make out the silhouette of a man standing with his back to her in the center of a bedroom.

A large black serpent was inked into his skin, slithering up his spine between his defined shoulder muscles. In his hand was a knife, and he was...slicing it across his ribs, moaning every time a new river of blood dripped down his side from the shallow wounds. A gasp fell from her lips, and the man's gaze snapped over his shoulder.

"Who's there?" he rasped.

Genevieve reared back, aghast, and spun on her heels. She swept through the foyer, rushing past an unexpecting Sevin.

"Cold feet?" Sevin called after her with a laugh.

Genevieve gave him the crudest gesture in her repertoire as she continued toward the drawing room, earning a boisterous laugh. When she reached the door she was looking for and hauled it open—

—she ran smack into Ellin.

"*There* you are," Ellin said as she steadied Genevieve. "Your wedding dress is here. It's time to get ready."

11

BRIDE

The sound of a pounding fist on the other side of the door echoed through the room.

"Ready yet?" Ellin called.

Despite Ellin knowing that all of this was fake, Rowin's sister had seemed to enjoy dressing up Genevieve like her own personal doll.

When Genevieve finally turned to face herself in the full-length mirror—which Ellin had Sevin drag into the drawing room earlier—she watched as her eyes widened in awe. The first thing she noticed was how bright the nervous energy crawling through her veins made the flush of her cheeks, complementing the teal of her widened eyes. The second was the dress.

It was absolutely *enchanting*.

The gown was made of a silk with an opalescent sheen that made it appear almost lilac instead of white. She had never had any particular desire to wear pure white on her wedding day, and the color certainly didn't fit her in the traditional sense, anyway. The bodice was cut snugly to her voluptuous curves, its boning coming to a "V" just below her navel. Its neckline dipped tastefully into her bosom and off her shoulders, which had been dusted with a pearlescent powder courtesy of Ellin. The silk skirts billowed from the waist in flattering pleats, stiff enough that she hadn't needed to add any crinolines beneath to keep its volume. Tiny pearls and crystals were scattered over the bodice and skirts, as well as the large bow that sat just above the bustle of the dress, underneath the swooping cut of the back. And the *sleeves*. Puffing dramatically at her biceps, they made her look as if she had fairy's wings before tapering in at her elbows and hugging her forearms all the way down to her wrists like a second skin.

Under any other circumstances her breath would've been taken away by how stunning she looked. Her glossy pink lips were perfectly pouty. Her golden-brown curls elegantly swept up into a strategically messy pile atop her head. The little pearls that dangled from her ears had been her grandmother's. Every detail was utterly perfect.

But at the moment it was the dread weighing on her shoulders that made her hardly able to breathe.

"*Hello?*" Ellin called again, impatience coloring her tone.

Genevieve finally yanked open the door, giving Ellin a disparaging glare, but when Ellin's mouth dropped open, it was hard to remain too annoyed.

"*Wow*," Ellin exclaimed, her eyes roaming admiringly over the gown as Genevieve shuffled out into the corridor. "Truly magnificent."

"Holy shit," Sevin exclaimed as he stood up straight from where he'd been lounging against the opposite wall. A wolfish grin spread across his face as he flicked his eyes over her. "Forget Rowin, what do you think about marrying me instead? Your chances of winning wouldn't be as good, but I'm *much* more fun."

"Shut up, Sevin," Ellin said with a roll of her eyes from where she was now throwing a blanket over the mirror. "The only difference between marrying you or Rowin is you hide your tortured soul much better than he does."

"And I'm prettier," Sevin added cheerily. "Don't forget that part."

Genevieve gave a slight shrug. It was true.

"Lesson number one about joining this family? Don't feed the egos," Ellin admonished Genevieve.

But Sevin *was* pretty, where Rowin was more sharp and handsome. Not to mention darkly alluring...

Genevieve shook off that train of thought before it went in a direction she did not want to explore and cleared her throat. "Why are you covering the mirror now?"

"I think you deserve a minute to collect yourself without any prying eyes," Ellin stated.

A brief flash of the scene in the powder room flickered through Genevieve's mind, and she shuddered at the idea of being so closely watched by those she couldn't see.

Ellin clapped her hands together now. "Alright. Go make sure Father and Rowin are ready in the garden, Sevin. I'm going to fix her a drink."

Genevieve raised her brows at that last bit.

Ellin shrugged. "You look like you need it."

Genevieve definitely wasn't going to argue. Gathering up her skirts, she let Ellin lead her back into the drawing room as Sevin headed for the front door humming a wedding march.

"I still cannot believe Rowin wanted to have the wedding outside," Ellin complained. "It's freezing."

"Probably because he wants to torture me," Genevieve muttered.

"Rowin isn't intentionally cruel," Ellin defended with a shake of her head. "Now, if it were Grave—absolutely. Which is why he's been explicitly banned from the wedding. But don't worry too much about the snow. Father has Remi and Covin shoveling as much of it as they can from the garden."

"Why bother?" Genevieve asked. "With any of this?"

"Knox," Ellin answered with a look that said *obviously.* "As soon as you walk down that aisle, you need to remember that every little thing you do has the possibility of being watched. And if you put on a good enough show, you might even be rewarded for it."

"Rewarded how?" Genevieve wondered.

"There are technically two prizes you can win in the Hunt. Winning the Hunt itself is a year of freedom, but there's also a vote for the player the spectators like most. The winner gets the title of Favored, and Knox grants them a boon from his infamous treasure trove."

Genevieve tilted her head. "What sort of boon?"

Ellin shrugged. "Magic trinkets. Jewels. Rare artifacts. You name it. Covin managed to win last year—it's usually Sevin—and he chose some ridiculous fucking potion that allegedly would enlarge his—"

"Is this shit still not over yet?" a gruff voice rang out around them.

Genevieve turned to see two men pushing their way inside the drawing room. The man who had spoken was the same one who had been watching her and Rowin from the top of the staircase earlier. Grave.

If Genevieve had to guess, she'd say Grave was a good two inches taller than Rowin, with a body built of pure, cut muscle. There were two onyx hoops pierced in his bottom lip, and his cropped hair was as white as Ellin's, with the addition of a single streak of sable running through the right side. His gray eyes were only a shade or two darker than the pale gaze of the man in the portrait with the owl—who Genevieve now realized was standing right beside him.

"It's technically her wedding day, Grave. Maybe try not to be an insufferable asshole until midnight at least?" Ellin suggested as she took two crystal glasses down from the cabinets behind the bar. Genevieve threw the girl a grateful look.

"Fuck off, Ellin. This is bullshit and you know it," Grave addressed his sister, though his eyes remained locked onto Genevieve in a way that made her want to run and hide. "I can't believe you're helping him with any of this. If he manages to win with *her*, we're all fucked."

"And what did you want me to do?" Ellin shot back at him. "Blow his cover to Knox and get her killed?"

Genevieve stiffened as a flash of intrigue flickered through Grave's eyes, but Ellin was already shaking her head.

"Knox has already sent out his invitations," Ellin warned. "At this point, if you tell everyone that the wedding is fake, Knox is going to be furious. This is about more than a single mortal, Grave. And more than your desperation to beat Rowin. But do whatever you want, I suppose."

Genevieve wasn't sure she was as grateful for Ellin's defense now, but there was no more argument from Grave, so Genevieve supposed whatever his sister had said worked well enough to placate his clear desire to remove her from this game. For now anyway.

"Now, whiskey or tequila?" Ellin offered Genevieve. "Grave? Wells?"

"Tequila," Genevieve answered automatically as both Grave and Wells declined in preference of a bottle filled with something purple.

As Ellin searched through the glass decanters in the cupboard, Grave leaned over the counter to get a closer look at Genevieve.

He glanced in the direction of the mirror, as if to double-check that it was fully covered, and then grunted, "How exactly did you end up here in the first place?"

"I came to Enchantra to return some correspondence your father sent my mother," she told him, her tone flat.

Wells cleared his throat. "Who is your mother?"

Genevieve took a deep breath and tilted her glass back to her lips, downing the burning liquid in a single gulp before answering, "Tessie Grimm."

A look of shock fell onto all three of their faces. Then a low whistle came from the doorway.

"I haven't heard that name in decades," Sevin said as he strolled into the room. Then he hooked a thumb over his shoulder and announced, "Father said we'll be escorting you out to the garden any second now."

A rush of adrenaline went through Genevieve at his words, and she reached out to Ellin with her glass, silently asking for a refill. Ellin obliged with a smirk.

"And you said you aren't Ophelia?" Wells confirmed as Genevieve took a slower sip of the liquor this time, relishing the warmth as it spread through her veins.

"No, I'm definitely not," Genevieve said.

"How is Tessie?" Sevin asked, fishing something from the pocket of his waistcoat. A red sucker.

He said her mother's name like he really knew her, not just *of* her—in the way children know *of* the adults who hang around with their parents just enough to remember their names. No, Genevieve was realizing now that they had all probably *known* Tessie Grimm themselves at some point.

"The better question is, why was Father writing her again?" Grave grunted.

"Well, he wasn't exactly writing to her," Genevieve revealed. "Since she died. A few months ago."

Sevin openly gawped as Ellin hid her surprise behind a hand. "*What?*"

Everyone snapped their heads toward the sound of Barrington's voice. He looked dashing in a crisp, dark purple suit, with a matching waistcoat and paisley cravat. The only thing out of place was the look of devastation on his face.

Genevieve winced at the sound her glass made as she set it down on the countertop and turned to face the man fully. "I'm sorry. I wanted to mention it before, but everything happened so quickly and—"

"When?" he demanded, his violet eyes shining with emotion as he rubbed a hand over his mouth in horror.

"Last fall. It was just before..." Genevieve shook her head as her words trailed off. "I can explain later. After the wedding. I think you and I need to have a conversation that doesn't involve this damned game."

Barrington squeezed his eyes shut for a moment, but before she could apologize again, he was already snapping his attention back to his children. "Wells, Sevin, come with me. We're going to get the doors and the gate open. Ellin, you can help Genevieve with her dress and escort her through the snow. Knox will be back any minute now."

Ellin exchanged a glance with Sevin. "Trade?"

Sevin nodded at his sister before flicking his eyes over to Genevieve with a grim smile. "Don't worry, you'll be in capable hands."

"Rowin hasn't given a single fuck about our lives over the past fifteen years, and all of you are really going to attend this fucking hoax?" Grave threw at them.

"Get out," Barrington barked. "This isn't the time to rehash this argument. And I swear to Hell, Grave, you better not give away anything to Knox about this marriage."

"Or what?" Grave taunted.

"Or there might be dire consequences for the *entire* family," Barrington emphasized.

The two men stared at each other for a long minute, making

Genevieve wonder what Barrington meant. Grave, to Genevieve's surprise, did just as his father asked and left—albeit with a scowl on his face. He snatched the bottle of liquor from his sister's hands as he went.

"Hey!" Ellin grumbled.

Grave swigged directly from the bottle in response as he and the others filed out one by one.

"Welcome to the fucking family," Sevin told Genevieve cheerily. "Ready or not."

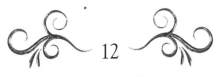

12

DREADFUL VOWS

Genevieve pushed back the blanket hanging off the mirror to give herself a final once-over. Admiring the light in her eyes one last time before she vowed herself away to a stranger made of darkness.

"Ready?" Sevin prompted softly from behind.

Genevieve squared her shoulders as he reached down for the small train that stretched out from the back of her gown. Before he could pick it up, however, she clucked her tongue and pointed to the sucker in his mouth.

"That has to go before you touch this dress," she chastised.

He sighed mournfully as he popped the candy from his mouth and tossed it into a crystal ashtray on the bar counter. He held up his hands to show her they were clean before crouching back down and carefully gathering up the excess material into his arms.

"So. Your brother wants me dead, huh?" Genevieve asked.

"Which one?" Sevin asked.

He shrugged as he straightened up to his full height once more. "I suppose we'll all want you dead when the game begins. But nothing that happens inside the parameters of the Hunt can be taken too personally. We have to perform a certain amount, or Knox will ensure we're punished for not raking in enough profits when it's all over. Try and remember that when you see us at our worst."

He extended the crook of his elbow out in offering, and she made herself accept it.

"And your performance starts now," he murmured as he escorted her toward the door.

There was a heavy tension sucking the oxygen out of the air when they stepped out of the room and moved into the outside corridor—which was now full of mirrors that had not been there before. Her heels clacking against the marble floor the only sound in the ominous quiet of the house. When they reached the foyer, Ellin pulled open the front door and waved them through. Sevin held Genevieve firm and steady as their shoes crunched over the fresh layer of ice outside. As the siblings guided her to the left of the villa, toward the stone gate that led to the back of the estate, a gust of chilling wind kicked up through the air. Genevieve knew she ought to have been shivering violently, but somewhere between the tequila and her nerves, she found that she was entirely numb.

Ellin knocked on the arched wooden door embedded into the stone wall that stretched from the house all the way to the silver fence surrounding the grounds. There was a clang and scrape of a metal latch on the other side before Wells pried the gateway open and waved the three of them inside.

"We can take our seats," Wells murmured to Ellin as Genevieve gaped at the sight before her.

A champagne velvet runner stretched from the gate all the way to the back of the house before hooking a sharp left into what looked to be a garden surrounded by the same sort of hedges that made up the labyrinth. Lining both sides of the runner were bushels and bushels of blush and gold roses. Between each bough of flowers were tall, gilded candelabras. Their flames seemingly untouched by the cold.

"How...?" she wondered as Sevin fixed her train over the carpet behind her before returning to her side to begin walking her down the aisle.

"Being a Devil's Familiar allows one access to quite the bag of tricks," Sevin explained.

"As well as good taste," she noted.

"Well, that part is Rowin," he told her.

When they reached the curve of the carpet, Genevieve nearly choked at the scene she found in front of her. The garden was stunning despite the snow. Perhaps even *because* of it. The hedges were dusted in glittering flurries of ice and surrounded a small square of checkered gray-and-white marble. Lining the hedges were silver latices intertwined with the same thorned vines that decorated Enchantra's front gates, the bright purplish berries dripping from the greenery like jewels. And in front of the latices were even more of the rose bushes as well as clusters of lit candles.

As they stepped into the illuminated square, Genevieve's eyes briefly roamed over the gilded chairs that had been arranged for Rowin's siblings. Ellin and Wells sat side by side behind Remi, who did not look like he was present by choice, while Barrington stood facing them all at the far back of the square.

Waiting at the end of the aisle, a wicked gleam in his golden eyes, was her soon-to-be husband.

Rowington Silver was a vision in obsidian against the white of the snow and marble beneath their feet. His black suit had an intricate, monochromatic silk filigree embroidered over the coat and trousers. All impeccably tailored. His cravat was a golden silk that matched the details of his cuff links as well as the earrings now dangling from his ears. Even his hair had been combed back handsomely, an effort that surprised her.

If he was equally as impressed by her wedding attire, his

expression didn't betray him. Though his eyes did linger ever so slightly on the bodice of her dress as Sevin handed her off, removing her hand from the crook of his arm and placing it in Rowin's waiting palm. Sevin eagerly left her with his brother and father, taking his seat next to Remi and leaving Genevieve to keep herself upright on her own.

As her heart thundered in her chest, she wondered how long she'd last.

"Breathe," Rowin demanded under his breath, giving her hand a subtle squeeze as his father cleared his throat.

She gulped down a single breath of air as Barrington announced, "We are gathered here today to witness the union of Rowington Silver and Genevieve Grimm in the sacred ceremony of Aeternitas. Eternal matrimony."

At the mention of *eternal* Genevieve's breathing became shallower.

"Rowin, we will begin with you. Please repeat after me," Barrington directed. "I, Rowington Silver, seal my fate with yours."

"I, Rowington Silver, seal my fate with yours," Rowin recited, his amber gaze fixing itself to Genevieve's and holding firm as he enunciated every word clearly.

"My soul is your soul. My heart is your heart. My blood is your blood. Eternally," Barrington finished.

"My soul is your soul. My heart is your heart. My blood is your blood. Eternally," Rowin told her.

They weren't dreadful vows—on paper. But Genevieve felt her stomach churning.

"Now, Genevieve," Barrington prompted. "I, Genevieve Grimm, seal my fate with yours."

Genevieve opened her mouth, tried to push the words out, but her tongue wouldn't work. For all she knew, she could be binding herself to a worse nightmare than Farrow. Not to mention that the word *eternally* was terrifying. She'd never really been entertained by anything long-term.

"Genevieve," Barrington urged gently, snapping her out of her thoughts.

Rowin was steadily silent.

Genevieve gulped down a few breaths, tried to focus on the bite of the winter air, the way it made her flesh pebble. The way it made her numb. She could get through this. She could play their game.

Rowin leaned down to whisper in her ear then, as if he could tell exactly what she was thinking. "Don't get caught up on the *eternal* part. Nothing is truly eternal. Not even when you wish it were."

So, Genevieve whispered, "I, Genevieve Grimm, seal my fate with yours."

Rowin dipped his chin in encouragement.

"My soul is your soul. My heart is your heart. My blood is your blood. Eternally," Barrington said.

She parroted the words, making her tone as lively as she could.

"And you both promise to protect each other, to choose each other, in sickness and in health, in light and dark?" Barrington continued.

"I do," Rowin said, the words loud and clear.

"I do," Genevieve agreed before she lost her nerve.

Barrington's smile was a sincere as it could be given the circumstances as he raised his voice and declared, "I now pronounce you husband and wife." He shifted his eyes over to his son. "You may now kiss your bride."

Barrington stepped away then, making sure the only thing in Genevieve's sight was Rowin. Her husband.

And then she felt it. The heavy eyes of a Devil.

Knox had arrived.

Her body went rigid with nervousness as she tried to glance away from Rowin, to look for where the Devil might be, but Rowin gave her hand a squeeze as if to say *focus*.

It felt as if Knox's gaze was pressing in on her from every side, but as Rowin reached out to tap a finger beneath her chin, lifting her face to his until their noses were nearly touching, that detail somehow faded to the back of her mind.

He slowly wrapped an arm around her waist and dragged her body up against his. "Ready?"

She wasn't, but she nodded anyway.

"Deep breath," he said.

She listened as he edged closer and angled his face down, their noses touching ever so slightly, and the rest of the world fell away.

And then his mouth was on hers.

For a kiss not born of lust, it was all-consuming. Every thought emptied from her head as the heat of his lips scorched her from the inside out. She felt him bury his free hand into her hair, tangling it through her pinned-up tresses in order to tilt her face to the exact angle he wanted. Every movement he made was sure, confident, and when he gently parted his lips to deepen the kiss, she didn't hesitate to follow suit. The taste of him filled her mouth as he dipped her back ever so slightly. She instinctively reached up to grasp onto his biceps, though it wasn't really necessary.

When the sound of a whistle rang out from somewhere in the distance, just as she went to flick the tip of her tongue against the hoop in his lip, Rowin suddenly ripped himself away.

She made an involuntary sound of disappointment as she blinked her eyes open, her breathing shallow as she searched his face for what was wrong. And then she remembered where they were. What they were doing. She smoothed a hand over her hair, embarrassed by getting so carried away. He, on the other hand, was wearing his usual mask of inscrutable composure.

This time it was too much.

How do you do that? she wanted to scream. *Pretend as if none of this has any effect on you?*

Someone appeared at her left: Barrington.

"All I need now is your signatures," Barrington prompted as he held out a thick piece of yellowish parchment in front of them both.

The top of the paper read *Certificate of Marriage* in shimmering gold. Both of their names were printed beneath two blank lines in the center, and at the very bottom were two signatures already scrawled in black ink. Sevington Silver and Ellington Silver. Their witnesses.

Rowin took a pen she hadn't noticed was clasped in his father's free hand and quickly scrawled his own signature on the blank line above his name. He passed it over to her next, and she gritted her teeth as she did the same.

With a sharp nod, Barrington rolled up the certificate and turned back to their audience. "Introducing Mr. and Mrs. Rowington *Silver.*"

A few cheers rang out amongst Rowin's siblings before she heard the scraping of chairs and a murmuring that sounded like, "Let's get the fuck inside."

As the rest of them went, so did the suffocating presence of Knox's gaze, and Genevieve let out a sigh of relief.

"Knox will probably be gone for a bit while he promotes our union to his patrons in Hell. But you have to be more careful," Rowin scolded her now that they were entirely alone.

"Of what?" she challenged.

"Of letting your real feelings show."

Genevieve looked away from him as the sound of midnight tolled, reverberating through the garden around them. She startled at the jarring sound.

Smoothing her hands over her hair, she muttered, "Now that the strangest day of my life is over, I think it's time to..."

Her words trailed off as a wave of exhaustion flooded through her body.

"Genevieve?" Rowin prodded.

She looked down at her hands and watched as her vision began to blur. A sharp, slicing pain speared through her temples a moment later, little black dots forming across her vision as she felt all the magic in her core drain away.

"*Rowin*," she pleaded. For what, she wasn't sure.

Right before she hit the ground, she felt a pair of solid arms wrap around her and his deep voice promising, "I've got you."

"You're a Demon. I wish I'd never met you. And now you'll fucking burn."

He dropped the match as she screamed, but the roar of the flames drowned it out. No one was ever going to be able to hear her cries.

THE SPRING EQUINOX

13

EAVESDROPPING

Genevieve woke in the drawing room to the buzz of a muffled discussion and something warm weighing on her chest. The fog in her mind was still thick, and it took several attempts before she was able to pry her eyes open and see—

—a wide, golden gaze staring right at her.

Genevieve squeaked as she heaved herself up, causing Umbra to scramble down from where she had been curled up on top of her chest. She brushed a hand down the silk corset of her now-creased gown and wrinkled her nose at the fox grooming itself at her feet.

"This house is truly run by animals," Genevieve muttered as she stood up from the tufted settee, an imprint of her body left in its velvet upholstery. The muted voices she had heard before were coming from the other side of the wall, and her curiosity was instantly piqued. Shuffling forward, she pressed an ear up to the damask wallpaper, seeing whether she could make out any of the words. Nothing.

Hauling the skirts of her wedding gown out of her way, she made for the door. Cracking it just wide enough to peek out into the hallway, she found that the corridor was empty, but the voices were instantly clearer. Umbra wiggled out of the sliver of space she'd opened and took off to the right. Genevieve followed, watching as the fox dashed through the open archway of the dining room and disappeared from sight. As a loud clatter echoed from the room, Genevieve slowed her steps and pressed herself flat against the hallway's wall, leaning forward just enough around the archway's frame to observe the scene without being noticed.

"Must you throw such a tantrum, Grave?" Ellin complained from where she sat at the end of the long dining table next to Wells.

"Look on the bright side—she's a brand-new person you might get to stab. You always enjoy that," Sevin pointed out from the head of the table, pulling yet another sucker from his mouth in exchange for a bite of a green apple. He was leaning dangerously far back on the hind legs of his chair, and Genevieve wondered how it was possible that he hadn't already crashed to the ground.

"The real question is whether Rowin would ever forgive any of us for killing her," Wells pointed out.

"Does it matter? It's not like he speaks to us outside of the Hunt anyway," Remi murmured from where he was standing behind Sevin.

"Don't fucking start," a familiar voice warned, making Genevieve's eyes snap across the room.

When her gaze landed on Rowin's face, she found the same stoic mask he usually wore. His amber eyes shrewd but filled with apathy. His mouth set in an irritated frown. The same mouth that had been on hers just earlier...

Her blood began to heat at the memory of their kiss. Her breath hitching in shock at having such a visceral reaction despite the fact that it had been nothing more than a very elaborate display of Rowin's dedication to their performance.

It was not even the most passionate kiss I've ever experienced, she admonished herself as she shoved the memory of it to the very darkest corner of her mind. *He's just a man.*

But that wasn't really true anymore, was it?

He was her *husband.*

The heat in her blood shifted from desire to something less desirable as she focused her attention back on the scene before her. As Genevieve glanced at each of the siblings, she noted that she'd never before seen the work of such strong genetics. She was sure she would have known that every person in this room was related to each other even if she'd met them separately, outside of Enchantra.

"And why shouldn't I start?" Remi asked Rowin, his expression mirroring his twin's perfectly. "Knox is in Hell, working out how to announce your faux marriage. I think this is the *perfect* time to start."

"Fine." Rowin crossed his arms over his chest, as he leaned back against the far wall. "My correspondence between games—"

"Or lack thereof," Ellin muttered to Sevin and Wells.

"—is not relevant to the matter at hand," Rowin continued, his words even but dripping with warning. "Whether you all decide to focus your attentions solely on killing Genevieve or not, the fact of the matter is you aren't just punishing me if she dies—you're punishing yourselves. She's a convenient tool. Nothing more, nothing less. If I can get free, you all stand to gain."

"When you find a cure?" Grave growled at his brother. "*Enough* with the cure. It isn't fucking real. The Crimson Rot has been infecting powerful Demons for centuries. Their families were just as desperate as us. And what did they find? Nothing. We continue to play the Hunt or our mother *dies*. End of discussion. So I hope your new ball and chain knows how to fight."

Even from her far-off vantage point, Genevieve could tell that Rowin's jaw was clenched tight. And for some reason the fact that he wasn't going to bother with a rebuttal infuriated Genevieve more than Grave referring to her as a *ball and chain*.

"Look, we all know how this is going to go," a raspy voice declared from the corner to Rowin's right, and Genevieve nearly let out a startled gasp as she spotted the man amongst the shadows. He had cropped black hair and crimson irises that, despite their eerie color, barely drew her attention. No, it was the giant ebony serpent spooling itself around his leg and torso that made her pause.

The man I spied slicing himself open with the dagger?

Which would mean this was the first time she'd seen all seven of the Silver siblings in one place. Because the discussion of her fate was now a family affair. She was also surprised to find that she only just realized the entirety of their discussion had been in their first language and that Barrington had been right—she'd hardly noticed the switch.

"How is it going to go, Covin?" Rowin addressed his brother's statement with a dark look in his eyes.

"You're either going to collect another win and we won't ever see you again, or your winning streak will come to an end, and you'll finally get a taste of Hell with the rest of our sorry asses. Either way, tomorrow's masquerade is our last chance to be civil with one another, so I say we put the bickering on hold and go out with a bang at the party," Covin stated, and while he spoke, Genevieve saw that his slithering pet wasn't the only one with a forked tongue.

She shuddered.

"Is that what you're thinking about right now?" Rowin lifted a brow. "Partying?"

"That's what *I'm* thinking about," Sevin chimed in.

Covin shrugged. "What else is there to enjoy in our circumstances? Between losing to you and Grave all these decades, and Sevin winning Favored nine times out of ten, I've grown quite fond of Hell and Knox's parties."

"You've grown fond of sharing Demons' beds," Ellin suggested with a roll of her eyes.

Covin shrugged again. "That too."

"If it makes you all feel better, Rowin's little romantic charade is almost certainly going to steal Favored from me," Sevin offered in condolence. "Which is a shame, because there's this nifty little pocket watch I've had my eye on in Knox's collection for a while. It's supposed to be able to tell whoever holds it how much time they have left until they—"

"Would you all shut the fuck up," Grave seethed. Sevin chucked his apple at Grave's head for interrupting him. Grave caught the half-eaten fruit one-handed and tossed it to the ground before turning to address Rowin directly. "You and your bride can sleep in peace tonight, but the moment the Hunt begins, you will not be getting any mercy from me. So I suggest you take Covin's advice and thoroughly enjoy the masquerade."

Rowin advanced a step toward his brother, a dangerous smile playing on the edges of his lips. "And I won't be showing *you* any mercy if you lay a finger on my wife."

A shiver went down Genevieve's spine.

Rowin stepped around Grave and began heading for the exit, making Genevieve duck out of view as quickly as she could before he caught her eavesdropping. By the time he reached the hall, Genevieve had barely managed to wedge herself back into the drawing room, heart still pounding like she'd been caught.

When Rowin burst through the door a few moments later, Genevieve knew two things. The first was that she was not built for quick getaways—she'd never needed to be before. And the second was that Rowin had known she'd been eavesdropping the entire time. A fact punctuated by the pointed look in his eyes as his gaze took in her flushed skin and the odd, constricted movements of her breaths against her boned bodice.

Before he could accuse her of anything, however, she asked, "Why did I faint?"

"My father suspects your system wasn't able to handle Knox's lockdown of your magic in combination with the magic that links our lives together for the Hunt," he told her. "I felt awful, too, for a moment."

"Why the Hell did Knox lock down my magic?"

"Not just yours," Rowin assured. "Everyone's. During the Hunt, our days will be broken up into two halves. The hunting hours and the safe hours. We are not allowed to access our magic during the hours between midnight and noon, since that is when the Hunt will take place. Starting now."

"*Fuck*," she cursed.

This was disastrous. In Phantasma she'd been able to walk right through all the levels without a single worry. Becoming invisible when the world around her became too intense had always been her saving grace and the only time she ever stayed out of trouble.

"Good, you're grasping the scope of the situation, then," Rowin approved. "I think it's time to retire to our bedroom for the night."

"What the fuck do you mean, *our* bedroom?" she demanded, voice rising.

He lunged forward to try to clap a hand over her mouth, but she batted him away with a withering look.

"Watch it," she warned darkly. "I bite."

His gaze narrowed. "Yes, I'm aware." Still, he stepped closer. "I implore you to keep your voice down. Knox is in Hell with my father right now, but he'll most likely be roaming the house later tonight while they go over the details of the masquerade. So whatever delicate sensibilities you have about sharing a room, you need to get over them now."

She snorted. It was not her sensibilities that were delicate. It was the fact that she didn't want him to be anywhere within hearing distance while she *slept*. Her nightmares tortured her enough; she didn't need him to witness them as well.

She tilted her nose up at him. "No."

His gold eyes darkened. "I wasn't really asking. Don't make me throw you over my shoulder again. I don't care how much you bite."

The moment those words were out of his mouth, someone burst into the room. Two someones: Sevin and Covin.

Covin let out a low whistle. "Biting. Nice."

Sevin tilted his head at Rowin. "And I thought choking was more your thing."

Genevieve gave Rowin a taunting smirk. "Now *that* I'm game to try. I've wanted to strangle you since the first time I heard you speak."

Rowin rolled his eyes as Sevin corrected, "I don't think you'd be the one doing the choking, sweetheart."

Genevieve felt the tops of her ears burn ever so slightly at the picture Sevin's words conjured in her mind, but before any of them could notice, a dark flash went through the room.

"I'm surprised you two lovebirds are still up," a rasping voice purred as a tall figure appeared between them all. "I thought surely there would be a headboard breaking somewhere right about now."

Even if Genevieve hadn't recognized the voice, the way Rowin stiffened at the sight of the newcomer would have told her exactly who this was.

Knox.

He was stunning. Most Devils were. But even by those standards he was exceptional. His face was all refined angles and sharp lines. His calculating violet eyes were framed by thick black brows and lashes, his obsidian hair longer than her own and hanging pin-straight down his back. Two curved horns jutted out from the crown of his head, and she immediately recognized them as his Devil's Mark.

"Back so soon?" Rowin questioned the Devil. "I thought you'd be spreading our wedding announcement to the entire Third Circle for the rest of the night."

Knox grinned. "I only came back to install a few more looking glasses for my eager patrons. Everyone is *very* excited about your nuptials."

"Wonderful. If you'll excuse us, Genevieve and I were just making our way to bed," Rowin said, before turning to Genevieve and imploring, "Ready, trouble?"

He offered his hand to her while Knox watched expectantly.

Genevieve gave Rowin a dazzling smile as she accepted his waiting palm. "Absolutely."

A spark of something flickered through Rowin's eyes, but before Genevieve could name it, it was gone.

As he began to pull her away, she drawled, "You all have a good night."

"Lovely to officially meet you, Miss Grimm," Knox said in farewell.

Genevieve paused to look back at the Devil, meeting his violet gaze as she corrected, "It's *Mrs. Silver.* And it's with utter disdain that I am officially meeting *you.* Good night."

With that, she marched Rowin out of the room.

As he began leading her toward the other end of the house, he said, "Not many mortals would be brave enough to talk to a Devil that way, you know."

She began to pick at her nails. "Well, I figure he wants me alive more than he wants me dead in order to play his little game, right? So why should I hold my tongue?"

"I wouldn't have even considered that was a thing you knew how to do," Rowin murmured as they reached one of the bedroom doors in the portrait-lined wing of the villa. He pushed the door open and waved her inside ahead of him. "After you, *Mrs. Silver.*"

14

THE RING

Genevieve and Umbra stared awkwardly at each other while Rowin fetched her trunks from down the hall. The fox was sitting on the black velvet comforter tucked neatly over Rowin's bed, the tip of the creature's fluffy black tail flicking from side to side.

"*What?*" she huffed at the Familiar.

Umbra only twitched her ears.

Peeling her eyes away from the shrewd creature, Genevieve glanced around Rowin's bedroom, struck by how pristinely kept it was and thankful there was not a mirror in sight. There were also no windows, or displays of art, just fussed-up walls with elaborate picture frame molding over the rich golden wallpaper.

His closet was enormous—something from her dreams— and perfectly organized, its doors painted a glossy ebony and embossed with two running foxes whose snouts met at its middle seam. The only sources of light were from the taper candles in the sconces bookending the bed.

And Hell, the *bed*. It was the largest bed she'd ever seen. It looked large enough to fit at least five people comfortably, and Genevieve's mind began to wander as she pondered whether it ever had. The headboard was just as intricately carved as the closet doors, the details carrying over to the four posts rising from each corner of the solid wood frame.

But it didn't matter how grand the bed was, or how comfortable it looked. She was not sharing it with him.

Right on cue, Rowin returned with her bags, setting them on the dresser across from the bed and giving her a pointed look.

"How much stuff did you *bring*?" he muttered.

"I don't take criticism of my packing habits from my sister, and I'm surely not going to take yours," she leveled at him as she went to unclasp both trunks and flip their lids open, propping the tops against the back wall. "You're lucky I *only* brought these. If it hadn't been for those damned birds, I'd have a proper wardrobe."

"The hex wouldn't have let the crows harm you," he reasoned.

"And how was I to know that?" she said, as the scene outside the Colosseum came roaring back to her. "I think it's time we lay to rest the discussion of what I should or should not have done before coming here. Unless you really feel like spending our honeymoon night fighting." She batted her lashes at him.

"Stop that," he ordered, his voice dropping in a way that made her raise her brows. "Turn around."

She propped a hand on her hip. "Why?"

"So I can unlace your corset."

She sputtered. "Are you mad? Absolutely *not*."

"Must you be difficult about *everything*?" he bit out.

"I am not going to fuck you just because we're married," she maintained.

He lifted a brow. "Tell me, trouble, what does you getting changed have to do with us fucking?"

She glared. "You're trying to get me undressed."

"I'm trying to get rid of the gown taking up all of the space in this room, yes," he agreed.

She looked around. He was right. The skirts of the gown took up half the floor around them, not to mention how encumbered they made her movements.

"I'm not sure I have any nightgowns that would be appropriate to wear in front of you," she finally said.

He snorted. "Whatever you have wouldn't be anything I haven't seen before."

"I hate when people say that," she told him. "It *is* something you've never seen before. Me. And I'm spectacular."

He gave her a considering look but didn't comment further.

Finally she huffed. "Fine. Unlace the ribbons, but if you even *think* about putting your hands anywhere else—"

In a blink he was right in front of her, so close that she could feel the warmth of him over every inch of the exposed skin of her neck and shoulders.

"Let's get one thing clear," he warned, eyes darkening with each word he spoke. "I have zero interest in putting my hands on you unless it's to keep you from harm or because you've asked me to. Understood?"

She glanced away as she gave a noncommittal grumble.

"Genevieve."

She huffed and looked back at him.

"If we are going to be partners in this game together, that means we have to *trust* each other," he emphasized.

She tilted her nose up. "Trust is *earned.* And what have you done thus far to earn it from me? Force me to marry you?"

"I let you marry me as a lifeline to help you survive this place," he reminded. "That falls under keeping you from harm, as I said. As for the latter bit—I said that, and I meant it. Which should instill trust by the sheer fact that it was absolute truth, whether you liked to hear it or not. I will not ever lie to spare your feelings."

"How romantic my husband is," Genevieve drawled dramatically, but she hated to admit that he wasn't wrong. The casual cruelness of honesty might be hard to hear, but the fact that he stood by his words was admirable, at least.

"We can win this," he told her. "I've won the last fifteen

consecutive years because, aside from Grave, my siblings have grown tired of the game. Right now they believe you might finally be the key to their success in breaking my winning streak. Don't prove them right."

"I was not planning to just roll over and die, if that's what you think," she told him.

"If you refuse to trust me, that's exactly what you'd be doing," he vowed. "From here on out everyone will try to pit us against each other, to isolate one of us in order to go in for the kill. Our trust has to be implicit. We are on each other's side first and foremost, even if someone else suggests otherwise."

Genevieve understood why this could be a detrimental pact for them to make.

"Unfortunately, the last time I trusted a man implicitly, he shattered my heart," Genevieve told him. "I'm not very eager to do so again."

"This game isn't about hearts," Rowin told her, a glint of something she couldn't read in his eyes at her revelation. "Hearts can never truly be trusted, anyway."

He gestured for her to turn around then, and his original request came back to her now. Her corset. Right. She faced away from him in silence, giving him access to the back of her dress.

As he began to slowly pull at the knots of the laces at her waist, he continued, "Hearts are not ruled by logic or loyalty. They can easily betray you."

As if to prove his point, her heart began thundering in her chest as his fingertips grazed the skin over her spine and loosened her corset.

"And you won't?" she wondered, looking over her shoulder at him. "Betray me? Even if your *family* asks you to?"

He stepped around her then, raising his hands between them to slide off one of the many rings he wore and hold it out before her in his left palm. She leaned in to get a better look at the onyx gemstone embedded into the thick, silver band, noting the unique swirling pattern carved in its polished surface. A signet.

"Consider this my wedding gift," he said as he lifted her left hand and slid the band gently onto her ring finger. It was just the right amount of snug. "I tried to give it to you before. If anyone who means you harm is close by, it will alert you. The hotter it gets, the closer they are."

Like the "hot and cold" game Ophie and I used to play.

"It's ice cold at the moment," she observed as she peered down at the shimmering, black stone.

A corner of his mouth lifted. "Precisely."

"I'd never usually say no to a man gifting me jewelry"—she gestured at the ring—"but this is . . . ugly."

"It isn't meant to be *fashionable*." He looked to the ceiling in exasperation. "It's meant to be helpful. I'm offering you undeniable proof of my intentions and you're concerned that it isn't to your taste?"

She scoffed. "No, I'm concerned people will think *I* chose it."

"How mortifying," he deadpanned.

She swallowed now. "Fine. I'm willing to . . . work with you. We have the same goal, right? Keeping me alive?"

"Correct," he agreed. "If we act up the romance from time to time, you might even win Favored. That way I'll win my freedom at the end of this, and you'll win a gift from Knox's collection. You might as well walk away with something."

"Unless he has something to erase unwanted memories in that collection, I couldn't care less about some silly little consolation prize. But I'll play along. You have my word."

He inclined his head. "I suppose we'll have to learn if your word is worth anything."

"It's worth much more than my heart," she muttered.

He stared at her for a long, silent beat, and she again found herself frustrated by the fact that she could never really read him.

Eventually he cleared his throat and murmured, "You should probably get changed."

She looked down at herself. "Oh. Right."

Grabbing her nightgown from her trunk on the dresser, she made her way into the en suite. Once she was safely closed inside the enormous white marble room, she let her wedding dress shimmy down over her thick curves, kicking it away as she replaced it with cornflower-blue chiffon. The sleeves of the nightgown were long and billowy, tapering in at her wrists before flaring out at the ends. There was a pretty silk bow that sat just beneath her bosom, but the square neckline was just low-cut enough to be inappropriate to wear in front of a stranger, as she had said earlier.

Except he *wasn't* a stranger anymore. He was her husband. A title that she needed to get herself used to by the time she saw Knox again.

When she returned to the bedroom, she stopped cold on the threshold, and a flush of heat rippled through her body after she saw that Rowin had also changed out of his wedding attire. Now, he was wearing a tight black undershirt, the material clinging around his biceps and torso like a second skin. She could see that there were inky black wisps, like swirling waves of smoke, covering every inch of his newly exposed arms and neck.

I want to trace them with my tongue.

She made a noise of shock at the thought before she could stop herself.

No, I most certainly do not.

Rowin gave her a puzzled frown, but Genevieve avoided his gaze as she asked, "Where should I put this?"

He jutted a chin toward the closet. "There. I'll take care of it tomorrow."

Once the dress was stowed away, Genevieve emerged from the closet to find that Rowin had separated the bed down the center with a pile of pillows. It seemed ridiculous, considering the bed's size, but she certainly didn't complain. When he extinguished the candle on his side of the bed, plunging them into near pitch-black, a sudden spike of adrenaline flooded through her veins.

"I can't believe after everything you've somehow managed to get me into your bed," she grumbled.

The corners of his lips curled up ever so slightly, though she was pretty sure he was trying to hide it.

"So, now we just...go to sleep?" she asked as he lifted the corner of the comforter on his side.

It went against every one of her instincts to crawl into bed with him. He could so easily harm her. She'd slept beside plenty of strangers before, but never without her magic. However, she felt safer here, in his bed, than she would anywhere else in this house of monsters.

Rowin's gaze locked with hers. "Is there something else you wanted to do? Was today not eventful enough?"

"Well, there is one last thing we need to address tonight, isn't there?" she prompted.

"Which is?" He tilted his head in anticipation.

And before she could stop the words from spilling out of her mouth, she blurted, "The matter of our consummation."

A brief look of surprise flickered over his expression, quickly replaced by one that was infuriatingly smug. "I thought you said that just because we're married doesn't mean we're going to—"

"*I didn't mean it like that*," she rushed to correct. "I just meant—you heard Knox earlier. Do you think he's keeping tabs on us tonight? Expecting any sort of evidence that we..."

"There are no looking glasses in our bedrooms. If he decides to spy on us, it would have to be in person. And I would sense it," he assured as he threw back the covers, letting Umbra spring onto the bed and curl up atop one of his pillows.

Genevieve made a face at the idea of sharing a bed with the creature, and she swore Umbra glared back.

"Not to mention that proof is rather arbitrary since anyone can be fucking," he continued as he stretched out next to the fox, reaching up to pillow his head back on his folded arms as he closed his eyes. "An emotional connection is what gives him the stakes for his game."

"That's unfortunate," Genevieve said as she moved to blow out the final candle so she could tuck herself into her own side of the bed. "The emotional connection is a lot harder to fake."

For once, the nightmare did not start with fire.

Genevieve was wearing her wedding gown in the middle of a frozen lake. As far as she could see, there was only darkness above her and ice beneath her feet.

"Would you like to dance?" a deep voice said from behind her.

Genevieve startled, whipping around toward the voice, the sound of crunching ice reverberating through the freezing clearing. Out of the corner of her eye she swore she saw a fissure crawling across the frozen surface, but the moment she spotted him, all thoughts of danger disappeared.

"We never had a proper first dance," Rowin said as he held his hand out to her.

Without hesitation, she placed her palm in his, and he spun her into an effortless waltz across the ice. She pressed herself as close as she could to his body heat as he twirled her around, and she found herself impressed by how graceful he was. As their movements slowed to a steady sway, she closed her eyes and rested her face against his shoulder.

"I appreciate you trusting me," he told her, the rumble of his deep voice vibrating against her cheek. "I know it can't be easy after everything that happened with Farrow."

She stiffened at the sound of Farrow's name, but for some reason she couldn't make herself pull away. When he began to speak again, something on her left hand began to grow strangely warm.

"Though you really ought to have been more careful when giving your heart away," he continued.

The ring, she realized. She blinked her eyes open and glanced over at where her hand was clasped in his. The hideous silver band felt like it grew ten degrees hotter with every word he spoke.

When she tried to pull back, he picked up their tempo once again and spun her out from him. "Rowin—"

Except when she finally stopped turning, she saw that it wasn't Rowin at all, and suddenly the frigid air around her turned absolutely scorching. The ice beneath their feet began to crack further, spiderwebbing out in every direction as he reeled her back toward him.

"You're one of them, Genevieve," Farrow said as he continued their dance. "You're a fun time, but believing I, or anyone else from a good family, would ever marry someone like you is just delusional."

"Let me go," she hissed at him, digging her feet into place as she stopped their spinning.

She tried to yank herself out of his grasp, but he wouldn't let go, laughing as she struggled against his hold.

"Let me go!" she cried again.

"I will, as soon as I take back what you promised me," Farrow told her.

And then he plunged his hand into her chest.

A garbled shriek bubbled out of her mouth as he ripped her heart out of her body and held it between them. Bright-red blood began to bloom across her corset as she gaped down at the hole he had made inside her.

"Why? You don't even want it," she seethed as she tried to snatch back the beating organ in his hand.

"Of course not. But I won't let you give it to anyone else either," he told her, and then he shoved her away.

She fell backward, slipping on the ground and crashing through the ice as a furious scream ripped from her throat.

Genevieve shot up in bed. Her chest was heaving as she tried to catch her breath from the nightmare, her temples slick with sweat while she scrambled to tear away the sweltering covers tangled around her limbs. She looked around wildly in the dark, taking a moment to remember where she was.

She glanced over to Rowin's side of the bed.

His back was facing her, his form as close to the edge as he could possibly get without falling off. His head was covered by one of the pillows, and she wondered whether he had unconsciously tried to block out whatever noise she had been making in her sleep.

At least he didn't wake up, she thought.

The same could not be said for Umbra.

Genevieve jumped when she finally spotted the fox, fully awake and unblinking from where she was still curled up.

Genevieve turned her back to the Familiar and settled into

her pillow, the covers still pushed down to her waist as she waited for her body to cool off.

Farrow had been wrong about one thing. Someone *did* marry her. But it had been nothing at all like the wedding she had imagined.

When she felt the corners of her eyes prick, she twisted her fists into the sheets, gritting her teeth until she staved off the traitorous tears. She would not cry. Not here.

She had a Devil's game to play. And this time, she wouldn't be leaving until she won.

15

GILDED PREY

Genevieve woke up to a snow leopard pouncing on the bed. She let out a piercing shriek as she scrambled away from the enormous feline and—

—rolled right off the edge of the mattress.

The pain of hitting the floor never came, however, because a second before impact, her entire body disappeared.

She shifted herself back to her solid state as relief flooded through her at the feeling of her returned magic. Glancing up, she spotted the leopard's dark eyes peeking just over the edge of the bed, ears flat against its head as its tail waved in anticipation.

"Sapphire, *heel*," Ellin's voice ordered the overgrown cat from somewhere on the other side of the room.

A moment later and the other girl appeared around Genevieve's side of the bed, the look on her face not nearly as regretful as Genevieve thought it should be.

"You're a heavy sleeper," Ellin said. "I didn't know what else to try."

Genevieve climbed to her feet, kicking away the linens that had slid off the bed along with her. "What did you try in the first place?"

Ellin shrugged. "I knocked."

Genevieve propped a hand on her hip. "How many times?"

"Once."

Genevieve glared.

"You're going to have to learn how to be more alert during

the Hunt," was all Ellin offered in lieu of any sort of apology. And, unfortunately, she was right. Genevieve had never had to worry about being a heavy sleeper before. Anytime her instincts sensed she was in danger, she'd trained herself to simply disappear. Aside from last night, she usually didn't even wake up from her nightmares. Enduring them until the sunlight broke the horizon or opting not to sleep at all.

Genevieve huffed and rubbed at her eyes as she tried to dislodge the sleepiness still lingering in her mind from waking up sometime during her slumber. The room around her was still dark, no windows or natural light to tell her what hour of the day it might be. Rowin and Umbra were nowhere to be seen either.

"What time is it?" she wondered.

"Half past four," Ellin answered as she scratched her Familiar behind its fluffy white ears, making the feline fill the room with its purring.

"I slept for over *twelve hours*?" Genevieve gaped. "Why didn't Rowin wake me up?"

"He was adamant about letting you rest." Ellin shrugged. "Something about you needing more of it since you're a mortal and all. Truthfully, I'm surprised you didn't wake up when the band arrived and Sevin and Covin decided to commandeer their trumpets."

"They're trumpet players?" Genevieve wondered.

"No."

Genevieve found herself grinning.

"A part of me hopes you might actually last past the first round, if for no other reason than I'll be all alone with these morons again," Ellin grumbled.

"I'm touched," Genevieve said dryly.

Ellin only smirked as she raised her hand and made a sweeping gesture through the air around the room. Genevieve watched in awe as the candles in the sconces sparked to life along with the feeling of crackling power over her skin like static electricity. It was a feeling very close to what she had felt the first time Rowin had opened Enchantra's front door.

"Fire?" Genevieve asked. "Can all of you do that?"

"Light," Ellin corrected. "And no. I'm the only Light Wraith in the family."

Genevieve filed away this information for later. "Which makes Rowin...?"

"Rowin, Wells, and Remi are Shadow Wraiths. The power of every Wraith tends to vary since we can inherit any number of things from our demonic parent," Ellin said with a dismissive wave of her hand, as if the subject was too boring to continue discussing. But Genevieve was kicking herself for not having learned more about them by now. "It's time to start getting ready. The masquerade starts in an hour and a half, and Rowin requested that I help you get dressed while he and the others help Father prepare for everyone's arrival, but I have to get myself ready, too, you know."

Genevieve was about to ask why Ellin would need to help her when she spotted the gown hanging against the bedroom door. It was the most elaborate dress she had ever seen—much more detailed than her wedding gown had been—and even more opulent than those at the Mardi Gras balls back home.

Ellin waited patiently for Genevieve to strip down to her undergarments before helping her step into the gown. The bodice was made of pristine gold silk, its boned panels tapering to a point at her waist in a salaciously flattering cut before giving way to the layers of billowing skirts. Ellin tightened the laces of the corset until Genevieve almost couldn't breathe, but the effect was worth the lack of oxygen, with the square neckline showing off a scandalous amount of her perfectly ample bosom. The corset's thick straps tied in bows at the tops of her shoulders, a detail she couldn't help but adore, though it was the hand-beaded, anatomical heart made of sparkling diamonds and pearls that made the gown a true masterpiece.

Pear-shaped gems emanated from the heart's center, scattering across the bodice and down onto the skirts, making it look like the heart was bursting into a thousand droplets of shimmering black blood. Genevieve gave a twirl, testing to see how easily the skirts moved. Like air.

"He was right. You *do* look good in gold," Ellin said matter-of-factly as she stepped back to admire the dress.

Genevieve opened her mouth to ask who *he* was, but Ellin was already moving on.

"Remember—the Hunt begins at midnight. Once it starts, you officially exist for *their* entertainment," Ellin warned. "I suggest you indulge during the party and enjoy the last bit of fun you might ever have."

Genevieve winced.

Ellin sighed. "I worry Rowin hasn't really prepared you for the consequences of playing this game together—win or lose. For all involved."

"Because of your mother? That's what this is all for, right? To save her from the Crimson Rot?" Genevieve said.

"It's more complicated than that," Ellin said. "But that's not your problem. You're not really part of the family."

Genevieve winced as if Ellin had slapped her, though Ellin didn't seem to notice. It wasn't that Genevieve thought, or wanted, otherwise, but she didn't think it was possible for such words to not sting deeply. Except for Rowin, it was clear that she was expendable to everyone here. It didn't matter that Sevin had walked her down the aisle. That Ellin had helped dress her up and defended her against her brothers. Or that Barrington had been so adamant about sparing her. In her experience, immortals had a way of making you feel like they were empathetic, attached even, when their hearts were actually made of impenetrable stone.

Genevieve imagined it was a necessary coping mechanism when one saw so much life and death come and go in their never-ending existences. Still, it was a good reminder of why she loved being so mortal. She enjoyed feeling everything so intensely. Well, almost everything. She could certainly do without the heartbreak.

"After you finish getting ready, my father requested that you meet him in his study," Ellin said, pulling Genevieve out of her thoughts. "But remember to be in the ballroom at six. Knox gets cross when anyone's late. He likes to make a grand entrance."

Ellin rolled her eyes at that last bit as she turned to leave, letting her Familiar escape into the hallway ahead of her.

Once she was alone, Genevieve noticed, sitting at the corner of the mattress, a silver gift box that she hadn't seen before, a pair of elbow-length gloves by its side. A purple envelope sat atop the box, its silver wax seal face up, and she hesitated.

The last time I opened such a tempting letter . . .

When she finally scooped up the envelope and turned it over, however, she saw that this time it was addressed to her. Well, addressed to *Mrs. Silver*.

She slid her fingernail beneath the flap to break the seal and pulled out the thick, black parchment inside. There were three sentences and a name scrawled in glittering, silver ink in the middle of the page.

Your husband requested the gold. I requested the mask.
I think it'll be rather fitting.
Knox.

She tossed the letter aside and pried off the box's lid to reveal the mask beneath. The sense of dread that flooded through her at the sight of it nearly made her choke.

A hare.

The Devil had dressed her up like shiny, gilded *prey*.

Genevieve did not expect to walk out of Rowin's room to a crowd of people.

As soon as she opened the door, a group of masked figures, all draped in opulence, turned toward her at once. It reminded her eerily of the crows.

Someone in the back gasped, "That *has* to be her. The bride."

They were all clutching onto what looked like handheld mirrors as well as various bubbling cocktails.

One of the figures, who was dressed in a gown made of feathers with the mask of a peacock affixed to the top half of their face, held up their looking glass and requested, "Show me the bride."

When Genevieve's image appeared in real time on the mirror's surface, everyone gasped. Including Genevieve herself.

Another of the figures stepped forward then, looming down over her as he scrutinized her like she was a specimen of bug he'd never seen before. His mask was a bright cobalt blue, the same color as his skeptical gaze and the rest of his three-piece suit. Unlike her hare costume, or the peacock's, the theme of his ensemble seemed to be . . . a man in a mask.

Rowin's ring suddenly began to heat, and she looked down at her finger in shock.

"You don't look like anything that fucking special," the man in blue scoffed.

Genevieve fiddled with the ring on her finger. "You know, I was just thinking the *exact* same thing about you."

He seemed amused by this, crossing his arms over his chest as he tilted his head at her. "Why should we place our wagers on you?"

Genevieve curled a lip in disdain. "The better question is, why should I give a fuck whether you do or not?"

His smile tightened. The ring grew hotter.

"Don't you want to win Favored?" he glowered.

Genevieve giggled. "Why would I want to impress a bunch of depraved assholes with nothing better to do than watch a family tear each other apart?"

"Oh, she's mouthy," someone with the horns of a stag attached to their head mused.

"I thought Rowington would like someone more...quiet," someone else chattered back.

Genevieve nearly laughed. *He definitely would.*

"Mortals," the man said with a disdainful roll of his eyes. "You think any of us care about being morally superior enough to take any of what you said as an insult? If you could live long enough, you'd see that there is no such thing as depravity or saintliness— just creative ways to pass the time."

A few toasts clinked around them.

"I'll leave you to do that, then," she said as she tried to step past them. "Enjoy your meaningless eternal existence."

The man shifted a step over to block her path. The ring was scorching now.

Before Genevieve could snap at him to move, he reached out and shoved her against the wall. Her shoulders and the small of her back bounced off the hard surface painfully, but all she could do was suck in a sharp breath in shock as she tried to regain her balance.

"Watch it, Cedric," the peacock warned. "Knox will kill you if you spoil his game."

"It's not like I'm going to maim her," Cedric said with a taunting smirk. "I just want to see what sort of fight she's got. I have a feeling her contribution is going to be pathetic."

Pathetic. There was that word again. It took everything in her not to launch herself at him.

Instead, she walked away. Refusing to give the crowd the satisfaction of watching her get all worked up. She was sure they'd get enough of that soon enough in the game.

"Hey, I wasn't done with you," Cedric called as he rushed after her. "Listen, maybe we got off on the wrong foot. I have an offer for you, and I wanted to make sure you wouldn't be a waste of time."

"I'm not interested," she said as she continued on without looking at him.

"Don't you want to know what it is, at least?" he pressed. "I can make us both rich. Well, I'm already rich. So rich*er*, I suppose."

"If you don't go away, I'll scream," she threatened cheerily.

"Could you just fucking stop for one second—"

"Rowin!" she shouted. "There's a strange man bothering—*mmf*!"

Cedric had slapped his hand over her mouth from behind.

She opened her jaw and sank her teeth into the sensitive flesh between his thumb and index finger as hard as she could.

"You little *bitch*!" Cedric howled as he tried to shake her off, but she only bit down tighter.

When he finally managed to dislodge her, she turned around to snap her teeth at him once more. "Stay the fuck away from me, or the next time I'll make sure I hit *bone*."

As she strode away, she looked down at Rowin's ring on her

hand and brushed the pad of her thumb over it. With every step she took, it grew colder.

By the time Genevieve made it to Barrington's study, there was less than an hour until the masquerade began.

The dim, candlelit room was quite drafty, causing a shiver to run down her spine as her eyes adjusted to the dark. Scents of wood, tobacco, and old books hit her a moment before the bitter smell of charred...something.

Her arms pebbled at the power she felt bleeding into the room from somewhere in the back. As her eyes traced over the bookcases behind the desk at the study's center, she found the source of the strange energy. A large, fathomless portal.

The portal's surface seemed to be rippling—like a vertical pool of black water. Genevieve was so enraptured, and disturbed, by the mysterious abyss that she failed to notice Barrington until he cleared his throat.

"Genevieve," Barrington greeted softly from where he stood by one of the bookcases. "Come. Sit."

She made her way over to a leather chair in front of the desk, perching on the armrest and leaving her gown to drape carefully down the side. She didn't want to crease the material too much.

"You look wonderful," he told her, but there was a sadness in his tone that was unmistakable. "You have Tessie's eyes. Well, the eyes she had when I first met her, anyway."

Because as soon as Necromancers completed the ritual to inherent their magic, the warm cerulean the women in her family had been born with turned an icy shade of blue. Grimm Blue.

Being Ophelia's younger sister, Genevieve had never thought

to worry about taking on the haunting irises that her mother had possessed their whole life. Grimm Blue did not go with her complexion or hair like it did with Ophie's.

"You have her determination, too," Barrington said, bringing her focus back to him.

"Ophelia would call it stubbornness," Genevieve muttered.

He tried to smile, but the gesture seemed almost painful.

A beat.

"What happened?" he finally choked out.

Though her own questions were being barely contained in her throat, Genevieve knew his was a fair place to start. "My father happened. We found out that he entered Phantasma again, and there's this level... Fraud. The consequence to losing was killing the person you loved most, and he..."

Barrington's grip on the arms of his chair became white-knuckled, the fury rolling off him barely contained as he snarled, "Is he still alive? Gabriel?"

"Ophelia and I aren't sure. And neither of us wants to search any longer at this point—"

"I'll find him," Barrington seethed. "I always knew that bastard would be the death of her. She should have *never* entered Phantasma. It's why we—"

He cut himself off, pressing his lips together.

"Tell me," Genevieve pleaded. "All of it. I want to know, *need* to know, what happened to make her the way she was. Why she never..."

Loved me?

No, that wasn't right. Tessie Grimm had surely loved both her daughters. In her own way.

Perhaps it was simply that I could have become anyone, anything, and she still would not have felt about me the way she did about Ophie? That was closer.

"I came here because I was looking for another family like mine," she revealed. "I thought...I was hoping you might be a Necromancer. And if you had children, at least two of them, I might find someone who felt just as lost as me. My mother told me *nothing*. She was so strict with Ophelia yet so unconcerned about me. It's been hard for us both to put ourselves together now that Mother is gone."

Barrington was quiet for a long moment. Then.

"Tessie and I met when I was doing a job for Knox. I needed the blood of a Necromancer."

Genevieve's heart raced. She was finally about to learn something about her mother's past.

"I was in New Orleans when Knox assigned me the task, and I had heard of the Grimm family through a mutual connection. Your mother hadn't received her magic yet, but her bloodline was what mattered. And she was happy to help. Your grandmother would likely have been furious to hear that she was helping a Devil's Familiar. But Tessie was wild and impulsive."

"My mother?" Genevieve raised a brow. "Wild and impulsive?"

Barrington nodded. "It's true. It's why we got along so well, in the beginning especially. We quickly became close friends. There's an entire decade of adventures we don't have time to get into. After the Hunt, perhaps. Why don't you ask your most pressing questions for now?"

"What caused your rift? Why *did* she enter Phantasma? Do you know anything about the locket she wore? You once wore one that matched it."

Genevieve reached into the hidden fold of her gown and pulled out the picture. Barrington swallowed as she handed it over, his fingertips barely gripping the edge of the delicate paper, as if he might accidentally ruin the only proof that their friendship once existed.

"This was the last photograph we took together," he whispered. "Our rift started because she wanted to enter Phantasma. Her Necromancy training was nearly complete, but she still hadn't received her magic. Still, she insisted on going into that damned competition. Like I said before, the Tessie I knew could be impulsive. But after she received her magic... and her locket... it doesn't surprise me if she changed."

"Do you know why her locket was so special? Was yours the same? And why don't you wear yours anymore?" Genevieve asked.

"The one I wore wasn't special. Not like your mother's was, anyway. What do you know about Soul Locks?"

"Soul Locks?" Genevieve repeated, tasting the term in her mouth for the first time.

"They are enchanted artifacts made to collect and contain souls. Only a few beings know how to forge them. The enchantment can be placed on any sort of item, though lockets *are* used quite often. The locket I'm wearing in the photograph was lent to me by Knox while I completed a piece of work for him. But your mother's was very different. It was shrouded with magic I'd never seen before, and she was certain it contained something incredibly powerful, something disastrous."

"Disastrous *how?*" Genevieve pressed.

Barrington shrugged. "Nothing she could ever explain, more of a feeling. She said your grandmother had felt the same. It doesn't surprise me if she became strict with your sister, to prepare her to bear that burden. A *great responsibility*, she'd called it. The last time I saw her, even when she was about to throw herself into Phantasma, she was talking about how intentional she'd have to be with her first child. How she'd have to train her for the day she took over the locket."

Genevieve, of course, knew what had happened with Ophelia

and her locket. How it had led to her sister's legacy. Her destiny. She wouldn't describe that as *disastrous*.

Or maybe it had been, by her mother's standards. Releasing the Prince of the Devils was probably disastrous to most people's standards.

But those people didn't know Salem. Or they didn't have his affection, at least.

"Your mother loved you, Genevieve," Barrington finally spoke again. "I can tell you that with certainty. If she neglected you, it was because of something that weighed on her since long before you were born."

Genevieve looked down at her hands as she nodded silently.

"But," Barrington continued, "that doesn't mean you aren't allowed to be angry with her about it now. Even if she's gone. You're allowed to feel that anger."

Genevieve's gaze snapped back up to his.

"Sometimes parents make terrible mistakes. And there's nothing we can ever do to fix them," he whispered to her. "The least we can do is let you be as angry for as long as you need."

"Thank you," she told him, sincerely. She didn't need his permission to feel this way, but it still felt nice.

"My children are not going to go easy on you in the Hunt," he said, changing the subject. "I see so much of Tessie in you, though. You and Rowin can win this. But you have to trust him. Don't let the others get in your head. You should watch out for Grave. He has brute strength and determination on his side. Covin too. Remi and Wells are quiet but clever. Ellin isn't ruthless, but she doesn't give up easily—watch her until the very end. And Sevin... Sevin is unpredictable."

Genevieve committed as much of this information to memory as she could before standing and turning for the door. Right before she left, she paused and looked back.

"Did you ever think about going to find her?"

"Yes."

"Why didn't you?" she pressed.

Silence.

Then, "Sometimes I think it's best not to chase after things. Sometimes all we can do is let them go and hope they come back on their own."

As Genevieve left the mournful silence of the room, she knew such a thing would never be good enough for her. She'd always want to be found. No matter how many times she ran away.

Knox's Annual Masquerade

The Hellmouth opens at six o'clock sharp on the night of the spring equinox & closes at twelve o' five | Anyone that remains in Enchantra after this deadline will be killed on sight.

The Hunt

All wagers start at one thousand Soul Coins | All wagers for the Champion, First Hunter, and First Eliminated must be placed before midnight at the Masquerade | All wagers for the Final Two, Most Kills, and Favored are flexible until there are less than four players left. The Favored will be announced right before the Final Match. | Once the Hunting Blade chooses the Hunter at the beginning of each Round, the Hunter will choose which game they'd like to play. The safe hours begin exactly twelve hours after. | All monitoring will be done through the one-way looking glasses provided with this invitation. Looking glasses must be returned to the Knoxium estate after the Hunt is over.

Betting Categories

Champion	Final Two
First Hunter	Most Kills
First Eliminated	Favored

The Players

Reigning Champion: Rowington Silver

Gravington Silver	Sevington Silver
Covington Silver	Wellington Silver
Remington Silver	Ellington Silver

The Bride

As promised, this year's Hunt has a very special surprise. Rowington Silver and Genevieve Grimm have said their vows, and she will be his partner in the Hunt. All wagers placed on the couple will therefore be doubled. Adjust your strategies accordingly. If Rowington manages his sixteenth consecutive win, this will be his final Hunt. Of course, the last time one of our beloved Silver siblings attempted the marriage loophole, it didn't end so well, did it?

The Night of the Spring Equinox

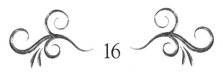

16

MASQUERADE

Enchantra was glittering.

When the bells tolled six, Genevieve stepped into the ballroom, her mouth open in wonder. The air all around her was filled with floating orbs of light that looked like twinkling fireflies, emphasized by the fact that in every corner of the room were enormous, gilded mirrors that made the lights seem endless. High above her head, sashes of silk stretched from the perimeter of the room's ceiling and gathered to a single point in the center, where a sphere of the glowing orbs slowly rotated.

Masked guests were draped over the balcony, watching those already dancing below them and howling with inebriated laughter. The dance floor was crowded with lively beings, all of whom paused their gossip and drinking to stare as she passed. An orchestra was playing a twinkling waltz, the melodies floating through the air like bubbles of champagne—which Genevieve now spotted flowing from a fountain across the room. She made a beeline for the display of refreshments, craving the ecstasy she knew was at the bottom of a few glasses of the golden, effervescent wine. Usually, she'd stop herself after a drink or two, but she knew she should take Ellin's advice to have fun tonight.

Besides, there were few things she was better at than enjoying a good party.

"Fuck you, Sevington Silver, it does *not*," Ellin growled just as Genevieve downed her first glass and stuffed a ripe strawberry into her mouth.

Genevieve's gaze snapped to where Ellin, Sevin, and Covin were huddled together a few feet away. Their ensembles were, unsurprisingly, just as intricate as hers—if not more so. Sevin's mask was of a silver wolf. Covin's was a striking serpent, its crimson scales the same shade of crimson as his and Sevin's eyes. And Ellin's mask was...

"Look, just in time—a nonpartial third-party opinion," Sevin pointed out when he spotted Genevieve, the sucker that usually hung from his lips noticeably absent.

Sevin curled two fingers in Genevieve's direction, beckoning her over.

Genevieve swiped another two glasses of champagne before approaching with a curious "Yes?"

Covin let out a low whistle as he looked her up and down. "You look positively *exquisite*, bunny rabbit."

"Careful, Covin. Despite the adorable disguise, I've heard rumors that our new sister bites," Sevin drawled.

"The rumors, as usual, are true," Genevieve confirmed before taking another sip from her glass.

"Lucky Rowin," Covin murmured with a smirk, and a sudden buzz of whispering sounded at Genevieve's back.

Her gaze snapped to the three onlookers behind her, all of them dressed like swans, all holding the same looking glasses as the crowd outside of Rowin's room earlier. The words *Rowin*, *bride*, and *bites* stood out from their conversation as they looked between her and the mirrors in their hands.

"Always watching," Ellin reminded under her breath.

Genevieve took a longer sip this time.

"We need you to settle something," Covin told Genevieve. "Can you tell us what you think Ellin's mask might be depicting?"

Genevieve couldn't, actually. The craftsmanship of the mask was a stark contrast to that of the marvelous silver gown Ellin was wearing. It was some sort of animal—that much was clear. A creature that could only be described as something between a deranged bear and a house cat.

"She made it herself, if you couldn't tell," Sevin said after a beat of Genevieve's silence, trying to hide a smirk behind his fist as he pretended to cough.

"It's supposed to be Sapphire, and you both know it," Ellin hissed. "Hell forbid I have hobbies other than fucking, fighting, or partying like the rest of you!"

"You might want to reconsider making arts and crafts one of them," Sevin drawled.

"Where the Hell is Wells?" Ellin growled.

"Uh-uh, you know the rules—twins don't get a deciding vote," Covin told her.

Ellin stomped off anyway.

Genevieve raised her brows. "Wait, Ellin and Wells are—"

"Yes," Sevin interjected before she could say the word *twins*. It took her a moment to realize he had interrupted because the question would have seemed suspicious to any partygoers eavesdropping on their conversation. "Alright, I'm going to find some vamps. I'm out of suckers."

As he strutted off, Genevieve shifted uneasily on her feet at being left alone with Covin.

"So"—Covin flicked his crimson gaze over her—"do you have a favorite amongst my siblings yet?"

"Whichever one of you I'm not currently talking to," she told him.

Covin smirked. "At least you've got a sense of humor."

Before Genevieve could say anything else, someone called Covin's name, and he strutted off without so much as a goodbye.

Manners must be a lost art in Hell, she thought as she quickly polished off both her glasses and discarded them on a passing waiter's tray. She made her way over to the streaming tower of champagne, filling up another glass before spinning back toward the room to search through the crowd.

Where is he?

"Looking for someone?"

Genevieve turned to find the face she'd been searching for, but not the man.

Remi was dressed in a golden suit, his sleeves rolled up to his elbows. Despite the fox mask he wore, she knew it was Remi and not Rowin from both the lack of any piercings and the fact that Remi seemed much less intentional with his appearance to her than his twin. Rowin's hair was always carefully disheveled, every detail of his outfits considered and refined—much like her own style. Meanwhile, Remi's hair had clearly been combed with his fingers, and his shirt was half-unbuttoned, with no cuff links or necktie.

"Would you like to dance?" Remi offered, lifting a hand in invitation.

Genevieve hesitated, the nightmare from the night before flashing in her mind. She absentmindedly reached over to play with the ring on her left hand, and when her fingertips brushed against cold, textured metal, she looked down in surprise to find Rowin's signet.

She'd gotten used to having a ring there, and now she'd apparently gotten used to missing it. But at least she had something to fidget with again. As well as something to tell her that Remi's intentions must be innocent enough, considering the band remained cold.

"Something wrong?" Remi prompted.

Genevieve shook her head and finally placed her hand in his, letting him lead her toward the dance floor as she shoved the images of the horrible dream to the back of her mind. Remi guided her in a simple, swirling waltz around the other couples, and she thought it ironic that she had arrived in this country hoping for a moment exactly like this. A handsome suitor who would dance her into a stupor before leading her away for a tryst in a hidden corner of a gilded room.

But Enchantra was not made of gold. Just ruthless Silvers.

"I'm sorry about this," he told her. "All of it."

She looked around at the crowds of onlookers, at the magic mirrors in their hands. "I can't think what you mean, Remi. I'm Rowin's wife. There's nowhere else I'd rather be."

"Really?"

Genevieve glanced up at him. "Why are you speaking to me, Remi?"

"Am I not supposed to?" he wondered as he expertly spun her out by one hand.

"Do as you please. But after our first encounter, I didn't think you'd *want* to," she pointed out as he began to reel her back in.

And then, over his shoulder, she spotted the man she *had* been looking for.

Rowin was like a blade of darkness cutting through the glowing ballroom as he scanned the crowd. She noticed that his suit had a gilded heart beaded over the left breast of his jacket in a similar vein to the details of her own gown, and she snorted at the connotation.

A heart of gold? Please.

Even beneath the onyx fox mask, she knew the moment Rowin's gaze found her and Remi. He didn't come over as she thought he might, however. He only crossed his arms and leaned a shoulder against one of the pillars that held up the balcony at the back of the room, watching intently as she and his twin continued to dance.

"Would you have been happy to meet someone you'd soon

have to see killed?" Remi murmured, bringing her focus back to their conversation.

"You can always try *not* to kill me," she said sweetly.

"There is no mercy in the Hunt," he told her. "But that doesn't mean that I don't feel rather sad for you."

Genevieve halted their steps and yanked her hand out of his grip. "If you're saying you *pity* me—"

"Would you not pity a mouse stuck in a trap?" he said, but his expression still seemed as apathetic as ever.

"You can keep your pity to yourself," she spat.

Remi had opened his mouth to say something else when a deep voice cut in.

"I believe it's my turn to dance with my wife."

She and Remi turned their heads toward Rowin in tandem, and Genevieve was shocked to find how much relief flooded through her at his sudden presence.

Remi waved a hand toward Genevieve. "She's all yours."

Rowin exchanged an inscrutable look with his brother as he pulled Genevieve into his own arms and whisked her away. Rowin pressed her into his body and the music morphed into something quite enchanting, its tempo slowly building as they traveled across the ballroom.

The world around them slowly became a blur of color while Genevieve followed his steps instinctually, her mind somewhere very far away.

"What did he say to you?" Rowin asked, his clipped tone slicing through her thoughts.

Genevieve blinked up at him before flicking her eyes over the dance floor around them. All the other couples had stopped to watch them.

"It was nothing," she finally told him.

He gave her a hard look. "If he upset you, I think it's important for you to remember that, as your husband, it's my *job* to defend your honor."

In other words, the optics of him sticking up for her were very important for their audience. Except Genevieve wasn't currently interested in crafting more of their false narrative off the very real feelings she was having. Not with the weight of so many eyes on her.

She stepped away from him as the song they were dancing to finally came to an end. "I need another drink."

Rowin sighed as he grasped onto her hand and pulled her off the dance floor, the crowd parting without hesitation as he led her back to where the refreshments were. When he stepped away to swipe another glass of champagne for her from the table, a group of masked spectators greeted him enthusiastically, and Genevieve watched while one of them boldly winked at him as he extracted himself from their conversation to return to her.

"I think you have an admirer," Genevieve whispered, ignoring the itchy feeling she suddenly felt crawling across her skin.

"One of many," he told her without so much as a glance back.

Genevieve clucked her tongue. "They must all be so disappointed with our recent nuptials."

He smirked. "Because beings of Hell hold the sanctity of marriage vows with the highest respect?"

Point taken. Which reminded her . . .

"For a ball being thrown by a Devil, I certainly expected more debauchery." As soon as she said the words, she tipped her glass all the way back to her lips, leading by example.

"Careful what you wish for," Rowin cautioned as he watched her polish off the drink. "Our bastard of a host hasn't arrived yet—"

On cue, all the lights in the room were extinguished at once. The music in the background began to simmer to something more sinister than before, and Genevieve braced herself for the Devil's appearance.

In Phantasma she'd had her fair share of dealing with Devils, but being in the same room as one was something you never really became used to. They seemed to take up so much space in any room they occupied, like their power sucked the air out of it. A warning that no matter how benevolent they appeared, they could still destroy you with barely a thought.

"Welcome, esteemed guests." Knox's crackling voice echoed through the hushed ballroom from somewhere she couldn't see. "As always, to those of you who make my masquerade your single annual excursion to this linear plane from the Other Side—I thank you greatly."

There was a brief flash of light; then the orbs slowly reignited around them, except this time their glow was carmine. Genevieve watched with thrilled fascination as the room transformed. Beds with mirrored headboards surrounded by sheer curtains to—poorly—give the illusion of privacy replaced the tables around the dance floor. Mirror balls made of thousands of tiny vermilion pieces began to spin from the ceiling above amongst the scarlet orbs, scattering winking dots of light in every direction. The tied-back curtains fell over the windows with a heavy swish to block the moon's luminescence and plunge everything into seedy darkness, while the orchestra's violins shifted to a sensual crescendo.

Things appearing out of thin air was nothing new to Genevieve, especially after spending time with Salem, but the way Enchantra had gone from a shimmering celebration to a writhing affair right before her eyes was *thrilling*. Most likely because of all the champagne that was now hitting her system, filling her veins with pure ecstasy, but she'd prefer not to worry too much about that.

She watched as pairs, trios, *quartets*, headed toward the beds—some not even making it that far as they sank to the floor—and her skin prickled at the sound of their moans joining the orchestra. No one had ever touched her in such an uninhibited way, but now she found that she was *craving* it. Compliments of the bubbly in her system, she was sure.

Just then, a waiter balancing a tray of glowing, pink cocktails passed by, and an instant need for whatever was in those glasses came over her.

"*Genevieve, wait*," Rowin ordered.

But she did no such thing, weaving through the throngs of masked patrons after the waiter like a moth chasing after a flame.

Knox's voice began to boom across the room again. "Usually, we start our evening in Enchantra with a toast—to the whole Silver family for another entertaining year of the Hunt. Tonight, however, I am delighted to finally introduce a very special addition to this year's game."

Genevieve was barely paying attention to the Devil's words as she flagged down the waiter, greedily pilfering one of the neon-pink cocktails off their tray.

"For the first time, the Hunt has a team of two. Our reigning champion has unexpectedly wed a lovely little *mortal*. And I know you've all been dying to meet her."

The room began to buzz with whispers, and Genevieve giggled as she pressed the cool rim of her new glass to her lips. The tart liquor tasted like citrus and berries.

Yum.

"And now," the Devil declared, his voice still floating ambiguously from somewhere in the far distance, "Mrs. Rowington Silver herself…"

A tall figure suddenly blinked into view right in front of

Genevieve, a large spotlight erupting overhead and making her startle and slosh pink liquid onto her skirts and across the marble tiles beneath her feet. Rowin's ring felt like molten lava on her hand.

"*Fuck*," she gasped down at her hand as she squinted through the too-bright light beaming from above her.

"What a wicked mouth," Knox purred. "Don't worry, I can take care of that."

He snapped his fingers and the stain—as well as her drink—instantly disappeared.

"I wanted that," she complained.

"I have something better," he said as he snapped his fingers again and a flute of something purple and fizzy appeared in his grasp. "Try this."

Her instincts screamed at her to reject the offering, to turn and go back to Rowin. Her first reaction when it came to Devils would always be flight. But maybe it was the liquor already in her system that made her desperate to try.

"What is it?" she finally asked as she took the glass and gave it a sniff.

"Passion fruit," he told her. "My favorite."

"I've never had it."

"Try it, then," he persuaded. "Just one sip."

She narrowed her eyes.

"I *insist*," he urged through clenched teeth.

She drank.

Extraordinary.

She went to down the rest, but Knox clucked his tongue. "Ah, ah, ah. We must toast your fellow players."

He gestured behind her with his chin, and she spun to see Barrington leading his family—sans Rowin—toward the circle of light. Their faces were all carefully blank, leaning toward apathetic, except for Sevin, who looked amused as he eyed the drink in her hand.

She opened her mouth to ask where Rowin was, a sudden need to see him erupting within her, but before she could get the words out, she felt the static warmth of his presence approach from behind.

"Move," he said against her ear as he began to guide her toward the rest of his family.

In a blink, glasses of champagne appeared in everyone's hands around the room as Knox announced, "I propose a toast to another lively season of the Hunt and a healthy year for dear Vira."

At the mention of their mother's name, Grave shattered his glass to pieces in his fist, sending a spray of black blood and bubbly to the ground as Ellin shifted closer to place a comforting hand on his arm. Remi and Wells didn't even bother glancing at the scene, while Sevin and Covin exchanged loaded looks.

Knox raised his glass in the air, and all around the ballroom the guests returned his gesture. The clinking of glasses rippled through the room as each of the Silvers took a customary sip of their champagne. Minus Grave, who was already storming away from the illuminated circle.

Genevieve tilted her own glass back and polished it off in one go.

After she licked the last drop from her lips, she blinked over at Rowin, who she now realized was simmering with barely contained rage beside her. She furrowed her brow at him in question as she searched for what might be wrong, but there wasn't a hair out of place. Even the champagne in his hand looked perfectly yummy—

—except it was no longer champagne. It was now the same bright purple liquid that Knox had given her.

"What's wrong, Rowin? Don't like the flavor of passion fruit?" Knox smirked. "I just wanted to make sure you and your new bride had a good time tonight. The honeymoon will be over as soon as the clock strikes midnight, after all."

Genevieve's head was swimming, and she couldn't work out what the Devil was getting at, as Rowin shoved his half-drank cocktail at a passing waiter before unceremoniously wrapping an arm around Genevieve's waist and yanking her across the dance floor.

"Are you alright?" she asked as he steered her toward the outer perimeter of the room. He looked like he was in physical pain.

"Fine," he said between clenched teeth, which was not at all convincing, but he only held on to her tighter and kept walking.

She could feel the impressive muscle of his bicep where she held on to his arm like a lifeline as she tried not to stumble, and before she could stop herself, she squeezed. He skipped a step in surprise, his eyes flicking down to hers. The music around them had begun to shift into something much more... intimate, and she found herself pressing closer to his side as their steps slowed to match it. Every inch of her skin that was covered suddenly felt much too hot, and she had the primal urge to rip off the suffocating cage of the dress then and there. Her teeth began to ache, her mouth watering for something she couldn't quite pinpoint, but the shape of it was awfully reminiscent of his name.

The desire was coming from somewhere intrinsically within, spreading through her veins until it took over her entire system and she could barely think of anything except for *him*.

"You have to fight it," he implored, his voice thick with... lust?

That couldn't be right, and yet, when she peered up into his eyes, she saw that his pupils had nearly completely swallowed the gold of his irises.

"*We* have to fight it," he gritted out again.

When she saw how hard he was clenching his jaw, the strain of keeping his breaths steady in his chest, she knew she was not the only one losing her mind. "I don't want to fight it."

"Fuck," he hissed. "Neither do I."

17

SCANDALOUS AFFAIRS

There was not an ounce of resistance from Genevieve as Rowin led them into the shadows of a hidden nook beneath the grand staircase. When he pressed her back against the wall, there was no protest ready on her lips, only a whimpering moan as her bare skin ached for his touch.

His answering groan filled her with desperate want, making her nipples harden painfully beneath her corset as his hands began roaming down her arms, tugging away her gloves and discarding them to the floor before moving on to brush over the curves of her hips. His fingertips explored up her bodice until the pads of his thumbs brushed deliciously across the material covering the taut buds aching for his attention. Her hips shifted forward involuntarily, grinding against him and eliciting a low rumble of pleasure from his throat.

A moment later something else began to caress her skin, tangling in her hair. Something cool and light as a feather that was vibrating with power. His shadows.

Her eyes squeezed shut as one of the tendrils gently circled her throat while his warm lips pressed to the underside of her jaw, sending a shiver down her spine.

Yes, yes, yes. This is what I've been missing. Pleasure. Passion. Sex.

Her own hands were nothing compared to the heat of his, the strength of them, the way they—

—suddenly disappeared.

Genevieve groaned in protest as she opened her eyes to see his shadows dissolving around them as he readjusted his mask over his eyes. Both of their chests were heaving with labored breaths from holding back.

"Why did you stop?" she complained, her lust-filled voice unrecognizable. "I don't care if people see."

"We are not going to play his game," he snarled as he began to back away.

"What do you mean? I thought that's exactly what we have to—"

"Not the Hunt. *This*. He drugged us. The passion fruit. If we give in, it could be *hours* before the magic would let us stop," he told her darkly.

Genevieve knew that he had not meant for the idea of being wrapped up passionately in each other for so long to sound as appealing as it did.

"Are you really trying to claim that you can last for hours?" she mused.

"For fuck's sake," Rowin gritted out as he rolled his eyes up to the ceiling, as if he was invoking a higher power to give him the willpower she obviously did not possess. When he looked back at her, he commanded, "Stay away from Knox and the drinks. *And do not follow me*."

A blink later he melted away into the shadows and entirely out of sight. If she thought the thread of desire tethering her to him would thin as soon as he disappeared, she was sorely mistaken. In fact, it only seemed to get *worse*. The need to find him intensifying until she felt like she might unravel entirely in his absence.

Righting her dress, she plunged back out into the party. In the few moments they'd been distracted, the heat of the ball had intensified. And by heat she meant the sounds of pleasure coming from behind the wispy curtains of the beds and the grinding couples on the dance floor. All of it only adding to the torture of her own unfulfilled lust.

As she scanned the crowd for Rowin, she spotted several of his siblings in compromising positions. Covin was lying back on one of the beds, the curtains left wide open, as two women bent over his waist, pleasuring him in tandem. Elsewhere, she almost didn't recognize Wells, whose face was practically being consumed by a man with bright blue hair while a woman kneeling between them attended to both of them at once. Ellin was straddling a man's lap as he fed her a strawberry.

"He went upstairs."

Genevieve whipped her head to the right to see Sevin leaning against the wall next to the foot of the stairs, sipping from a glass of thick red liquid.

Blood.

"Is the honeymoon already over?" He tilted his head at her with a crooked smile.

"Not if I have anything to say about it," Genevieve mumbled under her breath. But to Sevin, she questioned, "Aren't you going to partake in the...festivities? This seems like your kind of party."

"My ex is here. So I'm pining," he responded.

Genevieve raised her brows. Of all of Rowin's siblings, Sevin had the most charm. Not to mention his *looks*, and it surprised her greatly that he would be a wallflower at such an event. She meant to say as much, except Sevin's eyes had gone glassy, the same way Barrington's did when his mind had slipped back into the past. She was happy to leave him lost in his thoughts.

When she reached the top of the stairs, she found an entirely different array of scandalous affairs on the second-floor landing.

Vampires.

Everywhere Genevieve looked were clusters of the fanged paranormal beings lapping at each other's necks, thighs, breasts. Stains of crimson dripped from puncture marks pocking their skin, and Genevieve watched as they switched between drinking from their partners' wounds and from between their legs.

I may be in a little over my head, she thought as her gaze snagged on a nearby couple.

One of the women was swirling a familiar-looking lollipop around the peaks of her partner's breasts before bending forward to lick away the sticky, red trail of sugar it left behind. Except...Genevieve was pretty sure that the suckers were not made of sugar at all.

"Pretty little rabbit," the woman crooned as she caught Genevieve's eye, her partner continuing to tend to her breasts. "Do you want a taste? We have plenty more suckers if you're interested."

Genevieve wasn't sure which sort of *suckers* the woman was talking about, but she decided she should keep moving before she found out. The landing curved like a crescent moon, its railed balcony giving her a perfect view of the party below. She moved further into the expansive corridor where she'd first met Ellin and Sevin. Each side was lined with five rooms, and at the very end was a closed-off set of double doors.

In the first room, she found a couple shredding the sheets of a bed that hadn't been in the room when she'd explored the day before but was an exact match to the beds Knox had procured downstairs. Behind the second door, she found a full-blown orgy, and a sweat broke out at her temples.

The third room was surprisingly empty, and in the fourth she found...

Rowin.

And he was absolutely not alone.

He was lying against the headboard of a bed. His suit jacket had been discarded on the floor, along with his fox mask. His shirt was halfway unbuttoned and exposing more of the swirling ink of his tattoos over the defined muscles of his abdomen and pectorals. There was a woman standing to his left and she was... tying his wrist to a bedpost.

Genevieve's face flamed.

Even next to the sight of Rowin being *tied to the bed*, the woman herself was a sight to behold. Her fingertips adorned with what Genevieve could only describe as talons, and the ends of her long raven hair were made of dancing orange *flames*. Flames were also burning in the centers of her dark irises, flickering between orange and blue.

And her *face*. Her mask had either been discarded, too, or she hadn't bothered to wear one in the first place, which Genevieve couldn't blame her for. Not when she possessed the sort of beauty men started wars over.

A queen of Hell.

Genevieve felt a pang of unjust jealousy as the woman stepped back from her work and asked Rowin, "Tight enough?"

Genevieve cleared her throat now.

Rowin's gaze snapped in her direction.

"*Genevieve*," he snarled.

"Honey, I'm home," Genevieve said dryly, crossing her arms over her chest.

The woman glanced between the two of them curiously before recognition seemed to register on her expression. "You're the wife."

"For now," Genevieve said at the same time that Rowin stated, "Yes."

The woman threw her head back in a disarming laugh.

"*Leave*," Rowin seethed. But he wasn't talking to Genevieve.

The woman smirked now. "Are you sure?"

"Yes," he grunted, like the word was painful for him to say. "I can handle her."

"Thanks for rescuing me from Sevin," she told him, and as she stepped past Genevieve, she whispered, "Give him Hell."

"No worries there," Rowin said, glowering as the door shut behind her. "Didn't I tell you not to follow me?"

"Did you think tonight was going to be the night I started behaving for you?" she retorted.

His mouth pressed into a tight line.

"But I think the more pressing question here is, what's wrong with *me*?" she continued.

He reached over with his free hand and began to pull at the knot. "You'll have to be more specific."

She scowled. "You left me to come up here with someone else for whatever sexual game I just walked in on—"

"Who said we were doing anything *sexual*?" Rowin huffed a laugh. "That's the passion fruit clouding your mind. Which is exactly why I left you downstairs."

What did he mean, it wasn't sexual? He was just being tied to a bedpost by the most beautiful woman Genevieve had ever seen.

"Gwen was only trying to help me stay away from you," Rowin claimed as he finished undoing the knot and standing from the bed. "I should have known you'd come looking for me, given that I specifically told you not to."

As he stepped closer, his gaze dropped down and lingered a little too long on her lips, and warmth shot through her core once again, making her entirely forget her ire and whatever point either of them had been trying to make. Now, all she was wondering was what it would feel like to kiss him again. To have his shadows wrapped around her as she traced the tattoos running over his chest and stomach with her tongue.

"I couldn't help it," she whispered as she took a step closer to him. "I want this."

He stayed rooted in place, a labored heave of his chest the only indication that her proximity had any sort of effect on him. "Want *what*? Again, be more specific. There's no one watching us in here, so please don't hold back."

Heat instantly bloomed on her cheeks. She'd had plenty of lovers, but none who had ever asked her to tell them what *she* wanted.

"I want to know what it's like to kiss you when it isn't just for show," she told him.

"A kiss, how innocent," he taunted as he ran his gaze over her blushing cheeks. "But innocence is not what I'd be looking for tonight. Go back to the party."

She scoffed. "I am not *innocent*. I have plenty of experience."

He raised a skeptical brow. "Trouble, I suspect the only thing you have experience with is *sweet*. That's never what I'd be."

She wrinkled her nose at him. "Stop calling me *trouble*."

"Stop causing it."

"Or you could just join me in causing it," she crooned.

She saw the moment his resolve finally snapped, and before she could blink, he was in front of her, the tendrils of his shadows pushing her gently back into the wall.

"Hypothetically, if we were to do this, it would be nothing more than *fucking*," he told her, his amber eyes practically glowing with desire.

"I'm not sure you can consider it only fucking when we're *married*," she reasoned, her words breathless as whatever magic was in her system reacted to how close his mouth suddenly was to hers.

"Being contractually married and being emotionally attached are two separate things," he stated. "There cannot be any strings attached between us. The web we're caught in is too tangled as it is."

He's right. And I want release, not another man who will rip my heart out.

"Fair enough," she said. "To answer your question—as long as you make me come, there won't be any problem with just fucking."

The look he gave her now was absolutely *sinful*. His shadows began unfurling around them just as they had before, and her entire body began to vibrate with anticipation as he undid the cuffs of his shirt, one at a time, before discarding the shredded material to the floor. Next to go was his belt, which he removed with one hand as he nodded to her dress.

"That needs to go. Now."

Unlike the night before, she readily gave him access to the back of her gown this time. He made quick work of the laces, and within seconds the dress was sliding down her curves and piling onto the floor. Leaving her in just her lacy pink undergarments.

"Fuck," he cursed as his gaze roamed over her from head to toe.

Her blood began to boil as the lust within her became a frenzy of *need*. For a moment she thought she might perish if he didn't start touching her.

He muttered another curse at the sight of her arousal already soaking through her underwear before meeting her eyes and declaring, "You were right."

"About what in particular?"

"You aren't anything I've ever seen before," he said gruffly. "You're spectacular."

She hummed with satisfaction and watched as his shadows began crawling over her skin, caressing her in a way that made her want to pleasure *them*.

"Lean back against the wall," he ordered.

She did as he asked, pressing her shoulders against the cold surface and making her flesh pebble with anticipation. She expected him to step closer, but he stayed planted in place.

"Spread your legs," he directed next.

"Take off your pants," she countered.

The corners of his lips twitched. "Patience, trouble. I need to make sure I oblige your only request."

Her mind was completely blank on what he might be talking about. To be honest, she could hardly remember her own name at the moment.

"Making you come," he reminded her. "Which is why you're going to show me how to do it first."

Her breath hitched.

"You lead, I'll follow," he told her.

She began with her breasts, sliding her hands over her camisole to squeeze them until they ached. She watched his lips part in awe as she trapped her nipples between her index and middle fingers, squeezing them through the silky material and sending a shot of pleasure right to her core. She grew even wetter.

Her hands dipped toward her sex then, a finger making slow circles over the outside of her underwear, wringing out a whimper of satisfaction as she finally got the friction she so desperately needed. For a moment she forgot about Rowin entirely, her eyes fluttering shut with ecstasy as she continued her steady, circular rhythm.

She nearly cried as relief started to spread through her body. For a single breath the lustful frenzy in her mind cleared, but the second she opened her eyes and saw the pained look of *need* on his face, the cloud of desire came back in full force.

"There, I showed you," she said as she reached for him, the

racing beat of her heart from being interrupted only driving her more mad with want. "Now, *touch me*."

His shadows snapped out to wrap around her wrists, halting her hands before she could touch him again. "No."

Her cheeks heated. "You don't want—"

"It doesn't matter what I want. I'm not going to touch you as long as we have this stuff in our system," he maintained.

"You...you tricked me," she realized.

He gave her a pointed look. "You got to come, exactly as I promised, didn't you?"

"It isn't the same," she huffed. "You don't understand, it's like my entire body is on *fire*—"

"I assure you I fucking understand," he gritted out.

He might have been good at hiding the emotion on his face, but the unfiltered *torment* in his voice was undeniable.

"Fine. I'll go," she whispered.

She snatched her dress off the ground before either of them lost their resolve, then turned herself invisible as she plunged through the wall and out of the room.

Once she had found somewhere to dress—which was an entire ordeal given she didn't have Ellin's help this time—Genevieve spent several hours trying to sweat out the passion fruit in her system by dancing with anyone and everyone downstairs. Her eyes stayed peeled for any sign of Rowin as suitor after suitor twirled her around the dance floor. Half of her hoped he'd show up every time someone else took her in their arms while her other half hoped he was stronger than her and would stay away. When he was out of her sight, it was easier for her to understand how ridiculous she'd been upstairs. How furious she was with him for letting her be so vulnerable when he knew he was going to hold back.

Eventually she was too tired to go on and dragged herself off the dance floor. She slipped into a small powder room on the far end of the second floor's balcony, to freshen herself up.

At some point, someone knocked on the door, begging to be let in. To Genevieve's surprise, it was the man whose hand she'd bitten earlier.

"Hello, princess," he grinned. "Cedric. Remember me?"

The ring on her finger began to heat, and she made to close the door in his face. But he jammed a foot in the gap and forced his way inside. He kicked the door shut and crossed his arms over his chest, looking down at her. Rowin's ring was scorching now.

She backed away, as much as she could in the tiny room. "What the fuck do you think you're doing?"

"It's nothing personal," Cedric told her as he advanced a step. "But you wouldn't take my bribe."

"Get out. Immediately."

"What, are you going to call for your husband again?" He laughed.

He lunged then, shoving her back painfully into the edge of the vanity.

"*Hey*," she snarled as she turned invisible and passed through him.

He caught himself on the counter before spinning to face her, his face pallid as he suddenly realized that whatever power he thought he'd had to trap her was useless.

"No one mentioned you were a *Specter*," he stammered. "Fuck, I didn't—"

The door wrenched open before he could finish his sentence.

Rowin. Heat reignited in her belly.

You've got to be kidding me.

Cedric looked like he was going to throw up.

"Cedric Wrathblade, is that you?" someone said over Rowin's shoulder.

It was Sevin. She hadn't even noticed him.

Rowin's gaze never left hers as he asked, "Are you alright?"

Genevieve swallowed and dipped her chin in a nod.

"I want to hear you say it, Genevieve," Rowin implored. "Are you alright?"

"*Yes,*" she promised. "He was just being an asshole."

Cedric reached up to grasp what looked to be a key hanging around his neck. "If you touch me, the Daemonica—"

"Say another fucking word and I'll rip your head off your neck," Rowin snarled at him, the darkness saturating his tone making her feel almost sorry for Cedric. But not quite.

Cedric went silent. Sevin laughed.

"Listen to me carefully," Rowin told Genevieve. "You are going to go downstairs, and you are going to wait with whichever of my siblings you see first. Understand?"

She nodded stiffly.

"The Hunt starts in seven minutes. You cannot be even a second late," he warned her.

She didn't waste another moment as she bolted out of the room, passing Umbra a few feet from the door. Halfway down the stairs, someone winked in at her side.

Knox.

Just as the enchanted ring had begun to cool down, its magic flared to life once more.

"Enjoying the festivities?" Knox asked her as he matched her pace.

"It's so lovely to see that all Devils have the same terrible timing," she huffed at him. "And no. I am absolutely fucking *not* enjoying this."

"Pity. I was hoping I'd found the perfect wedding gift," he confessed.

She stopped on the final step, letting him pass her. Even when she stood two steps above him, he was taller than her.

"Trying to lock me and my husband in a sex-fueled haze, you mean?" she demanded.

"Passion fruit is a delicacy," he told her. "It makes you crave your deepest desires a hundred times over. I thought that perhaps you and Rowington would enjoy a little extra passion tonight since you won't be getting a honeymoon anytime soon. If ever. Your presence in the Hunt has brought a lot more spectators ready to empty their coffers, and I wanted to say thank you."

"You're a *bastard*. I thought passion fruit was a *flavor*," she hissed at him.

His smile tightened. "I was trying to be nice."

"Devils aren't *nice* unless it benefits them," she recited. "With rare exceptions."

Like Salem. But even then, her sister had technically paid a price to keep the Prince of the Devils—her mortality.

"And what do you know of Devils?" Knox purred.

She fixed him with a hard look. "My sister lives with one. His name is Salemaestrus. Does that mean anything to you?"

At the sound of Salem's full name, Knox's face turned ashen, and Genevieve's lips curled up in a triumphant smile.

"Play all the games you want with me, but you'll have Salem to deal with when I get out," Genevieve threatened. "And Salem *adores* me."

Salem had never said such a thing in as many words, but Genevieve did not doubt it was a fact.

"I have heard whispers that Salemaestrus had finally returned from his exile," Knox admitted, words tight. "I'm honored that a friend of the Prince would choose to enter my contest. Let there be no hard feelings. In fact...I might be able to offer you an additional bargain if you win."

The giggle that bubbled out of her mouth was mocking. "I am not the Grimm sister who makes bargains with Devils."

Before he could counter, she bounced down the last steps and strutted toward Ellin and Wells, who were waiting in the center of the dance floor. They each gave her an acknowledging nod as she took a place beside them. Barrington and the rest of Rowin's siblings appeared one by one, and stepped into the circle. Genevieve twisted the ring on her finger as she waited for Rowin.

When a sudden swirl of inky shadows began to manifest next to her, she nearly sighed. But when Rowin stepped out of them, he didn't even bother to spare her a glance.

The sound of midnight tolled through the ballroom moments later, and the face of the giant clock on the wall began to slowly turn. As the twelfth numeral flashed a glittering gold, Genevieve's body went heavy as she experienced the loss of her magic for a second time. And she knew exactly what that meant.

The Hunt had begun.

Round One of the Hunt

18

NUMB

If Genevieve had thought an air of shame might cling to the spectators as they pried themselves away from their bacchanalian activities to gather around the ballroom and watch the upcoming spectacle, she was very mistaken. Half of Knox's guests looked *more* smug, in fact, and under any other circumstances she would have been thoroughly entertained by the gossip that was sure to come out of an event like this.

Instead, as each of Rowin's siblings began to remove their masks, Genevieve felt that it was as if they were losing a bit of their armor. She might have preferred to strip herself bare than show everyone her flushed face.

She glanced over at Rowin's taut expression. "What happened? Upstairs?"

"Now is not a good time to talk," he told her.

"The Hunting Blade will now choose the first Hunter," Knox declared to the enraptured audience.

The Devil lifted a sparkling dagger into the air like it was a sacred offering before simply . . . letting it go. The enchanted blade hovered there as Knox and Barrington cleared out of the circle, and Genevieve held her breath as they all waited for the dagger's decision. The blade slowly turned itself horizontal, its point spinning around the circle, past Ellin and Wells and Covin, until finally stopping on . . .

Grave.

Rowin stiffened at her side.

The Hunting Blade shot through the air like an arrow, aiming right for Grave's heart. His eyes locked with Genevieve's as he grabbed it by its hilt mere centimeters before the tip pierced through him. A vicious smile broke across his face as equal cheers and groans of disappointment sounded from the onlookers.

"The masquerade is over," Knox announced to his spectators. "I would like to thank all of you for another wonderful equinox celebration. If your last name is not Silver, please head back to the Hellmouth *now*." The Devil's smile turned vicious. "If I find you lingering, you will not like your fate."

The crowds dispersed. A few of the masked revelers called out wishes of good luck to their favorite players, and it jarred Genevieve to see them act as if Rowin and his siblings were famed entertainers instead of hostages trapped in a tragic curse.

"What's your choice of game, Gravington?" Knox requested.

"Roaming rooms," Grave declared.

All the siblings groaned at once. Except for Rowin, whose expression was as smooth as stone.

"Fuck you, asshole," Covin grunted in Grave's direction.

Genevieve was sure that Rowin had explained this version of the game to her earlier during their brief tour, but the rules were evading her now. Too much had happened in such a short time for her to keep track of every little thing he'd said. And it didn't help that she always had the urge to tune him out.

"Roaming rooms grants you ten minutes to hide—which begins *now*," Knox declared, his eyes flicking pointedly to Genevieve.

Grave stayed planted in place while Covin and Remi dashed across the room in a single blink. Ellin and Wells ran off next— in opposite directions as the first two. Only Genevieve, Rowin, and Sevin lingered.

Rowin turned to her, leaning his mouth down to her ear to murmur, "Wait for me in the foyer. There's something I need to do."

"But—" Genevieve sputtered in protest as she watched him take off for the staircase.

"One tip, sweetheart?" Sevin offered as she gaped after Rowin. "If Grave is smiling, you should be *running*." With that, he strutted from the room.

One final look in Grave's direction was all it took to make Genevieve's feet finally start moving. She dashed in the direction of the foyer, pushing past the remainder of the exiting patrons.

A spectator in a white bear mask whistled at her from down the hallway. "If you and Rowin give us a nice little show, I'll vote you for Favored. I want to see if it's true that he's got five piercings in the head of his—"

"Choke and die," Genevieve sneered at them with a dismissive flick of her hand.

As the last of the rowdy guests disappeared, she paced back and forth in the foyer, counting down the minutes in her head as she waited for Rowin to appear. When she was down to the final two without a single sign of him, however, she became too anxious to wait any longer.

Damn him. Was this all a trick?

She wasn't going to wait to find out. No matter what she shared with Rowin—vows, kisses, beds—it was important for her to remember that she had to trust herself first and foremost.

She strode for the front door and plunged outside into the cold before the final minutes ran out. Despite the fact that she was likely going to contract hypothermia without her magic to help stave it off, hiding outside felt like a good strategy for that exact reason. Plus, whatever *roaming rooms* meant, the others had not seemed thrilled, so avoiding any semblance of a *room* seemed like the best way to go. Maybe.

She made for the labyrinth.

As she took in the snow-covered greenery, she was equally surprised to see it had been covered in mirrors at some point. Their gilded frames held up by the twisting branches and vines every few feet along the walls.

"Nosy f-fucks," she stammered aloud as she rushed through the outer hedge's opening, the chill already piercing down to her bones.

Has it gotten colder? she wondered, but she had a feeling she'd just been too preoccupied with her *wedding* to notice how cold it was the night before.

Her breaths came out in billowing, white puffs as she delved deeper into the maze, trying to commit its twists and turns to memory. Finally, she emerged into the square at its center and spotted the grand silver fountain. She nestled herself into a dark corner, against the shrubbery, ignoring the uncomfortable way the branches dug into her bare arms and shoulders as she settled back as far as she could. She tucked her underskirts tight around her legs like a blanket while using the top layer of her gown's fabric to wrap around her torso as best she could. The tips of her nose and ears had already gone completely numb.

She wasn't sure how long she could last out here without freezing to death. And the irony that she had been suffocating from the heat of the passion fruit just hours earlier was certainly not lost on her. The Devil and his audience must be laughing now.

⚜

The footsteps came what felt like an hour later. Followed by Rowin's signet nearly melting the flesh of her frostbitten finger.

Her head snapped up from where it had been resting on her knees, and she listened for the sound of someone approaching.

Footsteps.

There was someone else in the maze. And they were hunting for her.

Lurching to her feet, she found that the cold had seeped into her very core and drained almost every ounce of energy she had. She tried to take a step, the movement brittle.

The footsteps grew closer.

Genevieve took a deep breath and hauled her feet forward. Her joints loosened and her heart began to race, slowly thawing her out. She kept her steps as light as possible while she retraced her path, listening for whoever was pursuing her as she wove her way back out of the labyrinth. Glimpses of her reflection flashed next to her from the mirrors lining the walls within. And just as the exit, and the house, came into view...

"I know you're in here." A gruff voice, calling from somewhere behind her.

As she suspected. Grave.

Genevieve began to run.

As she broke free of the maze, it became instantly clear that she could not make it all the way up the stairs, across the porch, and inside the house in time. Worse, she realized exactly how Grave had tracked her from the house—her footprints. *How could I be so stupid?*

Grasping one of the branches protruding from a hedge to her right, she bent and twisted it until it snapped away in her hand. She hastily swept away the footprints in the snow behind her. It wasn't perfect—there was still a trail—but at least it wasn't a set of sharp, fresh tracks. Turning back to the house, her eyes snagged on a small gap between the house's walls and the giant lattice holding the vines that covered the façade. She lunged toward it and, sure enough, there was a hollow space just behind the crisscrossing woodwork.

She swept away the last of her footprints leading up to the lattice and, biting her tongue as hard as she could, wedged herself into the impossibly tight gap. The metallic taste of blood filled her mouth as the thorns ripped through her hair and skin. Holding her breath, she squinted through the slivers of space between the vines to watch the maze's exit.

Grave emerged.

The Hunting Blade was clutched in his white-knuckled grip as his calculating eyes roamed over the front porch. Then the ground. He prowled forward, and Genevieve forced herself to regulate her breathing as he got closer to her hiding spot. She swore the ring on her finger began to vibrate.

Knox's little test in the mirror-realm came back to her now in perfect clarity. The way that imposter version of Grave had said killing her would be so easy...

Except he walked right past her, along the outside of the lattice. He looked at the house's façade for a moment. Then he pivoted on the balls of his feet to head back inside. A single tear of relief ran down Genevieve's face.

And then he paused.

Of fucking course.

As he turned to face the crisscrossing lattice once more, Genevieve pressed herself back into the stone behind her, as if this would help her remain invisible. Holding her breath once more, she tracked every movement Grave's silhouette made.

And when the dagger plunged through the lattice, about three feet to her right, it took everything within her not to let out the scream of terror crawling up her throat.

He pulled the blade back out, ripping away some of the vines and letting moonlight spill into the shadows of her hiding place. A beat later, he plunged the dagger in again, closer.

The third time the knife came through, it nearly speared her right in the face, missing her eye socket by mere inches. Her hands shook as she ducked out of the way of the new hole while Grave continued stabbing into the trellis. He seemed to pick a few more random spots before *finally* deciding he could move on and go back into the house.

She waited a full ten minutes as the ring on her finger cooled down before trying to move. Despite the ring's reassuring temperature, she cautiously put her eye up to one of the small holes he'd pierced in the web of vines to see if the coast was clear, before squeezing out of her hiding spot and creeping along the house toward the porch.

Dashing around the corner for the steps, she ran headfirst into something warm and solid.

No, not something. Someone.

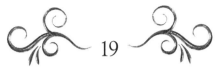

19

TWO TRUTHS

Rowin's hands snapped out to steady her, his gaze darkening as it snagged on the deep scratches and streaks of blood on her arms from the thorns.

"We need to get you inside, *now*," he muttered.

Before Genevieve could process what he was doing, he had her scooped up in his arms, cradling her against his chest as he carried her up the steps. He paused at the front doors, one of which was slightly ajar.

"The ring, it's not warm, is it?" he asked under his breath.

When she shook her head, he used the toe of his boot to gracefully pry open the door he left cracked and cautiously carried her into the house. His eyes flicked over every inch of the empty foyer as he hastily made his way to his bedroom—where Umbra was patiently waiting for his return atop the bed. He set Genevieve back on her feet before softly shutting the door, though she noticed he didn't bother with the lock.

"C-carrying me around like a damsssel in distresss for our audience, how ch-charming," she stammered between numb lips, the chattering of her teeth dulling her sarcasm.

"I told you to wait for me," he reprimanded, ignoring her look of annoyance. "Though I realize trying to give you a direction was very optimistic."

"I *did* w-wait for you! You n-never showed! Do you think I ssshould have risked getting caught out in the open?" she huffed, rubbing her hands over her bare arms for heat.

"So your brilliant idea was to hide in the *snow?*" he asked.

"I f-figured no one would look for me there, and it worked well enough, didn't it?" she said.

"You're blue," Rowin noted unhelpfully. "And I'm not sure it's your color."

"F-fuck y-you," she stuttered.

A corner of his mouth curled up for a moment before he turned to wave a hand at the rest of the room. "By the way, I do not appreciate the state you and Ellin left my room in. I'm not sure how this is even possible. I left you alone in here for less than a day, and you were *sleeping* for most of that time."

The room *was* littered with an explosion of her things. Hairpins, brushes, and scented oils were taking up the entire surface of the dresser. Articles of her clothing were strewn everywhere, undergarments hanging off the bedposts, corset ribbons pooled on the ground next to a pile of her shoes. There was also a lipstick stain on the carpet she'd tried her best to scrub out before she went down for the masquerade.

"It's not that bad," she defended herself. "My room at home is much worse. At least you can still see your floor."

"For Hell's sake," he muttered.

"If you're only going to complain for the rest of the night, I'd rather go back to freezing to death," she grumbled. "And where *were* you?"

How could you leave me for Grave to find alone?

"There was something I had to take care of before Knox did a final sweep of the house for any lingering guests. I didn't think it would take as long as it did," was all he revealed as he headed for the bathroom, gesturing with his hand for her to follow. "I've spent the last hour looking for you, but I never considered you'd be outside trying to catch hypothermia. But when I saw Grave go out there, I figured I should check. I'm impressed you managed to evade him."

"It was a close call," she admitted as she followed him into his en suite. "But your ring helped, so I suppose I should take back what I said about it being hideous. Even though it is."

He gave her a withering look.

"Speaking of Grave—what the Hell does this version of the game entail? Is the Hunting Blade the only weapon Grave can use to kill us? Shouldn't we be finding a less obvious spot than your bedroom to be hiding in right now? How *have* you managed to win for the last *fifteen* years if this is your strategy?"

She realized now that in all the fuss and frustration of preparing for their damned wedding, she had barely prepared herself for the Hunt.

"Breathe, Genevieve," he told her as he slid aside a pocket door within the pristine white bathroom to reveal a linen closet.

She stuck her tongue out at him. Then took a breath.

"Roaming rooms is Grave's favorite version of the game. Every four hours we'll be forced to switch the room we are hiding in. That's three mandatory changes during his turn. And staying hidden during the changes can be difficult." He handed her the folded stacks of towels that were piled at the bottom of the closet. "And the Hunting Blade is the only thing that can truly kill us in the game, yes. Though we can certainly all slow each other down however we'd like—breaking necks, slitting throats. Stabbing your opponent through the heart as quickly as possible is the best way to get a safe kill, but the spectators vastly prefer when things are a bit more...dramatic."

Genevieve ducked down to watch as he began pressing his fingertips along the wall at the back of the closet.

"And my room might be too obvious a hiding spot, yes, but the room next door won't be."

His words trailed off as he slid the panel of the wall to the side to reveal an opening to another bathroom. Umbra dashed through without hesitation.

He waved for Genevieve to go next, and she tried not to groan. She was not ready to shove herself into any more tight spaces. Her Specter abilities usually enabled her to avoid such circumstances, and the idea of struggling to wedge herself into another tiny passage right now made her stomach churn with dread.

Taking a deep breath, she knelt on the ground and began to crawl through the little hole. The jagged edges of the hole scraped painfully against the fresh wounds on her arms, and the bulky skirts of her dress hindered her as she wiggled her way through to the other side.

She felt her face heat as she stood and straightened herself out, not wanting to think about how ridiculous she must have looked. When she turned, however, the sight of Rowin trying to wedge his broad shoulders through the narrow space made her press a hand to her mouth to suppress a giggle.

He huffed in frustration as he flipped onto his back to place his hands against the wall and shove himself out. Like her, he was probably used to relying on his magic to avoid these sorts of situations. Truthfully, she couldn't believe he'd actually managed to make it through at all. Grave or Covin certainly wouldn't have been able to.

As Rowin covered up the secret passage, she wondered, "Whose bathroom are we in now?"

"Grave's," he answered.

She balked. "Are you out of your mind?"

"If we had tried to enter his bedroom from the hallway, we would have found two things," Rowin began, as he stalked over to the mirrored vanity to begin covering it with towels. "One, that it's locked. And two, the door is rigged with a particularly nasty trap."

"I'm assuming he is not aware of your little homemade entrance into his room?" Genevieve asked as Rowin led her toward the bathroom's exit.

"Correct," he answered.

"I'm surprised you and Remi don't have rooms next to each other. I was sort of hoping I'd get to see his."

Rowin paused in front of the bathroom door, lifting a brow. "Because?"

She shrugged. "It fascinates me that you have the same face and yet don't seem to be very...close? Plus, I wanted to see if he *also* has a rigid system for organizing his socks and underwear. Length, then color, then type of material, right?"

He glowered. "You went through my things?"

"I got distracted while I was doing my makeup for the masquerade," she confirmed cheerily.

"Remi and I are very different," he said. "Which reminds me—what is it that he said to upset you while you were dancing?"

"I'm surprised you even noticed I may have been upset," she admitted.

He gave her an odd look. "Why?"

Because despite always being surrounded by people, very few ever paid such close attention to me.

But she didn't say that aloud. Instead, she answered, "He said that he pitied me. That I was like a mouse in a trap. And I am tired of being referred to as a rodent. Also of pity from men who don't *really* care what happens to me. Who just think of me as a pretty girl someone else should rescue. And I say *someone else* because *they* never actually want to put in the effort of saving me."

Rowin was quiet for a long moment.

Then, "Saving you from what? Yourself? Because you seem to be able to hold your own."

Her breath hitched as his words hit a nerve she hadn't expected him to find. She was absolutely her own worst enemy. Every bit of danger she'd ever been in was a tangled web of her own creation. She didn't like how easily he'd figured that out.

"Is that what you were doing when you stopped things earlier?" she needled. "Saving me from myself? The passion fruit had no effect on you whatsoever?"

"I think it was very clear the effect it had on me," he told her, his voice deepening now.

She crossed her arms. "Because you would have never touched me otherwise?"

He gave her a taunting smile. "Is there a specific response you're looking for from me, Genevieve?" A step forward. "No strings attached. Wasn't that what we both agreed?"

She scowled. "It was."

He didn't look as if he believed her, but he didn't press any further. She watched in silence as he turned back to the exit and cautiously opened the door, poking his head into the room to make sure it was clear. The layout of Grave's room was nearly identical to Rowin's, with the single exception of the bed being a much more normal size. Everything in the room was painted black—even the furniture. No wonder the man was so unhappy. The darkness of the space was *suffocating*. The only thing that helped it feel a little less like a coffin were two mirrors propped against the wall facing the bed. Rowin fetched more towels and promptly covered them.

Genevieve moved to the doorway, searching for the trap he had mentioned before. Sure enough, there were two black chains attached to the top of the door that ran along the ceiling toward the opposite side of the room. The chains were rigged to pull taut when the door was opened in order to yank up a metal panel that faced the doorway. She couldn't see what the panel covered, but she could only imagine it was meant to maim whoever entered.

She rolled her eyes. *Dramatic.*

"Warm up," Rowin ordered, pointing at the bed. "You're still too pale."

Genevieve didn't bother to argue as she sat back against the headboard and pulled the comforter tightly around her. The relief was instant. A violent shiver racked her body as she realized exactly how cold she'd been.

Rowin settled himself into the large armchair in the corner of the room, reaching back to fold his arms behind his head as he let his eyes fall closed without another word.

After a long minute of silence, she asked, "Now we just... wait?"

"This would be the *hiding* part of the game, so yes."

A beat.

"For nearly three more hours?" she confirmed.

Without discussing anything that happened between us? Am I just supposed to forget that we almost . . . ?

"Correct," he stated.

Another beat.

"That's *forever*," she complained.

He sighed deeply. "You wouldn't handle being an immortal very well."

Only minutes ago she was being hunted for her life, and now she found herself... bored. It was an unsettling feeling. Perhaps Rowin had grown used to it, but the constant push and pull of emotions in this house was making Genevieve antsy. She needed to be distracted.

"Why don't we play a game?" she suggested.

His eyes blinked open. "We're already playing a game."

She gave him an exasperated look. "I meant one that doesn't involve *murder.*"

"That sounds dull," he told her. "But fine. What's the game?"

"Two truths and a lie?" she proposed. "I used to play it with my friends back home, and since you and I are supposed to be convincing partners..."

"Rules?"

"We each have to state three outrageous things—two of them true, one a lie—and then figure out what the lies are," she explained.

"I suppose it couldn't hurt," he allowed. "Since we're building trust with each other. Right?"

"Your words," she agreed.

They both took a moment to figure out what three things to say, the only sound in the room coming from Umbra bathing herself like a house cat. It made Genevieve miss Poe and Grimm Manor.

"Alright. I've got mine," Rowin announced.

She motioned for him to go ahead.

"Sevin and I accidentally officiated a wedding for a Demon marrying nineteen brides at once. I've never fucked anyone in my own bedroom. And the last time I traveled further than Florence was fifteen years ago."

She frowned. The first one was ridiculous enough to easily be true. But the last two...

"The second one has to be the lie," she eventually decided. "No way you have a bed that size and haven't *used* it."

He shrugged. "Wrong."

"*What?*"

"The bed in my room used to be Covin's before he upgraded to something even bigger. I don't like strangers in my personal space, so I've always taken my lovers...elsewhere," he admitted. "You're the first person I've allowed to stay in my bed in recent memory."

"Ah, the privileges of being a wife," she crooned.

He didn't smile, but she swore he wanted to.

"You're seriously telling me you have all the wealth and time anyone could ever want, and you haven't left this part of the country in *fifteen years*? You win freedom every time you play this game, and you don't use it to travel as much as possible? To escape this place?"

"It doesn't seem fair," Rowin murmured. "To enjoy all the things the others can't."

"You *do* care that your winning streak has kept them in Hell for so long, then," she stated.

His eyes locked with hers. "Of course I do."

She felt the truth in his words.

You're either going to collect another win and we won't ever see you again, or your winning streak will come to an end, and you'll finally get a taste of Hell with the rest of our sorry asses, Covin had said, but Genevieve was starting to suspect there was a lot more to Rowin's desire to win than anyone understood.

Silence stretched between them for a while, though Genevieve didn't necessarily find it to be uncomfortable. Only thoughtful.

When it became too much, however, she found herself blurting, "I just thought that the only real reason to own a bed that size was in order to host orgies."

He huffed a laugh. "Well, you weren't wrong, but multiple lovers is Covin's thing, not mine."

So she had seen.

"Alright," he prompted. "Your turn."

20

CHASED

Two hours later, when her body temperature had finally returned to normal, Genevieve was shut in Grave's bathroom, taking out all the carefully placed hairpins in her curls to give her aching scalp a break. She had uncovered the mirror, and she stared at her reflection as if she might get a glimpse of all the unseen gazes that were undoubtedly watching her.

She and Rowin had played their game of truths for two rounds before it clearly got a little too personal for him and he decided he preferred silence. What she *had* learned was that he and his brothers—Remi and Covin—once got so drunk they thought it'd be a good idea to steal the prized mascot of some sort of esteemed Demon institution in Hell. And that he had read every single book in the family library. And that the tattoos covering most of his body had been his way of differentiating himself from Remi. The most surprising fact, however, was that Grave was their mother's favorite.

It was when she had asked more about his mother that Rowin decided he didn't want to talk anymore.

Unlike her, he wasn't bothered by long stretches of silence, apparent by how relaxed he looked sitting in the armchair while Umbra slept curled up on his chest. Genevieve, however, had been on the verge of going absolutely mad by the second hour. So, she made up ways to entertain herself. It was something she'd often done as a child when Ophie was in Necromancy lessons. She'd rearranged Grave's closet by color—pitch-black, jet-black, and ebony—before folding all the writing paper in his desk into swans. Eventually, she'd moved on to her hair, which had come to resemble a bird's nest throughout the night, and as she gave her appearance one last look now, she frowned at the purplish circles forming beneath her eyes.

She had turned to leave the bathroom, to figure out what her next task would be, when the door suddenly flew open, making her jump.

Rowin strode in with purpose, Umbra darting in behind.

"What do you think you're—"

He raised a finger to her lips. Umbra was on high alert, ears twitching to listen for something Genevieve couldn't hear.

"Distraction," Rowin ordered down at his Familiar, his voice barely more than a whisper, but Umbra heard the direction perfectly and trotted back to the room to belly-crawl beneath the bed and out of sight. Leaning down until his mouth was right next to her ear, Rowin murmured, "When he opens the door, Umbra will run out of the room and create a diversion in the hallway to lead him back out. I'll follow and draw him further away. When his attention is completely on me, you *run*."

"Grave? He's here?" she whispered as he lowered his hand. "*Where should I run to?*"

"Doesn't matter. Just don't back yourself into any corners. The first switch is about to happen, and we'd have to change rooms then, anyway."

He closed the bathroom door until there was only a small sliver of space for them to peek through. When Genevieve moved forward to look, however, the crinoline dragging along the floor beneath her gown made a rustling sound that in the careful silence might as well have been an explosion.

Rowin cursed under his breath. He searched through Grave's bathroom cabinet and produced a steel razor. Crouched down, he started to slice away the long layers of silk and crinoline. Genevieve's heart ached watching such a beautiful dress get destroyed. But it was hard to protest when she was finally able to *move*.

The sound of the bedroom door creaking open made them both stiffen, and the ring on her finger began to burn. The rattle of the chains attached to Grave's trap made her hold her breath, but it did not seem to trigger.

Rowin gestured for her to stand against the wall behind the bathroom door. Footsteps approached on the other side. But when a loud thump sounded from somewhere further away, however, the footsteps changed direction in an instant.

She slid her eyes over to Rowin, and he gave her a reassuring nod before dashing out into the bedroom and heading for the hall. She peeked out from the bathroom as Rowin stood in the bedroom doorway, shouting to his brother before taking off to the left and out of sight. Grave's hulking figure sprinted past the open bedroom doorway, and she knew that was her cue.

Genevieve cautiously stepped out of the en suite. She crept over to the open threshold and poked her head out just enough to see Rowin and Grave at the end of the corridor. Grave was slashing the Hunting Blade at Rowin, his movements sharp and fluid. Rowin was dodging every blow.

Tiny, sharp teeth suddenly nipped at her ankles. Not enough to hurt, but enough to urge her forward.

She glared down at Umbra. "I'm going, you little menace."

Speaking was the wrong thing to do. As was often the case for her.

"For fuck's sake, trouble," Rowin growled. "*Run!*"

The moment she spoke, Grave's attention had snapped to her. A wide, toothy grin spread over his face.

If Grave is smiling, you should be running.

She flew down the corridor and through the foyer, looking for a route that wouldn't back her into a corner. Easier said than done. Especially when Grave was gaining on her.

The only thing working in her favor was that her pursuer was not really built for *speed*. Grave must have been two hundred pounds of pure muscle.

When the open archway of the dining room came into view, the only thing she could think to do was dive through it, rounding the large table so she could face Grave with a barricade between them. He laughed as he slowed to a halt, and she noticed that he was hardly out of breath.

Genevieve, on the other hand, was worried she might pass out. Little spots of light clouded up her vision as a cramp reverberated through her side. She wasn't sure she had ever run this much in her *life*.

Grave slowly approached the table, which was completely bare other than a ceramic bowl of fruit sitting atop its polished surface. Genevieve stayed on the balls of her feet, waiting for him to pick a direction of attack. Where was Rowin?

"Sorry, pal, but I have unfortunately chased, and been chased, around this table for enough hours of my lifetime to know"— in a single jump, he landed right atop the table with a heavy thud—"it's much easier to just go over it."

The action knocked the bowl of fruit to the floor, making the ceramic shatter noisily as its contents bounced over the ground by her feet. When Grave jumped to the ground only two feet in front of her, shards of the bowl crunching beneath his feet, it occurred to Genevieve that she should start to panic. For whatever reason, Rowin still had not appeared. Not that she was the sort who would usually pray for a man to save her, but in the current circumstances she thought it might be nice if he could do *something*.

She backed up a step. Grave followed.

"If it's any consolation, you lasting less than four hours means Covin and Sevin both lost a good bit of money. That's something we can all be satisfied with. And I'll make it quick. Consider it my wedding gift."

The blade came down.

Genevieve didn't know what possessed her as she dove down to grab one of the apples by her feet, ducking beneath his arm toward the table and out of the way of his blade's arc. They both spun to face each other once again. When the dagger came down this time, however, she slammed the apple against its sharp tip. The knife wedging itself into the fruit slowed down Grave's momentum just enough that she was able to stumble back out of his reach—right into the edge of the table, trapping her between it and him. He swung the dagger down on the table next to her like a hammer, splitting the apple speared on the end in half and leaving a thick scar in the mahogany.

"Grandmother would not be happy that you just ruined her table."

Genevieve whipped her head to see Rowin leaning against the archway's frame, casually watching the altercation.

"I don't give a fuck," Grave said as Genevieve began to inch to the side while his focus was on Rowin. "That woman has never liked me."

"She's never liked anyone," Rowin corrected. "At least you have the advantage of looking so much like Mother."

"*Help?*" Genevieve prompted Rowin as Grave lunged for her again, making her dash to the side and nearly stumble to the ground.

"Hey, trouble?" Rowin murmured.

"*What?*" she hissed as she righted herself and continued to back away from Grave.

"Could you step a little to the left for me?"

She did as he asked and, in two blinks, Rowin cleared the table. He landed in front of Grave and rammed a fist into his brother's jaw, making Grave's head snap to the side with a grunt. Genevieve watched, impressed, as Rowin slipped around his brother to wrap an arm so tight around the man's neck that Grave's face was blue in seconds. She swore she heard the snap of a bone.

Grave tried to buck Rowin off his back, and when that didn't work, he drove the dagger right through Rowin's bicep. Genevieve cringed.

Rowin, however, didn't even flinch.

"Thank you for that," Rowin grunted as he used his free hand to yank the Hunting Blade out of his arm.

With a pained hiss—as if the blade burned him—Rowin whipped it clean across the room, through the arched opening and out of the window across the corridor. Shattered glass rained down onto the floor as a cool draft kicked up around them.

Rowin released Grave just as four tolling bells rolled through the house, and Genevieve grinned.

21

ℒITTLE GAME

"Well, well, well, look who lasted the first four hours, after all—" Genevieve began to boast at the sound of the bells, but before she could finish, Rowin was hauling her out of the room by her upper arm.

"First rule of catching a bear in a trap—don't continue to fucking poke it," he told her as he pulled her toward the ballroom while Grave disappeared out of the front door to go find the blade. "When it eventually gets out, it'll be twice as pissed."

His tone was hard, admonishing, but she saw the glint of amusement in his eyes.

"He almost killed me!" she reasoned with an exaggerated huff as they continued toward the grand staircase, her pace barely able to keep up with his impossibly long strides. "Am I not allowed to gloat?"

"Not until we're the Hunters," he told her.

Halfway up the steps, a sudden flush of heat came over her and made her pause.

"It's just the magic of the game making sure everyone's switched rooms," he assured her from the step below. "If we hadn't left the bedroom or the dining room, it would have felt like your skin was boiling off."

"Oh, phenomenal," she said, tone dripping with sarcasm, "something else to look forward to."

When they made it to the hallway upstairs, Genevieve was

surprised to run into Ellin. Ellin, who could barely breathe as she bent over to place her hands on her knees.

"Fuck." Inhale. "Knox." Inhale. "And his games."

"What was it this time?" Rowin asked, apparently completely unconcerned by the state his sister was in.

"Desert oasis," Ellin told him as she straightened back up, brushing away the short strands of her white hair that were sticking to her face with sweat. "With about a million scorpions. And snakes. It was disgusting."

Genevieve gave a nervous giggle.

Rowin flicked his eyes over to the doors on their right. "Want to hide with us this round?"

Ellin shot him a dirty look. "So you can use me as bait during the next switch of rooms? Fuck off, Rowington Silver."

Rowin gave a rueful smirk.

"Where is he?" Ellin asked.

"Outside," Rowin answered. "Though I doubt for much longer."

Ellin nodded and disappeared.

"Desert? Scorpions? *Snakes?*" Genevieve questioned.

"Knox is heralded for his creativity even in Hell," he muttered, as if that offered any sort of clarification.

He strode toward one of the doors and threw it open, and Genevieve gaped in awe.

"Every spare room in the house is enchanted to transform into a different landscape. Knox comes up with new designs every season. It gives us more interesting places to hide than each other's bedrooms. Not to mention, each of the enchanted rooms contains a token that gives immunity from one round of the Hunt—if you can manage to find and retrieve it."

Genevieve barely registered his words as she took a step toward the doorway. The Devils that had run Phantasma's trials had created similar illusions in the haunted manor. But those illusions had been terrifying and bloody. This...this was like stepping into a dream.

The room, if it could even be called that, was an expansive, lush green meadow. A babbling brook snaked through the clearing in the distance, a silver bridge made of swirling filigree bent over it. As far as her eyes could see were species of colorful flowers completely foreign to her. Birds soared overhead, and fluffy white clouds rolled through the blue sky. She moved to step inside, but Rowin stopped her.

"Are we not going in?" she asked. "It seems like a wonderful place to hide."

"There's only one exit in and out of the enchanted rooms, and it's too risky when we need to switch," he told her. "Those rooms are deadly games all on their own. It might look beautiful and serene in there, but everything Knox creates is dangerous. Didn't you see the state of Ellin? She's lucky we left Grave preoccupied downstairs instead of waiting for her here."

"Why would Ellin risk it, then?"

"Because she figured the two of us would be Grave's focus, I imagine. And she was right."

He waved for her to follow him toward the set of double doors at the end of the hall. When Rowin pulled them open to reveal a library, she instantly got the unnerving feeling that they were being watched. But the ring remained cold. There was only a single mirror in the entire room—above the stone fireplace in the center of the back wall—but somehow she didn't think it had anything to do with the eerie feeling.

"Covin's on this floor somewhere," Rowin murmured as if he'd heard her thoughts.

"Where? How do you know?" she wondered as he strode toward one of the many bookcases on the left.

As far as in-home libraries went, the design was, surprisingly, rather boring. It was the one room that lacked the opulence of the rest of the villa. Here, the gilded, baroque details had been traded for something much warmer—mahogany shelves, plush couches, and a surprising lack of dust compared to other rooms in the house.

Genevieve perused the titles of the tomes on the shelves next to the fireplace as Rowin scanned the ones on his side of the room. She pulled out a thick hardcover that said *The Matter of Souls* on its spine and thumbed through the yellowed pages. There were chapters on how to harvest souls, where souls went after they were extracted, how to turn them into currency for Devils . . . she shuddered and clapped it shut.

"Satan is sleeping on one of the shelves up top," Rowin said, and it took her a moment to recall what her question had been. "Covin's probably in one of the other rooms."

"*Satan?*" she repeated in concern while she took a closer look at the title of a half-read, splayed-out novel on one of the couch's arms.

The Devil's Darkest Desires. Genevieve giggled, wondering which of the Silver siblings the bodice ripper belonged to. It reminded her of similar tattered copies that her sister used to hide from their mother.

"Satan is Covin's Familiar," Rowin clarified as he finally pulled out the book he'd been searching for.

Genevieve watched as one of the bookshelves began to spin— because what sort of enchanted estate would it really be without such a feature—and Rowin waved her over. She squeezed past the wingback chair of the sitting area in front of the fireplace and strutted over to the far wall, allowing him to pull her into his body atop the turning platform just before it finished spinning into a new hidden room.

The room they were now standing in was possibly the drabbest place Genevieve had ever seen. Bare stone walls. Creaky wooden floorboards. A couch that looked like it would give her tetanus if she sat on it. There was not a single comforting detail—no rug, or splash of color, or even the warmth of candlelight. Just, next to the couch, a gas lamp that Rowin lit with a match.

The only positive thing Genevieve could comment on about this particular hiding spot was the fact that there wasn't a mirror in sight.

"Want a drink?" Rowin asked as he made his way over to the corner and a fully stocked bar cart that she hadn't noticed.

She tilted her head. "What do you have?"

"Whiskey...or what I'm pretty sure is Sevin's piss from the last Hunt."

She nearly choked on her horror.

He smirked. "When the others get stuck in here for too long, sometimes they—"

"I get the picture," she interrupted. "That is *disgusting.*"

"After seeing the state of my bedroom, I'm not sure you're allowed to judge," he told her.

"Excuse me, I am *messy.* Not *gross.* There's a difference between leaving dresses strewn about and leaving a bottle of *urine* to ferment for a year."

"That's fair," he allowed. "But you never answered my question."

"What—? Oh. The drink." She felt her mouth twist in disgust. "No, thanks. I don't drink whiskey. Nor do I trust the rest of those bottles to not have been...contaminated."

He shrugged.

"What happens if someone else tries to hide in here? Or if the Hunter finds us and blocks our way out?" she asked.

"Once someone is inside, the door cannot be opened again from the outside unless it is reset. Plus, there's the trap door," he said before walking over to a spot in the middle of the room and reaching down to search for a groove in the floorboards. When he found it, he pried up the nearly invisible door in demonstration. "These stairs lead to a tunnel that can get you to and from the kitchen downstairs. It's one of the better hiding spots to be in." He lowered the door back down. "You might as well settle in, because we have a couple more hours to wait out before we move again."

This is Hell.

It took Rowin almost the entire decanter of whiskey before he decided he was tired of the silence.

"Why not?"

Genevieve was situated on one end of the couch, a spring biting into her hip from the cushion and her head pillowed on its armrest. At some point her eyes had drooped closed.

"Why not, what?" she murmured.

"Why don't you drink whiskey?"

She blinked her eyes open. "I don't like the flavor."

"Liar. If you didn't like the taste, you would've said that. You said you don't *drink* it."

"I thought you didn't want to share truths anymore," she countered.

"Hmm," he hummed as his amber eyes scrutinized her. "It's either because you overindulged once and got sick or... it's because of someone you don't like to think about."

"You're guessing," she said. But he was right on both accounts.

"What was his name?" Rowin asked.

Genevieve gave a heavy sigh. "Why are you so interested? Are you drunk? Or bored? If it's just out of boredom, I'm sure we can make up another game to play."

"I think it would take a damn distillery's worth of whiskey to get me drunk at this point," he muttered. "And you're my wife. I think it's reasonable to want to know you."

She knew immortals had an extraordinary tolerance to inebriation, but she wasn't sure she believed him. And she certainly didn't buy the *you're my wife* bit.

He sighed at her pointed look. "Maybe it's boredom."

"Alright, then how about a modification to our previous little game?" she proposed. "We each get to ask the other person three questions. Two of our answers have to be absolute truths, but we can choose whichever one to lie about."

"Deal."

She didn't bother to let him go first this time.

"I remember Grave mentioning something about a cure for your mother. He said he didn't believe it existed. And you do, right?"

Rowin was silent for a long moment. As if he was deciding whether he was still bored enough to play.

"Yes," he finally said. "The cure is the reason I've been so adamant about winning every year. I'm doing...research about it. I wouldn't be able to do that in Hell. Knox would have me doing his dirty work all the time. And I don't trust any of the others to do it."

"Since they don't believe in the cure, you mean?" she assumed.

"Partially. Even if we found a cure, Knox would probably find another way to keep us under his control. We're too valuable to his empire. Grave thinks that if we try to play Knox at his own game, he'll find a way to make things even worse. The game is bearable for him, so long as it's keeping our mother alive. But I..."

He pressed his lips together now, and Genevieve sat up straighter at the sight of the guilt coloring his expression.

"It's okay," she told him. "I promise I'm the last person who would ever judge you for having complicated feelings about your family."

He looked at her then. *Really* looked at her. And whatever he found must have been enough.

"I'd rather keep hope that the cure exists. That if my mother can be saved with it, if she's out of danger, then the rest of us could fight back against Knox." He shoved a hand through his hair as he spoke the hushed confession. "I know wanting to save her only as a means to save myself is not exactly the purest of intentions..."

"Some people would call that selfish," Genevieve agreed.

She could have sworn he flinched, but he only muttered, "You've called me worse."

"Oh, *I'm* not some people," she rushed to assure. "I've been here only a couple of days, and I would rather be anywhere else in the world. If you've decided you can't endure this for the rest of *eternity*...I think maybe you've earned the right to be a little selfish."

He snorted and then fell silent, and she tried to leave it, truly, but after a while she couldn't help herself.

"Is this why you've stopped visiting them, then? Because you're spending all of your time looking for this cure?"

"That and the guilt," he told her. "Facing my mother when I haven't been able to find a true lead in *fifteen years*..." He shook his head as his words trailed off.

"If we win, and you don't ever have to play this game again, would you still search for it?" she wondered.

"No," he said with a pointed look.

"You're not supposed to give your lie away so easily," she sighed. "It defeats the purpose of the game."

He shrugged. And then, barely loud enough for her to hear, "I wouldn't rest until I freed them all."

She tilted her head. "Whatever version of selfish anyone considers you, Rowin Silver, is one I very much admire."

He flicked his eyes away from her, and she couldn't help but smile. Watching him squirm when she praised him was even better than pissing him off.

"Now for my next question—" she began.

He shook his head. "You asked all your questions. It's my turn."

She pouted. "Wait, most of those were simply to clarify—"

"You're cheating," he drawled, all traces of vulnerability already tucked neatly away.

She gave an exasperated sigh. "*Fine*. You go."

"Why don't you drink whiskey? Why did you write my father letters pretending to be your mother? Who is Farrow?"

At the mention of Farrow's name, she froze.

"How do you know that name?" she hissed.

He lifted a brow at her reaction. "From you. Umbra found you, passed out from the demonberries, and when I was taking you back outside the gates, you asked if I was someone named Farrow."

"Is that all I said?" she pressed, stomach churning with the idea that words had been exchanged between them that she couldn't remember.

His expression stayed smooth as he said, "You were hardly coherent. I only remembered the name because it was so odd. My magic removed as much of the demonberries from your system as it could—Ellin's healing abilities are much more substantial than any of the rest of ours—but you were still a bit dazed."

She tucked away the information about their healing abilities in the back of her mind to revisit later, and begrudgingly told him, "I don't drink whiskey because of Farrow. I wrote the letters because my mother kept my sister in the dark about so much of her life and I couldn't stand it any longer. When I found out your father existed, I thought that perhaps he was also a Necromancer. That maybe someone in his family would know what it was like to be the spare sibling." She took a deep breath. "If I had known it would lead to all of this, obviously I would've left it alone."

He barked a laugh. "No, you wouldn't have."

She crossed her arms over her chest. "And how the Hell would you know?"

"In the last two days you have not *once* left anything well enough alone."

"The last two days bear no resemblance to the rest of my life. You don't know what you're talking about."

"There. You have to argue about everything," he pointed out with a smirk.

"I do not argue about *everything*—"

"Is this supposed to be you *not* arguing?" he interrupted. "If so, you're horrendous at it."

She pressed her lips together, indignant, but his eyes were suddenly shining with mischief, and something about the sight of it made her blood warm.

"Well?" he eventually said.

"Well *what*?"

His lips twitched. "You owe me an answer to my last question. Who is Farrow?"

And this was the question she'd been trying to avoid answering.

"He isn't anyone significant," she stated.

A beat.

"That's your lie."

She made a face. "I didn't think you were considering the rules so carefully. And why do you think that?"

"Because you wear all of your emotions on your face," he stated. "You don't seem like the type that would let some man get under your skin. So deep that you're letting him *ruin* pristinely aged liquor."

"Yeah, well," she said, looking down to pick at her nails as her voice grew quiet, "some people are poisonous that way. They touch you once and somehow infect every little thing you do thereafter."

Hell, she'd nearly lost all her friends because of that bastard. She'd nearly lost her spirit. Her sense of self. Thankfully, she'd found spite along the way.

"I sure as fuck hope he wasn't who you were referring to when you claimed to have *experience*."

She squeaked in surprise, her gaze shifting back to his. "And if he was?"

"Then you desperately need a different experience," he decided.

"Just because someone's a bastard doesn't mean they don't know how to fuck well," she snipped right back, thinking of the fact that she'd *had* the opportunity to have a different experience just a few hours ago, and he'd stopped it.

"That is very true," he murmured.

Before she could blink, Rowin had shifted forward, his hands bracing his weight on either side of her hips, caging her back into the couch as their faces hovered only inches apart. Close enough that if she reached out with the tip of her tongue, she could flick it against the golden hoop in his bottom lip.

Enough with the damned lip piercing, she chastised herself.

The look in Rowin's eyes, meanwhile, was absolutely sinful.

"With how strongly the passion fruit affected you, I'm inclined to believe that no one has made you come, properly, in quite a while."

There was no way in Hell that she was about to admit how correct he was, but the smirk unfurling on his face told her he already knew. With him this close, it was hard for her to think properly. The smell of him was too intoxicating. The warmth of his body too inviting.

The only thing she could think to say was, "And? Are you offering to rectify that mistake? To finish what we started at the masquerade?"

"In your dreams, trouble," he murmured, but she didn't miss the way his eyes flicked down to her mouth just before he backed off and stood.

"Then *why* are you flirting with me?" she accused.

"Am I?" The curl of his lips was arrogant now. "I think you just find me very attractive, and we happen to be talking about sex."

"When the fuck is the next switch?" she grumbled as she pushed herself off the couch. "I think I've reached my limit of you for the night."

A moment later the bells announced it was time to move.

22

Brutal

Genevieve and Rowin didn't speak a word the entire way down to the kitchen, escaping the little hidden room in the library through the trap door and along the dusty secret passage. Nor did they speak a word while he scrounged together enough food to make them each a semblance of a meal or in the hour that followed. And they definitely did not say a single word when Wellington Silver came bursting into the kitchen.

Rowin cursed as Wells slammed into one of the marble islands that sat in the center of the room, black blood smearing across its white surface from his hands as he steadied himself. Genevieve saw that one of his arms was hanging strangely, like it had been pulled out of its socket, but when she stepped forward to ask if he needed help, Rowin grabbed the back of her dress and tugged her into him.

"Get in the dumbwaiter," he ordered as he pushed her toward a small opening in the wall to their left.

She scoffed. "There is absolutely no way—"

"Now is not the time for arguing, Genevieve," he bit out.

Genevieve had opened her mouth to give a retort when the sight of Wells coughing up blood mixed with the sudden warmth of the signet on her finger made her pause. Without another protest she let Rowin boost her up toward the lift, wedging herself all the way to one end in order to make room for Rowin next to her. He dragged down the metal door seconds before Grave erupted through the kitchen door himself.

Genevieve pressed forward, squinting as she peeked through the sliver of open space around the dumbwaiter's door. She watched as Wells grabbed a glass bowl from atop the island and smashed it across Grave's face. Grave barely flinched. Blood spurted from his nose and glass crumbled to the floor. A grin spread over Grave's expression as defeat began to take over his brother's.

When the dagger came down, and the grunts of pain began to beat against the door of the hollow shaft, Genevieve pulled back. She could only watch as Rowin closed his eyes and clenched his fists until his knuckles were stark white, as if he could imagine away the sounds of his brothers fighting to the death. Wells's death.

Sitting there, helpless, was brutal.

That was when she really understood. Enchantra was a different sort of horror than Phantasma. More intimate. There might have been no hauntings here, or tubs of blood, or the wailings of strangers. But the death of people you loved was infinitely worse.

Glancing over at Rowin, Genevieve slowly reached out her hand to give his a gentle squeeze.

"I'm sorry..." *That you have to endure this. That your family has to endure this. Year after year.*

"*Don't,*" he snarled quietly.

She swallowed. When she began to pull her hand away, however, he gripped onto it tighter.

Her heart began thundering in her chest as she let him continue to hold on to her. At some point, Genevieve dozed off, her head against the too-hard steel walls of the tiny box they were confined in. When a metallic rattling echoed around her as someone lifted the dumbwaiter from above, however, she snapped awake in a second.

Rowin let out a string of curses as he lunged for the door,

trying to slide it open so they could jump out. But the platform moved too quickly, and their window of opportunity disappeared.

"Scoot over," Rowin ordered as he tried to shift in front of her, positioning himself to be nearest to the exit.

There was a moment of stillness as the lift finally stopped. Then the door slid open and Grave's solemn, pallid face came into view. Sweat dripped down his temples, and the single strand of black in his hair was pasted to his forehead. Blood covered the front of his shirt.

"Get out," he ordered Rowin, the hollowness in his voice sending a shiver down Genevieve's spine.

The dumbwaiter had brought them back into the library, right beside the fireplace. A room with access to books and snacks. Under different circumstances, she imagined her sister would love to visit Enchantra.

"I'm not just going to let you have her," Rowin told his brother.

Grave grinned. "Then I'll kill you both. Like stabbing fish in a barrel."

The dagger was between Rowin's ribs a second later, and he grunted in pain as Grave moved to wrench him out of the lift by the front of his shirt. Genevieve scrambled out after them, but the moment her feet hit the floor, Grave slammed his fist into Rowin's temple.

Grave spun for her next, and if he expected she'd be intimidated by the fact that he'd just knocked Rowin out cold, he was wrong.

"You could stab him right now and win, but you still want *me*?"

"I've killed him plenty of times," Grave told her. "Plus, killing you could help me win Favored."

He lunged. She dodged.

"Let me do it quickly," he seethed.

She had the urge to roll her eyes. She was not going to let him do anything. Genevieve was absolutely not going to win this fight. Not without her magic. But winning didn't matter if she could just run out the clock, and according to the one on the wall behind him, she had to make it only six more minutes without dying and her magic would be back.

An idea struck.

I should let him take a free shot.

There was the risk that any blow he landed would be instantly fatal, of course. Rowin could handle a dagger in his side, but that was *not* how things worked for mortals. Even paranormal ones. She and her sister had always been able to sleep off bad injuries. Broken ribs, arms, that one time Genevieve got bitten by a water moccasin. All healed overnight or with a few days of rest. But she knew whatever Grave did to her wouldn't be so tame that she'd be able to sleep it off.

Grave slashed at her again, regaining her focus as the tip of the blade grazed her arm. Blood trickled down her bicep, but her eyes never left him. She darted over to one of the bookshelves, grabbing an armful of tomes and whipping them at his head. The strength of her throws surprised even her, especially when one of the spines hit him square down the middle of his face and more black blood spilled over his mouth and down his chin.

It didn't make him falter.

He slammed her back into the shelf with a hand wrapped around her throat. Her head cracked against the wood, and little spots of black filled her vision.

"You're slowing down, pal," Grave taunted. "Ready to give up?"

"*Fine*," she whimpered dramatically, though her head *was* truly pounding from the hit. "But...the least you could do is let me breathe long enough to give you a message for my family."

He didn't protest the request, simply let go of her neck so she could suck in a deep breath.

When she was recovered enough, she looked up at him, chin raised, and stated, "I'd like them to know I loved them. Ophelia is to burn my diaries *immediately*. And I want to be buried in something pink, holding Mr. Daisy."

Grave lifted a brow at the last bit, though his expression remained tight.

"My childhood stuffy," she explained. "A teddy bear with a daisy in his ear."

In reality, Mr. Daisy had met his untimely end when she was ten and she threw him in the Mississippi River to go for a swim. May he rest in peace.

Grave dipped his chin in a nod of acknowledgment and then said, "You might want to close your eyes."

She shook her head.

There was a glint of respect in his gaze as he shrugged. "Suit yourself."

He raised the dagger. She braced. And when his swing came down, she jerked to the left as hard as she could. The dagger pierced right through her, just beneath her right clavicle, and out of her back. Pinning her to the solid wood shelf.

She let out a ragged scream of pain as bright-red blood spilled down the front of her dress, her throat becoming hoarse with tears while Grave tried to yank the blade out of the wood. His strength had been a little too forceful, however, because he found himself struggling to recover the dagger from where it was now stuck in the molding.

"You've got to be fucking kidding me," he growled.

Her vision was growing blurry.

"Who makes up a stuffed animal named Mr. Daisy?" He

grunted as he finally managed to get enough leverage on the knife to rip it out of her.

"Mr. Daisy was *very real*," she slurred as she began to slump toward the floor. Her entire body felt like it was on fire.

Grave poised himself to strike once more. "Let's try this one last time."

But when the knife came down, however, Genevieve completely disappeared. And so did the Hunting Blade in Grave's hand.

His fist passed harmlessly through her.

She'd made it. Six minutes.

Genevieve held on to her returned magic just long enough to step past him, and then solidified once more. Before she could hit the ground, Rowin was suddenly there, scooping her up to cradle her against his chest. It seemed his wounds had healed entirely in the last few minutes.

"Must be nice," she whispered, but the words came out garbled and incoherent.

There was a crash somewhere behind her and a long string of curses that she assumed was coming from Grave, but she was too weak to keep her eyes open any longer.

"Sleep," she muttered into Rowin's neck. That was the only way she was going to heal these wounds. If she even could.

"*Not yet,*" he ordered.

As usual, she didn't listen.

"*Why?*" *she pleaded.* "*Why?*"

"*You're a creature from Hell,*" *Farrow told her.* "*And you deserve to burn like one.*"

When Genevieve woke, it wasn't to the smell of smoke but the smell of mint. She bolted straight up in the bed, her heart thundering as she glanced around, trying to figure out where she was, what had happened—

"Careful."

At the sound of his irritated voice, she focused on Rowin standing by the armchair in the corner, Umbra hopping from his lap as he walked up to the foot of the bed and crossed his arms over his chest. His *bare* chest. Uninvited butterflies erupted in her stomach.

Genevieve wasn't sure what was sexier—his perfectly sculpted abdominals, the tattoos swirling across his skin that disappeared below the waistline of his trousers, or the golden hoops pierced through his nipples and belly button.

She realized she wanted to bite him again. Badly.

"What happened?" she questioned; her voice hoarse.

"What happened is that you almost fucking died," he said, tone clipped. "I had to bribe Ellin to heal you."

"What did you bribe her with?" She touched her hands to her throbbing temples. "And why are you complaining? I survived the first round, didn't I? Shouldn't we be celebrating?"

He shoved a hand through his hair in frustration. "Get dressed. We're missing dinner."

It occurred to her then that the only thing she was wearing was an ill-fitting black button-down.

Her cheeks heated as she asked, "What happened to my dress?"

"It was covered in blood," he said.

"You *stripped* me?"

She had meant for the question to sound annoyed but, unfortunately, with the current huskiness of her voice, it came out much sultrier than she had intended.

Still no smile, but there was a slight glimmer of amusement in his eyes as he said, "Don't get too excited, my *sister* stripped you when she was healing you and cleaning you up. I only provided the shirt."

She rolled her eyes at him, but before she could argue, her stomach growled.

"If you want dinner, everyone will be in the dining room," he told her as he headed toward the door. "Or I can bring something back—"

"No, I'll come," she told him as she waved for him to leave. "I want everyone who bet against me to see my face until they're sick of it."

23

ℒOOPHOLES

Genevieve entered the dining room to much fanfare.

"Ah, she lives," Sevin declared when he spotted her hovering in the archway, giving her an obnoxious slow clap.

"You lost a lot of people a lot of money, bunny rabbit," Covin said with a grin.

Genevieve shot him a dirty look as she walked over to the spread on the table. She was ravenous after sleeping through so many meals.

Covin, Sevin, and Remi were all sitting together at one end of the table, scarfing down their own dinners. Rowin watched everyone from where he was leaning against the wall, sipping that same purple drink she'd seen the others pull out from the bar before the wedding. On the opposite end of the table was Ellin, who was pushing around a pile of berries with her fork, a solemn expression on her face that Genevieve could only guess had something to do with her eliminated twin. Grave was nowhere to be seen.

"Heard you were quite the team last night," Covin said as he stroked his Familiar's scaly head. "Grave is not happy."

"He's having a meltdown as we speak," Sevin chimed.

Even Ellin cracked a smile at that.

Genevieve ignored them as they continued to jostle each other about the events of the past twenty-four hours. The highlights of which included: Covin taking on six simultaneous lovers at the party, Sevin almost getting impaled in one of the enchanted rooms, and Remi receiving multiple propositions to begin salacious affairs when others mistook him for Rowin.

Genevieve brought her dinner over to where Ellin was sitting, ignoring Rowin's stare as he tracked her movements. Ellin gave her a wary look.

"Rowin told me that you healed me," Genevieve murmured quietly, not wanting to attract the others' attention to this fact in case they didn't already know. "I just wanted to say—"

"I healed you because he offered to spare me if the two of you get chosen as the Hunter and we aren't the only ones left—*not* out of the goodness of my heart," Ellin explained, her words firm but not necessarily harsh.

Ellin scraped her chair back from the table and strode from the room then, leaving her untouched plate behind.

Sevin rolled his eyes at his sister's exit before glancing over at Genevieve. "She's just pissy that Wells already lost. He's the only one who gives her a break during the game."

"Lay off Ellin," Rowin warned his brother as he walked over to steal a few blackberries off his sister's abandoned plate. "Wells might give her a break from time to time, but that's because the rest of you are pricks."

"Leave me out of that," Remi muttered as he slouched back in his seat.

"Hey, I'm just as nice to our baby sister as I am to all of you," Covin claimed around a bite of food.

"A shining defense," Sevin scoffed.

A moment later Umbra came trotting into the room, making a high-pitched chirping sound until Rowin gave her his attention. The two of them seemed to have some sort of silent conversation, Rowin narrowing his eyes at the fox for a long moment before setting his crystal goblet down on the table and heading for the exit.

"I'll be right back," was all he offered as he and Umbra strutted from the room.

The others exchanged curious looks, and Genevieve decided it would probably be a good time to excuse herself and go back to the bedroom to update her diary.

"Genevieve," someone called just as she stepped into the foyer.

She spun to find Sevin strutting toward her.

"You can call me Vivi, by the way," she told him as he approached.

He gave her a dazzling smile. "Does this mean I'm your favorite?"

She snorted. "I think Ellin probably deserves to be my favorite. She's been the most helpful."

"She did single-handedly keep your heart from stopping last night," he allowed.

"You were there?" Genevieve wondered, her cheeks heating at the prospect.

"Only because I was hiding in the library," he said. "And what a show it was. Ellin almost didn't get to you in time."

"Rowin said the rest of you aren't able to heal like her," Genevieve recalled.

"Rowin, Wells, and Remi can control—and become—darkness itself, but their healing skills are pretty limited to things like absorbing poison or helping someone sleep. Covin and I are Blood Wraiths—our magic isn't a particularly savory subject to discuss right after dinner—but we do have a bit more capability than the rest of my brothers. Nowhere close to Ellin's abilities, though."

"And Grave? Or is he only capable of destruction?"

"Something like that," Sevin revealed. "He's a Void Wraith. Extremely rare. Extremely powerful."

"*How* powerful?"

"Just be thankful he doesn't have access to his magic during the Hunt," Sevin said.

"Good to know it could be even worse," she muttered.

"You have no idea," he told her, sincerely. "I've never seen my brother so volatile."

"Really?" she scoffed. "Because Grave seems like volatile is his middle name."

"Close, his middle name is Blade." His gaze turned pointed now. "But I wasn't talking about Grave."

Does he mean . . . Rowin?

"Anyway, I just wanted to tell you that you may have been underestimated in that first round, but no one is going to make that mistake again. No matter how this year's Hunt plays out, I have a feeling things are going to be irreparable at the end. So be sure you want to win."

And with that, he left her there. Staring after him, utterly vexed about what the Hell that meant.

When Rowin didn't make any sort of reappearance, Genevieve became antsy. Pacing his room for the last hour while she tried to untangle her thoughts.

What had Sevin meant by be sure you want to win?

Of course she wanted to win. It was the only way she could *live*, after all.

Despite the fact that she didn't even know if what she'd been doing this past year was really *living*. More that it had felt like drowning in the sorrow of her past with Farrow and feeling suffocated by her small life in New Orleans. . .

She felt her chest tighten now as she finally faced the questions she'd been too afraid to ask herself before. What *was* she really winning this game for? Living for?

What the fuck do I even want?

She'd been running away from her problems in New Orleans, her feelings of never being enough for anyone there, and now here she was, an important piece of *this* family's legacy. So if she couldn't think of a single thing from her life before Enchantra to fight for, why not fight for the ones here, who clearly had a million reasons they'd like to live free of this cursed game?

Sevin was right, no matter how this played out, whether she survived or not, the next game was going to be very different from this one. Why stop at only trying to free herself and Rowin from this game?

She'd long given up the hope that someone with a white horse would ever come to save her. But that didn't mean she couldn't be the knight in shining armor for herself. For them.

As soon as the idea sank its teeth into Genevieve's mind, a rush of adrenaline speared through her, and before she knew it, she was heading toward the library.

Genevieve scoured the indexes of at least fifty different books before she found one that mentioned Crimson Rot. And just as she'd really started to sink into reading—something that had never been easy for her—the ring on her finger began to warm. Naturally.

She hurried to shove the book into the pocket of her frothy green skirts as she waited for whoever it was to show themselves. When they didn't, however, she stood and glared at the empty room.

"Don't be a coward, come out," she told them.

"I must say, I do enjoy how cheeky you are, Mrs. Silver," Knox's voice rang out as he winked into view in the center of the library's seating area. "Some Devils might consider it a challenge to be called a coward."

"Not any of the Devils I know," she said with a shrug. "Perhaps you're just insecure?"

In a single blink Knox was looming over her, making her jump as his violet eyes narrowed just inches from hers. "The rules of the game do not allow me to rip you to shreds myself. And my patrons might find you entertaining thus far. But if you keep pushing my buttons, Mrs. Silver, I will not hesitate to show you that *every* deal has a loophole."

She swallowed but didn't cower, and his hostile expression melted into one of faux charm.

"Now, I've come here to offer a proposition," he told her as he took a step away.

"I told you, I don't make deals with—"

He held up a hand to cut off the rest of her sentence. "This isn't a bargain. I simply wanted to inform you that your audience is hoping for something a bit more titillating from you and Rowington. And I must say that I find it very *interesting* that you two lovebirds have been able to keep your hands off each other."

"I'm sure you've noticed that Rowin is not as ostentatious as some of his siblings," she told him, sticking as close to truths as possible. "Have you considered we're simply private?"

"I've considered a lot of things," he told her, his eyes narrowing in suspicion. "So, I suggest you make entertaining my patrons your highest priority. And soon."

Before she could really decipher the threat hidden beneath that suggestion, he was gone.

"One problem at a time," Genevieve murmured to herself.

First, getting back to reading about the Crimson Rot—

Squeak.

Genevieve blinked at the high-pitched sound.

If there's a rat in here, I'm never visiting this library again.

Squeak. Squeak.

Genevieve turned toward the direction of the noise just as a fluffy white head poked over the back of the armchair that sat at the head of the seating area. It was some sort of weasel—or perhaps a mink. A very large mink.

Squeak.

The critter tilted its head at her, its round ears twitching as it clawed its way over the fabric and pulled itself up onto the headrest.

"You are so *cute*," she cooed as she stepped toward it. But the closer she got, the more she realized how aware its gaze was as it watched her. Like a certain fox she knew.

And that was when she realized that the signet on her finger had never gone cold.

The light in the room began to flicker, and the air around her thinned, making her breathing labored. A swirling cloud of darkness formed a few feet away, stretching and stretching until a large muscular silhouette stepped out of it.

Grave.

"Just how I'd hoped to find you. Alone," he declared as the shadows evaporated around them like smoke. "You're dismissed, Lilith."

The white mink immediately skittered away.

Genevieve lifted a brow as she folded her arms over her chest. "And why would you want to get me alone? Don't tell me you've decided to confess your love. I'm not into the whole 'choose between two brothers' thing."

There was no hint of amusement in his expression. "This is your final chance to allow me to make this quick and painless."

She fought to keep her expression neutral, but fear sank into her belly like a stone.

I can use my magic during these hours, she reminded herself.

"Your vendetta is ridiculously misplaced," she stated. "I don't get why you can't sacrifice *one* more year in Hell to let him be free and help you all?"

"No, you really *don't* get it," Grave agreed. "This marriage loophole that Knox offered has never sat right with me. And I have no doubt that if Rowin manages to get out of this game, Knox will find a way to turn it against the rest of us. He won't just give up one of his pawns. Someone will have to pay. The others think I'm paranoid, but I won't take the risk."

"Trying to kill me during the safe hours because you've let Knox get into your head is rather dishonorable, don't you think?" Genevieve reasoned.

His smile was grim. "I've never particularly aspired to be honorable."

Genevieve mustered up every bit of bravado she had and shrugged. "Take your best shot, then."

He narrowed his eyes. "Has anyone told you what I am?"

"Sevin said you were a *Void* Wraith."

"And do you know what that means?" he pressed.

But before she had the chance to answer, Grave unsheathed a knife from his belt and whipped it right toward her heart. Genevieve waited for her Specter abilities to take over, to turn her invisible so the knife would pass right through her. But her magic never came.

The knife never came either. The blade had stopped in mid-air. She tried to blink, breathe, *scream*, but she couldn't move.

Time around her had halted to a standstill.

24

FICTION

The last time the world had stopped for Genevieve, she'd been wearing a hideous green dress.

The gown had been an effort to match Farrow's attire for the Mystick Mardi Gras ball, since it was supposed to be the first time she met his parents. His family's Krewe wore a particularly heinous shade of green—because they might have been the most elite and expensive organization in the city, but that certainly did not buy them taste. And while it had pained her, Genevieve had chosen an outfit in just the same color, to show them what it would look like if she were one of them.

She'd trekked all the way from Grimm Manor to her favorite spot on the Riverwalk in the heavy, ruffled atrocity to meet him. Not wanting to spend any spare change on a carriage when she knew how debt riddled her family secretly was.

It was why she and Farrow were such a wonderful match—she loved him, *and* his family was exorbitantly wealthy. At the time it had felt like fate. When she'd arrived, however, she knew fate had nothing to do with it. Just childish naivety.

I don't understand, she had told him.

My mother found out about your family. She's forbidden me to escort you tonight. All anyone cares about here is appearances. But we can meet afterward—at Basile's. Luci will be there, too—

If you cannot stand up to your mother about a ball, how will you stand up to her when we are engaged? she'd demanded.

He'd flinched at the mention of *engaged*, but quickly put on a mask of mocking indifference.

*You're one of **them**, Genevieve. You're a fun time, but believing I, or anyone else of good standard, would ever marry someone like you is just delusional. Oh, don't start crying. It's pathetic.*

Tell me, why wouldn't I believe it? she'd implored. *You made me promises. Of adventures. A grand wedding. Cradles. **Love.***

Haven't you ever said things in a lover's sheets that you regretted later? he'd reasoned. *I know you've had plenty of opportunities.*

She had been so shocked to hear those words coming from his lips that her tears had dried up in an instant.

*You know exactly what your reputation is. Luci and the others might ignore it, might ignore your family ties, but I am from a different world than all of you. I have a **real** legacy to uphold.*

Legacies were a con. Genevieve would rather have her whole self than a part of any sort of legacy that treated people like *that*.

You don't even like your family, she'd spat. *Isn't that why you've spent all this time with us? Your lowly, classless friends? Because you were unhappy and bored sitting in your grand mansion, utterly alone. You said you'd never even felt alive until you met me—*

I've grown out of all that, he'd interrupted. *I was waiting until after tonight to tell you, but I'm leaving for London next week. There's a girl there. The niece of my father's colleague. We are to be married this fall. Basile's party and tomorrow's parade are the final times we might be able to see each other. So come, or don't, but this is it for us.*

And she'd felt it as he walked away. The world slowing to a stop around her. Her heartbeat fading.

At least in her present situation she was wearing something pretty. Though it was still green.

Perhaps I should retire this color.

Grave cleared his throat, the sound slicing through the scenes playing in her head and bringing her focus back to the hovering knife between them.

"If it makes you feel better, time manipulation costs me a great deal," he said. "But it's a perfect counter to your little disappearing act."

When time began to move again, it was subtle. Her heart thudded a single beat in her chest, the knife floating before her shifted an inch closer, and her body flickered out and back in again. She reached deep into her core for her magic, grasping as much of her power as she could while Grave waved a hand between them and let another second tick by. In and out she flickered again. Then the shadows began to rise.

When Grave reached out to slam the frozen blade the rest of the distance to her heart, she unleashed everything she had at once.

The knife pierced through her, but there was no pain. Her body remained completely solid, but everything else in the room, including Grave, disappeared for a moment in a ripple of magic. And when Grave released his hold on the room around them, so did she.

Genevieve knew the moment the knife reappeared somewhere behind her when the sound of a metallic clatter reverberated through the room.

Grave's face was utterly stunned.

"What the fuck?"

Genevieve sighed in relief when she spotted Rowin on the threshold of the library's entrance, Umbra sitting at his feet with Grave's Familiar dangling between her teeth by the scruff of its neck. The little mink squeaked pitifully, and Umbra opened her maw to drop the critter, letting it scamper over to Grave and claw up his body to drape itself over his shoulder.

"He was trying to kill me," Genevieve pouted as she rushed over to Rowin.

"I meant, what the fuck did *you* just do?" he clarified as he lifted his arm so she could press herself into his side.

She gave him an exasperated look but certainly didn't turn down his invitation, tucking herself against his body as she glowered at where Grave was still standing, confounded.

"I protected myself," she said in a way that implied the word *obviously*.

"You *projected* your magic," Grave spat with irritation. "I'm over two and a half centuries old, and I've never heard of a Specter being able to do such a thing."

She lifted her nose. "I'm sure there's a lot of things you haven't heard in two and a half centuries. Someone telling you that you're fun. The sound of a lover's climax—"

Genevieve felt Rowin's chest move with a silent laugh. Until Grave took a threatening step forward, that was.

In an instant Rowin pushed Genevieve behind him and bared his teeth at his brother. "Do not get any closer."

"Or what?" Grave barked. "All of this over a girl you don't even—"

"*She's mine*," Rowin snarled, his shadows beginning to swirl in the air around him. "Whatever you might think of that, whatever problem you have with it, if you ever try to touch her again, I will make the rest of your eternal life even more fucking miserable than it already is."

Grave's eyes narrowed at the vehemence in Rowin's words. "For Hell's sake, Rowington. You've been married to her for mere days. I will be your blood for *eternity*."

"How unfortunate for me," Rowin bit out.

Genevieve watched the exchange between them with as smooth of an expression as she could manage, but, truthfully, hearing Rowin say the words *she's mine* with such conviction had her stomach twisted up in knots.

It isn't real, she assured herself. *No matter how real it sounded.*

"The last fifteen years you've claimed you can't return to Hell because your *research* takes up all of your time. You can't show up to give our mother a single token of affection, but you'll risk everything for *her*?" Grave shook his head.

Genevieve narrowed her eyes at Grave's words but remained silent.

"Our parents made their own beds," Rowin stated flatly. "She was thrown into mine."

The smile Grave gave his brother was bone-chilling, but it was Genevieve he addressed as he said, "You really should have just let me make it quick and easy."

A large obsidian portal opened in the air between them, and Grave stepped inside and disappeared.

"Well, that was fun," Genevieve eventually said, trying to keep her tone light.

Rowin turned back to her. "Are you alright?"

Genevieve shrugged. "Where did you go? Earlier?"

"Umbra sniffed out Lilith. Grave only lets her wander around the house when he's up to something. I wouldn't have known you were in trouble otherwise. Though you always are, aren't you?"

She propped a hand on her hip. "Hey, I was minding my own business up here. Knox and Grave sought *me* out."

His gaze darkened. "Knox was here too?"

She reached over to fiddle with the signet on her finger, twisting it around nervously as she nodded. "I am a rather hot commodity to seek out in this household, it seems."

He looked like he wanted to laugh.

"Let's go back downstairs," he suggested, holding out his hand in offering. "I need to change, and I don't think you should stay here by yourself before one of the others decide they feel like ambushing you, too."

She swallowed as she looked down at his upturned palm as if it were a serpent poised to strike.

She's mine.

How long had she waited for someone to proudly say such a thing about her? She wished she could've enjoyed the butterflies his words had produced, but, unfortunately, she wasn't confident that those butterflies were capable of understanding the difference between fiction and reality.

She glanced over at the fireplace, at the mirror hanging above it, then reached out and threaded her fingers with his. And she let him lead her all the way back to his room without a word.

As soon as the door was shut, and they were truly alone, she dropped his hand and said, "Do not *ever* call me yours again."

A flicker of an emotion she didn't recognize flitted over his expression, but he didn't offer any response.

She took a deep breath. "When someone says those words to me, I want them to mean them."

He looked away from her as he dipped his chin in a nod and vowed, "Deal."

ROUND TWO OF
THE HUNT

25

ASTUTE OBSERVATION

While Rowin went to change in the bathroom, Genevieve hid the tome she'd taken from the Silvers' library at the bottom of one of her trunks next to her diary and the grimoire. For some reason admitting her interest in helping to save his mother and family was just a little too... intimate.

She scooped out her diary before covering the book with her clothes and went over to sit at the writing desk, opening the diary up to the fresh page she'd wedged her pen inside. She began a new entry, the ink in her pen flowing perfectly fine for nearly half the page before becoming spotty, leaving blank indentions instead of words. She shook the pen vigorously. It didn't help.

Rowin must have some ink in here, she thought as she pulled open the desk's wide drawer. She brushed aside a few bits and bobs as she reached all the way back to search with her fingertips for something that felt like a jar. There were wax sticks, stamps, pens, and then something she couldn't quite identify at the very back corner. Like a slightly raised square in the wood. She pressed down and—

—the front panel of wood that ran right beneath the open drawer popped open.

A hidden compartment.

When she pushed the top drawer closed and slid the bottom one out further, she found a thick stack of papers covered in handwriting she swore was familiar.

She plucked one of the papers out and saw that it was a letter, dated a few months ago and addressed to... Ellin.

Dearest Ellin, I'm sorry that it's taken me so long to find the words to write to you after all this time. I've been sitting at this desk for the past five hours, unable to think of a single thing that would make it worth sending. I've made no progress with the cure, you see. Every time I find someone who might be able to help, they disappear shortly after or decide they're too scared to be caught by Knox.

Genevieve returned the letter to the drawer and pulled out another. This one addressed to Remi and containing only a single line.

Remington, I don't know how to repair this rift.

The final letter she pulled was addressed to Grave.

Grave. Please. I am begging you to consider that there is a possibility of truth to the rumors. Consider Mother's feelings as well. You know she does not wish for this to continue either.

Genevieve felt her throat tighten with the threat of tears. He had been writing them letters for the last fifteen years.

The click of the lock on the bathroom door made her jump.

While she shuffled the papers around, trying to make it look like she had never touched anything, something caught the corner of her eye at the very bottom of the hidden drawer. An envelope with a bright-red wax seal embossed with a rose. The address in the corner one she knew intimately.

Grimm Manor
Esplanade Avenue
New Orleans, Louisiana

Her breath hitched.

I'll come back to it later, she promised herself as she shoved the drawer closed.

When Rowin emerged, he made himself comfortable on his

bed without a word. Stretching back against the headboard while Umbra nestled herself into his lap.

Genevieve decided she could write another time, making her way over to the dresser to exchange her diary for the grimoire she'd brought from Grimm Manor before settling into the armchair in the corner and leafing through it. Not that she could focus on any of the words inside, since the words of his letters were still burning at the forefront of her mind.

They stayed that way for a while, Rowin's eyes closed as he seemingly napped along with Umbra, and she pretending to read about the magic of various paranormal beings. At some point both Sevin and Covin showed up at Rowin's door, barging in before either Genevieve or Rowin could protest and settling in on the bed with a plate of hors d'oeuvres from the dining room and an entire bottle of whiskey.

The four of them spent the remaining time before midnight playing a lively game of Pit. And in the midst of screaming out numbers and fighting over hands of cards, Genevieve found that she had almost forgotten where she was entirely. Toward the end Sevin whipped his cards at Covin's head and Rowin began tidying up while his brothers fought to convince Genevieve that the other had been cheating by stashing extra cards up their sleeves.

When midnight finally did call, however, everyone sobered in an instant.

Remi, Grave, and Ellin were already in the ballroom when the rest of them arrived, and as soon as the circle of siblings was complete, Knox blinked into the room with the Hunting Blade.

"Wellington sends his regards from Nocturnia," the Devil announced.

Ellin's face twisted with rage. "Nocturnia? What the fuck do you have him doing there, Knox?"

"Nothing he didn't ask for by being the first eliminated." Knox smiled, though his words were firm.

Ellin's fists balled at her sides, but she didn't say anything more, and Knox didn't bother with further ceremony as he launched his enchanted dagger into the air just as he had at the end of the masquerade. Genevieve watched the silver weapon with bated breath as it hovered for a tense moment before spinning around the circle and zipping right into Remi's grasp.

"Choice of game?" Knox prompted.

"Random starts," Remi answered.

Rowin turned to Genevieve, opening his mouth to speak, but the sound of his voice was lost in the rush of them both being transported from the room.

Genevieve blinked her eyes open and found herself in an unfamiliar space. Her head was swimming from Knox's magic, and it took her a moment to realize she was in some sort of butler's pantry. The walls were lined with tiers of oak shelving stacked with serveware and utensils, and Genevieve wondered whether Enchantra had a full staff outside of the Hunt. Or if Rowin lived out his days in complete solitude.

There was an exit at each end of the room. Genevieve spotted a spider's web that stretched from one of the doors all the way to the ceiling. She wondered if the fact that the web had remained intact through the last round meant that this might be a good place to hunker down. But a moment later she heard someone moving in the room on the other side of that door. She bolted for the opposite exit.

Pressing her ear to the cobweb-free door, she listened until she was certain there was no sound coming from its other side. She quietly turned the handle and slipped out into—

—the dining room.

How have I never noticed this door? she wondered, concerned for her lack of observational skills, but when she glanced back at the exit, she realized the panels had been designed to blend in perfectly with the walls. The seams in the molding were so indiscernible that if she hadn't just walked through the opening, she wouldn't have believed there was one.

She crept out of the room into the grand hallway, her skirts swishing around her ankles with the speed of her stride as she made her way toward Rowin's room. She hoped that maybe he would have the same idea, but if not, her backup plan was to grab the library book in her trunk and make haste for the secret room he'd shown her in the library.

As she grasped onto the doorknob, someone yanked the door open from within. A spike of adrenaline went through her, and she leaped backward, ready to bolt, until she saw their face.

"Good," Rowin sighed as he beckoned her inside. "I was worried it was going to take forever to find you."

"Should we hide somewhere else now?" she asked.

"Remi isn't going to hunt us down like Grave did," he told her, and as he spoke, she noticed a tiny drop of blood beading at the piercing in his lip.

She tapped at her own lip and said, "You're bleeding."

He swiped his thumb across his mouth. "I bit my lip when Knox transported us."

"Making everyone start in a random room is quite clever," she said begrudgingly.

"And it cuts out the hiding time we usually get," he agreed. "Remi prefers a quick start. Really, he prefers anything that gets the whole game over with as soon as possible."

"He seems to be rather apathetic about participating," she noted. "What happened there?"

Rowin shrugged. "The rest of us are still hopeful in one way or another. He gave up wishing that this would end a long time ago."

"Is that why the two of you aren't close anymore?" she asked.

"I suppose you'd have to ask him why we aren't close."

A nonanswer.

"Want to play two truths and a lie again?" she prompted, and so many questions that had been burning inside her over the last two days bubbled up to the surface again.

He tilted his head and advanced a step toward her, leaning down just enough so their eyes were level, a few of the disheveled tendrils of his raven hair falling into his eyes.

"I have a better idea of how we can pass the time," he murmured, his golden gaze flicking down to her mouth.

Despite the way her heart began to thunder in her chest at his suggestion, something was off. Notably the lack of heat he usually elicited from her whenever he was so close.

"You don't think we should save some excitement for our audience?" she snorted, crossing her arms over her chest to stop him from pressing himself any closer.

"If you'd like," he answered as he tried to tuck a wayward tendril of his hair behind his ear, but it was just a bit too short to stay put.

That's when her blood turned to ice. And the ring on her finger turned to molten fire. Or maybe it had been burning this entire time and she hadn't even realized because, well, he made her pulse erratic and a part of her had clearly begun to associate him with safety.

This is why he told me that I couldn't trust my heart here.

Genevieve curled her lips into a sultry smile. The one that men couldn't ever seem to resist. Farrow. Morello. Basile, on that awful night when she'd wanted to hurt Farrow.

And now Remington Silver.

Remi's gaze heated as she blinked up at him, laying on her sweet Southern belle accent as she purred, "Why don't you go decide on the perfect spot for our little show and then meet me back here?"

"Why don't we practice in here first?" he suggested as he tilted his face down and brought his lips to hover just a breath away from hers.

It was bait and she knew it. She backed away from him.

"What gave it away?" Remi tilted his head, a small smile playing at the corners of his lips.

She was careful not to glance down at the ring. "Did you really stick something through your lip just to trick me?"

He shrugged as he finally unsheathed the Hunting Blade from the inside of his boot. "It wasn't only to trick *you*, but it was convenient that I ran into you first."

And then he lashed out.

Genevieve dove to the side, but it wasn't quick enough, and she hissed at the pain as the blade sliced right through the side of her corset and into her skin. Before he could get in another jab, however, she reached out to grab the golden hoop in his lip and ripped it right through his flesh.

He yelled in pain, the blade clattering to the ground in his shock at her gruesome attack. She didn't waste any time as she reached down to pluck the dagger up from the ground, but the moment her fingertips brushed its hilt, a searing pain went through her entire body. *Fuck. So stealing the knife is against the rules.* She snapped her hand back to her chest with a colorful curse, kicking out to send the blade flying across the floor instead. As Remi dashed for the weapon, she threw open the door and darted out of the room.

26

MEADOW

Genevieve was so damned tired of running. She was also so damned tired of getting blood all over every single dress she owned.

Blood does not go with pink.

She had known there was no way she could've made it all the way to the ballroom and then up the stairs before Remi caught up with her. So she'd done the next best thing—made a bee-line for the dining room, where she proceeded to ruin her nails prying open the hidden entrance to the butler's pantry. As she had suspected, the opposite exit of the pantry led through to the kitchen, where she then found the hidden corridor that led to the stairs and up to the secret room behind the library that Rowin had showed her the night before.

As she climbed the rickety wooden steps up to the drab, stone room, she pressed a hand to the aching wound at her side, sighing in relief at the pressure. As she leaned dramatically against the banister, the loose ribbons of the choker she'd tied around her neck snagged on the sharp end of a protruding splinter without her notice, and when she hauled herself up the next step, they pulled a bit too tight around her throat. Before she could reach back to untangle herself, the decrepit board beneath her gave out, and her foot went right through.

She let out a strangled gasp as she fell, jagged pieces of wood scraping her trapped ankle raw while the ribbons turned into a painful vise around her throat. She clawed at the silk knot until it came loose, gritting her teeth against the pain of prying her foot from the hole in the hollow step. The muffled sound of someone else shouting from behind one of the walls sent a shot of adrenaline through her and she worried she'd made too much noise. There was a pressure behind her eyes as they begged for her to cry, a lump in her throat she was barely able to swallow while she righted herself on the stairs to keep going.

She refused to give Knox's spectators the satisfaction of her tears—and she knew they were watching. The strategically placed looking glasses in the nooks of this dusty passage no longer going unnoticed as she passed them.

It's only a few scratches, she screamed at herself. And aching bones. Hurt pride.

By the time she made it to the, *blessedly*, empty secret room, she had already made a decision. She limped over to the cart with the decanters, double-, triple-, quadruple-checking she was not pouring herself a glass of urine. But Rowin must have taken care of that disgusting little detail when he'd reset the room's door sometime during the safe hours, because all she found within the bottles was pristine maple whiskey.

She pulled out the bottle's glass stopper and poured a bit of the liquor in a glass. As she brought it up to her nose, she nearly gagged at the smell, but once she forced down the first sip and felt its burn, the good kind, spread through her system, promising sweet relief, she easily gulped back the rest.

Two glasses later and she was draped over the couch, her eyes drooping closed as the nightmare started anew.

⚜

Groaning as she sat up, Genevieve massaged her fingertips into her throbbing temples as her eyes adjusted to the dark.

"I thought you didn't drink whiskey?"

Genevieve sucked in a surprised breath as she searched for Rowin in the dark, finding him sitting against the far wall, elbows resting on his bent knees as he watched her with an unreadable expression. Umbra was curled up against his hip, sound asleep.

There was a beat of silence as Genevieve adjusted her dress, and he climbed to his feet to walk over to her. Umbra gave a chatter of protest at being disturbed.

"If you wanted to be choked, all you had to do was ask," he murmured as he crouched before her, reaching up to brush the pad of his thumb over the tender skin of her throat. "I wouldn't have left any marks."

She felt the tips of her ears heat at his words, but only glared as she waved him back so she could stand. A dull spike of pain shot through her ankle, but she tried not to let it show as she hobbled over to the bar cart. She snatched up the mirrored tray that was sitting atop it and held it up to inspect the blotchy, inflamed ring around her neck.

"This looks *terrible*," she whined.

"Are you *limping?*" Rowin demanded.

"I slipped on the stairs on the way up here," she explained as he crouched in front of her once more and swept her skirts aside to look at her swollen ankle. "My foot went through one of the boards and my choker got caught on a splinter sticking out of the banister. That Devil can forge wards stronger than steel on the front gates and create fantasy lands inside of bedrooms, but he can't take care of a few planks of rotting wood? Who does the upkeep around here?"

"Me. Knox only visits Enchantra during the Hunt. I get everyone's rooms ready before they return, but fixing broken steps in secret passageways has fallen by the wayside while I've been looking for the cure," Rowin said. He gently squeezed her ankle, eliciting a hiss from her despite his carefulness. "It's sprained. Let me see the cut on your side."

She stepped away from him as he stood. "I'm *fine*."

"You're good to move to another room, then?" he prodded. "To run if we have to?"

"Can't we stay here?"

"We've been in here for a while already. I think we should try and move to one of the enchanted rooms," he reasoned. "You shouldn't have let yourself pass out like that. If it hadn't been me who found you—"

"I know," she said, sincerely.

His gaze brightened with surprise, and she rolled her eyes.

"I had a weak moment and saw the whiskey and I don't know what came over me," she admitted. "I also ran into Remi earlier, and he was pretending to be you, so it's been a strange few hours."

"Did...did anything happen?" he demanded, the seriousness of his expression making her want to laugh.

"Define *anything*," she teased.

A muscle in his jaw ticced. "If he touched you—"

"If I didn't know any better," she interrupted before he could get too worked up, "I might think you were jealous, Mr. Silver."

He gave her a hard look, as if to say she'd lost her mind, but all he said was, "Are you going to be able to walk on your foot?"

"If I said no?" she asked.

He smirked at her. And before she could protest, he was scooping her up into his arms and bringing her over to the spinning bookcase.

"I thought this couldn't be opened again until it was reset," she said as they spun toward the library.

"I said it couldn't be opened from the *library* side until it was reset," he corrected.

Just as the wall stopped spinning and he set her back on her feet, Genevieve felt the burning sensation in her hand.

"Rowin—" she gasped, but it was too late.

"And to think I was coming in here to take a break," Remi said as he strutted into the room.

Rowin crossed his arms over his chest as he faced his twin. "I wouldn't pick a fight with me right now, Remington. Not after what you pulled with my wife."

"I'd say your wife and I are even after she ripped that ridiculous piece of metal out of my lip," Remi reasoned.

Rowin raised his brows and swung his gaze over to her. "You did *what?*"

Genevieve shrugged. "Be thankful I lived out that fantasy on him and not you."

Rowin's eyes lit up with a wicked gleam. Remi grunted in irritation, unsheathing the Hunting Blade and pointing it at Rowin. "Let's get this over with."

And then Remi was launching himself forward. He leaped onto the small coffee table in the middle of the seating area and used its wooden surface to propel him onto the armchair, rocking it backward with his weight until it fell and gave him the perfect arcing momentum to slam the blade down into Rowin's shoulder. Genevieve tried to swallow her yelp of surprise when the blade actually made contact, having expected Rowin to dodge the hit, but it was clear that this was exactly what Rowin intended.

As Remi went to yank the dagger back out of Rowin's flesh, Rowin grabbed his twin's straightened arm with both hands and *snapped it.*

Genevieve looked away and heaved a bit as the image of broken bone poking out of Remi's skin lingered in her mind. A scream of agony filled the air, then grunts of effort as the two of them fell to the ground in a tangle of limbs. Even with only a single useful arm, Remi held his own—so did Rowin, with the dagger still protruding from his shoulder.

Eventually Rowin managed to pin Remi to the floor, and Genevieve couldn't help but think how bizarre the sight was. As if Rowin was fighting himself.

"I'll sit here for the rest of the round if I have to," Rowin threatened.

In answer, Remi freed his good hand and wrenched the dagger from Rowin's shoulder before plunging it back into his brother's side. The grunt of pain Rowin made was impressively restrained.

Genevieve would've been cursing up a storm.

"I'm so fucking tired of this," Remi said from behind clenched teeth. "*I want out.*"

That last part was a desperate roar, and it was almost harder for Genevieve to watch than any snapping bone.

"Then let me end it," Rowin snarled back, and she wasn't sure whether he meant this particular fight or the Hunt altogether.

It didn't matter either way, because in a blink Remi mustered up the rest of his strength and bucked his legs hard enough that he managed to slam Rowin back into the ground. As he unsheathed the knife from Rowin's ribs, he poised himself to strike again, this time in Rowin's heart. Fortunately, the dagger never made it to its target because the case of books behind him came crashing down instead.

Genevieve blinked in disbelief at what she had just done as Rowin crawled out from beneath Remi's body and Remi flattened to the ground, unconscious, beneath the heavy shelf. Her chest was still heaving from the exertion as Rowin climbed to his feet, stunned.

"Those shelves are much heavier than they look," Genevieve complained before turning to him and saying, "Sorry. But I just couldn't stomach it any longer."

Rowin shoved a hand through his hair as his surprise finally wore off. "Let's go. He's going to have a headache, but that won't keep an immortal down for long."

As soon as Rowin shut the door to the enchanted room behind them, Genevieve gasped as she realized which room he'd brought her to. The meadow. Only now, instead of sunny, blue skies, the clear, inky abyss above them was sparkling with a million stars. The river was still softly bubbling somewhere in the distance, and the blanket of flowers over the hills was glowing with flickering fireflies.

It was heaven.

"Genevieve?"

She glanced over her shoulder.

"I just wanted to say you did well back there," Rowin said.

His expression, as usual, told her nothing about how he was feeling. The sadness in his eyes, however, made her chest tighten.

The line from his letter came back to her now. *Remington, I don't know how to repair this rift.*

Kicking off her shoes so she could feel the grass beneath her feet, she backed away, careful not to put too much weight on her bad ankle. "Two truths and a lie?"

He nodded as he shoved his hands into his front pockets and followed her toward the sound of the water. They were quiet for a while as she thought of her questions and took in their surroundings, a symphony of croaking frogs and crickets beginning around them. At some point she began to pull the petals off the lavender flower in her hand, getting all the way down to the final two petals before he spoke again.

"Where did you get this ring?" she began. "If the Hunt didn't exist and you could live anywhere, here or on the Other Side, where would it be? And"—she bent down to snap a purple flower from its stalk as she passed by—"what leads have you found for the—"

"Careful," he inserted. "There may be no mirrors here, but everything that happens within these rooms is being broadcasted with crystal clarity."

"For the"—she searched for a placeholder—"the super-rare birthday gift you're going to get me."

"I won Favored fifteen years ago—the same year my winning streak began—and the ring is what I chose as my boon from Knox's trove. Grave and I got into an argument at the masquerade that year, and it made for a pretty brutal game. Knox's audience clearly enjoyed seeing that side of me."

He looked up at the stars, and she wondered whether he was wishing that side of him didn't exist.

"I'm not sure where I'd want to live if I ever leave Enchantra. It's been so long since this has truly felt like home, and yet I cannot think of another place worthy of such a title either." He looked back at her now. "And that brings me to your . . . birthday gift. Unfortunately, all I've found are dead ends so far. I've been writing letters"—he flicked his eyes over to her, and she swore she saw guilt in them—"but most people don't even respond. And when they do . . ."

Everything he'd said had the ring of truth, and Genevieve was unsure whether he quite understood how to play this game. But all she said was, "What did you and Grave fight about at that masquerade all those years ago?"

"It's my turn," he reminded her.

Genevieve sighed and nodded as she tossed away the mutilated flower before continuing toward the ornate silver bridge just ahead. Rowin kept pace at her side. Umbra, meanwhile, was pouncing in and out of the grassy field around them, snapping at the fireflies, and Genevieve couldn't help but giggle.

Rowin still hadn't said anything by the time they reached the overpass, and Genevieve was too busy exploring to bother giving him a nudge. Up close, the bridge was much wider than she expected, the steady, streaming river beneath it surprisingly deep. The water's surface was glassy, reflecting the twinkling stars from above like a mirror. As she began to cross, one of the stones dropped down slightly beneath her weight, and nearly made her trip.

Rowin hooked a steadying arm around her waist just as a flash of gilded, luminescent fish swam downstream.

"Did you see that?" she gasped as she tugged at the sleeve of his shirt and stepped toward the railing.

She leaned over to peer into the water, but the only gold in sight now was the reflection of Rowin's eyes as he leaned over next to her. She frowned.

"I think you found the game within the game."

Genevieve glanced over. "The what?"

He waved toward the rest of the scene around them as he crouched to examine the sunken step. "Remember I mentioned that there are tokens Knox has hidden inside each of these rooms? Every room contains a puzzle. Solve it, survive it, and the token is yours."

"And the token would give us immunity from the next round," she recalled.

He nodded and then placed his palm against the stone, shifting his weight forward onto the loose step once more and sending another stream of glowing fish through the water.

"Do you think there are more triggers like that one?" she asked.

One corner of his mouth curled up with anticipation. "I suppose we'll have to find out."

27

Long Story

After half an hour of checking every loose stone across the bridge, they had discovered that each one released a group of the gilded fish—with the exception of three or four of the stones that released white fish amongst the golden swimmers as well.

At first Rowin had thought they needed to catch one of the white fish to locate the token, but after managing to snag three, even with his half-mended injuries, there were still no obvious clues. Now, they were lying back on the sloped bank, feet dangling in the running water. Rowin was still shirtless from diving into the river, and Genevieve was trying to focus as hard as she possibly could on the stars and *not* on his glistening abs. So far, she'd invented thirty-five new constellations.

"What happened the night you stopped drinking whiskey?"

His first question.

She turned to look at him, ignoring the scratchy grass on her cheek. "You're still stuck on that?"

"I'm nosy," he murmured.

Well, we certainly have that in common.

She took a deep breath. There were exactly four people in the world who knew this story. Herself, Farrow, Basile, and Salem. Five if Salem had divulged it to her sister despite Genevieve asking him not to.

"This story might make you think differently of me," she warned.

He gave her a sidelong glance. "You have no idea what I think of you now, trouble."

That was very true.

"It's a long story," she tried again.

"I think we've got the time."

"*Fine*," she gave in. "I suppose this means I'll have to explain to you who Farrow is, after all."

He smirked. Exactly what he had been hoping for, clearly. It only proved what she'd always known—men loved gossip and drama as much as women.

"I first met Farrow Henry when I was fifteen years old. I'd snuck into this charity gala at the Hotel Monteleone, off Royal Street. At the time it was my second favorite place in New Orleans. So many elegant people to watch."

She thought of all the women she'd seen at those types of parties, how many of them had informed her own personal style, her taste for opulent things . . . her distaste for the paranormal.

"I'd spotted him almost immediately that night," she continued. "Mainly because he was the only other person even close to my age, but also because he was in the middle of a very poor heist—trying to steal an entire bottle of bourbon from behind the bar. So, I decided to intervene."

"Shocking," Rowin murmured.

She kicked him with her good foot as she continued: "The bartender had caught him, and was getting ready to have someone throw him out, but luckily I'm rather good at pretending to faint."

Rowin snorted. "And how does one become good at pretending to faint?"

"Wearing corsets."

"Mmm," he allowed. "Continue."

"Anyway, I created a distraction. The bartender rushed over, and Farrow got away with his bottle. Once I *magically* recovered, I looked for him, but I couldn't find him."

If only that had been the case. She blinked up at the stars and steeled her nerves to tell the rest of this story. Despite seeing Farrow in her nightmares almost every night, talking about him aloud felt so much more torturous.

Something brushed the back of her hand: Rowin's fingertips. Gentle. Comforting.

She took a deep breath. "On my way home, I decided to stop on the Riverwalk. That's my *favorite* place in New Orleans. Under the stars and the glow of the gas lamps, looking out at the water, I could pretend I was at the edge of something bigger instead of stuck where I was. Where I had always been. And as fate would have it—the cruel bitch—that's where I found Farrow with a group of his friends. And of course the bourbon. It was the first time I ever got drunk outside of Grimm Manor. He brought me back to his house—this extravagant mansion in the Garden District. The type of glamour I'd always dreamed of. When his friends left, it was the first time I'd ever been alone with a boy. The first time I'd ever..."

Her words became thick with emotion. Her first sexual encounter had not been painful or awkward or wrought with shame. Farrow had been kind, and passionate, and everything she'd ever dreamed of for herself. At that delicate age, anyway.

He hadn't kicked her out of his bed the moment it was over. He hadn't refused to cuddle. And for a very long time she'd kept the memory of that first night of them together close to her heart.

Rowin waited patiently for her to find her next words, but she could tell she had his full attention.

"After that night, he promised to see me again," she whispered. "And he did. He courted me for the entire summer, taking me places I'd never been, giving me experiences I never thought I'd have. His family is enormously wealthy. The kind of wealthy that has a different set of dishes for every occasion you can think of. The kind that has their name on historic buildings and street signs. The kind that sends their sons off to prestigious out-of-state boarding schools for the best possible education."

"Ah," Rowin murmured.

She nodded at the sky. "I was devastated. Didn't leave my bed for a month. My mother hardly even noticed. Ophelia did, but I had never told her about him, or how far things had gone, so I lied and learned how to hide the truth from her. Farrow promised to write until he came back for me. The letters came weekly at first. Then a couple times a month. Then one last letter on my sixteenth birthday before . . . nothing. I spent years getting over him. Tried to use others to get him out of my system. And eventually it worked. I'd finally stopped thinking about him." She ripped out a handful of grass at her side. "And then that bastard came back."

She sat up in frustration now, sifting through the blades of grass in her hand and tearing them into tiny pieces. Rowin also sat, bending his knees up to his chest and propping his cheek on his fist as he looked at her.

"I assume this story takes a turn for the worse?"

She gave a bitter laugh of confirmation. "He came back and acted like nothing happened. Like he hadn't ripped my heart out when he left, and I hadn't spent years trying to get clean of him. I told him the moment he arrived to leave me alone. I'd made other friends—Luci, Iris, Basile—and I'd been just fine without him. It was the first group I'd ever really been a part of. And he had to poison that for me, too. He and Basile became inseparable. He'd introduced Iris to his brother, and she was *smitten*. She constantly begged me to go on outings with them. Luci was the only one on my side, but her family fell on hard times, and she grew distant for a while."

"Don't tell me you just gave in," Rowin drawled.

"Of course not," she scoffed. "I made him work for it. Grovel. For three whole months before I finally agreed to see him again."

"Three months? That's practically an eternity," Rowin agreed, tone dripping with sarcasm.

"Without any good sex it is," she muttered.

The corners of his lips curled up. "Try five years and get back to me."

She balked. "Five *years?*"

He looked away from her. "I've had more important matters on my mind, remember. Now, back to your story."

She had almost forgotten she was in the middle of her own sordid tale.

"Right. I agreed to see him again, and this time he swore he was there to stay. He had begun shadowing his grandfather's business and claimed he was ready for commitment. For months, I slept by his side, listening to his promises. How he was going to propose to me and build me the house of my dreams. Help me take care of my family. Because my sister didn't know it yet, but my mother was on the verge of plunging us into bankruptcy." Her breaths grew shaky. "And then on February twentieth of last year, he changed his mind."

She threw the grass in her hand out into the stream, watching as each blade sent tiny, overlapping ripples through the water. She was afraid the conversation she'd had with Farrow that day would not fade from her memories until she was dust in a grave.

"He said his family was too affluent to have someone with paranormal blood in their *pristine* family line. That I was delusional for ever thinking otherwise. He told me he was engaged to be married to some girl in London and that we could have two more nights together." Her face burned with shame as she focused on a spot far ahead. "Anyway, I sent Farrow a note saying I wanted one last hurrah before he left—asked him to meet me inside one of the Mardi Gras parade floats at six o'clock sharp. And then I got very, very drunk."

"On whiskey," he guessed.

"Yes." Tears pricked the corners of her eyes. "He found Basile and me in a *very* compromising position. I wanted to make him feel as horrible as he'd made me feel. To show him that I had moved on first."

Rowin's eyes narrowed, his jaw clenching as he asked, "What did he do?"

Genevieve swallowed her tears as she recited, "Called me every derogatory name in the book. Whore. Slut. *Demon*. Whatever. The names didn't matter." She wrapped her arms around herself. "I'd embarrassed him. And in response he set the float on fire with me and Basile locked inside."

Rowin's lips parted in disbelief. "Genevieve."

"I was too drunk to use my magic. I think maybe *that's* why I fainted the first night here—having my magic taken brought back that helpless feeling. I hate it."

A brief flash of guilt flitted over his face.

"By the time we were rescued, Basile had burns on over half his body. I, of course, recovered. Though it took *weeks*. But Farrow's father paid off the police department, and then a check arrived at Grimm Manor as well."

She took a deep breath and continued: "Basile asked me to help him use his own hush money to get a very expensive elixir for his scars, and while the elixir worked well enough, it didn't do much for my guilt."

"And Farrow? You just let him get away with that?"

"Fortunately, I've recently gained the sort of connections that I needed to enact the lasting sort of revenge Farrow deserved."

"I hope that revenge included lighting him on fire," Rowin told her firmly.

"Close enough," she murmured.

Salem had been a little too eager to burn down the Henry family's estate, honestly. Even with Genevieve's provision that there could be *no one inside* when it happened. She never made Salem swear on that provision, however, and there was a tiny part of her that hoped maybe he hadn't listened.

"Which part of that story was supposed to make me think differently of you?" he wondered.

"Is that one of your questions?" she asked.

"Yes."

"I'm not proud of any of it," she admitted. "I desperately want to forget, but I don't think I deserve to. Not when Basile has to remember. Since then I've been trying to find some kind of light in the darkness of what happened. But I think maybe the light will never be in my reach, and I need to accept that."

"The light isn't something you need to chase, Genevieve. The light is wherever you are," he told her.

A rush of surprise at the sincerity of those words went through her, and she had to look away from him.

"You do know that none of the blame is on your shoulders, don't you?" Rowin demanded. "It's that bastard's fault. Farrow. What a ridiculous fucking name."

"Pots and kettles, *Rowington*," she joked half-heartedly.

"I'm serious," he insisted, reaching over to tap a finger beneath her chin to make her look him right in the eyes, the gold of his irises earnest. "You know that you are not to blame for any of it, right?"

"Is that your final question?" she whispered.

"Genevieve."

"I don't know," she admitted.

He shook his head, expression darkening. "That better be your fucking lie."

28

TOKEN

Over the next few hours, Genevieve made enough flower crowns for a small army. She'd braided hers through her soft curls and even made one small enough to fit around Umbra's neck like a collar. Which the Familiar did not seem all too pleased with. Though definitely more pleased than Rowin, who was now wearing the strings of flowers atop his head, around his neck, and on each of his wrists. The soft pastel petals were so at odds lying against his tattooed skin, yet it somehow only enhanced his allure to her.

"Stop giggling to yourself over there," he ordered.

She pressed her lips together in amusement. He was currently walking back and forth across the bridge, sending waves of glowing fish down the stream over and over as he tried to figure out Knox's game.

"It has something to do with the white fish," he said for the thousandth time. "There's no other reason for them to be a different color."

"How many triggers are there again?" she called.

"Eight."

"And which ones have the white fish?" she wondered as she discarded another ringlet of flowers and stood.

"It's random." He pressed down on one of the stones, and a ripple tore through the water in response. "The first two release only golden fish. But the third has white fish as well. Then four is gold, five has white, six has white, seven is only gold, and eight has white."

"Are there the same number of white fish each time?" she wondered.

He paused. Then, "For fuck's sake."

She watched as he pressed down on each stone he'd noted produced the white fish. Sure enough, the numbers were all different. A group of three, a group of four, a pair, and one lone ivory swimmer.

Rowin quickly went to work stepping on the stones in ascending order. They waited, but nothing happened. He tried descending order next. Nothing.

"Try ascending order with each of the other stones in between," she suggested.

So, he did. One white fish. All gold. Two white fish. All gold. On and on until the entire sequence was complete.

And something happened.

All the fish flooded back into the river at once, and instead of disappearing somewhere downstream this time, they meandered around lazily. Their golden glow filled the meadow.

"That was…a bit anticlimactic," Genevieve said, hand propped on her hip. "I expected more—"

"Look," Rowin interrupted as he pointed at something in the water.

Genevieve squinted, searching beneath the surface for something new.

There. A single crimson fish.

"Umbra, fetch," Rowin directed.

Umbra looked up from where she was bathing herself a few feet from Genevieve on the bank. At Rowin's order, the fox lifted her back leg and scratched at the flower necklace around her throat until it tore away and then promptly dove into the water.

Genevieve made a noise of annoyance. She'd worked hard on that one.

They watched as Umbra paddled through the water, the Familiar's head darting back and forth as she tracked her scarlet mark. When she dove beneath the surface, Genevieve edged forward in awe, watching as Umbra caught her prey with quick precision.

The moment the fox's maw grasped onto her target, however, something shifted.

The stars in the sky began to wink in and out before turning a foreboding crimson color. The glow of the fish below them also changed, swathing everything in an eerie vermilion hue. Like blood. The fish slowly began to transform as well, their scales shifting from their luminescent gold to pitch-black, their faces suddenly locking all at once onto Umbra.

And then Genevieve saw the teeth.

Rowin shouted Umbra's name in warning, but it was too late. The fish darted all at once.

Before Rowin could dive over the side of the bridge for his helpless Familiar, the silver railing began to contort, striking out toward him and wrapping itself around his torso. A cage. Genevieve didn't know what came over her then. All she saw was the look of agony on Rowin's face as he struggled to free himself to help Umbra, and the cloud of dark red unfurling in the center of the river.

Genevieve dove in.

Her ankle was still sore, her side still aching from where Remi had caught her with the Hunting Blade, but she didn't stop swimming. As she hoped, the piranhas paid her no attention as she cut through their frenzy, their sights locked only on Umbra and the glowing crimson prize. She knew as soon as she reached the Familiar that she wouldn't have much time. The closer she got, the thicker the blood became, clouding her vision, making it hard to distinguish the red fish in Umbra's jaws.

As soon as Genevieve spotted wild amber eyes and thrashing black paws through the murk, she grasped as much of Umbra's flank as she could and ripped the Familiar from the swarm. Tucking the fox into her body with one arm and propelling herself forward with her other, she kicked them toward the bank, swimming as fast as she possibly could. The piranhas instantly gave chase.

She could hear the muffled sounds of her gown being shredded to pieces, the weight of the clinging skirts still hindering her momentum. Then came their jagged little teeth digging into her flesh. She screamed, sending all the air in her lungs back up to the surface in a swirl of bubbles, thrashing wildly as her own blood spilled into the water around her. She kicked and kicked as the vicious fish ripped into her flesh, but her grip on Umbra stayed firm, the Familiar's jaw around her token equally unwavering.

When they finally hit the bank, Genevieve used the rest of her strength to launch Umbra out of the river and onto the earth. As soon as the crimson fish was no longer in the water, the piranhas fell away, their scales slowly melting back into their previous golden glow. And as Genevieve bled out into the stream, sinking further and further down, everything went black.

The fog was so thick in her mind she couldn't tell what was real and what wasn't. But at least this time she wasn't dreaming of fire.

No, she was very, very cold.

The sound of tolling bells vibrated all around her, synchronizing to the slowing beat of her heart.

"She's so cold," a deep voice growled.

"She's lost too much blood," someone else said.

Something soft and fuzzy pressed against her side as scorching hands smoothed hair away from her face. She tried to say something, but the words wouldn't come out.

"I've got you," that first voice whispered. "I won't let you go."

"It's going to really cost you this time," someone said softly.

"You can have the token," a familiar voice swore. "*Just help her.*"

"And if I say no? And she dies?" the first voice wondered.

No response.

A minute later and a sharp, electric sensation began to ripple through her body. Starting at her fingertips and crawling up over every inch of her skin. Whatever sort of magic it was, it itched terribly, and she desperately wanted to scratch, but she still couldn't move.

"Hold still," the familiar voice soothed. "Just a little longer, I promise."

More silence. The zaps continued.

"I'm onto you, you know," the soft voice finally spoke again.

Again, no response.

Genevieve wasn't sure how much time had gone by when the itching finally stopped.

"You have to hold on for me," that voice demanded now. The one that was keeping her warm.

"What will you give me if I do?" she tried to say back.

A long pause.

"What would you request?" The words were nearly a whisper this time.

"Something real," she said.

Silence.

29

SHRINE

A comforting warmth was pressed along the length of Genevieve's back, and a heavy weight was wrapped around her waist. She'd never been more comfortable. Then something rough and wet dragged across her cheek.

Umbra's tongue.

"Ugh," she whined, opening her eyes and swiping the Familiar's saliva off her face.

"Umbra, enough."

For a moment Genevieve went rigid as her mind registered that it was *Rowin* pressed behind her. He lifted his arm to allow her to face him, and she was grateful that the room was dark enough to hide her flushed cheeks.

"You're on my side of the bed," she rasped.

"Flawless observation," he murmured.

She swatted at his arm, which he still hadn't removed from around her waist. "What the Hell happened?"

"You lost a lot of blood. Your body temperature dropped dangerously low for a mortal."

"And blankets couldn't have helped that?" she wondered as she began giving herself a once-over. Her dress had been removed yet again, replaced with one of his shirts, her skin cleaned of any blood.

"This was an easier way for me to make sure you warmed up properly," Rowin explained.

The smile that slowly took over her face earned her a glare, but she simply wasn't buying the excuse.

"Well, thank you for being so *considerate*," she told him.

"After what you did for Umbra, you deserve it," he said quietly.

The reverence in his eyes was so open and genuine that it made her throat tighten.

She reached out to lightly touch her fingertips to his cheek. "Thank you for saving me from certain death. Again. Or convincing your sister to do it, at least."

"You don't need to say thank you," he told her. "You and I are partners. We'll save each other."

Her heart stopped.

We'll save each other.

It had been less than four days, and yet he was the first person other than her sister to ever show up for her when she needed him to. Every single time. He was the first person other than her sister that she wanted to save as well.

She'd come to Enchantra to find someone like her, someone who might understand what it was like to be an outcast in their own family. But she'd found all of them—a family that was funny, and loud, and brutal, but that she knew was fiercely loyal and might be able to do great things if they weren't pitted against one another.

"But I would like to say thank you," he continued, his voice slicing through her thoughts in that way it always did. Like her mind was always waiting for his next words, whether she wanted to hear them or not. "For saving Umbra—"

"You don't need to say thank you," she repeated back to him. "You don't owe me anything, Rowin. Umbra is a part of you, and you are..."

He's what? Not mine. Not really. Not in any way that counts after this game.

"I am what?" he pressed.

"If you and I are partners, that includes your furry little menace," she finally answered.

She glanced over at Umbra, who was staring back at her, unblinking, with adoration.

Great.

Rowin flashed a smile at his Familiar before shooing her away and refocusing his attention on Genevieve to say, "Fine. I won't say thank you. But can I at least show you how grateful I am?"

Her breath hitched at those words, at the anticipation that suddenly fluttered through her body, but he didn't move. Only watched her expectantly.

"Yes," she whispered. "Please do."

As soon as the words were out of her mouth, he shifted their bodies until she was on her back, and he was hovering above. He leaned down to press a gentle kiss against the underside of her jawline, leaving a trail as he moved toward her throat. She saw his shadows begin to unfurl around them and nearly moaned with the anticipation of them touching her skin again. She felt him smile against her clavicle when they began to slither over her body and beneath his shirt, drawing a whimper from her lips. Her heart thundered as his hands began sliding over her as well, gripping the hem of the shirt and pushing it up and up, until it was over the swells of her breasts. His eyes darkened as he took her in, a hunger gleaming in them she had never seen in anyone else's.

She knew what he'd said, about hearts not being logical and that they couldn't be trusted, but she didn't fucking care. She wanted him so badly in this moment that she'd let her heart lead her into whatever perilous fires it wanted if he would just keep touching her forever.

Without warning, he leaned down and flicked his tongue

against one of her taught nipples, sending a shot of pleasure right to the apex of her thighs and making her twist her hands in the sheets to keep herself from writhing beneath him.

"I thought you said you wouldn't be sweet," she gasped as he began placing scorching kisses from one breast to the other before lathing at her other nipple in turn.

"Oh, I won't be sweet for long, trouble," he vowed.

"Because we're *just fucking*, right?" she tested.

He lifted his head to look into her eyes, and for a moment he didn't respond.

Just before a spark of hope could ignite inside her, however, he said, "Right."

When a wave of disappointment crashed through her, she knew that her promise of being okay with having no strings attached between them had been optimistic of herself at best. She also knew she could stop him right now if she thought she'd changed her mind. But then she would miss out on whatever experience he was about to give her, and that almost seemed more painful.

Before the disappointment could drown her, he leaned down and gently sank his teeth into her nipple. Her back began to arch off the bed as a moan of pleasure finally escaped her lips. As he moved to pull at her other nipple, his shadows wrapped themselves around her wrists and ankles, pulling her limbs taught until she was at his complete mercy.

He looked up at her again. "Can you snap your fingers?"

She lifted a brow. "Yes?"

"Demonstrate," he demanded.

She snapped a couple of times, his shadows never loosening. "Why?"

"You can tell me to stop at any time. And if you can't speak, snap, got it?"

She wondered what sort of things he was into to make such a system necessary. *And am I going to get a firsthand experience of them?*

As if he knew exactly what she was thinking, he explained, "Covin's a large proponent of the snapping. His tastes are a lot more sadistic than mine, but extra forms of communication are never a bad thing when mouths are...preoccupied."

She had to swallow another moan at the images his words conjured, and it made her realize just how wound up she really was. He huffed a laugh and ducked back down to lathe at her breasts once more, making her rosy buds tighten almost painfully as her arousal began to soak the sheets beneath her. He was careful to keep all his weight on his forearms as he worked her into a frenzy with his mouth, which meant she was not getting any friction where she needed it most.

"Touch me," she pleaded.

"I am touching you," he said, giving a lazy swirl of his tongue.

"*Fuck me*, then," she growled.

He had moved his hand between their bodies, his fingertips brushing ever so lightly over that most sensitive spot at her core. She tried to writhe closer, but his shadows only pulled her tighter, moving her wrists together and stretching her arms above her head as they spread her legs apart. He laughed again as he pushed himself up to kneel between her legs, roaming his eyes over her figure as he basked in her torment.

"I'm not going to fuck you," he told her as he splayed a hand over the plump curves of her belly. "Yet."

"But—" she began to protest.

"I'm supposed to be thanking you, remember?" He shifted his gaze back to hers. "Let me show you what it's like to have my gratitude, trouble." He moved the hand on her abdomen down, agonizingly slow, until his thumb brushed against that heavenly spot once again. "If you thought I was a tireless opponent, wait until you see me as a lover."

She could hardly focus on what he was saying as he finally gave her the friction she needed, pressing his thumb down onto her clit and rubbing tight, languid circles over the bud of nerves. She mewled in pleasure as she jerked against his shadowy bands, but they didn't give an ounce of mercy, and neither did Rowin. Without lifting his thumb, he slid his index and middle finger inside her, curling them forward and pumping them until she soaked his hand with her arousal.

"Please," she panted. "I need…"

"What do you need?" he murmured as he watched her squirm. "Be specific."

"I need you to taste me," she told him, the sultry voice coming from her lips nearly unrecognizable to her own ears. "I need to feel you *worship* me."

He smirked. "I'm a creature of Hell, worshipping is not usually in my nature." Then he lowered himself between her legs and flicked his tongue out to taste her. "But for whatever time you remain in my bed, I will make it your shrine."

"*Fuck*," Genevieve cried.

Several new tendrils of his shadows split from the others to begin stroking themselves over her skin, tightening around her nipples and tangling in her hair as Rowin worked his tongue over her over and over again. His technique was masterful, the tip of his tongue flicking slow circles over her clit until she was at the precipice of ecstasy. Just before she could crash over the edge, however, his shadow limbs tightened, just enough to be painful, cutting her pleasure and pulling her back from her climax. She felt him smile as he dipped his tongue toward her entrance next, working to build her back up to the edge.

He continued to devour her until she worried she wouldn't be able to take it anymore, his attentions as relentless as he claimed they'd be. And when she approached the threshold of her climax once again, he had his shadows pull her back once more.

"I swear I will kill you," she snarled, but he only laughed as he pulled away.

"Deep breath, trouble," he told her, his voice gruff with lust. "You're about to need it."

As he spoke, his shadows began to slither down her body—except for the ones holding her wrists and ankles—until they reached her sex. Rowin watched, on his knees before her, through half-lidded eyes as his magic began to pleasure her, working her back up into a moaning mess. And when they plunged *inside* her, giving her the fullness she was desperately craving, she screamed.

Waves of ecstasy crashed over Genevieve over and over and over again as his shadows pumped in and out of her, wringing out every last bit of breath she had to give.

When she finally started to come back down, the inky magic dissipated like smoke, and Rowin replaced their hold on her ankles with his hand, gently massaging the sting of their grip from her skin. Her chest heaved as she tried to catch her breath. Tried to form a single coherent thought.

When he moved to lie back down by her side, still fully clothed, she could feel the hardness of his arousal against her hip as he reached over to massage her wrists next.

"Are you alright?" he asked.

She turned her face toward him. Her eyes still a bit unfocused. Dazed.

His lips curled into a smug smile, and she glared.

"You're much too proud of yourself," she muttered.

"And you're much too satisfied to be complaining," he retorted.

She glanced away from him. He was right. She was *much* too

satisfied for something that was supposed to be *just fucking*. He might be able to switch the character he was playing on and off, in and out of this bed, but she suddenly had a feeling that no one else would ever be able to make her feel that incredible ever again. And that was a very dangerous feeling.

I will not let him ruin me.

"I need to take a bath," she said as she sat up, ignoring how her legs felt like gelatin, and slid out of the sweltering bed. As she pulled her shirt back down and padded toward the bathroom, she heard Rowin stand from the bed himself.

She twisted to look at him with a raised brow. "Where are you going?"

He pushed past her and went right for the black claw-foot tub that took up the entire back wall of the bathroom, running the water as he said, "Grave doesn't know about the opening between our rooms. But even so I won't take the risk of leaving you alone in here while you're still recovering."

She huffed. "I am not letting you watch me *bathe*."

He smirked. "It's me or Umbra. She's refused to leave your side since you rescued her, anyway."

Genevieve eyed the fox, who was, in fact, currently nuzzling her head against Genevieve's legs.

Sighing with defeat, Genevieve grumbled, "*Fine*. The fox can stay."

"Towels are under the sink. Use whatever soap you'd like," Rowin said as he left Genevieve and his Familiar alone together.

"At least look away until I'm in the tub," Genevieve said to the fox.

Umbra dipped her head as if to nod and spun in a circle to face the linen closet. Genevieve relaxed ever so slightly and turned to the tub as she unbuttoned Rowin's shirt. She peeled the garment away from her feverish skin and let it drop to the floor.

Wasting no time, she stepped into the steaming tub, sighing in pleasure as the water lapped at her skin and relaxed her aching muscles. She immediately opened one of the small vials of soap sitting on the tub's ledge and poured some of the pearlescent concoction into her palm before lathering it across her skin. As she inspected her body for any remnants of the piranhas' horrifying bites, she noted that there was not even a single scar.

Ellin is definitely my favorite.

The mental scars were still there, though.

Genevieve wasn't sure she'd ever be able to scrub the flashes of pain from a hundred little pointy teeth ripping into her flesh out of her mind. She certainly never wanted to see another fish again.

She sank deeper into the tub, until she was completely submerged, but the moment her face went under the water, the memory of being in the river with the piranhas flooded back, and panic began to claw at her chest. She let out a bubbling scream and thrashed in fear as she grasped the side of the tub to pull herself up. Before she could, however, two strong hands were there, grasping her arms and pulling her above the water.

She spluttered as she blinked away the droplets clinging to her eyelashes, her chest heaving with effort as she sucked air into her lungs, her face tight with the pain of unshed tears as she tried to keep them back.

"Genevieve, you're safe," Rowin assured her as he crouched next to her, swiping water and hair from her eyes. "I'm here. You're safe. No fish. No river. You're right here."

His words were an instant balm, as was his touch, and it only made her want to cry more. How had she let herself become so reliant on him?

She worked on settling her breathing for a minute before she could respond, and he waited patiently, his eyes never leaving her face to dip *lower*. It dawned on her then that she was still naked.

She brought her knees up to her chest, wrapping her arms tight around them as she requested, "May I please have a towel?"

He nodded, returning a few seconds later with the largest towel she'd ever seen. He unfolded it and stretched it open between himself and the tub, turning his head to the side to make her more comfortable as she stood from the water; then he wrapped the plush white fabric around her.

Once the towel was secured around her body, he offered a hand to help her out of the tub, and she accepted, sending water sloshing onto the white marble floor as she moved.

"Sorry," she said as he sighed and drained the water from the tub. "I swear I don't *mean* to always make such a mess."

He gave her a doubtful look but didn't seem too perturbed as he got more towels to clean up after her. Something about seeing him do such a mundane, domestic task made her belly warm, and she instantly spun away toward the vanity, to distract herself with her hair. She moved the corner of the towel covering the mirror to the side to see her reflection. One look at the horrifying state of her hair and she let out a piercing shriek, recovering the mirror before anyone else might catch a glimpse at the atrocity as well.

"What happened?" he questioned, appearing behind her.

She pointed to the impossible clump of knots in her brown curls. "My *hair*."

She began pulling at the strands to try to work them loose, but the more she pulled, the worse the knots became, and her stomach twisted with despair. There was no way she'd be able to get them out without cutting it, and that tragic thought made the tears she'd been keeping locked away for the last few days spill onto her cheeks.

"No, no, *no*," she cried, sniffling hopelessly as her hands began to shake.

It was all a little too much. A little too on the nose. Her emotions were a tangled mess. Her sex life was a tangled mess. Even though she'd promised there wouldn't be any strings to tangle in the first place. And now her *hair*.

Rowin's shoulders heaved with the weight of his exasperation as he brushed her hands away from the tangled tendrils and muttered, "Stabbed through the shoulder with a magic dagger and almost bleeding out: no tears. Nearly eaten by piranhas: no tears. But a few knots in your hair and—"

"Easy for you to say when you wake up every day looking like *that*," she huffed as she whirled on him.

He lifted a brow, a smirk playing on his lips as he taunted, "Like what?"

Her tears ebbed as her frustration spiked. "You know exactly *like what*. I'm not going to stand here and tell you how attractive you are when you definitely already know."

"As long as attraction is all it is." He nodded as he placed his hands on her shoulders and forced her to face the covered mirror once more. As he moved to take a fine-toothed comb out of the vanity drawer, her skin prickled at his words, the implication of them, and her anger only grew stronger.

"Because it would be so terrible if I actually enjoyed the company of my husband, wouldn't it?" she asked with a heavy dose of sarcasm, but she held her breath as she waited for his reaction.

Maybe it was the fact that she'd almost died, or the pleasure he'd given her afterward, pumping too much adrenaline in her system, but all she knew was that being around him made her feel *something*, and it wasn't just because he happened to be so sinfully handsome.

"Keep still," he told her. "And, yes, it would be terrible. For so many reasons. We're playing a game, Genevieve."

She turned toward him again, and his shadows suddenly whipped out into the air, circling around her wrists and waist to pin her back against the counter as he leaned over her with an exasperated look.

"Stop moving, or you're going to make it worse," he demanded.

She tried to shake off the hold of his shadow hands, but they wouldn't budge.

"For fuck's sake, trouble. What happened? Your mood changed before you even got out of bed—what happened? What did I do?"

"*Nothing*," she told him, her words nearly sticking in her throat. "You were—are—*ugh*. I don't know when you started to become tolerable in the last few days, but I *hate* it. I told you I wasn't the girl for this. I'm not good at pretending. I can't act like you didn't just give me the best pleasure of my life—oh, *stop grinning*." She glared as he tried to hide his smile by coughing into his fist. "This marriage is supposed to be a game, but I feel like a pawn and not a player."

"What is it you need from me?" he asked, sincerely. "Tell me and it's done."

She swallowed. The intensity in his gaze, his current proximity, and that strange, vibrating feeling of his shadows clasped around her skin—it was all too much for her to form coherent thoughts.

"I tell you that you can ask anything of me and *now* you want to be quiet?" he murmured.

"I don't think we should be intimate anymore," she whispered. "I'm not sure I can..."

Handle it, she almost said, but then Knox's earlier proposition came back to her, and she thought maybe what she actually needed to do was reframe things in her mind.

"Everything we do from here on out is for show," she decided.

"No *thanking* each other unless it's for an audience. When Knox sought me out before you found Grave attempting to murder me in the library, he made a proposition for you and me—to give his audience a little more *excitement*. So, if you're going to ruin me for all my future lovers, I at least want something out of it. I want to win Favored."

At least this way I'll have an excuse for craving his touch.

His expression went entirely smooth at her request. "If that's what you want."

She nodded and let his shadows turn her back around, giving him access to her hair once again. His shadow limbs pulled the towels away while he worked, so she could watch his progress.

"If you interrupt me again, though, you're going to have to deal with these knots on your own," he told her.

By how gentle his touch was, she knew he didn't mean it. But she didn't say another word.

It took almost an hour for Rowin, and his shadows, to smooth out her hair. Watching his shadows work was fascinating, and she thought that she also might be an unbelievable lover if she had five extra pairs of hands.

But the tenderness in which he worked made her furious, honestly. One moment it was clear she meant nothing to him, and then he took care of her like *this*? She wanted to bite him again.

When he was combing through the last few tendrils, she finally asked, "How did you get so good at that?"

He hadn't pulled too hard even once, and she was well-known in her family to be awfully tender headed.

"I used to do it for Ellin," he said. "Our mother couldn't always be around, and the rest of my brothers were too impatient."

He set the comb down on the counter and finally let her turn around again.

His eyes lingered on her face for a beat longer before he finally stepped away and admired his work. "There, you'll be perfectly presentable for dinner."

"Dinner? What time is it?"

He dug beneath his waistcoat to pull out a pocket watch, flicking open its lid to read, "Nearly five. You really didn't sleep very long."

"I must say, the worst part of nearly dying every night is the fact that it's impossible to keep track of time," she told him. "I couldn't even tell you what date it is anymore."

"The twenty-third," he supplied as he began to cover up the vanity's mirror once more.

When Genevieve froze, Rowin lifted a brow in concern.

"Tomorrow is my birthday," she realized.

"*What?*" He gave her a hard look. "Why didn't you tell me before?"

"Would you have cared before? And I do recall mentioning that you should look for a super-rare birthday gift for me."

He frowned. "I thought that was a code you were using to talk about *the cure.*"

"It was," she confirmed. "But it's also my birthday."

"Alright, well, I need to get a few things together," he said as he strode for his bedroom. "You should get dressed. For a celebration."

"What about a performance, as well?" she prompted as she followed after him.

He lifted a brow. "A performance?"

"Yes." She nodded. "Perhaps winning Favored can be my birthday gift this year."

30

QUITE PERSUASIVE

March 23

It is the eve of my birthday and I completely forgot. Right now, I'm supposed to be enjoying an opera at the Teatro Argentina back in Rome. My sister bought the tickets as a gift. And instead I decided to come to this accursed place. For the very first time in my life, I will be spending my birthday without my mother and Ophelia. There will be no celebratory andouille gumbo for dinner, no white chocolate bread pudding. If Rowin had not reminded me of the date, it might have passed without me even realizing.

Rowin has insisted that I let him and the others throw me their own sort of celebration tonight—mostly because there is no guarantee I will survive the next round of the Hunt so we can celebrate tomorrow. It's morbid, but if there's cake, I won't complain.

Apparently the Silvers have rigid family traditions when it comes to birthdays. Since his siblings have celebrated all of theirs in Hell the last few years, he's missed their festivities. He assured me that dinner will be nothing short of <u>marvelously entertaining</u>.

Of course, all that excitement pales in comparison to the fact that we will soon be ripping each other's clothes off in the hallway for all of his family and Knox's spectators to see. Hopefully whatever display we put on will be

*exciting enough to satisfy Knox's depraved audience. And
the unsatisfied craving I can't seem to shake.*

X,

Genevieve

Genevieve locked the tiny heart-shaped closure on her diary
and shoved it back at the bottom of her trunk. As she
carefully shifted her things around to cover it up, she caught a
glimpse of the book she'd taken from the library, the one with
the section on Crimson Rot, and vowed to look at it before the
next round of the Hunt. Or at least take it with her so when she
and Rowin were holed up somewhere, she'd have some sort of
entertainment.

Which meant she would need to mention to him that she
wanted to help. Even when the Hunt was over, if she managed
to keep surviving, she wanted to help.

*And speaking of things I need to mention to him . . . eventually
I'm going to have to bring up the letters that he wrote to his family,*
she thought. *As well as the envelopes from Grimm Manor . . .*

She was sure those envelopes were the ones for the letters
she'd written to Barrington . . . but what possible reason would
Rowin have for keeping them amongst his things?

She had definitely done the right thing in insisting that there
could be no more "no strings" encounters between them. It
wasn't just his unnerving ability to be caring with her in one
moment only to claim it was just sex in the next. No, it was more
than that. She had opened up to him, laid out her darkest truth
for him, but he was clearly keeping secrets from her.

"Ready, trouble?" Rowin asked from the threshold.

Genevieve startled at the sound of his voice, her nerves
buzzing with annoyance as well as anticipation of what they
were about to do. He'd left her with Umbra while he prepared

whatever it was he had in mind for her birthday celebration with the others in the dining room—right after their little *performance.*

Everyone will head to the dining room for dinner at seven sharp. Which means we need to be out there by at least a quarter till.

She was not ready. Not just for their impending act, but she still wasn't entirely dressed either.

The gown she'd chosen was the one she had told Ophelia she would wear to the opera. It was made of a teal velvet that matched her eyes, the drop-waist bodice tapering to a point just below her navel. A deep-cut sweetheart neckline showed off plenty of her décolletage, but its long sleeves restored a little modesty—voluminous at the shoulders before tapering in around her biceps and all the way down her arms. Its corset laced in the back, and she wasn't able to tie it on her own.

"Genevieve?"

"I need help," she sighed as he stepped into the room. "Can you lace this for me?"

He strode across the room to take a look at her dress, remaining silent as he began to tug at the ribbons. When she felt his fingers accidentally brush against the bare skin of her back as he wove the strings through the silk eyelets, she shivered.

"Deep breath," he directed her, and she obeyed as he pulled the ribbons taut before tying them in a neat bow.

She stepped away from him and did a small twirl. "How do I look? Overdressed?"

He didn't say anything for a long moment, his golden eyes roaming over every inch of her in a way that set those damned butterflies off in her stomach.

"No. You're not overdressed."

She made a face. That was not what she was looking for. *Perfect, gorgeous,* or *flawless* was more her speed.

"Ready?" he asked again.

Again, no, but she nodded anyway.

He seemed to realize her hesitation. "It's just you and me, trouble. Only a few days ago you *loathed* me because I'm a 'fucking brute,' remember? Just channel that passion and no one will know the difference."

She had said those things, hadn't she? But that was before everything that happened in his bed. It didn't feel right to say she *loathed* him whenever he'd made her feel quite the opposite just hours ago.

She loathed Farrow. The color of green olives. Humidity. Crows.

Rowin, she felt... vexed by. She didn't really know what box to keep him in within her mind anymore. They weren't husband and wife, not really, but they weren't friends. Were they?

"Just don't get too carried away," he reminded, cutting through her thoughts.

She scowled. "What makes you think *I'm* going to be the one to get carried away?"

He snorted, as if the notion that it would be him was ridiculous. Which sounded like a challenge to her.

As soon as Rowin led her into the foyer, he pulled her over to a dark crook between one of the pillars that bookended the entrance to the ballroom and the adjacent wall. He positioned their bodies so that she was backed up against the wall and he was leaning down over her, across from one of the enormous mirrors.

As much as she tried to remain unaffected by his proximity, the memories of his mouth on her just hours ago filled her with anticipation. She'd kissed plenty of people before—twenty-seven, to be exact—but, aside from Farrow, she had never thought about any of those kisses twice. And despite the fact that this was supposed to be *pretend*, her body had clearly still not grasped that concept. The way her heart skipped a beat as Rowin ran the tips of his fingers down her jawline and beneath her chin, to tilt her face up to his, was verifiable proof.

"Relax, trouble," he murmured right against her ear as he began to summon his shadows, curling them around their bodies, brushing them into her hair, circling them loosely around her waist. "Don't worry about whoever might be watching. Just focus on me."

She locked her gaze onto his.

"That's it," he murmured. "And remember that you can snap if you want to stop. If anything is too intense and it isn't something you're comfortable with others watching."

"Right back at you," she whispered.

He smirked. "I don't think that's something you'll have to worry about, trouble."

There was that challenge again.

The smile that curled onto her lips was innocent at first. Sweet. She settled her shoulders back into the wall behind her, lightly tilting her pelvis forward, in a way that wasn't overt, but simply her making herself comfortable. She had pinned up her curls into a loose French twist, so the only tendrils she had to twirl around her fingertips were the pieces that framed her face. She made do.

"You know what I think, Mr. Silver?" she hummed as she looked up at him through her thick lashes, tapping her index finger against her bottom lip as if she were being thoughtful. Purposefully trying to draw his eyes down to her mouth. It worked. Every time.

"What do you think?" he asked, his voice deepening ever so slightly.

"I think we should show everyone how willing you are to get

on your knees for me," she crooned, shifting her hips forward until they pressed into his a little firmer this time.

She wiggled her body back and forth, as if she were adjusting her stance, but when she saw his pupils dilate, and felt the hardness growing beneath his belt, she knew she had him exactly where she wanted him.

"You want me on my knees, trouble? Then I'll get on my knees. But first..."

He used his shadows to slip around her thighs, pulling her legs up and around his waist in one fluid movement without lifting a single one of his fingers. In fact, he placed both of his palms flat against the wall on either side of her waist, as if to prove a point that he could fluster her without even using his hands.

He leaned down to press a searing kiss against her exposed clavicle as other wisps of his shadows plunged into her hair, placing soft pressure at different points of her scalp, her temples, the sensitive hollows on the back of her neck. By the time his mouth started up the side of her throat, the ring in his lip scraping deliciously against her skin, her entire body was vibrating with desire. And when his lips got to the delicate spot behind her left ear, she felt his shadows slowly brushing up her inner thighs toward the throbbing apex between her legs. She found her body writhing closer to his. Her nipples were peaked, dying for friction. Her arousal soaked through her underwear as her core searched for the pressure it craved. He ground the hardened length within his trousers right into that sensitive bundle of nerves beneath her skirts, and in the same beat he tightened a collar of shadows around her neck, making her choke on the heady moan that was clawing its way out of her throat.

"*Fuck*," she choked out, practically panting as she felt him smile against her cheek.

"Quiet," he ordered as his shadows squeezed a bit tighter around her throat to emphasize his words.

"I'm being as quiet—"

His shadows tightened in punishment at her disobedience, and she whimpered, wishing that they would tighten in *other* places as well. She'd never felt so many overwhelming sensations in her entire life, and she needed *more*.

She dug her fingernails into his shoulders as his mouth shifted down to her jaw, pressing kisses there as he ground himself forward once again. His shadows climbed even higher beneath her skirts, brushing over her underwear with a feather-light touch. She accidentally let out another moan, and all the pressure he'd been giving her pulled away except for the punishing squeeze around her throat.

She'd had enough teasing.

She gripped the front of his shirt and ripped his mouth up to hers, their lips crashing together with hunger. As their tongues tangled together, her hands slipped up to his hair, twisting the longer tendrils around her fingers and tugging as payback for his teasing. He tasted just like the honey in his scent. He grunted with pleasure, and she swallowed the sound, pulling harder as his body responded with enthusiasm, grinding her further into the wall. When he pulled back ever so slightly to let them both breathe, she bit onto the little gold hoop in his lip and gently tugged on it with her teeth.

By the way that every muscle in his body tightened, and the curse he let slip out of his mouth, she guessed he had enjoyed that.

She giggled, and he recaptured her mouth with his, muffling the sound as he finally, *finally*, put his hands on her. One hand began to hike her skirts up to her hip while the other splayed on the side of her face to angle her mouth into a better position for him to deepen the kiss. The muscles in her stomach tightened the closer his hand got to the source of her arousal, and it took all her self-control not to *beg* him to touch her there.

When she pulled back to gulp down another shaky breath, his lips didn't miss a beat, trailing over her cheek until they were at her ear, whispering, "I . . . I've always been right about you, you know. You're going to be nothing but trouble for me."

"It's time for you to get on your knees," was all she managed to say.

He steadied her on her feet and did exactly that. And she'd be lying if she said it wasn't the most incredible sight she'd ever seen.

He slowly pushed up her skirts, raising them to her navel as he placed a kiss to her inner thigh.

"Are you sure—" he began.

But the rest of his words were cut off as someone cleared their throat, and that was the moment Genevieve realized the ring around her finger was *burning*. The two of them whipped their heads to the side to find Ellin, who looked intensely disturbed, and Sevin, who was grinning around the sucker in his mouth. And just behind them? Grave. A look of utter disgust on his face.

Genevieve scowled right back at the man. As if he had any right to judge her.

"Happy birthday, indeed," Sevin said before giving their performance a slow clap and strutting away.

Rowin untangled himself from Genevieve while Ellin remained planted in place, letting Genevieve fix her skirts as he eyed his sister warily.

"Interesting," Ellin told Rowin, a knowing smile playing on her lips. Genevieve wasn't sure what that meant.

When his siblings finally disappeared in the direction of the dining room, Rowin turned back to Genevieve with an approving dip of his chin.

"Good job, trouble," he muttered before following after the others.

As she watched him walk away, without a single backward glance, she realized he'd been absolutely right—she'd gotten carried away. And she wanted nothing more than to do it again.

31

TRADITIONS

The dining room table had been decorated with a centerpiece of pink and gold roses. Every chair was set with matching plates, and a feast of vibrant, mouthwatering food stretched across the center. Pink and gold silk hung from every wall, covering all the room's mirrors.

"We've put on enough of a show during the first two rounds. I think we deserve a break," Rowin told her when she mentioned that last little detail.

Genevieve took her place next to him at the table, across from a very amused Sevin. Before Sevin could tease her about the scene he'd interrupted in the hallway, however, Remi arrived, and everyone immediately turned their attentions on Rowin's twin. Since Remi hadn't managed to eliminate anyone during his turn, it apparently meant he'd have to deal with his siblings' ridicule for the remainder of the night. And though he looked like he'd rather be anywhere else, he stayed put—as far away from Rowin as he could get.

When everyone was present, Covin trickling in last, the festivities finally began. And it probably should have been unsurprising that the Silver family's birthday traditions were pure *chaos*.

"Shouldn't *I* get to decide how we celebrate?" Genevieve asked the others as they bickered over where to start.

"If you're going to be a Silver, sweetheart, you're going to have to deal with the fact that birthdays are a family affair," Sevin reasoned. "We celebrate as if it is *all* of our birthdays."

She crossed her arms. "Because?"

"Because otherwise someone would pitch a fit and unleash a pack of Hellhounds in the house," Rowin said with a pointed look at Sevin and Covin. "It's easier if you just let them do what they'd like."

She sighed. "Alright then. What's first?"

It started with the birthday ham.

In choosing who received the honor of carving it, all of them stood around the table and passed the hulking piece of pork around like a game of hot potato until everyone was eliminated except for Covin. Genevieve was eliminated after round one when she dropped it—to many groans—because she refused to smell like *ham* for the rest of the night. She also refused to eat the ham afterward because, well, she had *dropped it on the ground*. Honestly.

After dinner—which was quite good, despite how much she missed her mother's gumbo—Barrington arrived, a small box with a pink bow in his hand.

"Children," he greeted the others before nodding at Genevieve and handing her the present. "It's only chocolates. Your mother's favorites. Happy birthday, dear girl. Though I must admit the timing of your birth is quite unfortunate for me."

"Why?" she wondered as she set the gift aside, trying not to think about them being her *mother's favorites*.

"Because every time we celebrate a birthday, Father gets a knife in his back as a gift to all of us," Covin explained as Barrington's expression grew taut. "You're a Silver now. So it counts."

Genevieve was just about to ask if Covin was kidding when

Grave reappeared from the kitchen with seven large knives in his hand.

"Hell," she gaped as Rowin fought a smile at her shock.

"Alright, best secret gets to go first," Sevin announced. "Ellin got proposed to by Gareth Serpentine at the masquerade."

Ellin's face turned pink as everyone whipped their heads to her. "Sevington Silver, you little fucking *gossip*. Who told you that?"

Sevin grinned. "I don't give away my sources."

"Our baby sister is getting hitched next!" Covin raised his glass of wine.

"I didn't say yes, you ass," Ellin huffed.

"Why not? The Serpentines are one of the most powerful Demon clans in Hell," Remi chimed in from where he was leaning against the wall. "Maybe if you married one, you could try for the loophole next year."

"I'm not joining that family. They're archaic. They have traditions that make ours look normal," Ellin answered Remi. "Covin ought to know—he's been fucking Nessa Serpentine for a while now."

They all turned to Covin in shock, and Genevieve was sure she'd have the same sort of expression on her face if she knew who they were talking about.

Ellin grinned. "I've been saving that one for a while."

"*Nessa?*" Barrington glared at him. "Covington, do you know what the Serpentines would do to you if they knew you—"

"I'm aware, Father, thank you," Covin bit out.

"See? Archaic," Ellin echoed. "Gareth could fuck anyone and they wouldn't bat an eye."

"Gareth is not going to inherit the Serpentine empire. Nobody cares about anything he does," said Sevin.

"Whatever," Ellin muttered.

"Get on with your secret, Covin," Rowin prompted, and Genevieve glanced over to see his leg bouncing beneath the table impatiently.

"Grave stopped visiting Mother months ago," Covin declared.

Grave's face turned murderous as his eyes shifted to Covin. "I knew you followed me, you fucking bastard."

"I've been meaning to discuss that with you," Barrington said to his eldest son.

"As if I give a shit about what you might have to say," Grave snarled at his father before shifting his gaze back to Sevin. "Remi's the one who stole your stash of blood, Sevin."

"*I knew it*," Sevin exclaimed as he lunged for Remi and nailed him in the shoulder with his fist. "Where did you put it?"

"Don't bother," Grave continued. "He traded it for Demon's Breath."

"Remi," Ellin chastised. "Aren't you a bit old for such dull recreational drugs?"

"Yeah, don't be a baby, get into the hard stuff," Covin goaded.

"The Demon's Breath wasn't for me," Remi told them.

"For a friend, right?" Sevin laughed.

Remi didn't deign to respond further.

"Remi? Secret?" Ellin urged.

"Pass," Remi said, tone thick with boredom now.

"Alright, Rowin? Genevieve?" Ellin moved on.

"No, thanks," Genevieve blurted at the same time that Rowin revealed, "I killed Cedric Wrathblade at the masquerade, and Sevin helped me get rid of the body."

Sevin huffed. "I had a feeling you were going to pull that one out."

Grave choked on his wine, and Barrington nearly turned purple. Ellin, however, looked elated.

"Rowin has my vote," she said.

"You did *what?*" Barrington shouted at his sons.

Sevin shrugged. "Believe me, he deserved it."

"Messing with a Daemonica legacy is fucking asking for trouble," Barrington growled. "And a Wrathblade? Did you both lose your fucking minds?"

"We dumped the body in the middle of a bunch of high Vampires," Rowin said. "If anyone hears about it, they'll think Cedric got in over his head during initiation and the vamps got carried away."

As Barrington launched into a string of curses and the others began to vote for who deserved the title of Best Secret, Genevieve leaned over to hiss at Rowin, "You killed him because he was going to hurt me?"

"He touched my wife without permission," he bit out. "I'd have killed him for less than that. Whatever the risks of turning Daemonica against me."

"What *is* Daemonica?" she asked.

"A prestigious secret society for Demons," Ellin inserted. "Like one of those university clubs, with ominous cloaks and a special handshake. They're pricks, but they throw the most incredible parties. Sevin has always wanted to join."

"*Why?*" Genevieve swung her gaze to Sevin.

"Did you not hear the bit about the parties?" Sevin grinned, but it didn't quite reach his eyes. She thought back to how he'd stayed on the sidelines at the masquerade and couldn't help but think there was something much deeper going on with Sevin than anyone in this room knew.

"Alright, Rowin," Barrington said, voice tight. "Looks like you win this year."

Rowin grinned as he stood from his chair and walked over to the knives, which Grave had neatly laid in the middle of the table. Genevieve watched with rapt curiosity as Rowin picked up one of the blades and walked over to his father. She decided this was not going in a very fun direction.

"Happy fucking birthday, Mrs. Silver," Rowin said to her before spearing the knife right into Barrington's ribs.

Genevieve gasped, but Barrington stayed upright with barely more than a flinch. An immortal's endurance never failed to amaze her.

Sevin laughed in delight. "Welcome to the family, Vivi. Don't forget to make a wish for each knife."

Rowin returned to her side as the others took their turns with the knives. Barrington gritted his teeth against each one but did not cower away or protest. When there was only one left, Covin offered it in Genevieve's direction.

"Absolutely fucking not," she said.

"Dibs!" Sevin called immediately.

Once the final blow was struck, Barrington muttered, "Happy birthday, Genevieve."

Then he pulled the knives from his wounds and left the room, leaving a trail of blood in his wake.

All Genevieve could think to say was, "I do not understand this family."

But in another life, I think I might have really loved to be a part of it.

"He's the reason we're trapped in this fucking game," Ellin explained with a shrug. "It's only fair that he suffers occasionally."

"Alright, who's ready for cake?" Sevin asked.

An hour later, Genevieve and Rowin went back to his room, to change and rest before the next round of the Hunt. He stripped his bed of its old sheets as she took the pins from her disheveled hair.

"Do you need help with those?" Rowin asked when he was done, brow raised at the way she was now struggling to reach for the laces behind her back.

She paused. "Is this why you laced them so tight? So you'd get to unlace them as well?"

There was no hint of amusement in his face as he motioned for her to turn around, however, and she bit her lip, unsure how to read his mood. She felt him slowly pull on one of the laces until the knot came undone, then meticulously unweave them until the corset loosened enough for her to breathe properly again.

"Two truths and a lie?" he asked.

She turned, surprised at the suggestion coming from him. "Okay."

"Did you enjoy yourself? What's been your favorite birthday so far? What was the best moment of the night?"

"It was...interesting," she said in response to the first question. "A far cry from birthdays at home. My mom would make my favorite meal while I played games with Ophie. My favorite birthday was probably my thirteenth. That was the year my mother started letting me go into town by myself."

As he listened, he unbuttoned his waistcoat, shrugging it off and folding it atop the dresser. Next went his dress shoes and cravat.

"And the best part of the night..." She trailed off as she tried to focus on anything but him undressing.

"Mm-hmm?" he asked as he began unbuttoning his shirt.

Having your mouth on me. Hands down.

"Watching Covin swallow a knife as long as my forearm," she lied.

That incident had actually been extremely stressful and not at all something she cared to see again.

"His usual party trick," Rowin said. But from the way he watched her, she could tell he knew that she wasn't telling the truth. To his credit, he let it go.

"Your turn," he tossed back.

"Do you really hate your father as much as you all seem to?" she started.

She didn't have the guts for her other question quite yet.

"It's...not that black and white," he admitted. "But sometimes I do. Not because he made a rushed mistake in a moment he feared for his wife's life, but because he can't even be bothered to be *around*. He's too ashamed of what he's forced us into. But mistake or not, when you lock your family into a curse like the Hunt, you should at least look them in the eyes more than twice a year."

Genevieve nodded. "My mother never told us about our father—how she met him in Phantasma and the curses that broke our family apart—or the debt she'd accrued on our family's home. And then she died and just left us here to deal with it alone. She abandoned us, left me completely unprepared for life."

Rowin crossed his arms over his exposed chest and leaned back against the dresser in contemplation. "It's never easy to realize that the people who are supposed to protect us are the ones who can create the deepest scars."

Genevieve sighed. That was something she'd tried to come to terms with for a very long time.

"I think that's why I was still so determined to come inside despite your warnings," she admitted to him. "I wanted to find others like me. And I wanted to meet your father because I thought his proximity to my mother could give me some insight on why she...did what she did. But instead I found out—"

"He's equally as fucked up?" Rowin finished.

"Yup," she said, popping the "P" at the end of the word. She tried to find her way back to a lighter mood. "How long do we have until midnight?"

"Less than an hour," he told her.

"I'm going to change. There's no way I'll be able to run in this dress." She pointed down at herself.

"Genevieve?"

She flicked her eyes back to him. "Yes?"

"You still have two more questions."

And I was avoiding them, thank you very much.

"I'm not sure I have anything else to ask tonight," she said instead, a bit too casually.

"Lie. You're a never-ending well of questions, Genevieve Grimm," he stated.

She shrugged. "Maybe the well has run dry."

She tried to step by him. He blocked her.

"You're being annoying," she huffed.

"And you're not playing the game right," he shot back. "You want us to build trust? Then ask me a question. What is it?"

Why aren't you having as hard of a time with just fucking as I am? she thought, but the one she had the nerve to actually say was, "Why do you have letters from Grimm Manor hidden in your desk? My letters."

He froze at the question, but before he could answer, the stroke of midnight came.

ROUND THREE OF THE HUNT

32

REFLECTIONS

The chimes of Enchantra's gilded clock had quickly become synonymous with Hell in Genevieve's mind.

Rowin's jaw was still clenched by the time they made it downstairs to the choosing ceremony. Which was barely in the nick of time.

Knox blinked into the room.

"I heard it was someone's birthday," the Devil said and grinned over at Genevieve. "I hope you made a wish, Mrs. Silver."

"Well, my wish was to never have to see your face again, so this is quite disappointing," Genevieve said.

Knox's smile tightened as Sevin and Covin laughed. Rowin, however, was refusing to look at her.

Ellin cleared her throat. "I have a token to redeem, Knox."

Knox flicked his eyes from Ellin to Rowin and back, but he said nothing as Ellin pulled out the crimson fish. The one Genevieve and Umbra had almost died to retrieve. Only now it was no longer a fish. It had transformed into some sort of palm-size gemstone in the shape of a fish.

Ellin tossed the token over to Knox, who plucked it out of the air.

"Ellin has immunity this round," he announced. "Now, for the rest of you..."

He lifted the Hunting Blade into the air as per the ceremony she'd grown accustomed to, and this time the blade went straight toward Sevin, who grinned.

Knox waved him on. "Game?"

"Solitary confinement," Sevin answered before looking over to Genevieve with a wink. "Consider this my birthday gift, Vivi. You're welcome."

"Well, I'll see you assholes later." Ellin yawned as she strolled away. "I'm going to take a very long bubble bath. So don't even *think* about barging into my room."

Everyone made to leave, apart from Sevin, who had to wait ten minutes before pursuing them. Rowin led Genevieve silently toward the stairs. At the top, Umbra was waiting for them.

"Solitary confinement?" she finally asked. "That means we have to choose one room and stay there, right?"

It was one of the different game types that he had explained to her before their wedding. Now, as he guided her down the corridor of doors, he didn't bother to answer.

"You're being a baby," she muttered under her breath as he went to open a door to their left.

Before he could, however, she slid between him and the entrance and said, "I am not going in there until you speak to me."

"Genevieve, we have eight minutes to choose a place to hide," he warned.

"Wow. You give up on the silent treatment very easily," she commented. "You should have seen how long my mother could go on with it."

He glowered at her before grasping onto her hand and pulling her down the hallway, into the upstairs powder room where he'd found her and Cedric during the masquerade.

As he closed the door, she asked, "Does this mean we're going to have to be stuck in here for this entire round?"

"The magic doesn't lock us in until our lead time is up," he told her, using a hand towel to cover the mirror over the vanity.

He turned to her and crossed his arms. "You went through my things."

"Well, yes, I told you that before," she reminded him.

"You went through them *again*," he clarified.

"Maybe," she admitted, twisting his signet around her finger.

"Those letters weren't for you to see," he admonished, though the hint of guilt in his own eyes took any heat out of his words. "Have you known about the hex this entire time?"

The hex. Did he mean...

"Wait, wait, wait," she said, a bit breathless now. "You're talking about the hex on the invitation that *brought me here*? Those fucking crows were *your* doing?"

She remembered a fleeting thought she'd had when she first found the letters to his siblings, how the handwriting there seemed oddly familiar...

The invitation.

"*You're* the one who invited me here?" she realized.

"I said that you were my burden to bear," he reasoned. "Because of the way you came here. I never meant for *this* to happen. My father was never going to read the letters, Genevieve, and even if he did, he would have recognized that the handwriting wasn't your mother's. It was the first thing I checked as well. But I've been trying for so long to find people who could help me find the cure. And even if I realized it wasn't Tessie writing to me, I thought maybe Ophelia..."

The world tilted around Genevieve, and she stumbled back a step from him. "Ophelia?"

"I assumed—"

"*Of course* that invitation was intended for Ophelia." Genevieve laughed. "Of course. Because not even a *curse* could have been meant for me."

"Genevieve, I didn't know you *existed*," he argued. "Do you have any idea how grateful I am that it was you that walked through that door and—"

"No," she interrupted. "Don't do that. Don't lie to me. You wanted me to go. You were pissed that I disobeyed your demands to leave."

"Yes, I was," he agreed. "Until I met you. You're stubborn, and hardheaded, and determined, and you really might be my one shot of getting free from this game. I sent that invitation because I'm trying to save my family. I can't apologize for that."

"Then you should at least apologize for keeping it a secret," she told him. "*You're* the one who talks about building trust, and yet you continue to keep secrets from me."

"I know," he said. "But for so long I have been living in this Hell. Either completely alone or with my family trying to kill me. And clearly that has hindered my ability to just start trusting someone no matter how much I'm trying to. You might find it easy to talk to me about anything but—"

"It only seems easy because, somehow, I've started to *like* you, Rowin!" she told him. "Do you know how much of a travesty that is? When the last time I opened my heart to someone he…he…"

"*I am not him*," Rowin snarled. "I want to find him and flay all the flesh from his body and set *him* on fire for what he did to you. Don't ever compare me to him."

She swallowed at the conviction in his voice, the truth. Still, she said, "You're not him. But when I fell in love with him, do you think he seemed like the person he turned out to be? You told me not to trust my heart here so all I have is to trust your actions, what you say to me—what you omit. I've given you trust, my marriage vows, my loyalty in this game. What have you given me in return? And don't you *dare* say anything to do with sex."

The look he gave her was quite exasperated, but he only said, "You're right."

She wasn't expecting that.

"I should have found time to tell you that I wrote the invitation. I probably should have tried harder to make you leave in the first place. But I need you to keep trying to trust me. Another chance?"

She swallowed. He sounded sincere.

"We need to get back to the enchanted rooms," he reminded her now. "Come on."

He led her back to the corridor and over to the same room he had been ready to choose earlier. And when he pulled the door open and ushered her inside, her jaw dropped at the scene around them.

A gloomy forest, made entirely of twisting black trees and... mirrors.

Fantastic.

The looking glasses were everywhere she glanced, reflecting back twenty different versions of her. None of them quite *right*. The trees had tangled branches that drooped all the way to the ground. Their limbs, holding gray and ebony leaves the size of her head, reminded her of the live oaks back home. Easy to climb, dripping with spongy Spanish moss.

Rowin closed the door behind them as she padded across the carpet of leaves to approach a particularly large mirror straight ahead. The version of her that watched from its reflection was eerie. In the mirror, she wore the same white gown, had her exact same coloring, face, and hair, but her eyes... were entirely black. No irises or pupils or whites to be seen. Just depthless darkness.

Rowin approached behind her, and she saw his gaze had become the same. An unblinking abyss. She shuddered.

"What do you think these are all about?" she whispered to him just as Umbra appeared between their feet, tilting her head at the mirror as if she couldn't figure out what it was.

If it were possible, she found the fox's gaze even more unsettling than theirs. Probably because the black of her reflected eyes blended in with her shadowy coat a little too well.

Umbra chirped and skittered away from the oculus. Genevieve followed, moving deeper into the forest, passing reflections on every side. They reminded her of the Ghosts she'd seen in Phantasma. Solid but clearly unnatural. There was a small oval mirror embedded in one of the tree trunks that showed her with white hair and a black gown. A square one wedged in the crook of a branch that made her eyes golden like Rowin's. One showed her with horns crowning her head.

But the one that made her stop in her tracks showed a reflection that changed her eyes to an icy, all-too-familiar color. Grimm Blue.

She approached the mirror, her fingertips reaching up to her face and gently brushing beneath her haunting eyes. She had never realized how much she looked like her sister, not even when Ophelia's gaze had been the same shade of cerulean as her own, but she saw it now. How alike they really were. The future she might have had if she had been the eldest instead of Ophie.

Genevieve was hit by a wave of gratitude toward her sister— for being the model daughter she never could have been. She wondered sometimes whether the pressure Ophelia had been under would have simply crushed her.

I ought to get Ophie a very nice present if I see her again.

If? No. When. Because she *was* going to get out of here. Even if Rowin was a cagey pain in the ass, she was going to drag him to the finish line like he dragged her down the aisle.

The sound of a twig snapping underfoot made her flinch, but when she spun, she saw it was only Rowin.

"How do you think we find a token here?" she wondered as he strode closer.

He shrugged. "I'd say look for something out of place in one of the mirrors, but there must be a thousand here."

"And they all contain something strange," she pointed out.

He nodded. "I told Umbra to watch the entrance. She'll let me know if Sevin shows up. We might as well settle in. We've got twelve hours to kill."

Their eyes locked at that statement, Sevin's *you're welcome* echoing in the back of her mind as Rowin's gaze heated. It made her want to tell him to forget their fight, to ask him to kiss her again and distract her from all the complicated feelings she couldn't seem to stop from bubbling to the surface every other minute. On the other hand she still couldn't decide where they stood, if she trusted him, if it even mattered whether she did or not, because at the end of the day they were stuck playing together either way.

She sighed and moved to sit against the trunk of a tree. Her thoughts were an absolute mess.

Rowin remained standing, shifting on his feet, as if he were waiting for her to tell him that it was okay for him to come closer.

"Rowin?"

"Yes?"

"Did you mean it? When you said that you wanted me to give you another chance to trust you?" she asked.

"Yes," he said. No hesitation.

"Then tell me everything there is to know about Crimson Rot," she said, patting the spot next to her. "I want to understand how it has affected your mother."

He had refused to talk about anything to do with his mother before, but if he wanted her trust, he'd have to start somewhere.

He nodded. "Alright."

Sitting next to her, his side pressed along hers, he began. She eyed the reflection in the mirror across from them. It was the largest one she'd seen yet. Stretching up nearly six feet and framed with baroque molding that reminded her of Enchantra's gates. The differences in their reflections were instantly apparent, and Genevieve rolled her eyes at the clear game Knox's enchantment was playing. They were dressed in their exact attire from the masquerade ball. Rowin as a dark fox, she a gilded rabbit.

And perhaps it should have been the most harrowing reflection of all. The sly fox sitting right next to the wide-eyed hare. The hare so trusting in his presence.

But Genevieve couldn't help but think that a real fox would give pursuit. Instead of setting a glittering trap and luring her in, then burning everything she was starting to believe to ashes.

33

Fox Says

"That's another point for me," Genevieve bragged as her tiny gray pebble bounced into place next to a large, flat stone.

Rowin grunted at his fourth consecutive loss. He claimed it was because he'd never played bocce before—not that this was a very faithful version of the game, given their limited resources—but, really, he just didn't understand what throwing *softly* meant.

They'd spent the first couple of hours going over everything there was to know about Crimson Rot. He'd told her all the rumors there were of its origin. He'd explained how the Rot slowly infused itself with a Demon's blood so that their very life force was what killed them—rotting them from the inside out. The temporary fix that Knox administered to his mother after the Hunt cleaned the Rot out of her system, but over the course of a year it would consume her once again.

His willingness, and patience, in answering all her questions had slowly settled whatever lingering skepticism she had about his omittance of the hex. It helped that he had tried to get her to leave Enchantra when she first arrived and that he had convinced Ellin to save her life *several* times. It was also hard to remain upset with him when she knew what it was like to feel the need to keep so many secrets. How many had she kept from Ophelia over the years? How many was she *still* keeping?

After the heaviness of their conversation, Genevieve thought that playing a game might help to lift the mood.

"Fuck." Rowin's curse cut through her thoughts as he threw his next pebble.

She tried to hold in her giggle this time. "You're truly *terrible* at this game."

"You're being a very sore winner," he admonished as he dropped the rest of his pebbles to the ground. "Let's play something else."

"You are *so* competitive," she teased. "But fine. What game do *you* want to play? Or would you rather do something . . . else?"

A wicked gleam entered his golden gaze at that question. "Whatever are you implying, Mrs. Silver?"

Genevieve glanced around them. "Well, it seems to me that perhaps this would be the perfect place for our audience to get to see how well we . . . work together."

The heat in his gaze boiled over now, and she had a feeling whatever sort of challenge she'd just invoked for this next performance was not going to be as tame as the last.

"Are you sure?" he implored as he brushed a strand of her hair out of her face. "You want to show them everything?"

"Yes," she agreed. The word firm. Confident.

Truth be told, Genevieve hadn't ever thought about whether she'd mind such a thing. Of course she knew they had already put on quite the show for Knox's spectators, but they'd been fully clothed the entire time. Regardless, Genevieve had always enjoyed sex and expressing her sexuality. Because why shouldn't she? The masqueraders certainly hadn't had any qualms about their sexual endeavors being on display for all to see, so Genevieve couldn't imagine shocking any of them.

With the hungry way Rowin was currently looking at her, she wasn't thinking about anyone else anyway.

"Have you ever played Fox Says?" he asked as he began circling where she stood.

She crossed her arms. "Isn't that game a bit juvenile?"

"Not the way we're going to play," he murmured.

His masked figure in the large mirror ahead of them mimicked his prowling movements. A fox indeed.

She met Rowin's gaze as she lifted her chin and said, "Show me."

Rowin's grin widened. "Fox says remove your dress."

Her blood began to heat.

Ah, so we're cutting right to the chase.

He continued circling her, his hands clasped behind his back as he observed every little movement she made. She reached up to untie the bow at her gown's collar, pulling the ribbon until it came loose. Then she began slowly unbuttoning each satin-covered button that ran in a line down to her navel. When the gossamer dress pooled onto the forest floor at her feet, she couldn't even be bothered to care she was ruining yet another favorite article of clothing. Not when the expression on his face promised it would be worth it.

"Now, remove the rest," he told her.

She didn't budge, a smirk playing on her lips as she raised a brow. She wasn't new to the game. He grinned.

"*Fox says,*" he allowed.

She removed her camisole and underwear then, and, once again, she was completely nude while he remained fully dressed. Such a thing might have felt like a power imbalance. But by the way Rowin's body instantly reacted to the sight of her, bare, she knew she held the power between them despite the illusion that he tried to maintain.

He stepped square in front of her now and gently nudged her stance wider with his foot. She obliged despite the lack of verbal direction.

"Fox says"—he leaned down until his mouth was near her ear, the metal of his piercing cool against her heated skin and making her shiver—"put a finger inside that beautiful pussy for me."

She was instantly wet. It should not have come as a surprise that a being of Hell could have such a perfectly sinful mouth, but the way he could elicit such a potent reaction from her with only a few words shocked her every time.

She did as he said, reaching down to pump a finger inside of herself, once, twice, before sliding it out to draw a slick circle against the tight, throbbing bundle of nerves between her legs—

"I don't think so," he chided, hand snapping out to grasp her wrist. "I didn't say to touch yourself *there*. If you don't play correctly, you're going to get punished."

"That only makes me want to do it more," she breathed.

He made a low, guttural sound deep in his throat before warning, "Behave, trouble, or our little game won't last long enough for either of us to get what we want."

She stuck her tongue out at the order, and to her surprise he *bit* it. Hard. She squeaked in shock as she ripped it back from between his teeth, sucking the sting out of it as he grinned.

"Behave," he warned again.

Her body was practically vibrating with how badly she wanted to throttle him and to fuck him then and there. He had let go of her wrist, and she returned to her task, plunging a finger inside herself, gasping at how wet she already was.

"Good," he murmured. "Now, taste yourself."

She didn't hesitate, pulling her finger back out and bringing it to her mouth, sucking away her glistening arousal with a moan.

A low rumble of laughter sounded in his chest, and she froze, realizing her mistake. He didn't say *Fox says.*

He slowly lowered himself to his knees before her. "You really are a glutton for punishment, aren't you?"

She wasn't sure if she should tell him that watching him get on his knees was the opposite of a punishment. A second later, however, and the tip of his tongue was drawing a slow, teasing circle around her clit, and every other thought emptied from her head.

She plunged her hands into his hair, needing something to hold herself steady as he nibbled and sucked at her. Her legs began to shake as his mouth moved against her, his tongue expertly penetrating her in a way that made her eyes roll to the back of her head. It took only a moment for her to reach the edge of her climax, and she tightened her hands in his hair as she prepared to crash over—

—and then he stopped.

He pulled away and stood, licking his lips as he smirked at her enraged expression. "Punishment, remember?"

"This isn't punishment, it's *torture*," she snarled.

He ignored her as he ordered, "Fox says get on your knees."

She crossed her arms, refusing to move as he walked around behind her, looking at her through their masked reflections. She wondered how many other pairs of eyes were on them in this moment, if any of Rowin's admirers from the ball were amongst them, watching as she was about to get what so many had likely craved for years.

But he's mine.

Her partner. Her lover. Her husband.

He stepped forward to press the length of his body against the back of hers now, his cock hard against her lower back through his trousers, and she watched in the mirror as he reached over to clasp a hand around her throat. He pressed kisses across her shoulder as his hand tightened around her neck with authority.

"You're being a brat, again," he murmured against her skin. "You can either listen or tell me to stop."

She didn't want to listen. She also didn't want him to stop. Ever. And the war of those two facts battled it out inside her before she finally, slowly, knelt to the ground. He unwrapped his hand from her throat as she went, remaining standing as she spread her knees far enough apart that he could access her sex from behind. She watched her mouth part in the mirror, her chest heave, as he unbuttoned his pants and pushed them down just far enough on his hips to release his thick length. The chiseled muscles of his abdomen flexed as he pumped his cock into his fist, once, twice, three times, the tattoos of his chest and stomach writhing with his movements. That was when she noticed the golden hoop he had pierced through the head of his cock.

Holy shit.

When he finally knelt, behind her, the tip of him nudging at her entrance, the metal of his piercing made her gasp as he wrapped one arm across her stomach, reaching up to pinch one of her taut nipples while his other hand wrapped her hair around his knuckles so he could angle her face to the side. He captured her mouth in a scorching kiss as he tugged roughly on her curls, eliciting a loud moan from her throat.

He broke the kiss and said, "Let's play a new game now. The Quiet Game."

She whimpered as the hand on her breast switched sides, rolling the neglected rosy bud between his thumb and forefinger until she nearly came from the fusion of that pain and pleasure alone. He released her hair, draping it over her shoulder, and freed his hand to position himself at her entrance.

"Ready?" he asked. "For everything?"

She nodded eagerly. *Yes. Please.*

He thrust forward, and she had to bite down on her cry before she got herself punished again. He was large and she was tight, and it took a bit of adjusting before he was able to pump the full length of himself into her. He pressed an encouraging kiss to her temple as she took his strides without fuss, and she splayed a hand over her own tummy to feel the movement of him inside her. He reached his own hand between her thighs to draw lazy circles over her clit, and the moment he touched the slick bundle of nerves, she accidentally let out a mewl of pleasure.

He sighed and shook his head. "That wasn't very quiet, trouble."

He removed his fingers from between her thighs and, in one fluid motion, switched her position on his cock. Pressing her forward until her forehead was against the ground with her back arched up in the air, he thrusted into her relentlessly. She dug her fingers into the earth, dirt wedging itself beneath her pristine fingernails as she tried as hard as she could not to make another sound. When he gripped painfully onto her waist for more control, she nearly lost that battle. She loved the little stings of pain that were chased away by the pleasure.

After a long minute of nothing except his grunts of satisfaction, his fingertips gripping onto her for dear life, and the thunder of their hearts, he finally pulled her up once again. One of his hands immediately went back to the aching bundle of nerves at her core, making up for the last minute of neglect and wringing an orgasm out of her in an embarrassingly short amount of time. He muffled his smug laugh against her shoulder as she nearly convulsed with the effort of swallowing the scream of ecstasy trying to erupt from her throat.

When it was over, she slumped back against him, but he didn't stop. Only continued his lazy circles over her clit, the steady rhythm of his attentions almost agonizing now. Through heavy eyelids she watched him thrust into her in the mirror, over and over and over again, her breasts bouncing with the effort. She traced her gaze over the flushed, red marks his fingertips had left against her hips, the sight of them sending another flood of wetness between her legs. An inhuman sound of pleasure came from his mouth. His gaze met hers through the glassy surface, and she swore she'd never been so turned on by a sight in her life than by the two of them admiring their moving bodies together.

"This time," he said gruffly, his voice so thick with lust it was barely recognizable, "you're allowed to say my name."

Without warning, he pinched her clit, hard, and she did in fact scream his name, her voice hoarse from choking down her last cry. As she rode the rest of her climax, he pulled out of her in one fluid motion, his fist reaching between them to pump himself to completion, but she didn't give him the chance. She twisted around, dropping to her knees and sucking him into her mouth, tasting her own arousal as his seed began to spill down her throat. He watched her in awe. When he was done, she pulled back, licking her lips as she gave him a smile.

"That was my favorite game yet," she drawled.

He brushed away dirt from her face before pulling her forward to capture her mouth in another heated kiss. She felt his hands start to massage the places he'd been holding on a little too tight, and she hummed against his lips with affection.

"I'm sorry if I left marks," he told her as he pulled back.

"Don't be," she assured. "Maybe I can leave a mark on *you* next time."

He stood now, offering a hand to help her up along with him. "As long as it doesn't involve biting," he agreed.

She pouted now. "But you're so fun to bite."

He gave her a withering look as he picked up her undergarments and handed them over.

As they both redressed, she wondered, "Do you think that will win us Favored?"

"Only one of us can win Favored," he corrected as he rebuttoned his shirt. "Knox might let us win the Hunt as a pair, but he would never give up more than one boon from his treasure trove."

"What does Sevin usually do to win?" she asked as she smoothed her hands over her gown.

The moment the words were out of her mouth, she felt the ring around her finger beginning to warm. Fast.

"Rowin—the ring!" she shouted as it grew ever hotter.

A second later, Sevin stepped out of the woods, absolutely *drenched* in black blood and grinning from ear to ear.

"Genevieve, *run*," Rowin told her.

"It's just Sevin," Genevieve reasoned, but even as she said it, she noted the wildness in Sevin's crimson eyes, so different from the usual mirth she found there.

"That's right, Vivi, it's just me," Sevin drawled. "Have you decided if you want to win?"

Genevieve swallowed as she inched back a step. "Yes."

"Good," Sevin told her sincerely. "That means you'll fight harder."

A twig snapped from somewhere behind him, and Genevieve nearly choked at the sight of an enormous silver wolf emerging from the trees, with Umbra wriggling in its jaws. So this was Sevin's Familiar. The wolf tossed Umbra to the ground, and to Genevieve's surprise the fox skittered over to her, not Rowin.

"*Genevieve, run*," Rowin ordered again.

Sevin's smile was grim. "Dante. *Sic*."

The wolf lunged forward.

34

ᴵMPOSTER

The wolf's pursuit was relentless as Genevieve tore through the forest, the sounds of Rowin and Sevin struggling against each other echoing behind her. Umbra was running parallel to her, checking behind them every so often to gauge how close Sevin's Familiar was getting to their heels.

"The trees!" Genevieve shouted to the fox. "We have to get off the ground!"

Genevieve knew she could not outrun a wolf—*especially* a paranormally altered one—by any stretch of the imagination. But she could climb a tree. Had spent many days in the limbs of the live oaks in New Orleans. She scanned the thicket around her for one that had a branch close enough to the ground for her to start.

Just ahead to the right was the perfect specimen. Its lowest branch was nearly touching the ground, gnarled and easy to use as leverage to the ones higher up. Genevieve stepped up onto its rough bark, Umbra following, the Familiar's golden eyes remaining trained on the wolf. Just as Genevieve began to pull herself up, her limbs still gelatinous from her and Rowin's poorly timed passion, she felt a sharp-toothed maw clasp around her ankle.

She shrieked in frustration and kicked wildly at the wolf, trying to make it release her leg. Umbra was there a moment later, launching her lithe form right onto the wolf's head and scratching at its eyes until it let Genevieve go with a vicious growl. Once Genevieve made it up high enough, adrenaline shooting through her veins like lightning, she peered down to search for Umbra. She did not save that little critter from piranhas to lose her now.

Thankfully, she found Umbra scrambling up the tree only a branch below. Genevieve leaned down and stretched out her arm for Umbra to cling onto, scooping the fox up into her chest as the wolf tried to climb up from below. Umbra nuzzled her cold snout against Genevieve's neck affectionately.

"Yeah, yeah," Genevieve grunted at the fox.

The wolf didn't seem to be a great climber, which Genevieve was grateful for as she tried to catch her breath, but her peace didn't last long when Sevin broke through the tree line moments later. He laughed when he spotted her standing on the branch above as he strode over to pat his Familiar on the head.

"Look at you go," Sevin called as he hopped up onto the first branch and then swung himself nimbly onto the next. He paused to glance into a mirror embedded into the trunk on his level, frowning at whatever he saw there. "This room is creepy, don't you think?"

"Yep," she answered as she pushed Umbra up onto the next branch before starting to ascend once more.

"Sweetheart, I don't think climbing higher is going to do anything for you," Sevin told her, his tone genuine.

"Where's Rowin?" she demanded.

"He'll probably be here in a minute," Sevin said conversationally as he pulled himself to the next branch. "He got away from me for two seconds, and I lost him in the shadows."

"Why are you covered in blood?" she asked, hoping to stall him while she tried to work out what to do next.

As she scanned the rest of the forest, she spotted a rather large mirror in the tree parallel to theirs, but something about the reflection made her pause.

"Oh, right," Sevin said as he looked down at himself. "I killed

Remi. Accidentally caught him a little too close to his carotid artery. Well, maybe not *accidentally*. Since you two started getting all handsy in the corridors, I figured I'd need something special to win Favored. Plus he stole my entire fucking stash of suckers."

Genevieve barely registered his words as it finally clicked what was so different about the mirror she was studying. It wasn't mimicking her movements. No, the reflection of herself was *watching* her. As if it were waiting for her. Genevieve traced the length of the branch she was standing on, seeing that it angled down toward the branch just below the mirror on the other tree, only a small gap between the two of them. One that looked close enough to jump.

Sevin said something else, but whatever it was, she didn't hear. She was already taking off; one foot in front of the other, she walked down the branch like a tightrope.

"*Hey*," Sevin shouted as he climbed up after her.

Genevieve's balance had always been better than most, aided by the fact that she wasn't as tall as her sister. She wobbled a bit as the branch tapered toward the end, but she kept going. Sevin landed on the limb behind her, jumping a few times to try to make her lose her balance. She dropped to grip onto it with her hands before she fell.

"Keep moving," Rowin's voice rang out from below.

She leaned over to peer down at the forest floor, spotting him instantly in the shadows on the ground, his jaw clenched tightly as he watched his brother behind her. She took a deep breath and began to crawl forward, the delicate fabric of her gown snagging on the branch, her hands and knees scraping painfully on the rough bark. When she glanced over her shoulder at Sevin, she saw he had his hands shoved deep in his pockets, his stride seemingly unencumbered by gravity as he made his way toward her. She lurched forward, bracing herself as she made it to the end and leaped from her branch to the next tree.

"*Climb down*," Rowin called to her, and she knew she ought to listen. To get back on solid ground where he was able to reach her. But something inside her was screaming for her to make it to the mirror she'd seen.

For all the strangeness of the other mirrors, they still reflected her own movements.

She began to climb again.

Rowin cursed. "*Damn it*, Genevieve, now is not the time to give me trouble."

Sevin laughed. "Don't listen to him, sweetheart. He secretly likes being defied. It gets him off."

"I promise that is not a secret," she told him as she heaved herself up just as Sevin jumped across.

He was only seconds away from catching her now, could probably already have caught her if he was really trying, but he didn't seem to think there was anywhere else for her to go. When she turned on the branch to fully face the mirror, her heart began to race at the spine-tingling feeling it gave her. There she was, inside the glassy surface, not a detail out of place except for the fact that the reflection seemed to have a mind of its own. Genevieve lifted her hand toward the surface—the mirror version of herself watching her actions intently but refusing to follow them—and placed her fingertips against the cool glass.

The surface rippled and she gasped, the warm feeling of magic buzzing over her skin as she pressed her hand forward—*through*—until she was completely sucked inside.

꙳

There was a high-pitched ringing in her ears.

Genevieve was standing in an eerily quiet version of the forest she'd just come from. The silence was the first thing she noticed. How there was not a single thing to sense around her. The smell of leaves and petrichor was gone, the slight breeze winding between the trees nonexistent. Even the tree she was standing on, a direct replica of the one from a moment ago, was somehow a lesser version of itself.

And then there was *her*.

The imposter made Genevieve's skin crawl. Her stare was the same cerulean as her own, but it was blank. Like there was not a single thought behind her eyes.

"Hello?" Genevieve whispered.

"Hello? Hello? Hello? Hello? Hello? Hello? Hello?" the imposter parroted.

The piercing sound in her ears became worse.

"*Stop,*" Genevieve pleaded as she plugged her ears with her fingers.

"*Stop. Stop. Stop. Stop. Stop. Stop. Stop.*"

Genevieve lunged forward, meaning to clap her hand over the imposter's mouth to make it stop talking. But the moment she touched its skin, the nightmare truly began.

She watched in horror as the imposter's exterior began to flicker in and out, revealing a monstrous shadow creature below its surface. As the replica of her own face melted away, the faceless creature made a low keening sound that made her flesh prick with terror. Its new form looked nearly transparent, like some kind of Apparition.

Time to go.

But before she could whirl back to the mirror, something crimson flashed within the monster's chest cavity, between the shadows writhing over its form.

The token.

She gulped as it solidified into a stone shaped like a black heart. This would be the second time she'd risked her life for a chance of a day's immunity from the game.

But what a great birthday gift it would be to have a day off.

Damn it.

"Here goes nothing," she muttered.

As soon as the words fell from her lips, the creature let out a monstrous howl. She gritted her teeth against the sound and dove forward, plunging her hand into its chest and feeling around until she grasped the token. The moment it was in her grip, the creature became solid once more.

The monster clawed at her face, sending a slicing pain through her right eye as her vision went completely dark on that side. She let out a cry as she ripped the token from its chest, through slimy sinew and crunching bone.

The imposter began to burn away into a cloud of billowing black smoke. Her chest heaved as she clutched at her face, her good eye blurring with tears. She found the mirror and rushed toward it, not caring that Sevin was likely waiting on the other side. She was in too much pain.

When she stepped through the portal, however, she found that she had not arrived back in the place she had left. No, she had stepped out of a completely different mirror. The one right in front of the exit that would lead her back into Enchantra's upper corridor.

"Genevieve."

She spun, still clutching her eye with one hand, her other cradling the token to her chest protectively.

"What happened?" Rowin demanded as he reached her, brushing her hand aside so he could assess her injury.

"I found the token," she sniffled as she dropped her hand away and allowed him to prod at her face.

His expression didn't give her any sign as to how bad the damage was, but by the explosive pain still radiating through her head and the almost imperceptible way his pupils tightened as he looked at her, she didn't think it was good.

"Ellin isn't going to help us this time," he told her, tone regretful. "But I'll do what I can, alright? We need to go back to my room."

"Don't we have to wait for noon to come?" she choked out. "And where is Sevin?"

"How long do you think you were gone for?" he asked, cautious.

"Minutes," she told him. "Why—?"

He winced. "You've been missing for hours here. It's already afternoon. I've been pacing this forest since you disappeared. Sevin and I were in a standoff for hours before he gave up on trying to catch me and decided to hunt the others. I tried to go after you, but as soon as you went through, the mirror went completely *black*."

A sob caught in her throat, her chest tight as she tried to slow her breathing.

"Hey, you're here now, it's okay," he told her, smoothing her hair back from her face. "You got the token. You did perfect."

Her breath hitched at the compliment, and she let her eyes flutter shut as she leaned into his cool hands. "Rowin?"

"Yes?"

"Thank you for waiting for me," she whispered.

His only response was to lift her into his arms by the back of her thighs, wrapping her legs around his waist. Tucking her face into the crook of his neck as blood and tears ran down her cheeks.

35

SOMETHING REAL

Rowin had told her, before he healed her, that the wound would likely scar. Still, Genevieve had been horrified to see her reflection. The monster's claw had left a four-inch mark from the top of her eyebrow almost to her chin. When she'd cried at the sight, the only comfort he'd been able to offer was that she was lucky not to lose her vision.

Surely Salem can fix it, she'd told herself.

Now, she was moping over her diary in the dining room—where Rowin had taken the time to cover all the looking glasses while she ate so she didn't have to catch any unwanted glimpses of herself—while Rowin and Ellin played cards.

March 24

Happy twenty-second birthday to me. I just read my entry from a year ago and it's hard to believe how different my life looked then. Heartbroken. Grieving. Feeling stuck in New Orleans. In Grimm Manor.

That certainly isn't the case now. No, now I'm stuck in this cursed estate with people I cannot tell if I hate. With the man who has given me the best sex of my life. A man I still cannot trust, whose secrets I'm still uncovering.

After everything that has happened here, one little scar shouldn't be weighing on me so heavily, but I suppose it's the evidence that so much has changed in so little time and yet I have not changed at all. I remain as vain as ever. As jaded.

I just want to go home, but I'm not sure home could even be a comfort at this point. What would I find there? My sister, yes. And the reminder that she has a purpose in New Orleans that I will never have. Where do I fit into that? She and Salem had to get rid of me just to enjoy their time together.

Farrow wanted to get rid of me. My mother.

If Rowin could have gotten rid of me at the start, he would have despite however he feels about me now. And I hate that I've begun to enjoy his company. To like him. Because I do. He's competitive and pushy but also clever and nurturing. And I fear that even winning the Hunt and freeing him will not be enough to keep him. His guilt will always chain him to this place. As mine chains me to Grimm Manor.

X,

Genevieve

"Genevieve?"

Genevieve glanced up from her diary to find Rowin and Ellin looking at her expectantly.

"Were you talking to me?" she asked, her tone a bit clipped.

"Yes," Rowin answered. "Do you want to play a hand of cards?"

"No, thank you," she told him. "I'm tired of games at the moment."

She scraped her chair back from the table and tucked her diary beneath her arm. Ellin and Rowin exchanged a loaded look. She made her way out of the room, just as Sevin rounded the corner, sucker in hand. She nearly bowled him over.

He sidestepped out of her way, giving her a curious tilt of his head when he noticed her sour expression—and the scar on her face.

"I was coming to tell you what a good time I had last night," Sevin revealed as he pointed to her wound with his sucker. "That looks—"

"Shut the fuck up, Sevin," Rowin barked, his mouth curling up in anger.

"What?" Sevin asked innocently. "I was going to say *badass*. Gives her some edge, don't you think? Like she survived a battle with a monster or something."

"I did survive a battle with a monster," she growled.

Sevin nodded as he popped his candy back into his mouth, waving his hand in the air as if to say *yes, that's what I just said.*

"Go be a bastard somewhere else," Rowin snarled at his brother.

"Aren't the two of you fucking?" Sevin shot at Rowin. "I'd hoped that might make you less disagreeable for once. It's certainly made you first in line for Favored."

"And you know this how?" Rowin asked flippantly as he placed a card on the table in front of Ellin.

"Knox just showed up to let me know I'm in danger of losing my title," Sevin told him. "He also wants all the mirrors uncovered in here. Expeditiously. His word, not mine."

Rowin did not look happy at the request.

"From what I heard of your performance in the woods, I thought that order might make you excited," Sevin taunted.

Genevieve made a face. "You're being uncouth."

"No, what's uncouth is the fact that I bet money against Covin on the fact that Rowin would be able to resist sleeping with you because he swore he never would," Sevin complained. "And yet here we are."

Genevieve swung her gaze to Rowin. "What?"

"I'm going to fucking kill you," Rowin seethed at his brother.

Sevin lifted his brows. "What did I say?"

Ellin sighed deeply, slapping her hand of cards face down on the table as she turned to Genevieve and said, "Those fools had a pool going the moment Rowin mentioned the wedding to them. Covin bet that the two of you would fuck despite...the circumstances. Sevin bet you wouldn't."

"Because I'm a gentleman," Sevin added. "But then Covin offered Rowin half his winnings if you did and I said—"

"You're getting paid?" Genevieve looked at Rowin in disbelief. "That's why you...why we..."

Rowin was up from the table immediately. "*No*. Hell, Genevieve—"

But she was already leaving. Needing to be anywhere else.

"*Damn it*, you two," she heard Rowin growl.

"What? It's my fault you're over two centuries old and still have no idea how to treat women?" Ellin retorted.

Genevieve didn't know where to go, but she certainly didn't want to go back to his room. So, she went to the first place she could think of instead. The hedge maze.

March 24

Forget whatever I wrote earlier in my misguided youth.
I hate him.

X,

Genevieve

When Rowin found her a couple of hours later, she was sitting on the edge of the fountain, shivering.

"You're very determined to get frostbite while you're here, aren't you?" he murmured as his boots crunched through the snow.

"Leave me alone," she told him. The cold had made her numb again, and she was trying to enjoy it in peace.

He crossed his arms over his chest. "Do I get a chance to explain?"

"Another one you mean?" She laughed a low, humorless laugh. "You know, I know I dug through your private things when I probably shouldn't have—"

"Probably?" he snorted.

"—but if I hadn't, would you have ever told me? About my letters? The hex? If Sevin hadn't brought it up, were you ever going to tell me you were making money off of us fucking?"

"I didn't agree to my brother's ridiculous bribe, Genevieve. In fact, I told them both to fucking choke on it at the time. I didn't even remember they made that bet until now because I tend to ignore half the shit they say. I don't think this one should count against me."

She looked down at her hands. He was right.

Rowin crouched in front of her. "Genevieve. Look at me."

She didn't. He sighed.

"I know you must feel like things are out of control. Like you're constantly being used or played with. That's the nature of being under a Devil's thumb." He shook his head bitterly. "But you and I *have* made our own choices. No matter what they're saying, or wagering on, or voting on, *we* have chosen our path here. I cannot imagine how hard this has been for you. How exhausting it probably is thinking you finally have a handle on your emotions, only for the game to turn everything on its head an hour later. And I know a lot of that is my fault. But you're not alone."

She swallowed as she slowly spun the ring on her finger around and around.

"I have a scar on my face that might never go away because of a game that I—and the rest of you—don't even want to play. This is my first time missing a birthday with my family, without my *mother*"—her voice cracked—"and I've almost died too many times to count. Only surviving because other people have allowed me to. I don't want to survive anymore. I want to *live*.

And not for my mother or my sister or anyone else. I just want to find a reason to live for *myself*. Something *real*."

He was quiet for so long she had to look up to check if he was still there.

"Genevieve, you have to choose to live for *yourself*. *You* are the most real thing you'll ever be able to experience. Your light. Your determination. You can search every corner of the universe for something else and it will never be enough if you're trying to escape yourself. I don't know who told you that you weren't good enough, but they were fucking wrong. You're more than good enough. Your heart is more than good enough. No matter how many times it has been burned. How many scars it might have. It will keep on beating, brave and passionate, if you will only let it."

Tears pricked her eyes now as she whispered, "I thought you said you couldn't ever truly trust your heart."

"I meant when it comes to other people," he corrected. "Not when it comes to yourself. I think you know your heart is good. I think that's why you hold on to it so tight."

Her breath hitched.

He stood and offered out his hand to her. "We won that token, you know. We get to sit out this round. I thought we could get out of here. Pretend the Hunt doesn't exist for a bit."

She raised her brows as she took his hand. "Get out of here? How? Where?"

He began pulling her back toward the house. "You'll see. Plus, you're turning a concerning shade of purple."

"At least purple *is* one of my colors," she grumbled to herself. And then an idea popped into her head. "Hey, Rowin?"

"Yes, trouble?"

"I'll race you," she told him, and before he even took another step, she shifted into her Specter state and she ran.

ROUND FOUR OF THE HUNT

Immunity

36

HELL

March 25

I'm going to Hell today. <u>Ha.</u>

Also, you'll find that I've scratched out the previous entry. I don't hate Rowington Silver.

I hate how easily he gets under my skin. How hard it seems to be for him not to keep secrets. How, unfortunately, we have that in common.

And, most of all, I hate that the idea of going to Hell with him seems fun. A year ago I would never have written such a ludicrous sentence.

I don't think I know this new version of me. So maybe going to Hell will be a good place to start looking for her.

X,

Genevieve

Genevieve wasn't sure how one was supposed to dress to go to Hell, but pink was a fitting color for any occasion. She'd put her hair half up with a golden comb and dabbed some powder over her face in hopes that it would dull the shiny, angry scar. It did not.

The gown she'd chosen was a perfect shade of mauve, with a sweetheart neckline and embroidered butterflies over the glistening fabric.

She gave a small twirl. "How do I look?"

Rowin flicked his gaze over her, slowly. "Like you do not belong in Hell."

"Perfect," she said. "That's the sort of style I was going for—an Angel who got lost."

"I wouldn't say you look angelic either."

She gave him a grin. "Is Umbra coming with us?"

"Umbra doesn't enjoy Hell very much," he said. "She's become spoiled."

Genevieve tilted her head. "Where does she go, by the way? When she isn't around?"

"She's always around, in the shadows, you just don't see her. I don't like to keep her on a string like some of the others, if that's what you mean. Familiars are part of their host's soul. We can recall them *within* us whenever we'd like."

Midnight tolled then, and they strolled to the ballroom together. Genevieve with a spring in her step and Rowin with an amused smile.

When Knox appeared, Rowin had the token ready.

"We want access to the Hellmouth," Rowin told Knox.

The Devil dipped his chin in a nod. "Very well. I'll meet you in the study."

Rowin led Genevieve out right away, leaving the other four to finish the choosing ceremony alone. When she glanced over her shoulder at the rest of them on the way out, Sevin threw her a wink.

"When we get there, do not look *anyone* in the eyes, understood?" Rowin said as he led her to the study. "The beings that hang out around Hellmouths are not ones you want to associate with."

"It's probably hard to believe, Rowington Silver," she crooned as they pushed their way into the room, "but *no* beings in Hell are ones I want to associate with. I'm only going with you out of pure boredom and a touch of curiosity."

"Well, save your curiosity for when we get to Knox's estate."

"Is *that* where we're going?"

"Yes, it's where my family resides when we're in Hell," he explained. "Knox's residence is in the Third Circle—Greed."

Salem and Ophelia would *not* believe she was about to do this.

"Hello, my lovebirds," Knox's voice greeted them before he fully manifested in the room. "Taking a little romp through Hell today?"

"We don't need the small talk," Rowin told the Devil.

"Touchy." Knox smirked. "Looking forward to a tearful reunion with your mother? And then there are your brothers, of course . . ."

"Oh," Genevieve realized. "Wells and Remi will be there?"

"Yes," Knox informed her. "Wellington just returned from an errand of mine this morning, actually. Much quicker than I assumed. But I won't bore you with *business*. Are you excited to see how the Other Side lives?"

"I'm excited to get out of this fucking house," she answered cheerily.

Knox stepped up to the swirling black portal in the back of the room, and she watched with rapt attention as he reached into the inky abyss, whispering something under his breath, and turned it a ghostly shade of blue.

"After you," Knox said, tone firm.

Rowin reached down and threaded his hand in hers, giving it a reassuring squeeze as he pulled her toward the entrance to Hell.

"Deep breath and close your eyes," he told her.

She obeyed, squeezing them as tight as she could while he

gently tugged her forward. The portal felt like it was made of a thick gelatin, and Genevieve could only hope it would not ruin her hair or dress. The power around her was unmistakable, and for a moment fear crept into her bones, her fight-or-flight instincts emerging as they sensed danger nearby. Rowin only squeezed her hand tighter.

Then it was over.

"Open your eyes."

She did, waiting for them to adapt to the dark around them. The first thing she saw was Rowin—and she gasped when she took in his appearance. The tattoos inked across all his skin were now *alive*. She'd always thought the swirling lines looked like shadows or wisps of smoke, and now they writhed around his exposed forearms as if they really were.

"Whoa," she whispered as she brushed her fingertips on the ones curling around his throat. "How—?"

"Infernal Ink," he told her. "It comes to life in Hell."

"Fascinating," she murmured.

Knox stepped out of the portal behind them then.

"Your deadline here is noon," the Devil said to them as he waved a hand in their direction.

Genevieve watched in horror as glowing, violet cuffs appeared on each of her wrists.

"If you even think about trying to stay a second longer, these will drag you back. And it will *not* be fun," Knox threatened them both before shifting his attention solely on Genevieve. "You're leading the vote for Favored by leaps and bounds, Mrs. Silver. That little romp in my enchanted forest caused quite a stir." His tone was approving.

"When do you announce the winner?" she asked.

"Before the final round," Knox said. "When you arrive at my estate, remind me to show you something."

Before Genevieve could ask what he meant, he blinked out of sight.

"Come on," Rowin told her. "We need to catch the ferry."

Genevieve began to soak in their surroundings as he led her forward. They'd stepped out into an alleyway that opened into some sort of outdoor market or village. The buildings were mostly gray, the ground beneath their feet made of cobblestones. A starless night sky stretched above them. It was precisely what she thought Hell might look like. Gray and boring. Except for the people. The myriad of beings roaming past the alley were surprisingly colorful, draped in jewel tones and adorned with gems.

"Apulchra adomin, epulchra icapill," a grating voice rasped from down the alley.

Genevieve startled as Rowin shifted his body toward her, his stance protective. She'd completely missed the little Demon at first. They must have been about three feet tall, with grayish skin that blended in with the wall where they leaned. When they moved, however, their complexion warmed instantly into something more human, and their hair grew longer in seconds, shifting to a mundane shade of brown. She knew Rowin had told her not to look at anyone they might meet, but she couldn't help it as she watched the angles of their face morph into something softer, their eyes going from black to a light shade of blue. They almost looked like a regular, plain mortal now—some sort of demonic chameleon.

"What did they say?" she asked Rowin.

"Oh, *mortal*," the Demon rasped in English as they stepped forward, their pointed teeth dripping with saliva as they licked their lips. "Pretty lady, pretty hair. Pretty *eyes*."

Gross.

Rowin bared his teeth. "Take another step and I'll rip your head off your shoulders."

"I want her eyes," the stranger whined as they watched Genevieve hungrily. "I don't have that color yet."

At that last statement, the Demon's irises flickered through a rainbow of colors, and Genevieve's stomach began to turn at the idea that all their features had been *stolen* from others.

"Touch her. I dare you," Rowin snarled.

The Demon turned to Rowin, as if checking to see how serious he was. If looks could kill, they would have dropped dead immediately. Seeming to realize the danger, they slunk back to the side, giving Rowin and Genevieve space to pass.

Rowin wrapped an arm around her waist and guided her to his other side, putting as much distance between her and the Demon as possible. He walked them toward the end of the alley. Rowin didn't take his eyes off them for a second as he strode by, and Genevieve didn't relax until they were less than two feet from the exit.

The moment the sigh of relief left her lips was precisely when the Demon struck.

Genevieve cried out as a clawed hand grasped her hair from behind.

In a split second, Rowin had the being pinned by the throat against the wall. She didn't understand how he'd possibly moved that fast, but then she noticed how his arms and hands were now completely made of shadows, slowly solidifying back into their normal state as he grinned down at the squirming Demon.

"If you were looking to part with your life that badly, you could have just asked," Rowin snarled.

"No!" they cried as they clawed at Rowin's hold. "I just wanted her eyes! One will do. I won't take any more. Please don't—"

Genevieve cringed at the sound of bones and tendons snapping as Rowin ripped the Demon's head from their neck, as promised. She glanced away as he dropped both the head and corpse to the ground with a sickening thud.

Rowin turned back to her, looking down at his hands and grimacing at the black sludge that covered them. "Let's go," he said. "I need to find a place to wash up."

She gaped at him. "Was that truly necessary? Are you not concerned about getting in trouble?"

He smirked at her in amusement. "We're in Hell. This is just a regular night. And, yes, it was necessary. Not following through on threats here makes the predators too bold. Remember that."

"Ugh," she let out, but didn't protest further as he guided her from the alley. She was surprised to find how large the street was when they stepped into the fray. All sorts of shops lined either side, leading to what looked to be a town square that reminded her of the Quarter. Everywhere she looked was a sight she'd never seen before. There was a place advertising *fresh blood* on its sign outside, another offering to polish the skulls of your loved ones. She peeked into other alleyways as they passed and saw everything from people fucking against walls like animals to people bathing an . . . ostrich?

"What in the world?" she asked as she spotted a Demon lathering up the large bird.

"Perfect," Rowin muttered, as if there was nothing odd about the scene.

He led her over to the Demon and the ridiculous-looking animal. She watched as he borrowed the hose to wash the Demon blood from his hands, trying to convince herself she wasn't once again passed out in Enchantra, having a fever dream.

The ostrich tilted its head at her. She eyed it back suspiciously. *Why would anyone need an ostrich in Hell?*

She must've spoken the words aloud because the Demon patted the ugly bird on its bald head and answered, "Mouse here eats the mice around my shop for me."

Genevieve raised her brows. "You named your mice-eating bird *Mouse?*"

The man shrugged. "Kept it simple."

"Mm-hmm," was all she managed to respond. The ostrich glared at her.

As Rowin took care of the blood on his hands, Genevieve peered over at the shop next door. There was some sort of odd blue substance leaking onto the ground along the front façade from the old wooden gutters. The smell was sickly sweet, and when Genevieve tilted her head back to read the sign that said *Poison and Potion*, she spotted puffs of blue and purple smoke coming from a chimney above.

Genevieve glanced over at Rowin, still scrubbing at the blood on his hands, then inched toward the shop. Pushing her way through the front door, a bell tinkled in the air above to announce her arrival. There was no one inside that she could see, just shelves and shelves of different colored liquids in small glass vials. All of them had labels—all in languages she couldn't read without Knox's magic.

"Genevieve?" an unfamiliar voice gasped, followed by something in a language Genevieve didn't understand.

Genevieve turned to see a woman with wine-colored hair and a choker made of teeth.

"It *is* you," she exclaimed, switching to English before hurrying toward the shop door and yanking it open. "Mathilde! Astoria!"

Genevieve tried to turn herself invisible, but as she flickered in and out, she realized Knox's cuffs wouldn't allow her magic to work properly. It was too late anyway as the redhead, and as two other women, who must be Mathilde and Astoria, were already swarming her.

"I'm Gladys," the redhead said. "This is Mathilde and Astoria."

She pointed to her friends in turn. Genevieve was rather certain Mathilde was a vampire, judging by the size of her fangs, while Gladys and Astoria were some sort of Demon, but it was hard to tell.

"We just adore you and Rowin together," Gladys gushed. "I've bet on you the entire time. I knew Rowin wouldn't marry a mortal if they were useless."

"Astoria didn't think you'd survive after that first round," Mathilde said.

"I changed my mind when you dove in after Umbra," Astoria defended herself. "I didn't think you were anything special at first. But we *love* Umbra. She and Sapphire are our favorites of the Familiars."

"Is the sex with Rowin incredible?" Mathilde wondered.

"It certainly looks incredible," Gladys inserted.

"I've always been rather keen on him," Mathilde sighed dreamily.

"My favorite is Grave." Astoria grinned. "I want him to hate me like he hates everyone else. All the way through a mattress."

As they all became enraptured with discussing the details of the Hunt, both past and present, they slipped back into their first language as Genevieve slowly began inching away.

Genevieve made a break for the door and pushed her way outside. Rowin was just finishing up.

"Thanks for your help," Rowin told the man with the ostrich.

"Did you know we have *fans?*" she said. "Because I was just ambushed by a group of them."

The corners of Rowin's mouth lifted in amusement. "Of course we have fans. Look at us."

"Well, yes," Genevieve allowed as she flicked a piece of her hair over her shoulder. "But it's strange that they just acted like they knew me. Is this how it is for all of you here all the time? I mean, even before you stopped coming." She rushed to say the last bit.

"When you provide any sort of entertainment for people, some of them start looking at you as a commodity. They treat you in the way they think you deserve based on how well you entertain them. It's another reason I started staying away from this place."

Genevieve gave his hand a comforting squeeze. He lifted her hand to his lips and pressed a kiss against her knuckles.

"Are we going straight to Knox's estate?" she wondered.

He shook his head. "There's a place I need to stop at before we catch the ferry."

The little store he brought them to was a *dream*. The outside wasn't much to look at, but inside it was mesmerizing. Everywhere she looked something glittered, and lining the walls were glass cases filled with rare gemstones and trinkets.

The woman asked Rowin something from behind a counter in the same language the women at the potion shop had spoken, a smile on her cherry lips as she gave them an assessing look.

Rowin walked over, waving at Genevieve to look around as he bent his head toward the woman and whispered something. Genevieve watched him closely for a moment, but soon something sparkly caught her eye in one of the cases. Several minutes later, the saleswoman brought out a box from the back, and Rowin slipped something that looked like gold coins into her hand before turning for the door.

"Ready?" he asked.

She eyed the box as she dipped her chin at him. "Knox's estate now?"

Rowin nodded in answer. "It's time to pay a visit to my mother."

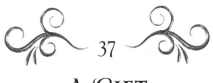

A GIFT

Knox's estate was really a *castle*. Complete with turrets, towers, and a very dramatic drawbridge.

"Welcome to true Hell," Rowin told her as they hopped off their second ferry and onto the stone dock.

The first ferry ride had been rather uneventful, aside from the information from the captain that if she fell into the water, she'd be drowned by the demonic sirens that lived beneath the surface. She'd clung to Rowin the entire time.

On their second ferry, Rowin explained that all the Circles of Hell were structured in much the same way: two rings of land that surrounded a larger, solid center of the realm, a river wedged between the pieces of earth. She hadn't caught the name of the first river they'd crossed, but the second one Rowin had called the Avarice and said that if one were to drink from it, the sin of greed would consume them entirely.

The very outer ring of land where they'd first arrived had been the Outskirts, where most of the demonic residents in each circle lived and worked. The outer ring held more powerful Demons; the inner more powerful Devils. The latter was where they would find Knox's home: *Knoxium*.

"He named his house after himself?" she deadpanned.

"His name isn't really Knox," Rowin revealed as they approached an iron lever beside the drawbridge. "We call him Knox *because* of Knoxium. Devils don't use their True Names."

Right. Ophelia once mentioned that Salem used to be known

by another name. His True Name. But once Phantasma had come crashing down, everyone instantly forgot it.

Rowin paused in front of the lever contraption. A sharp spike protruded from the handle, and Genevieve watched as he wrapped his fist tight enough around it that his blood flowed freely down the shaft, then yanked it back.

"It only opens for those it recognizes," he explained. The chains rattled as the bridge slowly flattened over the ground, inviting them into the belly of the beast. The castle was covered in the same demonberry vines that surrounded Enchantra, its style very reminiscent of the Silvers' home. So much so that Genevieve suspected the Devil had a hand in helping construct the other estate as well.

When they finally stepped inside, Knox was already there, prepared to greet them both.

"Welcome back, Rowington. It's been too long," he commented as he waved them inside the threshold. "Pixie, bring us some wine."

"Do not," Rowin said before a small Demon with pink pigtails could scamper away to fetch Knox's request. "Genevieve will not be eating or drinking anything, Knox."

"Oh, my mistake." Knox feigned innocence. "I completely forgot about that silly little rule."

Rowin glared at Knox in a way that made it clear he knew the Devil was full of shit.

"If you're looking for Wellington and Remington, you'll find them in your family's wing of the house." Knox waved a dismissal at them. "Feel free to explore—but don't touch anything, unless you'd like to have your hands fed to a member of my staff. And don't forget, before you leave, Mrs. Silver, I would like to show you my trove."

Rowin narrowed his eyes at the Devil but Knox didn't even acknowledge the look before winking out of sight.

"C'mon," Rowin muttered. "Let's go see what my brothers are up to."

_✦_

"_Rowin?_" Wells exclaimed.

They found Wells and Remi lounging in a sitting room in the east wing of the house. Dinner had apparently just finished because there was a team of butlers and maids clearing up trays and glasses. Genevieve wondered whether the time here was different from that at Enchantra.

Remi straightened from where he had been lying against a black leather couch as he spotted his twin in the entryway.

"What the fuck are you doing here?" Remi asked. "And with her?"

Genevieve frowned. She thought she and Remi were on decent terms. Though, considering she'd ripped a piece of metal out of his mouth and shoved a bookcase on top of him in the last couple of days, maybe not.

"Genevieve found another immunity token. And she's my wife," Rowin told him. "Where I go, she goes."

"How adorable," Remi said, tone bored.

"We came here to get a break from Enchantra," Rowin leveled at his brother. "Don't fucking ruin it."

"I'm not sure here is much better than there," Wells chimed in.

"And...I came to see Mother," Rowin told them. "I figured she should hear about our marriage. From me."

"Give me a break," Remi muttered as he stood. "I'm going to bed."

Rowin's fists clenched at his sides, and Genevieve bit her lip, reaching out to place a comforting hand on his forearm. He relaxed. Barely.

"Mother's awake, I was just visiting with her. Father's around here somewhere. I got back from Nocturnia today," Wells told Rowin.

"So we heard." Rowin eyed his brother. "Anything interesting happening in the heart of Hell?"

"More than you'd think," Wells murmured. "We'll talk later."

Rowin led Genevieve out of the sitting room and down a drafty corridor. Every detail of the house was either black or a rich shade of violet, the same color as the Devil's eyes—undoubtedly his signature shade. The windows were stained-glass portraits in purple and black, the velvet curtains and jacquard runners all an ebony color. Even the walls were black.

Rowin stopped before an ornate door at the end of the hall. And that was it. He just stood there and stared.

"Rowin?" she whispered.

He didn't say anything for a long minute, and then, "I haven't visited in so long. I don't know how much worse it's gotten . . ."

She reached out and brushed the back of his hand. "You aren't doing this alone."

He glanced sideways at her. His eyes were shining with an emotion she couldn't quite name—a mixture of terror and grati-tude, maybe?—but he only nodded and raised his fist to knock.

A pause. Then, "Come in."

Rowin pushed the door open, and the moment they stepped inside, Genevieve could tell someone sick lived there. The chill of death clung to the air, and the smell of something sharp and sterile burned her nose as they approached. Genevieve could see a woman through the black gossamer that draped down from the bed's canopy. She was wearing a scarlet nightgown and would have looked exactly like her portrait in Enchantra if she weren't so frail. Genevieve saw now what Rowin had meant when he'd said Grave was the spitting image of her.

"Remington?" The woman furrowed her brow, and then she gasped.

Genevieve saw recognition and disbelief move across her face as Rowin brushed aside the floating curtain next to the bed. He crouched down until he was eye level at the woman's side.

"Hello, Mother, I hope this isn't a bad time to visit," he told her.

Then he said something in their first language, gesturing to where Genevieve lingered at the foot of the bed.

"Oh, Rowington." Tears began to slide down his mother's cheeks. "Are you really here?"

He kept his eyes trained on Genevieve. "Yes. I'm here. And this is my friend."

Genevieve stepped forward, and his mother's eyes shifted right to her face. A delighted smile curled onto the woman's mouth.

"Hello, dear," his mother whispered. "I'm Vira."

Genevieve nodded. "It's a pleasure to meet you. I'm Genevieve."

"Rowington has never brought anyone to meet me before," Vira said as she eyed Rowin with a soft smile. "You must be special. What is your full name? Genevieve . . . ?"

"Silver," Rowin declared.

Vira sat up a bit straighter now. "Are you saying—"

Rowin nodded. "Genevieve and I were married. A few days ago."

"We never truly discussed me taking his last name, for the record," Genevieve said. "Everything went so fast. I think he should take mine, in fact. Rowington Grimm. Has a nice ring to it, don't you think?"

"Don't be a brat," he said dryly.

"You love when I'm a brat," Genevieve drawled with a grin.

Vira smiled at Genevieve conspiratorially. "You are utterly charming."

Genevieve beamed. "Thank you."

Rowin snorted. "Don't let her fool you, Mother. She's been nothing but a menace the entire time I've known her."

Genevieve scoffed. But before she could tease him more, Vira began to cough. Full-body heaves that splattered ink-like blood onto her hands and the sheets. Rowin turned his head and closed his eyes. Like the sight physically pained him.

"Sorry, dear," Vira whispered when the fit was over. "It gets worse this time of year. When the Fix is almost out of my system. You should come visit me after the Hunt. That's when I'm at my best. I can even stand up then."

Rowin winced. "We'll let you get some rest, Mother. Save your energy."

Vira reached out to grasp onto her son's hand. "Please come back soon. Evald et odesider."

"I've missed you, too," he said, but he made no other promises.

Vira seemed satisfied enough with his words, however. She turned and nodded at Genevieve.

"It was wonderful to meet you, dear. Welcome to the family," Vira said.

Genevieve's chest ached as she nodded and said, "It was a pleasure to meet you as well."

As soon as Rowin had closed the door behind them, Genevieve turned to him and asked, "Why didn't you give her the present?"

"What are you talking about?"

"The shop we went to. You bought something. I thought it might have been a gift for her."

He sighed, reaching into the pocket hidden inside his waistcoat to pull out the box from the shop. "I was going to wait to give it to you back at Enchantra."

Her breath hitched. "You got me a gift?"

He held it out to her in offering. "Happy birthday, trouble."

She carefully took the box from his hand and pried open the lid.

"*Rowin*," she choked out, nearly dropping the box.

Inside, nestled against a black velvet cushion, was a thin golden cuff. Between a line of white diamonds on one side and black diamonds on the other, there was an inscription.

The light is wherever you are.

"Here," he said, taking the bracelet from the box to help her clasp it around her wrist.

She launched herself into him, throwing her arms around his neck. His arms came sweeping in around her, crushing her body into his as he pressed his face into her hair.

"Thank you," he told her. "For visiting her with me."

She nodded. She understood. When mortals had to watch their loved ones grow sick and die, such experiences were usually over months or years. She could not imagine what it would be like to watch over an *eternity*.

He pulled back from her, just enough to press a sweet, lingering kiss against her mouth.

"Rowin?" she said as they started back down the hall.

"Yes?"

But before she could say anything else, an agonized scream echoed through the castle.

38

TRAGIC ENDING

Sevin had arrived in Hell, and he was screaming bloody murder. His stomach and chest were covered in crimson, but that wasn't the cause of his sickening wails. It was the fact that every inch of his flesh was bubbling and steaming, as if he had been dropped in a vat of acid. Genevieve almost lost the contents of her stomach on the rug beside him.

Rowin, however, barely even blinked. He grabbed a thick blanket from the back of an armchair in the sitting room and tucked it around Sevin's body as it convulsed. Then he grasped one of his brother's hands and just held on. A few minutes later, Wells and Remi joined them.

"What's going on?" she asked the others quietly.

"This is what happens when the Hunting Blade goes through our hearts," Remi explained.

"It's very painful," Wells said as if that weren't *very obvious*.

Sevin roared in agony once again. Sevin, who always had a smirk on his lips and a joke on his tongue. He was pale now, his eyes unseeing as pain ripped through him over and over again.

"How long does this last?"

"Hours sometimes," Wells told her.

Remi and Wells both slipped out of the room, leaving her and Rowin to watch Sevin shudder through the pain. It took about half an hour before he was finally quiet, though he still held Rowin's hand.

Knox suddenly blinked into the room. He barely spared a second glance at Sevin, beckoning to Rowin instead.

"Come," he ordered.

Genevieve curled a lip in disdain at the Devil. "Can't it wait?"

"No," Knox said before disappearing once more.

Rowin gently pried his hand out of Sevin's and stood.

"Can you stay with him?" he requested.

She nodded. "Of course."

As they left, she went over to kneel by Sevin's side. She picked up his large hand and cupped it between both of hers. He forced his eyes open.

"Being an immortal is a privilege, don't you think?" he rasped.

She gave him a sad smile. "I never have, no."

He tried to nod, wincing as he did. "You'd be right. Mortals are lucky. You live, you love, you *die*. Living forever just means there's infinite time for people to inflict pain on you."

"I thought Grave was supposed to be the serious one," she tried to joke.

"Ah, yes, you're right. I just died, you see. But I shall return to my post as the family jester right away."

She began to rub soft, soothing circles over the back of his hand, and he gave her a weak squeeze of encouragement, letting her know to continue.

"If Grave is the serious one and you're the jester, what does that make the others? Shall we give them all titles?" she suggested, trying to distract him as he braced himself against another wave of pain.

"Covin is the bad boy," Sevin panted. "Or the harlot. Whichever sounds more fun."

She thought of Covin's forked tongue and alleged scandalous affair with whoever Nessa Serpentine was. "Agreed. He certainly scared me on that first day."

"Oh?" Sevin asked. "How?"

She blushed. "I saw him, um, cutting...himself?"

Sevin jerked with a pained laugh. "You saw him releasing, you mean."

She let out a squeak of embarrassment. "*What?* You mean, he was—"

Sevin tried to smile. "Not *that* sort of release. We're Blood Wraiths. Our magic collects in our blood, and if we don't bleed a certain amount, it can build up. Which isn't good. We consume blood as well, but that's a different thing."

"Yes, your suckers. You get them from Vampires, right?"

"Yes." He winced as he tried to nod. "I really should've let you believe the other thing, though. Covin would've gotten a kick out of it."

"You're a menace," she muttered.

"And you're very cute when you're flustered," he said.

"Stop flirting with me."

"Ah, yes, I forget you have eyes only for Rowington. The romantic one."

It was her turn to laugh. "In what world is Rowin the romantic one?"

"In the world where he nearly bit my head off after you disappeared through that mirror in the forest. And then vowed he wouldn't be leaving the room until he got you back," Sevin said. "I thought you were a goner, to be honest with you. Not to mention that he snapped almost every bone in Cedric Wrathblade's body after that bastard cornered you at the masquerade. He claims the both of us had a hand in that job, but really all I did was snap Cedric's neck to put him out of his misery."

"Very dramatic," Genevieve approved at the mental image. Then, after a beat: "Sevin?"

"Yes, sweetheart?"

"Can I ask you a question?" she asked.

"That was a question," he answered.

"I swear you and your siblings are the most insufferable people in existence," she huffed.

A smile curled up on Sevin's lips. "We've earned it."

That's true.

Genevieve bit her lip. "Do you think it's possible to love someone after only a few days?"

"We're certainly capable of hating someone in a short period of time—on sight, even. I don't see why love should be any different," Sevin told her. "But I'm afraid I don't feel that way about you, sweetheart. You're not my type."

Genevieve sighed deeply, rolling her eyes up to the ceiling. Then, unable to help herself, she asked, "What *is* your type?"

"Sadistic and unavailable," he muttered. "Why are you asking me about love? Did my brother manage to get under your skin?"

"I don't know," she whispered. "Rowin said everything is heightened in Enchantra, and he's right. I can't tell what's adrenaline and what's real emotion. Hell, I can't even tell if I can trust him or not."

"Everything is *real*," Sevin said. "Heightened, sure, but just because the Hunt is life or death doesn't mean your decision on how you feel about each other afterward has to be. Let yourself fall in love. Let yourself fall out of it. You never know when you could lose someone and not have the opportunity to do so again. Believe me."

"Are you not afraid of breaking your heart so much you won't be able to put it back together? If you fall in and out of love so easy?" she wondered.

"If there's no risk in life, I don't think it's worth the journey," he told her.

She was quiet after that. Mulling over his words.

"Rowin hasn't come to see us or our mother in years," Sevin said eventually. "He's been lonely. A lot lonelier than he would ever let on, but I know him. And I know whatever the partnership between you two is, it has changed something in him again."

"I think that's the case for both of us," she whispered.

She'd kept herself surrounded with fair-weather companions and meaningless lovers anytime the loneliness became particularly cold, but all of them had been like striking a match. Warm for a short, blissful second, only to burn out quickly before being tossed away. None of those people had ever truly understood anything about her. They knew what she let them—nothing more. Lately it had been the same with Ophelia. Maybe Rowin would be able to get to know the real her. Maybe they could win the Hunt, free him from that curse, and then decide exactly how entangled they were willing to become.

Almost an hour later, Sevin had drifted to sleep, and Rowin was still nowhere to be seen.

Knox blinked into the room.

"Come, girl, it's time to go to the trove," the Devil ordered, a hint of frustration in his tone.

"I can't just leave him," she said.

"It's fine," Sevin said, his eyes blinking open. "Choose something fun."

She smiled and patted his hand before getting up and following Knox out of the room. He led her down the stone corridor, through a hall, dipping his head to enter a low archway in the corner.

As Genevieve approached the passage, she saw that the opening led to a narrow spiral staircase. She picked up the front of her dress and began to follow Knox up the steps. When they reached the top, she found a small round room with an ornate mirror leaning against the far wall. Its frame was an intricate work of art, carved with twisting vines and serpents, branches of fruit and flowers. As she stepped before it, the surface began to ripple like water.

"Before we proceed," Knox said, "you will need to agree to a little bargain."

Genevieve pried her eyes from the mirror to meet the Devil's gaze. "How many times must I tell you I will not make a bargain with you?"

"Please, lovely. This is a mere formality. One that all the others have agreed to in the past. I am granting you a boon from my collection. A free choice. All I ask in return is that you agree to lose all memory of the time you spend inside the trove. You will remember only the single item you select as your reward. It's a matter of security. I'm sure you can imagine that I don't want all my belongings to be public knowledge. There are some remarkably greedy and clever beings in this Circle of Hell, and they might get ideas about taking what's mine."

"So I won't remember my time inside the trove specifically? Only the one item I decide to take? That's it?"

"Yes."

Genevieve turned his words over in her mind, over and over, while spinning the signet on her finger. The band was a constant, scorching reminder of exactly whom she was dealing with.

If only I'd had this when I met Farrow.

"Fine. I agree. Let's see what you've got."

Knox grinned and stepped through the reflective surface. Genevieve plunged into the portal behind him.

꧁

"Welcome to my treasure trove," Knox told her as he swept his arm through the air at the glittering room around them.

Everywhere Genevieve looked there was something magnificent. Jewels, colored potions, furniture made of silver and gold, magical artifacts she didn't even have a name for.

"I can choose anything?" she asked him.

"Any one item, yes," he confirmed.

Genevieve held her breath as she watched Knox walk further back into the room. She crept along behind him as he followed a narrow path through the piles of treasure. She tried to take in as many of the artifacts and jewels as she could, hoping that something would stand out to her. There were daggers carved from bones and random potions. Compasses that didn't even seem to work and magic dice. Dolls made of hair and locked books with languages on the cover she couldn't read.

"What is it your heart desires?" Knox asked her. "Perhaps a pocket watch that allows you to travel back ten minutes in time at the cost of memory for each use?"

As he spoke, the item he described blinked into his hand. Then he tossed it to the side and walked further into the clutter. When she made to follow, the toe of her shoe accidentally clipped a bauble and sent it flying across the ground; she glanced down to see where it had landed. And froze.

It was a small golden locket with a black jewel nestled in the front. A Soul Lock. Perhaps even the one she had seen Barrington wearing in the photograph.

She crouched down to pluck the necklace from the floor and dangled it by its chain before her, wondering what souls it might have contained.

Ophie and I could match, she mused, a little sadly. How long had she wished for a locket like this?

Genevieve stood and nestled the locket atop one of the piles.

"Mrs. Silver, do come here."

She rushed along the path to where Knox was waiting for her.

"I have coin purses that can never be emptied, potions that grant otherworldly strength and beauty, arrows that are enchanted to never miss their targets," he offered, each artifact popping into the air between them as he spoke. "Or a potion that can erase a single person from your mind and you from theirs?"

Genevieve's breath hitched as she locked onto the vial of shimmering red liquid.

The Devil smiled. "Ah, is there someone you wish to forget, lovely?"

Farrow. A million times over.

"But before you make a final decision, there *is* one thing in particular that I thought might interest you, and your husband, more than all the others..."

The objects floating before her disappeared as he took something out of his pocket. A glass vial in the shape of a skull. Inside, there was a glowing blue liquid.

Somehow, Genevieve knew what he was showing her the moment that she saw it.

The cure.

"You're a fucking bastard," she seethed at the Devil. "You've had this *all along*? You could have cured Rowin's mother at any time?"

"I am a Devil, Genevieve Silver," he postured. "You should know enough about Devils by now not to be surprised at our nature. After all, our Prince is currently playing house with your sister."

"Yes, I believe I told you that," she huffed.

"But how was I to know you weren't lying?" Knox tilted his head. "I know now, of course, that your little threat was very much real. Wellington just returned from Nocturnia to confirm the information for me himself. The King knows that Salem is free, and he is very angry that his son has chosen not to return to Hell. But what can he expect after cursing the Prince so cruelly, hmm?"

Genevieve narrowed her eyes; she had no idea where he was going with this.

"Unless Salem comes back to the Other Side of his own volition, the King cannot touch him. Ancient traditions, you know. So you can imagine how excited the King was to discover that the sister of the very girl that Salem has tethered his soul to is currently in *my* possession. He offered me a deal I can't refuse, and so I'm going to offer you a deal that you can't either."

Genevieve's stomach churned with dread as Knox shook the bottle, causing a tornado of bubbles to float to the top of the glowing liquid.

"If you agree to convince Salem to return to Hell, I will let you choose this vial when you win Favored," Knox offered. "Rowington's mother will be cured. Everyone wins. But if you won't help me . . ."

Knox let the bottle fall from his grasp.

"*No*," Genevieve yelled as she dove forward, hand outstretched, but the vial never hit the ground.

A single snap and it was back in Knox's grip.

". . . everyone loses," the Devil finished.

"You're asking me to convince my sister's husband to abandon her. Which I will *never* do."

She would never *ever* take away her sister's happiness. She'd rather die.

Knox scoffed. "The Prince would be welcomed with open arms. Everyone knows the King has a soft spot for him."

"I will not betray her," Genevieve said. "Now that I know the cure exists, Rowin and I will simply find it ourselves."

"But *do you* know it exists?" Knox's smile turned chilling. "Don't forget…the moment you step back into Knoxium, our entire conversation will be erased from your memory."

"We'll find it ourselves," she maintained.

His violet eyes became hostile. "Do you know how Crimson Rot began, girl?"

She crossed her arms. "Nobody does."

"Oh, but I do." Knox swept himself into a dramatic bow. "Because I am its creator."

"*Why?*" Genevieve choked, aghast.

"I told you—when I lose, everyone loses," he echoed once again.

Genevieve knew she shouldn't be shocked that he'd created something so heinous. She'd known Knox was a villain, but she realized that she should have been thinking of him as *the* villain.

"Over the years I've bargained away a few vials to others who were willing to meet my desired price," Knox revealed. "Enough to start the rumors of a cure, but not enough that anyone would be able to track it down."

"So you're saying there are others out there," she said. "Which means I don't need you."

Knox watched her for a long, tense moment. He glanced at the vial.

"Well, if you're sure," he said.

And then he crushed it in his fist. Genevieve gasped as the liquid dripped over his knuckles and forearm.

"Take one last look around before I return you to your husband, Mrs. Silver," Knox said with a tight smile as he shook the shards of glass from his fist. "And don't worry, no one else will ever know the chance you've wasted here."

Genevieve forced herself to turn away from the evidence of the ruined cure. She knew in her bones she'd made the right decision, but it didn't assuage her guilt at the fact that she had been inches from the one thing Rowin had been looking for for over the better part of two decades and she'd just let it go.

What else would I even want from here?

The potion Knox had described earlier popped into her mind first, of course. The idea of being able to forget Farrow had been something she wished for over and over again . . .

"It's time to go," Knox prompted. "Have you made your decision?"

She took one last glance around and then nodded.

"I guess we'll see if you win, then. It's time for you to leave now," he said, pointing toward the portal.

Genevieve slowly backed away from him. Swallowing thickly as she twirled and made haste for the exit. Before she stepped through, however, she told herself she had to remember what just happened. Had to commit every detail in her mind.

The cure exists. The cure exists. The cure exists. The cure exists. The cure exists.

She stepped through.

The cure exists. The cure exists. The cure . . . the . . . the . . . hmm . . . where . . . am I?

Genevieve blinked at the dusty old room around her.

"What the Hell?" she muttered to herself as she turned to see the large mirror behind her.

She had been looking at her reflection and then . . .

Her deal with Knox. He took her memories.

"*Genevieve.*"

She spun at the sound of Rowin's voice.

"I've been looking everywhere for you," he told her, his expression carefully blank in a way that put her nerves on edge. "We need to go. Now."

She nodded numbly and let him lead her down the narrow tower, glancing back only once at the haunting emptiness of the room.

Rowin brought her to a different corridor, one that was empty except for the Hellmouth swirling at the end.

"What did Knox want to discuss with you earlier?" she asked quietly as they strode down the hall, side by side.

"Family matters," he answered, his tone clipped in a way that made it known he wanted this to be the end of the conversation.

"About the Hunt? About your mother's cure?" she pressed again as he pulled her to a halt in front of the portal. "Also, why did we end up in that alleyway if Knox has a Hellmouth here in his house?"

"This one is only for leaving, not returning," he informed. "A safety precaution."

"And my other questions?" she prompted.

He still didn't answer, only grabbing her wrist and pulling her through the portal. They stepped back out into Enchantra, the study manifesting around them just how they'd left it.

But she didn't make any effort to move, watching him expectantly. What had Knox wanted to talk to him about back at the house? Had it been about the two of them? Was Knox growing suspicious? Had he offered Rowin some kind of bargain?

How many more secrets is he keeping? And which one is going to be the nail in my coffin?

He shoved a hand through his hair. He was nervous.

"Wells went to Nocturnia for some information, and he got it," he finally said.

She tilted her head. "Why are you so cross? Was it not good information?"

"Depends on who you ask."

"I'm asking *you*," she shot back.

"Today was a lot," he told her. "I shouldn't have taken you there. I should have just left you here to rest."

She dropped her arms, hurt. His eyes softened, but his clenched jaw didn't.

"I think we should probably both get some sleep," he told her. "The next couple of days are going to be longer than most."

She didn't say anything more as they went back to his bedroom. As they lay down on opposite sides of the bed, a seed of dread began to bloom inside her. Something was very wrong.

She ran her fingertips over the words engraved onto the bracelet still clasped around her wrist and couldn't help but wonder that if she was where the light was, why did she suddenly feel so in the dark?

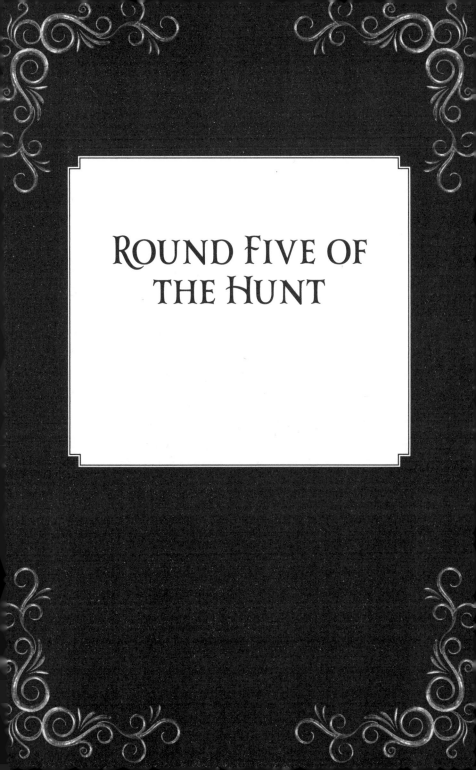

ROUND FIVE OF THE HUNT

39

ANYONE ELSE

When the next choosing ceremony came, Rowin was still acting strangely. They hadn't had a proper conversation, and yet he wouldn't let her out of his sight.

They'd spent most of their time in silence, trying to avoid his siblings, lingering in the library where she was finally able to show him the book she'd found on Crimson Rot. He'd seemed shocked that she'd bothered to track something down on the subject but didn't bother to say much else on the matter. Unfortunately, she hadn't learned anything about the virus that Rowin hadn't already told her, and it frustrated her to no end.

There was an inexplicable nagging feeling in the back of her mind that she was missing something.

Eventually the two of them left the library to eat dinner with Ellin, who spent the entire meal divulging all the gossip on the infamous Serpentine family Genevieve had heard so much about at her birthday celebration. She wondered if this was how Ophelia felt whenever Genevieve used to return home with stories of rowdy parties or gatherings with her friends.

After dinner, Genevieve chronicled the events of the past week in her diary, filling in with meticulous detail all the information she'd been neglecting. She tried to set down her feelings for Rowin, but she still couldn't define them, especially now that she was paranoid he'd made some sort of insidious deal with Knox. The Devil had offered her plenty of opportunity for bargains, after all, and everyone else had made it abundantly clear

Knox's first interest was in creating a good show for those paying to watch.

"And then there were five," Knox noted when he finally appeared in the ballroom with the rest of them, dragging Genevieve back to the present.

Without preamble, the Devil launched the Hunting Blade into the air, and they all watched as it went right to Ellin.

"Oh, Covington Silver"—Ellin flicked a piece of her platinum hair out of her face—"you'd better run after last night."

Covin grinned. "Bring it on, baby sister."

"Game?" Knox asked.

"Birds and stones," Ellin declared.

Knox nodded. "Begin."

Grave and Covin ambled off as usual, but Genevieve was surprised to see Rowin do the same without waiting for her. Grave seemed to notice as well.

She ran after Rowin, watching as he slipped into the powder room and closed the door before she could catch up. As she knocked on the door, she heard a resounding crash from within.

What the Hell?

The door swung open.

"Were you really not going to wait for me?" she huffed at Rowin. "Or explain what the hell *birds and stones* means . . . what did you *do?*"

The mirror over the vanity had been completely shattered. Its surface no longer reflective but a dormant black color. Shards of glass littered the countertop as well as drops of black blood. She glanced down at Rowin's fist. The skin of his knuckles was split open, but already healing.

Rowin pulled her into the powder room, shutting them inside. When Genevieve glanced pointedly at the mirror, Rowin shoved a hand through his hair.

"Ellin's game is a play on two birds, one stone," he explained, monotone, as if that was the most pressing topic. "If you had let me finish the tour a few days ago, you'd know that. If you see any other players at any point during the round, you have to stay with them for the remainder of the time. Makes it easier for the Hunter to get everyone rounded up. Though it's usually a game best played earlier on."

"Rowin, what *happened?*" she demanded. "In Knoxium, what the fuck happened? Because you certainly weren't acting like this before."

His expression gave nothing away. "How was I acting then, trouble?"

"Like...like..."

"Be *specific*," he taunted.

"Do not act as if you do not care for—" she began.

In a flash he had her backed up into a wall.

"And that's exactly the problem," he said, tone gruff. "I *do* care for you, Genevieve."

It was an incomplete thought, but he didn't seem able to make himself say anything else. Her mind went back to the thought of his meeting with Knox. The Devil must have offered him something. But did Rowin *take* it?

"You're a coward," she finally told him. "Whatever it is you aren't telling me...you're a *coward*."

His eyes flashed with anger.

Before he could give her another cryptic response or vague excuse as to why he was yet again refusing to open up to her, she spat, "Get out."

He lifted a brow. "You want me to leave?"

"Yes," she told him. "Find your own spot to hide."

He nodded, and without another word he slipped from the room. She stood there for a long moment, staring at the torn wallpaper from where he had detached the mirror. Eventually she left, her feet leading her back into the foyer and to the front door. And before she even realized what she was doing, she found herself back in the heart of the labyrinth, lying in the snow, looking forward to the numbness she'd soon feel again.

She thought she might actually have done it this time.

Contracted hypothermia.

She'd accidentally fallen asleep in the snow, dreaming about a forest full of mirrors, every one of their reflections showing a golden-eyed fox holding a dead rabbit in its maw. At least Farrow wasn't haunting her any longer. In fact, she hadn't dreamed of him since...

Since she'd woken up with Rowin wrapped around her.

The revelation jolted her, but she couldn't focus on that right now. She needed to focus on the fact that she couldn't feel her body. She flipped herself over, her limbs so stiff she cried out as she tried to stand. She hadn't meant to stay out here so long this time, but she knew it wasn't a place the siblings often looked, and she had needed to clear her head.

They don't look out here because none of them are foolish enough to hide in the snow and freeze to death, she chided herself.

She crawled over the threshold, relishing the warmth of the house as she made her way to Rowin's bedroom. She needed blankets.

Unfortunately, as she passed the first door in the hall, the ring on her finger began to warm. The heat against her cold skin was excruciating, and she yanked at the silver band, tears pricking at the corners of her eyes, until it flew off and sailed back across the foyer. It hit the far wall, bouncing to the ground with a clatter before rolling a few more feet and landing on its side. She dashed for it as fast as she could in her current state.

The moment she plucked it off the floor, however, she found that it was burning. And then she heard a sigh.

Genevieve lurched to a stand, eyes snapping down to the dining room's archway to find Ellin walking out, alerted by the noise of the ring. The Hunting Blade glinted in the candlelight as Ellin strutted closer.

"I was really hoping it wouldn't come down to this," Ellin said, sincere regret in her words. "I've actually enjoyed your company."

Genevieve backed away a step as she curled her hand around the burning ring. It had heated up next to that first room. Which meant someone else who wished her ill was in there, and Ellin's choice of game would mean they'd have to stay near her.

Ellin followed her movements.

"Did you know there were ostriches in Hell?" Genevieve blurted out.

Ellin lifted a brow. "Are those really what you want your last words to be?"

"What about 'I apologize that the world is about to be a lot duller' instead?" Genevieve suggested as she took another step back.

Ellin matched it. "Better…"

Genevieve took another step. "While we're on the topic, I'd like my tombstone to read 'Here lies Genevieve Silver. Unless you're a grave robber. Then here lies someone much less fabulous.'"

Ellin sighed again. "Alright, we're just going to have to get this over with, I think."

Genevieve took that as her cue to turn and run. She dove toward the hallway, making it to the door where she'd sensed one of Ellin's siblings and twisting the knob to—of course—find it locked. She kicked at the door as hard as she could, but her bones still felt like they were made of glass, and she hardly had any energy left.

No more going outside.

Ellin reached her now, blithely slashing the Hunting Blade down toward her chest. Genevieve tried to duck and tripped backward, falling hard onto her tailbone. Ellin was on top of her in seconds, straddling her waist and angling the point of the blade toward Genevieve's heart.

Ellin gritted her teeth as her charcoal gaze filled with tears. "I really am sorry."

Genevieve swallowed her pride and did the only thing she could think of.

"*Rowin!*" she screamed as she reached out and fought against Ellin's hold while the knife continued to lower. "*Rowin!*"

Ellin was strong. It was not surprising—her body was corded with lean muscles. And Genevieve knew she was not going to be able to hold on much longer. Then it was too late, her strength was waning quickly, and the blade was at the top of her bodice now, pricking her skin and drawing a drop of blood.

Genevieve squeezed her eyes shut.

Dying numb is better than the fire, at least.

The weight on her chest suddenly disappeared, and Genevieve blinked open her eyes to find Rowin holding a thrashing Ellin back from her. He had one arm curled around his sister's throat and the other gripping the crown of her head.

"Forgive me, Ellin," he grunted, and he snapped the girl's neck.

Genevieve cringed at the crunch of Ellin's bones breaking, and the sight of her body falling limply to the ground.

"Let's go," he ordered Genevieve.

Genevieve swallowed and stood, stepping over Ellin's form as they ran to find another place to hide.

Once again, Genevieve found herself sitting, annoyed, on the dingy couch of the secret room in the library. Rowin had not spoken a word to her after the incident with Ellin, but the way he was pacing around the room certainly said enough. Umbra watched him move from the corner of the room, back and forth, back and forth.

Genevieve was determined not to break their silence first.

She lasted an hour.

"Would you just fucking say something," she snapped at him, standing from the couch to block his path.

That did it. He strode toward her with such purpose she found herself tripping over her feet to back away.

"Anyone else," he told her. "*Anyone fucking else* in the world could have opened that fucking letter and it had to be you."

At first she thought the words were said with fury, but when she looked up into his eyes, she saw they were filled with pain.

"Just *tell me*, Rowin," she pleaded. "Don't make me call you a coward again—"

"Knox offered me a deal."

She felt the blood drain from her face now. She knew it. She *knew* it.

"Wells warned me that Knox was looking for a way to eliminate you from the Hunt. And that I should consider whatever his offer was carefully. Knox asked me to turn on you in exchange for . . ."

"For what?" she demanded.

"For my freedom," he told her, blinking open his eyes to lock his golden gaze onto hers. "He can't kill you himself while you're within the Hunt. It has to be one of us."

She held her breath.

"I turned him down, Genevieve," he murmured. "I would never...I could never..."

Tears pricked in Genevieve's eyes. Because even though those were the words she'd wanted to hear him say, it also hit her now exactly what he'd given up.

"You barely even know me Rowin," she forced herself to say. "He offered you eternal freedom and—"

He shook his head. "Nothing is eternal. Except for the fact that you've *ruined* me. All I've ever wanted was freedom from this wretched game, and I didn't even hesitate for a *second* to give it up."

"Why didn't you tell me? You promised you were—"

"Because I was trying to protect you. Can't you see that? I'm convinced you were made by the King of Devils himself to torture me for my sins."

"You're such a self-centered bastard." She scoffed at his presumption and poked a finger into his chest. "I deserve to be the center of my own story. I was not made for *you*."

"Truth, truth, lie," he told her.

Her heart skipped a beat.

You're such a self-centered bastard. Truth. *I deserve to be the center of my own story.* Truth. *I was not made for* you. Lie.

"I was *not* made for you," she repeated, though it was much less convincing this time.

"Then maybe *I* was made for *you*," he implored, as if he were angry about that fact. "How else have you managed to get so deep under my skin in such a short amount of time? Why is it that every time I try to imagine what it would be like to sever our vows, I feel like the Hunting Blade is piercing my heart? Fifteen years I've lived for everyone else around me. I've withered away in this damned place. Until you showed up and you made me laugh. You gave me hope."

Genevieve wanted to tell him it was a ridiculous notion that he was made for her. But then she remembered that he had been waiting here, in the same exact spot, for her to show up at his door. She remembered the way his body felt inside hers, the ecstasy he could bring her to that no one else ever had. Their shared scars. Their understanding of each other. Their vows.

My soul is your soul. My blood is your blood. Eternally.

"Shadows can only be seen in the presence of light," he told her, the words agonized. "I worry when you leave, there will be no one left to see me."

She wasn't sure which of them moved first.

40

SCORCHING

If she had been worried about hypothermia before, she certainly wasn't now. As Rowin expertly unlaced her corset and peeled away her dress, he deepened their kiss, scorching her with desire from the inside out. She clawed at the buttons on his shirt, before ripping them open and sending them flying across the room as he huffed a laugh at her fervor.

When neither of them had a stitch of clothing left, he bent down to slip his hands beneath her thighs and lifted her so she could wrap her legs around his waist. He walked them over to the side of the couch, setting her down on the armrest as he knelt all the way down to the floor.

"Lift," he demanded as he gripped her hips.

She did, and he pulled her forward until she was perched on the edge, her knees spread wide open to give his mouth access to the core of her. He didn't bother with any preamble, just buried his face between her legs, lapping at her clit until she was dripping wet, lifting a hand to slide two fingers, rings and all, inside her. He curled his fingers as he pumped them in and out, his tongue continuing to lathe at her like a man starved.

"You're my favorite fucking flavor," he murmured against her as his strokes became lazier, torturous. "Hell, I could stay here forever."

At his words, her climax hit her fast and hard, her hands gripping at the couch as she rode his face through the aftershocks. Her chest heaved with effort as she came back down, but he didn't bother to stop. She was so wet that the couch beneath her was soaked.

"Rowin," she cried. "Please."

"Please what?" he asked as he continued to suck at her tight bundle of nerves.

"Fuck me, *please*."

He finally pulled back, a smirk on his lips. He scooped her up beneath her thighs and sat back against the couch cushions, keeping her straddled over his lap. He kissed his way down her neck to her breasts as she wriggled against his hard length, looking for friction. He sucked one of her nipples, making her moan. A little too loudly.

"If you aren't quiet, I'll have to stop," he warned, switching to her other nipple.

She whimpered, softly this time. He grazed the tight bud in his mouth with his teeth in approval. She reached between them, wrapping her hand around the head of his cock, and squeezed. His hips bucked, and this time he was the one being a bit too loud.

She gave him a haughty grin.

"Oh, you've done it now, trouble," he told her as he moved his hands to either side of her waist and lifted her away from his lap—

—to slam her all the way down onto his cock.

She screamed his name, and he quickly covered her mouth with his hand.

When he was sure she was done, he folded his arms behind his head and said, "Ride me."

She leaned forward to place her palms against his chest, for leverage, but he shook his head.

"Reach behind you and grab my thighs. I want to be able to see you fucking yourself on my cock as hard as you can."

She did as he directed, arching her hips and chest forward as she grabbed onto his legs behind her back. She rolled her hips forward, once, twice, his cock hitting places inside her she didn't think it was possible to reach.

"That's right," he encouraged. "Now, faster."

She adjusted her pace, grinding against him in a steady rhythm until her muscles were burning with the effort, her temples beading with sweat. After a minute, she began to whimper with need.

"I know," Rowin murmured, as he pried his eyes away from her writhing body to meet her gaze. "I know. You're taking it so well." He groaned. "You're the most stunning person I've ever seen."

The only thing she could think to say was, "Obviously."

The smile he gave her now was brilliant. He shifted them suddenly, in one fluid motion, his cock staying sheathed inside her as he pressed her back against the couch. He picked up his pace then. Relentlessly fucking her until she was *begging* him for her release.

"Please," she whimpered. "Please. *Rowin.*"

He reached between them and pressed the pad of his thumb against her clit, wringing another orgasm out of her just before he pulled out and—

"Oh, *for fuck's sake*," a deep, displeased voice echoed through the room.

Covin and Rowin were still arguing an hour later while Genevieve etched yet another tic-tac-toe grid into one of the floorboards with her fingernail. Since Ellin's choice of rules required all of them to stick together for the remainder of the round,

Genevieve had been attempting to distract them with various games to keep them from bickering.

"You go first this time," she told Covin.

He paused his fight with Rowin long enough to look down at the game and carve an "X" into the center. She wrinkled her nose. He always took the center.

"Grave did not eat his twin in the womb," Rowin said for the tenth time. "Sevin made that up to scare Ellin when we were kids."

"I'm telling you, Mother told me that it wasn't just a story. And Sevin overheard Father talking about it once."

"Maybe that's why he's so large," Genevieve quipped.

Covin gestured to Genevieve as he emphasized to his brother, "*See?*"

After yet another game ended in a tie, Genevieve got up from the floor and walked toward where Rowin was sitting on the couch, now fully clothed. He lifted his arm in invitation, and she immediately tucked herself into his side.

"You two make me sick," Covin said, though his tone was rather chipper. "Are you not worried this is about to end in tragedy? You know Knox does not like to lose. I can't imagine the tricks he will have up his sleeves if either of you make it out of here."

Genevieve and Rowin exchanged a loaded glance.

Covin had asked a similar question earlier, when he popped up through the trap door and found them in the most intimate position possible. Rowin had nearly ripped his brother's head off for interrupting them at such an inopportune moment, but, of course, Covin wasn't able to leave due to the rules of Ellin's version of the game.

"Stop talking about Knox," Rowin snapped.

Covin lifted his hands in innocence. "Just making conversation."

"Make it about something else," Rowin muttered.

"Oh! I have one," Genevieve chimed in. "Your tongue—did that hurt?"

Covin grinned, letting the split tips of his tongue flick out between his teeth like a snake's. "Not really. But then I have a *very* high tolerance for pain."

Genevieve glanced at Rowin now. "What about your tolerance for pain? Is it high?"

"Being born in this family has all but guaranteed that," Rowin confirmed.

Covin stood and walked over to the bar cart to fix himself a drink.

Genevieve leaned into Rowin's ear and whispered, "What about the piercing on your..."

Rowin smirked. "Okay, that one hurt like a fucking bitch."

"How long have you had it? Am I the first one who's..."

"Seen it? Licked it?" Rowin murmured. "Yes."

"I can hear you whispering. Can you not talk about Rowin's cock anymore in my presence? I think I've suffered enough today. Enough for an eternity, really," Covin grumbled as he tipped his head back and downed his glass of whiskey.

That was fair.

"How much time do we have left?" Genevieve asked.

The two of them checked their pocket watches at the same time.

"Fifteen minutes," Covin said first.

"We can probably just head downstairs now," Rowin suggested as he stood from the couch and stretched. "I'm in the mood to go to bed. Maybe read a book."

Covin gave him a look that said, *Yeah, right.*

"Missing your copy of *The Devil's Darkest Desires?*" Genevieve teased.

"Yes," Rowin answered. "I left off at the part where the Devil takes his mistress to his throne room and shoves his—"

"If you say the word 'cock,' I'm going to beat the shit out of you," Covin threatened.

Genevieve started to laugh, until she felt her ring warming on her finger. One look at her face and Rowin seemed to understand what was happening.

He cursed as he rushed for the trap door, but it was too late.

"Well, well, well," Ellin laughed as she climbed into the room, pulling the door shut behind her. "Looks like I've found the party. Do none of you realize you're supposed to be *quiet* during hide-and-seek?"

"We got bored waiting for you to be good at this game," Covin admitted.

"Ellin—" Rowin began, but Ellin bared her teeth at him and cut him off before he could finish.

"Save it," she snapped. "I'll deal with you next."

She turned her sights on Covin.

"Hey," Covin said defensively, "I was only kidding."

"You cut off my *ear*," she screeched at him. "You *know* how long body parts take to grow back! It's worse than Rowin snapping my neck!"

Genevieve looked at her closer now, trying to see which side the aforementioned ear might be missing from, but Ellin's haircut covered it very well.

"The left," Rowin whispered.

"Shut *up*," Ellin snarled at Rowin.

Covin used the brief seconds her gaze was off him to lunge, but Ellin was quick. She dodged to the side, jabbing out with the blade and burying it in his abdomen.

He cursed, hunching forward to yank the dagger from his stomach as he snarled, "Rowin, a little help?"

Rowin didn't move. "No, I think you've got this."

"You're a prick," Covin seethed as he dodged another one of Ellin's stabs.

This went on for a while, the two of them wearing each other out and rearranging the furniture with their wrestling as Rowin kept Genevieve strategically out of harm's way. Eventually, though, Covin did get the upper hand: or a fist in Ellin's gut, to be exact. Ellin let the knife clatter to the ground as she vomited up her dinner from Covin's hit.

Genevieve winced and grasped onto Rowin's hand.

"Fuck, El," Covin said regretfully. And Genevieve could tell watching Ellin in pain truly did destroy him.

Ellin began to sniffle as she finished retching. "I'm done. I'm *done*. Whoever's turn it is next, you can just have me! I hate this fucking game!"

Covin took a cautious step forward as Ellin straightened herself up, tears streaming down her face. "El, it's going to be okay—"

"*No*," she spat at him. "It's not! Rowin has more at stake than any of us, and he's going to be the next Hunter! I lost my *ear*, Sapphire is still injured from her run-in with Sevin's bastard wolf, and I am *done*. I want this to be *over*."

Covin took another step forward, and Rowin gave Genevieve's hand two squeezes in quick succession. As if to say *watch*.

Genevieve noticed it then, how the toe of Ellin's right foot had subtly wedged itself beneath the hilt of the dagger. In a split second, Ellin kicked the knife up into her waiting hand and rammed it right through Covin's heart just before the bells announcing the safe hours rang through the house.

Covin and the Hunting Blade disappeared in a blink, and Genevieve gaped at the other woman in awe.

"Baby sister guilt." Ellin winked a watery eye at Genevieve. "Gets them every single time."

Something about her words made Genevieve pause, but a moment later Rowin was leading her away.

Genevieve and Rowin spent the rest of their day in his bedroom. Specifically in between his sheets.

Later in the evening, as Genevieve was falling asleep against Rowin's chest, the spark of an idea began to form in the back of her mind. She mumbled something to him about it, but he'd worn her out enough that she couldn't make herself bother to check whether his own eyes were even open.

At some point, however, Rowin got out of bed. She pried her eyes open ever so slightly, to watch as he got dressed and then lifted a very sleepy Umbra from her place on the chair in the corner. He placed his Familiar next to Genevieve's head, and the fox gave her an affectionate lick on the cheek.

"Where are you going?" Genevieve whispered.

"To find Ellin," he murmured before tucking the covers tighter around her in the bed. "Go back to sleep."

He quietly slipped out, the click of the lock reverberating in the darkness, and she let her exhaustion pull her back under.

41

FOR DEAD

It was the ring that woke her.

At first, she thought the nightmares about Farrow had come back, the fire that used to engulf her every night in her sleep returning to ruin the first week of peace she'd had in a long time. As she cracked open her eyes in the dark, however, she knew she wasn't alone, and the burning around her finger was very real.

"Good, you're awake," Grave said from the foot of the bed.

She shot up, adrenaline pumping through her veins as she clutched the sheets to her naked chest. Umbra was nowhere to be found.

"How did you get in here?" she demanded.

"I can create my own portals," Grave reminded her.

Right.

"Where's Umbra?" she demanded.

Grave flicked his eyes to the left, and Genevieve followed his gaze to find Umbra's limp body lying on the floor next to the wall. She gasped in horror, shooting out of bed to go to the fox, but when she saw Umbra's chest rise and fall, a jolt of relief went through her.

She spun back to Grave with a glare. "*Why* are you here?"

"Because Knox confirmed my suspicions. About his damned loophole." Grave crossed his arms. "I knew there had to be a catch. There was no way he would let someone out of this game without taking something in return. And I was right. Knox explained it all to me as a little gift—that only *one* of us could get out of serving him each year. If Rowin gets free, forever, then Knox won't be bound to let anyone else out of the game. We'll be forced to play every year with no true winner. Every year we'll go back to serving Knox in Hell."

Shock went through Genevieve. Knox had truly thought of everything.

"So, if anyone is getting the fuck out of here, it's going to be *me*. Which unfortunately means your time here is up," Grave told her.

"You've tried killing me once before," she said. "And it didn't work out very well, remember?"

"But now I know all your tricks. You don't have the element of surprise anymore, do you?"

Genevieve froze. Or, rather, she was *frozen*.

"Go ahead, try using your magic," he encouraged.

She did and—nothing. Not even a flicker. Whatever hold he had on her body made everything except her thoughts entirely still.

She tried to speak. Nothing came out.

He lifted her off her feet then, not with his hands, but with his magic. And Remi had been right—Grave was powerful. In a way that she could feel in the very marrow of her bones. The only other beings she'd ever felt such power from were Knox and the Prince of the Devils himself.

"It will be over before you realize," he promised.

And then everything around her exploded.

When Genevieve came to, she could not see or hear anything.

The room around her was filled with roiling shadows. And amongst them a single flash of gold. Rowin's eyes were glowing.

"What's happening?" she tried to ask, but her voice was drowned out by the thunder of power crackling around her.

Then someone burst through the door, and the shadows disappeared in a blinding flash of light.

"What the *fuck* is going on in here?" Ellin screeched.

White light was emanating from her hands as she sucked away Rowin's shadows so they could all see.

"*He was trying to kill her,*" Rowin snarled at Grave.

"What's new?" Ellin shouted. "You two cannot kill each other over some girl you've known for less than a week." She threw an apologetic look in Genevieve's direction. "No offense."

Genevieve rubbed her pounding temples. "None taken."

In fact, she sort of agreed. She'd made fun of Ophie relentlessly for nearly dying over a hot Ghost with green eyes whom she'd only known for days. She definitely owed her sister an apology. Love did not give a single fuck about time.

"Then how about I kill him over the fact that he's going to trap our entire family?" Grave spat.

"What the Hell are you talking about?" Ellin asked.

"If Rowin is released from the Hunt, baby sister, then the rest of us will keep playing without any true winner," Grave explained once again. "Knox confirmed it himself."

Ellin went slack-jawed as she flicked her eyes between her brothers. "Fucking Hell."

"Let's finish it here and now," Rowin told his brother. "I already told you once, Grave, she's *mine*. You are not going to take her from me."

Genevieve's breath hitched.

Ellin seemed to sober then. "You need to walk away, Grave."

Grave looked at her in disbelief.

"Play to win if you want," Ellin said. "But I won't let you

murder her outside the game either. I like her. She's earned her spot in this game."

Genevieve's pride swelled at Ellin's words.

Grave seemed to give the decision a great amount of consideration before finally, blessedly, releasing his hold on Genevieve. He transported from the room without another word.

Ellin looked at Rowin and said, "Get your shit together. If I'm going to trust you, I need to be certain you know what you're doing."

Then she left, too.

"Is Umbra okay?" Genevieve whispered.

He nodded, turning to wave a hand in the fox's direction, and Genevieve watched as the Familiar dissolved into smoke.

"I won't be able to summon her for a while. Until she heals. Broken bones and poison aren't fatal to Familiars. Not like getting eaten by piranhas would have been."

He strode over to the bed, pulling her into his arms to bury his face in her neck.

"Are you alright?" he asked.

She nodded. "That was, what, his—fourth? fifth?—attempt to kill me? I'm getting rather used to it." A pause. "So you spoke to Ellin?"

"I did. She didn't like it but...well, you heard her. We're almost there."

Genevieve whispered: "This is all my fault."

"No, it's not," Rowin murmured. "I started this a long time ago. You just sped up the ending."

She swallowed. "Rowin?"

"Yes?"

"You called me yours again," she whispered.

He looked away. "I'm sorry. I know you told me not to."

Before she could say anything more, he kissed her on the temple.

"Go back to sleep. I'll be here this time," he vowed.

As she curled back up against his chest in the bed, she found that this time she couldn't go back to sleep. Not because of Grave's attack or because she wasn't still exhausted, but because of the excitement of everything to come.

And his words still echoing in her mind.

She's mine. She's mine. She's mine.

ROUND SIX OF THE HUNT

42

FAVORED

When Genevieve couldn't go back to sleep, she and Rowin went to the library. Discussing anything and everything except the Hunt. Eventually, Genevieve dozed off in Rowin's lap while he read *The Devil's Darkest Desires*. Waiting for midnight to finally come around once again.

Just before the bells tolled, they walked to the ballroom, running into Ellin along the way. Grave arrived moments later, then Knox, the latter twirling the Hunting Blade in the air. When the choosing ceremony began and the knife shot straight for Rowin and Genevieve, Rowin caught it easily.

"Game?" Knox requested.

"Ready or not," Rowin stated. He'd explained earlier that this was the game he would choose because it didn't allow a head start like most of the others.

Knox dipped his chin in a nod. "Begin."

Genevieve watched as Ellin lifted her chin and strutted right up to Rowin. Grave watched with a look of astonishment.

"This is between the rest of you," Ellin told them all. "Rowin, as we agreed."

Rowin didn't hesitate. He shoved the blade right into her heart. She disappeared in an instant.

A snarl of frustration sounded from Knox, but no one paid the Devil a second glance.

Rowin turned to Grave next and said, "I can chase you all over this house now, if you wish, or you can agree to leave us the fuck alone until the final showdown tomorrow, and we can Hunt each other in a real match."

There was a long, tense pause.

Then, finally, Grave grunted, "Done."

"Have all of you forgotten what your job is here?" Knox inserted.

"Don't worry," Grave told the Devil. "This just means all our energy is going to go into making an extra-explosive finale."

That seemed to placate Knox, though not by much.

Once Grave and the Devil had disappeared, Genevieve turned to Rowin and said, "What now?"

"Now we wait for the end," he told her, his tone solemn.

Whether he meant their end or the game's, she wasn't sure.

Sometime in the middle of the witching hours, Genevieve found herself in the library with Rowin yet again. She'd never spent so much time around books in her entire life, but she found that she had a taste for reading once she'd discovered the right books.

Rowin was right, The Devil's Darkest Desires *is a masterpiece.*

She also found that she enjoyed sitting next to him in their understanding silence more than she enjoyed silence with anyone else, but, of course, it could only last so long before she was itching to talk to him again.

"Are you scared? For tomorrow?" she eventually whispered. "About how this will end?"

"Yes," Rowin admitted. "I am."

"Everything will be okay, though. Right?" she implored. "Because there are no more secrets between us?"

A pause.

"Right," he agreed.

Genevieve woke with her cheek resting on Rowin's chest, his arm wrapped tightly around her waist. She yawned and stretched.

"I don't remember falling asleep in here," she said, voice thick with sleep, as she glanced up at his face.

"That's because you didn't," he told her. "You fell asleep in the library. I carried you back."

She nodded.

"Genevieve, I need to tell you something," he murmured.

"Yes?" she asked.

"I'm glad you didn't listen to me, when I told you to leave that first day," he said. "No matter what happens, I need you to know that you've saved me."

"You've saved me too," she told him as she ran her thumb over her ring and then her bracelet.

He pulled her mouth to his, kissing her in a way that he never had before. Like it might be their last.

Round Seven of the Hunt

The Final Match

43

THE FOX

W elcome to the final match," Knox said when he appeared in the ballroom at midnight, making Genevieve's ring blaze to life.

Rowin had been quiet for most of the day, though he made sure to indulge her every whim. Playing cards with her over lunch, taking her for one last walk through the maze and snow, making fun of the oil portraits of his family. She hadn't realized, until then, that she'd never bothered to really look at his. Umbra outshone him, she'd said. He'd agreed.

Now, the two of them stood, facing Knox and Grave, braced for a fight to the death.

"First I would like to say *congratulations*, Mrs. Silver," Knox told her. "You've officially been voted as this year's Favored. It's time to claim your prize. I hope you can remember what it is…"

"I can," she told him.

"Picture it in your mind, then, and it should appear on your person," Knox directed.

She did exactly as he instructed, and a moment later she felt something heavy sitting in the pocket of her dress.

"This finale is rather special," Knox continued. "Usually this round of the Hunt is a clean duel. You each get a chance to race for the blade, and last man standing wins. But since not one member of this family has been able to complete the simple task of killing a *mortal girl*, I've decided to make an amendment to the rules. And the prize."

Genevieve froze now. Rowin's face remained a mask. Grave smiled.

"If I die, Salem *will* come after you," Genevieve told the Devil.

Knox grinned at her. "Not if I keep your soul and threaten to torture it for all eternity if he so much as *looks* in my direction."

Genevieve looked to Rowin, but he was staring straight ahead.

"So, here's my offer, boys: If she dies, within the hour, I'll release you and the rest of your siblings from your contracts to me. Forevermore. Effective immediately."

Genevieve's chest tightened. The Devil was pulling out every ace he had.

"And I'm going to make it very easy for you," Knox continued. "The Hunting Blade will deliver her soul to me. Rowington, I've lifted the enchantment binding your life to hers. I'll even give you both your magic back. Since she seems to be so slippery."

Genevieve stumbled back a step as Grave swung toward her—no. Not toward her. Toward *Rowin*. Who had still not given a single reaction to Knox's words.

"You want the honors?" Grave asked his brother. "Or do you want me to take care of it?"

"How noble," Knox said as he pressed a mocking hand over his heart. "Not making your brother kill his own wife."

Genevieve shook her head as she backed away from the circle. "*No.*"

Knox smiled smugly at her, and the beat of her heart began roaring in her ears.

Rowin turned to her then, his mask of apathy finally slipping away.

He was grinning like the fox who'd finally caught the hare.

"I want you to know, for what it's worth, that I am deeply sorry for what I'm about to do," he told her.

44

THE HARE

Genevieve took off running. Just like the prey the Devil always hoped she'd be.

Her mind was racing as she burst into the foyer and ran for the front door. Pushing her legs until they burned, she sprinted out to the labyrinth. At this point she knew every twist and turn like the back of her hand.

As she ran through the maze, she caught glimpses of herself in the mirrors that lined the thorned walls within. A wild girl in a beautiful gown being chased by the fox that had stolen her heart.

As she crashed into the center of the labyrinth, she found Rowin already waiting for her.

Grave blinked into view right behind his brother.

Knox appeared next, right beside Grave, grinning from ear to ear. Her ring was so hot now it was nearly melting through her skin.

"Thank you," Knox told her, sincerely. "This is going to make for a truly grand finale."

Rowin started forward. And Genevieve backed away, until she hit one of the hedges.

Hell was made of swirling darkness and secrets just like the man in front of her.

"I loathe you," she swore as the black tendrils of magic that slithered from his hands wrapped around her wrists and throat, shoving her back into the labyrinth's wall. The sensual energy that always buzzed over her skin whenever he was this close made her grit her teeth as she resisted the shot of attraction slowly heating up her veins. The last time his shadows were wrapped around her like this, there was much less clothing between them.

He followed after his shadows, stalking forward until his chest pressed into hers.

"Love. Loathing. Same passion, different names," he told her. "And how easily and swiftly the line can be blurred, don't you think?"

"No," she seethed. "I don't think it will ever be anything but crystal clear to me that I *hate* you."

Leaning down slowly, until his lips were right next to her ear, he said, "Prove it."

Knox laughed behind him in delight.

Then Rowin whispered to her, "Two truths and a lie?" Over his shoulder, she saw Knox and Grave share a look of confusion.

"Go fuck yourself. As if I would ever believe a single word from your mouth after this."

"C'mon, trouble, play the game with me," Rowin taunted, a sly grin on his mouth.

"Fine." The smile she gave him now was vicious. "Go ahead."

"You love me," he started.

Her throat became tight with shock.

He reached out and cupped her face, gently, brushing the pad of his thumb over her cheek as he spoke. "You *are* mine."

He leaned his forehead against hers.

"And finally. Your plan is brilliant, but I don't think it's going to work."

Genevieve's heart was still racing from the first two things he said. When they'd concocted this plan over the last couple of nights, she'd told him to surprise her with the secrets he chose. One last little game just for them.

"What the fuck is going on?" Knox snapped, taking a step forward.

Genevieve smiled as Rowin loosened his hold on her, and she dug out the Soul Lock from her pocket. "Truth. Truth. *Lie.*"

"*What is going on?*" Knox snarled.

Behind him Grave raised a hand. And froze the Devil in place.

Knox roared, and Genevieve saw every muscle in Grave's body strain with effort, the veins of his biceps bulging so much she thought they might burst.

"Do it," Grave said between gritted teeth. "I can't hold him for long."

Genevieve clasped the necklace around her neck and pried open the locket. It had all started when she first saw the Soul Lock. But when she told Rowin her idea, they both knew they would have to convince Grave. It hadn't been easy, especially after the fight in Rowin's bedroom. It had taken them hours, about a million promises, and invoking Salem's name countless times, but finally they'd convinced him this was their final chance at saving his *entire* family.

Grave had gone to Knox first thing this morning and planted the idea of capturing Genevieve's soul instead of killing her. He'd also suggested that Knox could turn both brothers against Genevieve. That he could lift their magic to leave absolutely no doubt. Knox's audience would be transfixed.

He can't resist a good show, Rowin had said. And he'd been right.

"Ready?" Rowin asked.

Genevieve began to nod and then paused. "Rowin?"

"Yes?" he whispered.

Genevieve had gone to Enchantra looking for the reason that she felt she had never belonged in her family. And she had found *him.* Someone who made her a part of his own family. Whether she had been ready or not.

She'd spent a lot of time in the last year wanting to be the girl she had been before Farrow broke her heart. Before he set her hopes and dreams on fire and plunged her into the darkness. But Rowin was right.

The light was wherever she was.

"Would the two of you hurry the fuck up?" Grave seethed with effort now.

"I *am* yours," she vowed. "Take good care of my soul, alright?"

Then she reached down to wrap her grip over his hand, the one holding the blade, and without hesitation she forced him to run the knife through her heart.

45

FADING

Every inch of her skin felt like it was on fire as she gaped down at the blade sticking out of her chest. And for once the flames did not scare her, because *he* was the one igniting her.

As if she were watching herself from above, she saw Rowin pull the knife from her body, a glowing blue light being extracted along with it. Rowin raised the open locket toward the strange blue energy, and the Soul Lock immediately sucked it inside before snapping shut.

I've got you, he whispered.

She saw tears in Rowin's eyes. But before she could lift a hand to comfort him, everything began fading slowly to black.

Rowin.

Rowin.

Row . . .

Ro . . .

. . .

. . .

BACK TO THE BEGINNING

46

Deep Trouble

When Genevieve woke, it was to a fuzzy mind and a familiar place. She blinked her heavy eyelids open, squinting into the dark of her childhood bedroom. Her limbs felt heavy, her mouth dry, as she slowly sat up against her headboard. She reached up to rub her fists over her groggy eyes, trying to clear the fog in her brain as she searched her memories for a clue of how in the Hell she'd gotten home.

The last thing she could recall was a carriage leaving her in front of a silver gate, an invitation clutched in her hand...

"Ah, you're finally awake."

Genevieve gasped, hand flying up to clutch her heart at Salem's sudden appearance a few feet away. She hated when he blinked in and out like that, but he didn't have the self-satisfied smirk on his face that he usually wore when he managed to catch someone off guard. In fact, he looked rather serious. Which was awfully unnerving.

"You are in deep trouble," he drawled, like a disapproving older brother. He casually reached into a brown paper bag and pulled out a piece of what looked to be...black licorice?

Genevieve eyed him curiously as he popped the candy into his mouth, wincing as he chewed. "Didn't Ophie threaten to throttle you if you didn't lose the obnoxious Southern accent?"

He swallowed and reached for another piece of candy. "Ophelia is currently out in the Quarter. Which means you get to deal with me and my horrible accent as punishment."

"Punishment?" she prompted as he bit into the candy once more and grimaced. "And do you not like licorice or something? You look like you're in pain."

He glared down at the bag. "Ophelia likes the red pieces, but they only come mixed with the black ones, from that candy store on Chartres Street. She always gets excited at the fact that we can split a bag, because she eats all the red ones—and I eat all the black."

"Except you clearly hate them," Genevieve reasoned.

"Something neither of us will ever tell her," he said pointedly as he popped another one into his mouth. "Understood?"

Genevieve snorted. "Couldn't you just snap your fingers and make them disappear? Instead of suffering."

Salem fixed her with an intense look. "I will suffer a million times over if it makes your sister happy. Which means I will eat a million pieces of this Hellish candy." A pause. "Or I'll just burn down the store. I'm still deciding."

There was a sudden, inexplicable ache in her chest as she watched him fold down the top of the bag and shove it into the inner pocket of his viridian coat for safekeeping. She knew how easy it would be for him to take every shortcut at any given opportunity, to will whatever he or her sister wanted into existence with just a single thought. But taking the extra time to do even the simplest of things, especially when they might be unpleasant, was how he loved Ophelia.

Now, he crossed his arms over his chest and narrowed his eyes down at her. "Speaking of making your sister suffer, what in fucking Hell were you thinking straying from the itinerary she made for you?"

"I . . . wanted to find something," she whispered.

"Vivi," Salem said pointedly.

"You and Ophie wouldn't get it," Genevieve whispered. "You

have each other. You *understand* each other. I wanted to find that for myself."

He sighed deeply. It wasn't as if he could argue with her.

"What happened?" she finally asked. "How did you find me? When did I get back here?"

There was a hard glint in his emerald eyes now. "What do you remember?"

She thought about that question. Truthfully, she wasn't sure. It was as if moths had eaten holes in the fabric of her memory. One day she was in Rome, being stalked by crows, the next she was waiting before a grand gate, plucking strange berries from thorned vines . . .

That must be it. The berries had done something to her. Poisoned her.

She explained as much aloud, but when his expression didn't change, she asked, "What? What's wrong?"

"The demonberries have nothing to do with this," he explained cautiously. As if he were afraid he'd spook her. "You . . . died, Genevieve."

"*What?*" she exclaimed in amused disbelief. "Stop toying with me."

"About four days ago, Ophelia and I were enjoying a very nice afternoon when two large men tore a portal into the den and delivered your *corpse.*"

Genevieve gaped at him. He seemed serious.

"Fortunately, you were only *temporarily* dead, because one of the men also delivered a locket containing your *soul,*" Salem told her, his tone exasperated. "Do you have any idea how difficult it is to revive a mortal body after the soul has been taken from it?"

"No," she whispered, still in shock at the words he was saying.

"Very," he deadpanned. "Very difficult. And very costly."

Genevieve tossed the covers off her legs and stood from the

bed onto shaky feet. The ache in her chest grew hollower by the second.

What is that?

When she felt steady enough, she lifted her chin at Salem and implored, "I feel...different. What happened to me?"

Salem shook his head. "Forging your soul and body together required more magic than I have at my fingertips. To do it, to sustain the enchantment, I was forced to take something from you."

"What?"

"All your memories of a person you love. And you're lucky I didn't have to take more."

"Who?" she beseeched. "Who is the person that was erased?"

She flicked through all the people she loved most in her mind. Ophelia. Salem. Luci. Basile. Iris. Poe. Her mother...

Everyone was still there.

Then what is this hollow feeling inside of me?

"The fabric of memory is fragile—believe me, I know," Salem told her solemnly. "Overwhelming you with details now could cause more harm than good."

"You just expect me to remain ignorant, then? With no recollection of what happened? Of events that were apparently *life altering?*" she demanded.

He had opened his mouth to respond when a familiar voice suddenly rang out from downstairs. "Salem?"

Salem's mouth instantly curled into a grin at the sound of Ophelia calling his name. "Up here, angel. Guess who's finally awake?"

A pause. Then footsteps pounding up the stairs.

The moment Ophelia stepped into her bedroom, she ran for Genevieve. "*Vivi.* Thank Hell. I've been worried sick."

Genevieve wrapped her arms around her sister as tight as she could, Ophelia's presence an instant balm to the ache still lingering in her chest. "Ophie, your Devil won't tell me what happened."

"Tattletale." Salem smirked.

Ophelia pulled back with a glare, but it wasn't for Salem; it was for Genevieve. "That's because he's trying to undo all the trouble you've gotten yourself into. What the *Hell* were you thinking, Genevieve? Traveling to a strange place without telling anyone?"

"I just . . . I wanted answers. About Mother. About myself. If there are others like me. Like us."

Ophie's eyes softened now. "I know Mother never gave you what you needed or deserved. I know that. But *I* will give it to you, Genevieve. I'll give you anything. If you'd just stay out of trouble for *once*."

Genevieve closed her eyes and leaned her forehead against her sister's. "I know, Ophie. I just needed to find something for myself."

"I understand that, too," Ophelia said back. "We can talk more later. For now, you should get freshened up and then read the first letter."

"First letter?" Genevieve wondered.

Salem slid something out of another of his coat pockets. An envelope. One with a very familiar-looking seal on the back.

"Start here," Salem directed. "We all agreed that it would be best if you got the entire story in installments."

Genevieve wrinkled her nose as she snatched the letter out of his hand. "This is a ridiculous waste of time. Why can't you just spit it out already?"

Salem grinned. "He'd said you'd be difficult about this part. That's why he didn't give us all the details of what happened. Even if we wanted to tell you everything, we couldn't. But don't worry, each week another piece of the story should arrive."

Before she could ask who *he* was, or argue further, Salem blinked both him and Ophelia out of the room, leaving her to stare down at the mysterious envelope alone. As she tore open the seal and unfolded the thick parchment inside, she swore she recognized the handwriting on the page, the way the letters curled elegantly in an exact replica of the penmanship belonging to that damned, hexed invitation. But as she glanced at the signature, it was not Barrington Silver's name that she found at all.

Rowington.

The moment she read the name, a shiver ran down her spine. The reaction so visceral that she stumbled back until her thighs hit the edge of her bed. She lowered herself onto the mattress as she scanned the rest of the letter voraciously.

Dear Genevieve,

You do not know me, but I very much know you. I know you're likely wrought with impatience that you will have to wait to hear this story one letter at a time.

She was.

I know that upon waking, every sentence from your lips has likely ended in a question mark.

They had.

And I know despite your proximity to the peculiar world of the paranormal, you will likely find the story I'm about to tell you hard to believe. But I assure you every single word is truth. The truth is something precious, especially between you and me. Something you'll soon see.

Why don't I start at the beginning?

He did.

47

CORRESPONDENCE

Their story came in waves, like the colors of spring and the heat of the Louisiana summer.

But her memories did not.

Those first few weeks, Genevieve would wait for the mail to arrive, ripping open the sealed envelopes before they could even hit the front porch, desperate to read the tale of her time in Enchantra, and the wicked game they'd had to play. At first, she found herself gripped by his ability to make her feel known, seen, though she had no recollection of them ever meeting.

By the end of June, however, dread had set in. It was after he revealed to her the nature of their relationship. Their forced nuptials. Since then, it felt as if she had been punched in the gut every time a new letter arrived. She'd hoped that as more came, her memories might finally click into place, like puzzle pieces, and she'd feel whole again. But with each new bit of correspondence, the devastating longing had grown only worse.

But Genevieve felt neither affection nor hope for the faceless stranger sending the letters—her *husband*—no matter how much she wished she did. And she did wish. Desperately. For his sake, since she'd apparently cared enough for him that she let herself be *killed* to save his family. But her hope was also selfish, since the burning nightmares of Farrow had returned.

Now, she was lying in bed, at a quarter past noon, as she waited for the next letter. The one he said would be his last.

"Vivi?" Ophelia called from downstairs.

Genevieve squeezed her eyes shut for a long moment, before hauling herself out of bed and making her way toward the stairs. As she descended, she watched as Salem brought over a very curmudgeonly-looking Poe to Ophie, who scratched the Ghost cat behind his ears. Ophelia smiled at the cat before letting Salem press a lingering kiss to her lips.

Genevieve cleared her throat as she stepped down into the foyer. "You called for me?"

Ophelia pulled away from Salem and reached out her arm. There was a parcel in her hand.

"This just came for you," Ophelia said.

The package was addressed in his handwriting, but it was much thicker than all the rest of his letters had been. And when she tore into the parchment of its wrapping, she saw why. Inside, there was a small black box enclosed with his usual letter. Ophelia and Salem exchanged a curious look as Genevieve opened the box first.

Nestled inside was a golden cuff with the inscription *the light is wherever you are.*

Genevieve swallowed thickly.

Then she unfolded the letter.

Dear Genevieve,

The final part of our story is where things fall apart. When Knox confirmed that the Prince of the Devils was, in fact, connected to your sister, he became desperate to control you. And that made him vulnerable.

You came up with a plan that was almost perfect. No one gives you nearly enough credit for how well you extract information from people and retain it.

It was your visit to Knox's trove that gave you the idea.

You wondered if we could leverage Knox's greed so he would offer us all the one thing he knew we wanted most—our freedom from the Hunt. If we could convince him to try and keep your soul hostage, then he would want us to extract your soul rather than killing you. If we could place it in a Soul Lock and escape, your friend Salem could bring you back.

Extracting your soul would fulfill the technicality of his bargain, and we could all walk away.

So, we went to Grave. Which was a risk. But at the end of the day, my brother is still my brother. And you're you. You convinced him we could pull this off. That he could plant the seed in Knox's head—ironically thanks to the fact that he had nearly killed you so many times before. That if Knox agreed to set <u>all</u> of us free, it was time for him to make the right choice.

When I spoke to Ellin of your plan, she agreed to forfeit when she realized returning to Hell would mean she could get Wells and Sevin to help remove our mother from Knoxium. Knox would still be forced to complete his end of the bargain after the Hunt was over and give our mother the Fix, but at least she would no longer be in the Devil's lair itself.

And so the last person we needed to convince of my betrayal was Knox himself. Just long enough for him to give Grave and me our magic.

Taking your soul was a risky move. Salemaestrus nearly killed Grave and me for delivering you to your home in such a state. I think only your sister convinced him to spare our lives.

But as well as our plan worked, Genevieve, there is one thing that went horribly wrong.

Salemaestrus did exactly what you suspected he could: extracted your soul from the Soul Lock and returned it to your corporeal form. I don't think I've ever been in so much pain as I was in those minutes before your heart started beating again. But then it did and you woke up and you . . . did not recognize me. And that was nearly unbearable.

It is a cruel thing. To be looked on as a stranger by the one who knows you best. It is cruel that I was given a taste of what my eternity could have been filled with—your smile, your pleasure, your humor—only to have it ripped away from me in seconds.

It is cruel that if your memories never come back that it would only be fair to let you go.

The problem is, Genevieve, that I can't.

That I never will.

And I know your memories have not come back even with these letters, and that means they likely never will. But I will never stop searching for a way to get them back for you. I will search for the rest of my eternity if I must, because it belongs to you already. I pledge it to you in my vows.

I understand if you do not feel the same. If you need to move on with your life. Our vows may have said "eternally," but as I told you then, nothing is ever truly eternal.

Except my longing for you.

Sincerely,
Rowin

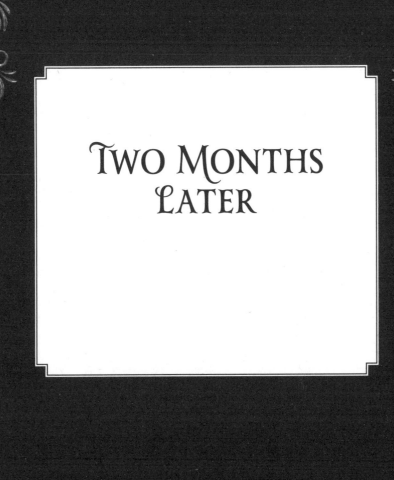

TWO MONTHS
LATER

48

HER RING

Genevieve was currently trailing through the French Quarter behind Salem and Ophelia. The two of them on their way to a specialty bookstore they loved to linger in well past Genevieve's patience for old dusty things.

Salem paused in front of a street act with moving cups and little rubber balls, driving the magician mad every time Salem guessed the incorrect cup, yet somehow a ball still managed to appear. Ophelia pressed her face into Salem's chest to keep from laughing.

"I'm going to get a praline from Laura's," Genevieve told them when she spotted the candy store on the corner.

"Get me one, too?" Ophelia asked.

Genevieve nodded, fiddling with her bracelet as she headed toward the shop, her thoughts somewhere far away as she meandered through the tourists. When she approached the shop's door, someone suddenly reached out ahead of her and pulled it open.

"Thank you," she said automatically as she looked up at the stranger's face.

She froze.

He was perhaps one of the most beautiful people she'd ever seen. His eyes an unusual amber color. His disheveled raven hair a bit unruly at the ends. And the single gold hoop pierced through his full bottom lip made her stomach flip.

He gave her a smile as he flicked his eyes down to the bracelet she was fidgeting with on her wrist.

"Hello," he murmured.

"Hi," she greeted back.

He had opened his mouth to say more when the sound of something metallic plinked on the ground between them. They both glanced down at a thick silver ring.

He crouched to pick it up. "Is this yours?"

It was a signet, its band carved with swirling filigree around a flat onyx stone.

She shook her head in amusement. "I would never wear something like that. It's..."

"Hideous?" he supplied.

She flicked her eyes back up to his golden gaze. "You think so, too?"

But he didn't answer. He only tilted his head and stared at her expectantly. As if he were waiting for something.

After a long beat, she asked, "Is there something wrong?"

Disappointment flashed in his strange gold eyes, and she couldn't help but think that he looked...devastated. Still, all he said was, "Are you going to go inside?"

"Oh." She blinked, realizing he was still holding open the door. "No, actually. I think I've changed my mind."

He nodded. "I hope you have a good day, then."

"You too."

He let the door shut and brushed past her without another word, and she watched as he disappeared down the street. But the further away he got, the more something began to nag at her. Something telling her to go after him. And before she knew it, her feet were moving. Slowly at first. A few tentative steps. Then she was running.

"Wait!" she called.

He spun.

"I made a mistake," she told him, a bit breathless. "The ring... is mine. I just forgot."

Hope flickered over his face as he reached into his pocket and procured the silver monstrosity. When he handed it over to her, she swore his expression contained the smallest bit of *relief*.

He watched her intently.

"Thanks," she told him.

Without wasting another second, she turned and dashed toward the Quarter to find her sister. Before the stranger changed his mind and took it back.

For two weeks after that trip to the Quarter, Genevieve couldn't sleep.

She tossed and turned as visions of labyrinths and mirrors played in her dreams. The same shadowy figure by her side in each one. And then one night, there was a flicker.

Of a man. With gold eyes.

She shot up in bed.

It was well past midnight as she threw off her covers and dashed over to her vanity, yanking open the top drawer to dig out the ugly ring that the stranger had given her that day in the Quarter.

She stared at it for a very long moment, her heart racing. Then she did something odd. She slid it onto her ring finger.

And the memories began to flower in her head.

They came back all at once, like smoke filling in every corner of her mind. Making her dizzy as the scenes unfurled one after the other.

Arriving at Enchantra's gates.

The first time she'd ever seen his face.

Putting on her wedding dress.

Their vows.

Their first kiss.

Dying in his arms.

She cried out as she crashed to her knees on the ground, gripping her temples as the pain of her memories weaving themselves back into her mind nearly made her pass out.

Yet she had never been more grateful to feel pain before. How could she when he finally returned to her? In one breathtaking vision after the next.

49

MEMORIES

The scene in Hell, however, was not from her own memory, but his.

"*I am told you've come to make a bargain with me, Rowington Silver.*" *The King of Hell smirked down at Rowin from his throne, the flames that surrounded the room rising with the volume of his voice.*

"*Yes,*" *Rowin confirmed.* "*I would like to bargain something to bring back a loved one's memories.*"

"*Your wife's memories, correct?*" *the King mused.*

"*Yes,*" *Rowin stated proudly.*

"*Memories are delicate things,*" *the King told him.* "*Once they leave the mind entirely, they dissipate like smoke on the wind. It's why hiding memories is a lot more advantageous than destroying them. Recovering them takes a lot of magic.*"

Rowin waited.

"*I don't particularly approve of creatures of Hell consorting with mortals,*" *the King decided.* "*But perhaps for the right price I'd consider helping you.*"

Rowin lifted his chin. "*Name it.*"

The King's smile was wicked. "*I want you to use your newfound proximity to my son to convince him to pay me a visit.*"

Rowin glowered. "*No. If Genevieve found out I betrayed her sister in order to get her memories back, she would never forgive me.*"

The King shrugged. "*That sounds like a personal problem. If you cannot agree to my terms, you can seek help elsewhere.*"

Rowin balled his fists. There had to be something he could give. He would stand here for the rest of time if he had to. Until—

An idea sliced through his mind.

"What about my immortality?" he offered the King. "If you don't think creatures of Hell should be with mortals, then why don't you tie my lifespan to hers?"

The King perked up at this. "Interesting."

They stared at each other for an uncomfortable amount of time, the King seemingly willing to make Rowin keep his promise to wait there forever.

Then finally, "I accept your trade. Do you have a token I can draw her memories into?"

Rowin glanced down at his hand and plucked the signet right off his finger. The one that used to be her wedding band. He handed it over to the Demon guard standing at the base of the dais, and they passed it up to their ruler.

"Here's the catch," the King began as he shifted the ring back and forth over his knuckles. "You must deliver it to her personally, and she must choose to put it on herself. When she does, your lifespans will be merged. Do you agree to these terms?"

"Yes," Rowin said, his voice ringing out clear.

"Very good. And when you inevitably see my son again"—the King's smile tightened now—"do tell him I'm waiting patiently for his homecoming."

Rowin dipped his chin in a single nod.

The King raised his hand to Rowin then, and at first Rowin felt nothing. Then His Highness tightened his fist, and Rowin felt the King of the Devil's ancient magic spear through his body. He nearly vomited all over the polished floors as a vital piece of him was pried away from his soul, extracted from his magic and drained from him entirely.

When it was over, the King turned his focus to the signet Rowin had given him, but Rowin could barely pay attention to what happened next. *The weight of mortality crashed over him, churning his stomach. He felt weak, barely able to stand. He reached inside of himself and prodded at the magic in his core and sighed in relief that it, at least, remained untouched.*

A bright flash of power erupted in the King's hand and rippled throughout the room, making Rowin cover his eyes. When it was over, the King held the ring up between them. Admiring his work.

"An eternity in exchange for such a brief moment in the life of a mortal," *the King mused as he tossed the ring back to Rowin.*

Rowin snatched it out of the air with a smile.

Rowin bowed and turned to leave. When he got to the grand entrance, however, someone slid into his path. A Devil with slitted, crimson eyes and long dark hair.

"Give Salem a message from me, too, would you?" *the Devil snarled.*

Rowin narrowed his eyes. "Who are you?"

"It doesn't matter," *the Devil said.* "Just tell him I'm coming."

50

TRUTH

Genevieve dashed from her room and bounded down the stairs.

Rowin. Rowin. Rowin.

Her footsteps must have been rather loud, because Salem winked into sight as she was hauling on her coat in the foyer.

"What the fuck are you doing, Vivi?" he demanded. "It's midnight."

"Rowin," she rushed out. "Rowin. My memories. Enchantra. Knox. Oh fuck."

"*What?*" Salem questioned as she froze.

"The *cure*, Salem. *The cure!* I have to tell Rowin. I have to tell Grave. Knox took the memory of it from me, but the King's magic must have returned it," she mumbled to herself.

Salem was watching her like she'd gone mad. And maybe she had.

Then, as she looked back at his concerned viridian gaze, something else rushed to the front of her mind. A name she used to call him.

Genevieve shook off the realization. That was a conversation for them to have another time.

"Vivi? Salem?" Ophelia's groggy voice said as she descended from the top of the stairs.

"Go back to bed, angel," Salem said gently. "Your sister is just having some sort of epiphany. I'll handle it."

"Salem," Genevieve said carefully. "I have to go. *Please.*"

Salem gave a sigh. "You better not come home married to another stranger or half dead this time."

Genevieve plunged into the balmy night.

By the time she saw the glow of the gas lamps lining the River-walk, she was a disheveled, sore mess. She wasn't sure what on earth she was thinking.

"This is absurd," she whispered to herself as she tried to catch her breath, chest heaving from her trek. "Why on earth would he be here?"

She looked around. There wasn't a single soul in sight.

"I should go back," she told herself. "This is—"

Her words cut off as a figure suddenly poured out of the shadows in a cloud of dark smoke.

"Hello, trouble."

Genevieve stopped dead in her tracks as she met his amber eyes. A sob tore from her throat.

The moment Rowin spotted recognition on her face, he lunged forward, wrapping her up in his arms so tightly she could barely breathe.

"You came back to me," he said, voice gruff. "When I saw you a couple weeks ago and you didn't put on the ring, I thought—"

"It just took some time," she whispered to him, tears pricking in her eyes. "It just took time. But I remember. I remember. *Rowin.*"

He pulled back, just enough to see her face, the tears that were now flowing down her cheeks. "I was stuck in that house, in that fucking game, for centuries, and yet these past couple of months have felt like the longest of my life."

He kissed her then. Desperately. Plunging a hand into her hair as he showed her exactly how much he had missed her. When he pulled away, she could barely stand upright on her own.

"How long have you been waiting here?" she wondered.

"Since the day we brought you home," he told her. "Lingering in the shadows until you found me."

"How could you? How could you trade your immortality for me?" she whispered. "What were you thinking?"

He reared back in shock. "You saw that?"

"I saw *everything*," she told him. "I can't believe I didn't recognize you, that day in the Quarter. I hate that you must have been..."

"Devastated," he admitted. "Ophelia warned me that you still didn't remember. But even that didn't prepare me for the way you looked at me and there was just...nothing."

"That's not true," she swore. "Even without any of my memories, I felt drawn to you. We could be enemies, or husband and wife, or just fucking, but *never* nothing, Rowington Silver."

His smile was brilliant. "Before you, I was going to spend my eternity alone, in the darkest parts of Hell. I'd much rather spend a single lifetime in your light. Or, at least, for however long you'll have me." Then he leaned his forehead against hers. "I want you to know, I really would have waited for you, right here, forever if that's what it would have taken. I would have stood in this spot until I could no longer distinguish my own soul from the shadows. Until your light came back to me."

She smiled. "I know." Truth. "Does that mean...does that mean there are strings now?"

"As many as you want, Mrs. Silver. And tie them down as tight as you'd like," he told her.

She gave him a devious smirk. "I was sort of hoping the tying down might be the other way around..."

"Oh, trouble, we're going to have a lot of fun."

EPILOGUE

Light

Genevieve adored Louisiana right before the turn of summer. The blooming magnolias, bright fashion, last crawfish boils. She especially enjoyed the fact that it wasn't a hundred degrees outside, which meant she could take strolls without her hair becoming a terribly frizzy mess.

"Who's coming, again?" Luci asked, pulling her long flaxen hair out of her face as they walked back to Grimm Manor from the Garden District.

Umbra was trotting just ahead of them. These days Umbra was more her shadow than Rowin's.

"Grave and Sevin," Genevieve answered Luci. "They're Rowin's brothers. You'll definitely like Sevin. Grave maybe not so much."

"For this cure, right?" Luci recalled. "You said they only have a year?"

"Less than that now," Genevieve corrected. "Since the Silvers still played in the Hunt this year, Knox was forced to give their mother one last dose of the Fix, at least. And Grave's been on the hunt nonstop but hasn't had any luck. Rowin and I are afraid he's going to drive himself—and everyone else—mad if he doesn't get a lead soon."

Their strides slowed as they approached Grimm Manor, where Luci herself had recently taken up residence after a few unfortunate events had occurred in her life over the past couple of months. Grimm Manor was a safe haven, after all, and Ophelia was particularly keen on trying to help Luci after the strenuous start of their relationship back in Phantasma.

She and Luci barely set foot inside the house before Rowin was there, wrapping Genevieve up in his arms for a kiss as Luci stepped past them with a sad smile.

"I missed the fuck out of you," Rowin murmured as he set Genevieve back on the ground. Umbra chirped at his feet, and he reached down to pat the fox on her head. "You too."

It had been two weeks since they'd seen each other. He'd been running around with Grave and Sevin, all of them desperate to find their mother's cure now that the family had been released from Knox's hold. Well, except for Barrington—whom none of them had been able to get in contact with since Genevieve's trick set them free and Knox's Hellmouth disappeared from within Enchantra. Something that made her stomach turn.

Someone behind them cleared their throat.

When Rowin refused to let her go, Genevieve stood on her tiptoes to peer over his shoulder. "Hello, Grave."

"Hi, pal," Grave murmured.

"Hi," Luci offered from where she stood as well. "I'm Luci. Genevieve told me all about you. Welcome to New Orleans."

Grave flicked his eyes over to Luci. He didn't offer more than a single dip of his chin in acknowledgment.

Genevieve threw Luci a look of apology as she asked, "Where is—"

"*Vivi*," Sevin exclaimed as he shouldered Grave and Rowin out of the way. A sucker was hanging from his grinning mouth as he wrapped his arms around Genevieve and spun her in a circle.

"Enchantra has been a little less exciting without you," Sevin said as he put her back on her feet and tapped the tip of her nose affectionately. "And Rowin a *lot* more insufferable."

Rowin rolled his eyes.

"Unsurprising on both accounts, honestly," Genevieve laughed.

"I do have a letter for you from Ellin. Though it's mostly just petty gossip," Sevin told her as he produced an envelope from his waistcoat.

Genevieve snatched the letter up greedily and found that it had already been torn open.

"Did you read it?" she accused.

"I got bored. My brothers are rather dull travel companions," Sevin reasoned with a shrug. "Page three is particularly exciting."

Genevieve gave him an exasperated look, but before she could offer a response, a movement caught her attention out of the corner of her eye. She glanced over to see Salem blinking into view beneath the open archway that led to the den.

He raised a brow at the sight of all of them. "Ah. You're all already here. My apologies, I was visiting an acquaintance in town."

By the smell of tobacco clinging to him, Genevieve would bet good money that acquaintance was Jasper.

Salem strutted over to the stairs to call, "Angel?"

They all watched as Ophelia appeared at the top of the stairs, her red dress swishing as she bounded down. Salem offered a hand to assist her off the final step, pressing a quick kiss to the tips of her fingers before letting go.

"Impeccable timing." Ophie smiled at Salem.

Salem reached out to shake Rowin's hand in greeting. When Salem let go, Rowin gave a subtle flex of his fingers, and Genevieve could only assume the Prince of the Devils had made his grip just a little too tight. It had taken some time to convince Salem to help the Silvers, particularly after he'd learned of everything that had transpired within Enchantra, as well as the message Rowin had brought from Salem's father.

Not to mention how angry Ophie had been that she came home from a vacation *married*.

"Does this mean you remember everything now?" Ophelia asked after Genevieve ran home from the Riverwalk in the middle of the night.

"Yes," Genevieve confirmed.

"Wonderful." Ophelia nodded. "Because now I'm going to throttle you, Genevieve Lila Grimm—"

"Well, it's Silver, now." Genevieve winced.

"Yes! Because you got married," *Ophelia huffed. "Are you mad? I don't care if it was for survival. I missed your wedding!"*

Ophelia elbowed Salem in the side now, bringing Genevieve's attention back to the present.

"Behave," Ophie chastised Salem as he gave Rowin a smug look.

Salem huffed a laugh. "And here I thought you preferred it when I misbehaved, angel."

Ophelia sighed heavily as she flicked her eyes over to Rowin and Grave. "You'll have to excuse him. Devils cannot be taught manners."

"We have that in common," Sevin chimed.

Salem pressed an affectionate kiss to Ophelia's temple before looking to Rowin and his brothers "Any news?"

"We've heard whispers that one of the cures is on reserve with a member of the Daemonica," Rowin told them all. "Which means—"

"You're looking at the soon-to-be newest pledge of the most elite Demon institution in Hell." Sevin grinned.

Rowin and Genevieve exchanged a loaded look. Grave, on the other hand, did not look happy.

"For the record, I still think you should let me go," Grave argued.

"Divide and conquer, brother," Rowin recited for what was likely the millionth time. "Breaching an ancient organization that prioritizes partying and making reckless decisions is practically Sevin's calling."

"Besides," Sevin said as he took the lollipop out of his mouth, "they would never let you in. There isn't a single ounce of fun in your entire body."

Grave grunted.

"Come, let's all get a drink," Salem inserted, waving them toward the drawing room.

Rowin made to leave with the others, but Genevieve tugged on his arm, holding him back for a moment alone.

"Yes?" he murmured as he tucked a strand of hair back from her face.

"I've missed you, too," she told him. "Terribly. Especially at night. My hands have just never been as skilled as yours—"

"You're going to get yourself into trouble if you keep saying things like that," he warned, his golden eyes sparking with wicked intent as she slid her palms up his chest, toward his quickening heartbeat.

She gave him an innocent smile. "What's new?"

As he scooped her up into his arms and headed for the stairs, she laughed. Grateful to herself for clawing her way through the darkness, and the light that followed them everywhere now.

Acknowledgments

Hello, my twisted little friends! Can you believe we're already at the end of yet another book of me yapping about all the sexy demons and magical beings that live in my head? Because I can't! When my editor told me it was time to write these acknowledgments, I had to take a moment to collect my shock, because I swear we were just roaming the haunted halls of *Phantasma* yesterday, but alas, time truly does fly when you're having fun. And I did. I had *so* much fun writing this book. That is, when I wasn't crying, or torturing myself over whether it was good enough to follow my last book. But such is the burden of being an artist, I suppose. Always trying to one-up yourself can be nerve-racking and exhausting, but I can genuinely say that I absolutely adore Vivi and her story, and I can't wait to see what else is to come of this world and these characters!

Half of this book was written to reruns of *Buffy the Vampire Slayer* and moody Lofi Girl playlists. The other half was written to *Howl's Moving Castle* playing in the background eleven times a day. And all of this book was written during a pretty chaotic period of my career—the good sort of chaos—and would have genuinely not happened without all the incredible people around me.

To Iz, always. No, I still have not gotten the matching tattoo for anyone who might be keeping tabs. But I *did* finally read that book you were begging me to read and watch that show you were begging me to watch, and I feel like that's its own sort of romantic gesture, right? (I know, I know, I'm literally booking the tattoo appointment right now.) Also to Kai, our favorite boy. You're the best pup in the whole entire world, please live forever.

To the friends who kept me actually sane during the drafting of this book and swore I would not be a failure when I worried it would be too different from *Phantasma* for anyone to love— Night, Becca, Darci, Deanna, Em, Elba, Hayley, Andrea, Dev, Loretta, Hannah, Gabi, Matou, Meryn. Night, our late-night phone calls literally got me through the hardest parts of drafting and editing this; Becca, our daylight conversations and never-ending voice memos saved my peace when I needed it most. I love you both so much.

To the icon that is Emily Forney, can you even believe this is our fourth book together?!? Five years, four books, endless screaming about *Danny Phantom*, *The Vampire Diaries*, and the snacks at Disneyland. I can't wait for all the other stories to come. Thank you for always being the best champion. Yeehaw.

To my editor, Jack Renninson, for being the most wonderful collaborator and always knowing exactly how to guide me toward the best possible story even when I was having a crisis about it in the eleventh hour (as usual). Also, this is where we all collectively say *Thank you, Jack!* for pushing me to make all my love interests *more* romantic and not letting me kill off any of our little animal friends. We don't need to talk about the version of this book in which Umbra died...

To my team at Second Sky for being such an amazing support system. To Noelle Holten, my publicist, who did such incredible work for *Phantasma*. As well as everyone else who had a hand in making *Phantasma* such a success. It's a pleasure working with you all!

To my team at Forever, for also being such incredible partners.

Sam Brody, my editor, and Caroline Green and Brieana Garcia, my publicists for all your amazing work. I'm so grateful!

To the very talented Laura Horowitz, who brought these audiobooks to life. I genuinely adore you and am forever in awe of how incredible your work on these books is.

To Rositsa Popova (Rosalynnarts) for your incredible work bringing all my characters to life with your art. I will never get over how talented you are, and I hope we get to collaborate together forever.

To Lily, my sister-in-law, always. I think you might actually be a bigger book nerd than me at this point, and I am just over the moon about that. Our chaotic phone calls are always my favorite. To my family, I'm sorry I had to move across the country. But I love you all so very much.

To every bookseller and librarian who recommends my books to readers—if you ever need a soul, you can have mine! I am endlessly appreciative of everything you do and your tireless work in this community!

And finally, to you, dear readers. Oh goodness, I don't know if there are enough words to tell you all how thankful I truly am for everything you've done. Not only did you all read *Phantasma*, you screamed about it, posted about it, loved it, and took it to places I never thought it'd go. To each and every one of you who reached out to tell me your own stories about living with OCD and how much you saw yourselves in Ophelia—I want you to know your love for my book and these characters is something that's touched me so deeply it's hard for me to really convey. I just adore you all so much. I hope Genevieve's story was just as fun for you as Ophelia's, but most of all, no matter what, I hope you'll stick around and come on more adventures with me. I'm so enchanted to be here with you all.

PS: Like most acknowledgments, these were written in the

last stages of developmental edits, right before the book went off for copy edits and proofreads. Since then, so many wild and wonderful things have happened for this book as well as all the other amazing books I have planned for both this world and brand-new ones. Writing a book is a very solitary endeavor at times, but publishing a book and bringing it to life and getting it into the hands of readers takes so much support. *Enchantra* was quite the journey for so many different reasons—I've never had a book so anticipated before, and I wanted to make sure I put every ounce of blood, sweat, and tears I had into this one—but it would never have happened without the incredible work of my editors, Jack and Sam, and my agent, Emily. How lucky I am to be surrounded by such an incredible team. I just wanted to say an extra *thank you*.

About the Author

Kaylie Smith (she/they) is a writer and lover of all things fantasy. They grew up in Louisiana, where they frequently haunted bookstores and practiced her craft. After college she decided to pursue her lifelong dream of becoming an author, but when she isn't writing or reading, she can be found at home with her menagerie of animals, fussing over their houseplants, or annoying people about astrology.

You can learn more at:
KaylieSmithBooks.com
Instagram @KaylSMoon
TikTok @KaylSMoon
X @KaylSMoon